Praise for the
Morganville Vampires Novels

Carpe Corpus

"Ms. Caine offers readers an intriguing world where vampires rule, only the strongest survive, and romance offers hope in the darkest of hours. Each character is brought to life in superb detail, with unique personality quirks and a full spectrum of emotions. *Carpe Corpus* is well-described, packed with action, and impossible to set down."   —Darque Reviews

"Rachel Caine has carved out a unique niche in the urban fantasy subgenre with her super young adult Morganville Vampires. The latest thriller contains plenty of action, but as always in this saga, *Carpe Corpus* is character driven by the good, the bad, and the evil."   —*Midwest Book Reviews*

"The pace is brisk and a number of loose ends are tied up as one chapter on the town of Morganville closes and a new one begins."
—Monsters and Critics

Lord of Misrule

"We'd suggest dumping Stephenie Meyer's vapid *Twilight* books and replacing them with these."   —*SFX Magazine*

"Book five of the Morganville vampires is filled with delicious twists that the audience will appreciatively sink their teeth into. . . . Rachel Caine provides a strong young adult vampire thriller."   —The Best Reviews

"A sinister book. . . . Although marketed to teens, this series is sure to capture plenty of adult fans with the fast-moving story line, hints of romance, and well-developed characters."   —Monsters and Critics

continued . . .

"Fast-paced and filled with action. . . . Fans of the series will appreciate *Feast of Fools*."   —Genre Go Round Reviews

"Thrilling. . . . In sharing her well-imagined world, Ms. Caine gives readers the danger-filled supernatural moments they crave while adding friendship, romance, and teen issues to give the story a realistic feel. A fast-moving series where there's always a surprise just around every dark corner."

—Darque Reviews

"Very entertaining. . . . I could not put *Feast of Fools* down. . . . There is a level of tension in the Morganville books that keeps you on the edge of your seat; even in the background scenes you're waiting for the other shoe to drop. And it always does."   —Flames Rising

"I thoroughly enjoyed reading *Feast of Fools*. . . . It was fantastic. . . . The excitement and suspense in *Feast of Fools* is thrilling, and I was fascinated reading about the town of Morganville. I greatly look forward to reading the next book in this series and catching up with the other books. I highly recommend *Feast of Fools* to paranormal readers for a delightful and fun read that you won't want to put down."   —Fresh Fiction

Midnight Alley

"A fast-paced, page-turning read packed with wonderful characters and surprising plot twists. Rachel Caine is an engaging writer; readers will be completely absorbed in this chilling story, unable to put it down until the last page. . . . For fans of vampire books, this is one that shouldn't be missed!"
—FlamingNet

"Weaves a web of dangerous temptation, dark deceit, and loving friendships. The nonstop vampire action and delightfully sweet relationships will captivate readers and leave them craving more."
—Darque Reviews

The Dead Girls' Dance

"[Glass Houses] left me emotionally spent, in a good way. The intensity is cubed in [The Dead Girls' Dance]. It was hard to put this down for even the slightest break, and forget what happens to the kid with the scar and glasses, I want to know what happens next in Morganville. If you love to read about characters with whom you can get deeply involved, Rachel Caine is so far a one hundred percent sure bet to satisfy that need. I love her Weather Warden stories, and her vampires are even better."
—The Eternal Night

THE MORGANVILLE VAMPIRES NOVELS

Glass Houses

The Dead Girls' Dance

Midnight Alley

Feast of Fools

Lord of Misrule

Carpe Corpus

Fade Out

Kiss of Death

THE
MORGANVILLE
VAMPIRES

VOLUME II

Midnight Alley
and
Feast of Fools

Rachel Caine

 NEW AMERICAN LIBRARY

New American Library
Published by New American Library, a division of
Penguin Group (USA) Inc., 375 Hudson Street,
New York, New York 10014, USA
Penguin Group (Canada), 90 Eglinton Avenue East, Suite 700, Toronto,
Ontario M4P 2Y3, Canada (a division of Pearson Penguin Canada Inc.)
Penguin Books Ltd., 80 Strand, London WC2R 0RL, England
Penguin Ireland, 25 St. Stephen's Green, Dublin 2,
Ireland (a division of Penguin Books Ltd.)
Penguin Group (Australia), 250 Camberwell Road, Camberwell, Victoria 3124,
Australia (a division of Pearson Australia Group Pty. Ltd.)
Penguin Books India Pvt. Ltd., 11 Community Centre, Panchsheel Park,
New Delhi - 110 017, India
Penguin Group (NZ), 67 Apollo Drive, Rosedale, North Shore 0632,
New Zealand (a division of Pearson New Zealand Ltd.)
Penguin Books (South Africa) (Pty.) Ltd., 24 Sturdee Avenue,
Rosebank, Johannesburg 2196, South Africa

Penguin Books Ltd., Registered Offices:
80 Strand, London WC2R 0RL, England

Published by New American Library, a division of Penguin Group (USA) Inc. *Midnight Alley* and *Feast of Fools* were previously published in separate Signet and NAL Jam mass market editions.

First New American Library Printing (Double Edition), October 2010
10 9 8 7 6 5 4 3 2 1

Midnight Alley copyright © Roxanne Longstreet Conrad, 2007
Feast of Fools copyright © Roxanne Longstreet Conrad, 2008
All rights reserved

 REGISTERED TRADEMARK—MARCA REGISTRADA

Set in Centaur
Designed by Ginger Legato

Printed in the United States of America

MIDNIGHT ALLEY

For the people who got me through my own personal Morganville years: Elizabeth Sandlin, Andy Sealy, Mona Fluitt, Bruce Tinsley, Luis Hernandez, Gary Wiley, Scott Chase, Marsha McNeill, Rachel Scarbrough, and many more who made the days bright. Also to the memory of sitting next to Stevie Ray Vaughn, hearing him make magic when few people were even listening.

For the people who are getting me through *these* Morganville years: Cat Conrad, Kelley Walters, Marla Stair, Katy Hendricks, Claire Wilkins and Baby Griff, Becky Rocha, Laurie Andrews and her lovely girls, P. N. Elrod, Jackie Leaf, Bill Leaf, Joanne Madge, Irene Ferris, Ter Matthies, the Alphas, ORAC, Douglas Joseph, Sharon Sams and her son Boardman, Ann Jackson and her son Trey, and literally too many LiveJournal and MySpace friends to even attempt to list. Every one of them a special, undeserved gift.

And to Charles Armitage and Kevin Cleary, for making Morganville an even more exciting place.

ACKNOWLEDGMENTS

Fast turnaround reading and commenting from a select group of people, including (but probably not limited to) Jackie, Sharon, Donna, and Lisa. Especially Donna, who reminded me that if you put a knife on the table in the first act, you'd better not switch it to a gun in the third . . . Thanks, Donna!

ONE

The instant the phone rang at the Glass House, Claire knew with a psychic flash that it had to be her mother.

Well, it wasn't so much a psychic flash as simple logic. She'd told Mom that she would call days ago, which she hadn't, and now, of course, it could only be her mother calling at the most inopportune moment.

Hence: had to be a call from Mom.

"Don't," her boyfriend—she couldn't believe she could actually call him that, *boyfriend*, not a boy friend—Shane murmured without taking his mouth off of hers. "Michael will get it." And he was giving her a very good argument in favor of ignoring the phone, too. But somewhere in the back of her mind that little voice just wouldn't shut up.

She slid off of his lap with a regretful sigh, licked her damp, tingling lips, and dashed off in the direction of the kitchen door.

Michael was just rising from the kitchen table to head for the phone. She beat him to it, mouthing a silent apology, and said, "Hello?"

"Claire! Oh my goodness, I've been worried sick, honey. We've been trying to call you on your cell for days, and—"

Crap. Claire rubbed her forehead in frustration. "Mom, I sent you guys an e-mail, remember? My cell got lost; I'm still working on getting another one." Best not to mention how it had gotten lost. Best not to mention anything about how dangerous her life had become since she'd moved to Morganville, Texas.

"Oh," Mom said, and then, more slowly, "Oh. Well, your father forgot to tell me about that. You know, he's the one who checks the e-mail. I don't like computers."

"Yes, Mom, I know." Mom really wasn't *that* bad, but she was notoriously nervous with computers, and for good reason: they had a tendency to short out around her.

Mom was still talking. "Is everything going all right? How are classes? Interesting?"

Claire opened the refrigerator door and retrieved a can of Coke, which she popped open and chugged to give herself time to think what, if anything, to tell her parents. *Mom, there was a little trouble. See, my boyfriend's dad came to town with some bikers and killed people, and nearly killed us, too. Oh, and the vampires are angry about it. So to save my friends, I had to sign a contract, so now I'm basically the slave of the most badass vampire in town.*

Yeah, that wouldn't go over well.

Besides, even if she said it, Mom wouldn't understand it. Mom had been to Morganville, but she hadn't really *seen*. People usually didn't. And if they did, they either never left town or had their memories wiped clean on the way out.

And if by some chance they started to remember, bad things could happen to them. Terminally bad things.

So instead, Claire said, "Classes are great, Mom. I aced all my exams last week."

"Of course you did. Don't you always?"

Yeah, but last week I had to take my exams while worrying that somebody was going to stick a knife in my back. It could have had an effect on my GPA. Stupid to be proud of that . . . "Everything's fine here. I'll let you know when I get the new cell phone, okay?" Claire hesitated, then asked, "How are you? How's Dad?"

"Oh, we're fine, honey. We miss you, is all. But your father's still not happy about your living in that place, off campus, with those older kids. . . ."

Of all the things for Mom to remember, she had to remember *that*. And of course Claire couldn't tell her *why* she was living off campus with eighteen-year-olds, especially when two of them were boys. Mom hadn't gotten around to mentioning the boys yet, but it was just a matter of time.

"Mom, I told you how mean the girls were to me in the dorm. It's better here. They're my friends. And, really, they're great."

Mom didn't sound too convinced. "You're being careful, though. About those boys."

Well, that hadn't taken long. "Yes, I'm being careful about the boys." She was even being careful about Shane, though that was mostly because Shane never forgot that Claire was not quite seventeen, and he was not quite nineteen. Not a huge age difference, but legally? Huger than huge, if her parents got upset about it. Which they definitely would. "Everybody here says hello, by the way. Ah, Michael's waving."

Michael Glass, the second boy in the house, had settled down at the kitchen table and was reading a newspaper. He looked up and gave her a wide-eyed, *no-you-don't* shake of his head. He'd had a bad enough time of it with her parents the last time, and now . . . well, things were even worse, if that was possible. At least when he'd met them, Michael had been half-normal: fully human by night, an incorporeal ghost by day, and trapped in the house 24-7.

For Morganville, that *was* half-normal.

In order to help get Shane out of trouble, Michael had made a terrible choice—he'd gained his freedom from the house and obtained physical form at the time, but now he was a vampire. Claire couldn't tell if it bothered him. It had to, right? But he seemed so . . . normal.

Maybe a little too normal.

Claire listened to her mother's voice, and then held out the phone to Michael. "She wants to talk to you," she said.

"No! I'm not here!" he stage-whispered, and made waving-off motions. Claire wiggled the phone insistently.

"You're the responsible one," she reminded him. "Just try not to talk about the——" She mimed fangs in the neck.

Michael shot her a dirty look, took the phone, and turned on the charm. He had a lot of it, Claire knew. It wasn't just parents who liked him. It was ... well, everybody. Michael was smart, cute, hot, talented, respectful ... nothing not to love, except the whole undead aspect. He assured her mother that everything was fine, that Claire was behaving herself—his eye roll made Claire snort cola up her nose—and that he was watching out for Mrs. Danvers's little girl. That last part was true, at least. Michael was taking his self-appointed older-brother duties way too seriously. He hardly let Claire out of his sight, except when privacy was required or Claire slipped off to class without an escort—which was as often as possible.

"Yes, ma'am," Michael said. He was starting to look a little strained. "No, ma'am. I won't let her do that. Yes. Yes."

Claire had pity on him, and reclaimed the phone. "Mom, we've got to go. I love you both."

Mom still sounded anxious. "Claire, are you sure you don't want to come home? Maybe I was wrong about letting you go to MIT early. You could take the year off, study, and we'd love to have you back home again. . . ."

Weird. Usually she calmed right down, especially when Michael talked to her. Claire had a bad flash of Shane telling her about his own mother, how her memories of Morganville had started to surface. How the vampires had come after her to kill her because the conditioning hadn't stuck.

Her parents were in the same boat now. They'd been to town, but she still wasn't sure just how much they really knew or understood about that visit—it could be enough to put them in mortal danger. She had to do everything she could to keep them safe. That meant not following her dreams to MIT, because if she left Morganville—assuming she could even get out of town—the vampires would follow her, and they'd either bring her back or kill her. And the rest of her family, too.

Besides, Claire *had* to stay now, because she'd signed a contract pledging herself directly to Amelie, the town's Founder. The biggest, scariest vampire of them all, even if she rarely showed that side. At the time, she'd been Claire's only real hope to keep herself and her friends alive.

So far signing the contract hadn't meant a whole lot—no announcements in the local paper, and Amelie hadn't shown up to collect on her soul or anything. So maybe it would just pass by ... quietly.

Mom was still talking about MIT, and Claire didn't want to think about it. She'd dreamed of going to a school like MIT or CalTech her whole life, and she'd been smart enough to do it. She'd even gotten early acceptance. It was drastically unfair that she was stuck in Morganville now, like a fly in a spiderweb, and for a few seconds she let herself feel bitter and angry about that.

Nice, the brutally honest part of her mocked. *You'd sacrifice Shane's life for what you want, because you know that's what would happen. Eventually, the vampires would find an excuse to kill him. You're not any better than the vampires if you don't do everything you can to prevent that.*

The bitterness left, but regret wasn't following bitterness anytime soon. She hoped Shane never knew how she felt about it, deep down.

"Mom, sorry. I've got to go; I have class. I love you—tell Dad I love him, too, will you?"

Claire hung up on her mother's protests, heaved a sigh, and glanced at Michael, who was looking a little sympathetic.

"That's not easy, talking to the folks," he offered. "Sorry."

"Don't you ever talk to your parents?" Claire asked, and slid into the chair at the small breakfast table across from him. Michael had a cup of something; she was afraid it was blood for a second, but then she smelled coffee. Hazelnut. Vampires could, and did, enjoy food; it just didn't sustain them.

Michael looked suspiciously good this morning—a little color in his face, an energy to his movements that hadn't been there last night.

He'd had more than coffee this morning. How did that happen, exactly? Did he sneak off to the blood bank? Was there some kind of home delivery service?

Claire made a mental note to check into it. Quietly.

"Yeah, I call my folks sometimes," Michael said. He folded the newspaper—the local rag, run by vampires—and picked up a smaller, rolled bundle of letter-sized pages secured by a rubber band. "They're

Morganville exiles, so they have a lot to forget. It's better if I don't keep in contact too much; it could make trouble. I mostly write. The mail and e-mail get read before they're sent; you know that, right? And most of the phone calls get monitored, especially long-distance."

He stripped off the rubber band and unfolded the cheap pages of the second newspaper. Claire read the masthead upside down: *The Fang Report.* The logo was two stakes at right angles making up a cross. Wild.

"What's that?"

"This?" Michael rattled the paper and shrugged. "Captain Obvious."

"What?"

"Captain Obvious. That's his handle. He's been doing these papers every week for about two years now. It's an underground thing."

Underground in Morganville had a lot of meanings. Claire raised her eyebrows. "So . . . Captain Obvious is a vampire?"

"Not unless he's got a serious self-image problem," Michael said. "Captain Obvious hates vampires. If somebody steps out of line, he documents it—" Michael froze, reading the headline, and his mouth opened, then closed. His face set like stone, and his blue eyes looked stricken.

Claire reached over and took the newspaper from his hands, turned it, and read.

NEW BLOODSUCKER IN TOWN

Michael Glass, once a rising musical star with too much talent for this twisted town, has fallen to the Dark Side. Details are sketchy, but Glass, who's been keeping to himself for the past year, has definitely joined the Fang Gang.

Nobody knows how or where it happened, and I doubt Glass will be talking, but we should all be worried. Does this mean more vamps, fewer humans? After all, he is the first newly risen undead in generations.

Beware, boys and girls: Glass may look like an angel, but he's got a demon inside now. Memorize the face, kibbles. He's the newest addition to the Better-Off-Dead club!

"The *Better-Off-Dead* club?" Claire repeated aloud, horrified. "He's kidding, right?" There was Michael's picture, probably directly out of the Morganville High yearbook, inset as a graphic into a tombstone.

With crudely drawn-in fangs.

"Captain Obvious never comes out and tells anyone to kill," Michael said. "He's pretty careful about how he phrases things." Her friend was angry, Claire saw. And scared. "He's got our address listed. And all your names, too, though at least he points out none of you are vampires. Still. That's not good." Michael was getting past the shock of seeing himself outed in the paper, and was getting worried. Claire was already there.

"Well . . . why don't the vampires do something about him? Stop him?"

"They've tried. They've arrested three people in the last two years who said they were Captain Obvious. Turned out they didn't know anything. The captain could teach the CIA a thing or two about running a secret operation."

"So he's not that obvious," Claire said.

"I think he means it in the ironic sense." Michael swallowed a quick gulp of coffee. "Claire, I don't like this. Not like we didn't have enough trouble without this kind of—"

Eve slammed in through the kitchen door, which hit the wall with a thunderous boom, startling both of them. She clomped across the kitchen floor and leaned on the breakfast table. She wasn't very Goth today; her hair was still matte black, but it was worn back in a simple ponytail, and the plain knit shirt and black pants didn't have a skull anywhere in view. No makeup, either. She almost looked . . . normal. Which was so *wrong*.

"All right," she said, and slapped down a second copy of *The Fang Report* in front of Michael. "Please tell me you have a snappy comeback for this."

"I'll make sure the three of you are safe."

"Oh, *so* not what I was looking for! Look, I'm not worried about us! We're not the ones Photoshopped onto tombstones!" Eve looked at the picture again. "Although yes, better dead than that hairdo . . . God, was that your prom photo?"

Michael grabbed the paper back and put it facedown on the table. "Eve, nothing is going to happen. Captain Obvious just loves to talk. Nobody's going to come after me."

"Right," a new voice said. It was Shane. He'd come in behind Eve, clearly wanting to watch the fireworks, and now he leaned against the wall next to the stove and crossed his arms. "By all means, let's keep on shoveling the bull," he said. "It's trouble, and you know it." Claire waited for him to come over to the table and join the three of them, the way things used to be.

He didn't. Shane hadn't willingly stayed long in the same room with Michael since . . . the change. And he wouldn't look at him, except in angles and side glances. He'd also taken to wearing one of Eve's silver crosses, although just now it was hidden beneath the neck of the gray T-shirt he was wearing. Claire found her eyes fixing on its just-visible outline.

Eve ignored Shane; her big dark eyes were fixed on Michael. "You know they'll all be gunning for you now, right? All the would-be Buffys?" Claire had seen *Buffy the Vampire Slayer*, but she had no idea how Eve had managed; it was contraband in Morganville, along with every other movie or book featuring vampires. Or vampire killing, more to the point. Internet downloads were strictly controlled, too, though no doubt there was a hot black market in those kinds of things that Eve had tapped into.

"Like you?" Michael said. He still hadn't forgotten the arsenal of stakes and crosses that Eve kept hidden in her room. In the old days, that had seemed like good sense, living in Morganville. Now, it seemed like a recipe for domestic violence.

Eve looked stricken. "I'd never—"

"I know." He took her hand gently in his. "I know."

She softened, but then she shook it off and went back to frowning at him. "Look, this is *dangerous*. They know you're an easier target than those other guys, and they're going to hate you even more, because you're one of us. *Our* age."

"Maybe," Michael said. "Eve, come on, sit. Sit down."

She did, but it was more like a collapse, and she didn't stop jittering

her heel up and down in agitation, or drumming her black-painted fingernails on the table. "This is bad," she said. "You know that, right? Nine
point five on the ten-point scale of make-me-yak."

"Compared to what?" Shane asked. "We're already living with the
enemy. What does that score? Not to mention you probably get extra
points for banging him—"

Michael stood up so fast his chair tipped and hit the floor with a clatter. Shane straightened, ready for trouble, fists clenched.

"Shut up, Shane," Michael said, deathly quiet. "I mean it."

Shane stared past him at Eve. "He's going to bite you. He can't help it,
and once he starts, he won't stop; he'll *kill* you. But you know that, right?
What is that, some freak-ass Goth idea of romantic suicide? You turning
into a fang-banger?"

"Butt out, Shane. What you know about Goth culture you got from
old episodes of *The Munsters* and your Aryan Brotherhood dad." Great,
now Eve was angry, too. That left Claire the only sane one in the room.

Michael made an effort to dial it back. "Come on, Shane. Leave her
alone. *You're* the one hurting her, not me."

Shane's gaze snapped to Michael and focused. Hard. "I don't hurt
girls. You say I do, and you'd better back it up, asshole."

Shane pushed away from the wall, because Michael was taking steps
in his direction. Claire watched, wide-eyed and frozen.

Eve got between them, hands outstretched to hold both of them back.
"Come on, guys, you don't want to do this."

"Kinda do," Shane said coolly.

"Fine. Either hit each other or get a room," she snapped, and stepped
out of the middle. "Just don't pretend it's all about protecting the itty-
widdle girl, because it isn't. It's about the two of you. So get it together,
or leave; I don't care which."

Shane stared at her for a second, eyes gone wide and oddly hurt, then
looked at Claire. She didn't move.

"I'm out," he said. He turned and walked through the kitchen door.
It swung shut behind him.

Eve let out a little gasp. "I didn't think he'd go," she said, so unsteadily that for a second Claire thought she was going to cry. "What a freaking *idiot.*"

Claire reached over and took her hand. Eve squeezed, hard, and then leaned back into Michael's embrace. Vampire or not, the two of them seemed happy, and anyway, this was *Michael.* She just couldn't understand Shane's anger. It seemed to bubble up when she least expected it, for no reason at all.

"I'd better . . ." she ventured. Michael nodded.

Claire slipped out of her chair and went to find Shane. Not like it was difficult; he was slumped on the couch, staring at the PlayStation screen and working the controls on yet another zombie-killing adventure. "You taking his side?" Shane asked, and splattered the head of an attacking undead monster.

"No," Claire said and settled in carefully next to him, with enough open space between so he didn't feel pressured. "Why are there sides, anyway?"

"What?"

"Michael's your friend; he's our housemate. Why do there have to be sides?"

He snapped his fingers. "Um, wait. I've got this one: because he's a bloodsucking, night-crawling leech who *used* to be my friend?"

"Shane—"

"You think you know, but you don't. He's going to change. They all change. Maybe it'll take time. I don't know. Right now, he thinks he's just human plus, but that's not what it is. He's human *minus.* And you'd better not forget it."

She stared at him, a little bit stunned and a whole lot saddened. "Eve's right. That sounds like your father talking."

Shane flinched, paused the game, and threw the controller down. "Low, Claire." He wasn't exactly his dad's biggest fan at the best of times—he couldn't be, with the number of cruel things his dad had done to him.

"No, it's just true. Look, it's *Michael.* Can't you give him the benefit of the doubt? He hasn't hurt anybody, has he? And you have to admit, having a vampire on our side, *really* on our side, couldn't hurt. Not in Morganville."

He just glared at the screen, jaw set. Claire was trying to think of another way to get through to him, but she was derailed by the ringing of the doorbell. Shane didn't move. "I'll get it," she sighed, and went down the hall to open the front door. It was safe enough—midmorning, sunny, and relatively mild. Summer was finally starting a slide toward fall, now that it had burned all the green out of the Texas landscape.

Claire squinted against the brilliance. For a second she thought that there was something deeply wrong with her eyes.

Because her archenemy, Queen Bitch Monica Morrell, flanked by her ever-present harpies Gina and Jennifer, was standing on the doorstep. It was like seeing Barbie and her friends, blown up life-sized and dressed like Old Navy mannequins. Tanned, toned, and perfect, from lip gloss to toenail polish. Monica had on a forced pleasant expression. Gina and Jennifer were trying, but they looked like they were smelling something rotten.

"Hi!" Monica said brightly. "Got plans today, Claire? I was thinking we could hang."

That's it, Claire thought. *I'm dreaming. Only this is a nightmare, right? Monica pretending to be my friend? Definitely a nightmare.*

"I—What do you want?" Claire asked, because her relationship with Monica, Gina, and Jennifer had started with being pushed down the stairs at the dorm, and hadn't improved since. She was a crawling bug to the Cool Girls. At best. Or . . . a tool. *Was this about Michael?* Because his status had changed from "hermit musician" to "hottie vampire" in one night, and Monica was definitely a fang-banger, right? "You want to talk to Michael?"

Monica gave her an odd look. "Why would I want to do that? Can he go shopping in broad daylight?"

"Oh." She had no idea what else to say to that.

"I thought a little retail therapy, and then we all go study," Monica said. "We're going to check out that new place, not Common Grounds. Common Grounds is so last century. Like I *want* to be under Oliver's thumb all the time. Now that he's taken over as Protector for our family, he's been all hands-on, wanting to see my grades. Sucks, right?"

"I—"

"C'mon, save my life. I really need help with economics, and these two are boneheads." Monica dismissed her two closest friends with an offhand wave. "Seriously. Come with. Please? I could really use your brainpower. And I think we should get to know each other a little better, don't you? Seeing as how things have changed?"

Claire opened her mouth, then closed it without saying anything. The last two times she'd gone anywhere with Monica, she'd been flat on her back on the floor of a van, getting beaten and terrorized.

She managed to stammer, "I know this is going to sound rude, but— what the hell are you doing?"

Monica sighed and looked—how weird was this?—contrite. "I know what you're thinking. Yes, I was a bitch to you, and I hurt you. And I'm sorry." Gina and Jennifer, her constant Greek chorus, nodded and repeated *sorry* in whispers. "Water under the bridge, all right? All is forgiven?"

Claire was, if anything, even more mystified. "Why are you doing this?"

Monica pursed her glossy lips, leaned forward, and dropped her voice to a low, confidential tone. "Well . . . all right, yeah, it's not like I had a head injury or something and woke up thinking you were cool. But you're different now. I can help. I can introduce you around to all the people you really need to know."

"You're kidding. I'm different *how?*"

Monica leaned even closer. "You signed."

So . . . this wasn't about Michael. Claire had just become . . . popular. Because she'd become Amelie's property.

And that was terrifying.

"Oh," she managed, and then, more slowly, "Oh."

"Trust me," Monica said. "You need somebody in the know. Somebody to show you the ropes."

If the only other person left on the planet was Jack the Ripper, Claire would have trusted him first. "Sorry," she said. "I have plans. But—thank you. Maybe some other time."

She shut the door on Monica's surprised face, then locked it. She jumped when she turned to find Shane standing right behind her, staring at her as though he'd never seen her before.

"*Thank you?*" he mimicked. "You're thanking that bitch? For what, Claire? For beating you? For trying to kill you? For killing my sister? Christ. First Michael, then you. I don't know any of you anymore."

In true Shane fashion, he just took off. She listened to the heavy tread of his footsteps cross the living room and then go up the stairs. Heard the familiar slam of his door.

"Hey!" she shouted after him. "I was just being polite!"

TWO

"So," Eve said as she drove Claire to school, "what was up with the Monica thing? I mean, maybe you ought to watch your back with her. Even more than you already do."

"She sounded like she really kind of meant it. It took a lot for her to come eat crow like that."

Eve shot her a look. One of *those* looks, doubly effective coming from a girl wearing rice-powder makeup and flawless eyeliner and black-cherry lips. "In Monica's world, being friends means doing whatever Monica wants, when Monica wants to do it. Somehow, I can't see you as one of her brain-dead backup singers."

"No! That's not—I didn't say I was *going* to be her friend, just—you asked." Claire crossed her arms and settled back in the bucket seat of Eve's ancient black Caddy, shooting for a stubborn look. "She's not my friend, okay? You're my friend."

"So when Monica starts bringing the in-crowd to hang at your study table, you'll get up and leave? No way. You're too nice. Before you know it, you're tagging along with them, and then you start to actually feel sorry for them. You'll tell me how Monica's not bad—she's just misunderstood. And before you know it you're braiding each other's hair and giggling over boy bands."

Claire made a retching sound. "I wouldn't do that."

"Please. You like everybody. You even like me. You like *Shane*, and let's face it: Shane's kind of an idiot, at least right now." Eve's eyes narrowed as she thought about that. "And about Shane, I swear, if he doesn't snap out of it, I'm going to punch him in the face. Well, punch him in the face and then run like hell."

Claire played that out in her head and nearly laughed. Eve's best possible punch wouldn't do more than surprise Shane, she figured, but she could just picture the wounded look of confusion on his face. *What the hell did I do?*

"I'm not popular," she declared. "Monica's not my friend, and I'm not hanging with her, ever, end of story."

"Swear?"

Claire held up her hand. "Swear."

"Huh." Eve didn't sound convinced. "Whatev."

"Look, if we're friends, how about buying me a mocha?"

"Mooch."

"You're the one with the job."

Midafternoon, and it was raining, which was kind of a rarity—a cold early-fall rain that came down in glittering sheets. Claire, like about 90 percent of the other students, hadn't thought to bring an umbrella, so she sloshed along miserably along the Quadrangle, past the empty benches and rain-soaked message boards, toward her chem lab. She loved Chem Lab. She hated rain. She hated being soaked to the skin and, frankly, living in this part of Texas made it usually not that much of a risk. There was no room in her backpack for anything frivolous, like a raincoat. She worried her books were getting soggy, but the backpack was supposed to be waterproof. . . .

"You look cold," said a voice from behind her, and then the rain cut off, and she heard the hollow thump of raindrops hitting the thin skin of an umbrella. Claire looked up, blinked water out of her eyes, and saw she was walking under a golf umbrella big enough for four or five of her . . . or one of her, plus the guy holding the umbrella. Because he was *huge*.

Also cute, in that big-boned football player kind of way. He would have made Shane look small. Well proportioned, though, so the height (had to be at least six feet five, Claire thought) and weight just seemed right on him. He had chocolate brown skin and gorgeous brown eyes, and he seemed . . . kind of nice.

"I'm Jerome," he said. "Hey."

"Hey," she said back, still amazed that somebody who was clearly *somebody* would stop to hang an umbrella over her head. "Thanks. Um, I'm Claire. Hi."

She juggled her dripping backpack to her other hand and offered him her right. He took it and shook. His was about three times as large, big enough (she bet) to cup most of an entire football.

He was wearing a TPU athletic department T-shirt. No mystery about his major.

"Where're you heading, Claire?"

"Chem Lab," she said, and pointed at the building, which was about a football field–length away, on the other side of the Quad. He nodded and steered that direction. "Look, it's nice of you, but you don't have to—"

"It's no problem." He smiled at her. He had dimples. "I hear the Science Building is nice this time of year. And anything for a friend."

"But I'm not—"

Jerome nodded to a group of girls standing huddled together under the awning of the Language Arts Building. Pretty girls. In the center of them was Monica Morrell, and she blew Jerome a flirty sort of kiss.

"Oh," Claire said. "*That* friend." Her estimate of Jerome fell by several dozen notches, hit bottom, and started digging for China. "Look, I appreciate it, but I'm not sugar. I won't melt."

She veered away and walked fast. Jerome took about two long strides and put the umbrella over her again without comment. She glared at him.

He lifted an eyebrow. "I can play this game all day."

"Fine," she said. "But I don't need favors from Monica."

"Girl, it's an umbrella, not a Lamborghini," he pointed out. Way too reasonably. "I'm not even lending it to you. It's not really that much of a favor."

She kept her mouth shut, head down, and walked fast. Jerome stopped at the foot of the Science Building's stairs, and she bounded up and darted under the concrete porch, which was already choked with other students hiding from the rain. She looked back down. Jerome smiled and waved, and a bronze or copper bracelet caught her eye.

He was Protected. Probably a native of Morganville.

"I'm not her friend. That was not my fault," she complained, defending herself to an Eve who wasn't even there.

And then she sneezed, sniffled, and dragged her soggy butt to class.

The rain kept up all day and all night, but the next day dawned bright and shiny, with a pale silver sun not quite as fierce as Claire expected. Kind of nice, actually. She'd already showered by the time Eve stumbled into the bathroom, looking more like the walking dead than most vampires. Eve mumbled something and ignored Claire as she started up the shower again. Claire finished at the sink and hurried downstairs. She found Michael at the coffeepot, emptying the filter of cold grounds. Deeply weird that he was *more* of a morning person as a vampire. Maybe he was just enjoying having a morning again, instead of becoming a floaty ghost at dawn.

"Eve's up. You'd better make it so dark the spoon melts."

Michael shot her a half smile, still almost lethal enough to stop a girl's heart. Luckily he knew just how much current to use on his charm. "That bad, huh?"

She thought about it for a second as she took down a bowl and the box of Rice Krispies, and found the milk behind the bottles of beer—contraband, from Shane—in the fridge. "You've seen that movie where the zombies eat people's brains?"

"*Night of the Living Dead?*"

"The zombies would run if they got a look at her."

Michael spooned extra coffee into the fresh filter. He looked good, she thought. Strong, tall, confident. He had on a nice blue shirt and some not-so-ratty blue jeans, and he was wearing shoes. Running shoes, sure, but shoes. Claire stared at his feet. "You're going out," she said.

"Got a job," Michael said. "Working at JT's Music over on Third Street, ten to close. Mostly I'll be demoing guitars and selling them, but JT said he'd let me do some private lessons if I wanted."

That was so . . . normal. *Really* normal. And he sounded happy, too. Claire bit her lip and tried to organize the explosion of questions in her brain. "Ah—what about the sun?" she asked. Because that seemed to be the first hurdle.

"They issued me a car," Michael said. "It's in the garage. Fully sun-proofed. And there's underground parking at JT's. There is most places."

"Issued—who issued you a car?" He shot her a *you're not stupid* look. "The town? Amelie?"

He didn't answer directly as he slid the filter compartment shut and turned on the *brew* switch. The machine began wheezing and trickling into the pot. "They tell me it's standard procedure," he said. "For new vampires."

"Not that there have been any for fifty years, right?"

He shrugged. It was obvious that she was making him uncomfortable with the questions, but Claire couldn't help herself. "Did you ever find out why—why there haven't been any in so long?"

"I don't think it's a great idea to be too curious right now."

She understood that—and understood he meant it for her as well—but she couldn't stop asking questions, somehow. "Michael—did they get you the job, too?"

"No. I know JT. I got the job all by myself. They offered—" He stopped, clearly thinking he'd already said too much.

Claire finished it out, guessing. "They offered you some kind of job in the vampire community. Right? Or—" Oh God. "Or they offered to make you a Protector?"

"Not right off the bat," he said, still staring at the coffeemaker. "You have to work up to that. So they say."

Michael. Owning people. Skimming off their wages like some Mafia don. She tried not to let him see how sick that idea made her feel, that he'd ever really consider doing it.

His eyes suddenly cut toward her, as if he'd read her mind. "I didn't do it. I found the job at JT's, Claire," Michael said, and suddenly moved toward her. She flinched, and he took a deep breath and held out his hand in clear apology. "Sorry. I forget sometimes—it's hard, okay, learning how to move around people when I can go so much faster. But I wouldn't hurt you, Claire. No way."

"Shane thinks—"

Light caught and flared in Michael's eyes, eerie and frightening, and then he blinked and it was gone. He obviously made a real effort to keep his voice quiet. "Shane's wrong," he said. "I'm not changing, Claire. I'm still your friend. I'll look after you. All of you. Even Shane."

She didn't answer him. Truthfully, as much as she liked him—and it verged on love—she felt something different about him today. Something complicated and agitated and strange.

Was he . . . hungry? He was staring at her. No, he was staring at the thin skin of her neck, wasn't he? Claire put her hand to it, involuntary but irresistible, and Michael got a very slight pink flush in his pale cheeks and looked away.

"I wouldn't," he said, in a far different tone than before. It almost sounded scared to her. "I wouldn't, Claire. You have to believe me. But—this is hard. It's so hard."

She did believe him, mostly because she could hear all the heartbreak and sorrow in his voice. She took a breath, stepped forward, and hugged him. He was tall; the top of her head only brushed his chin. His arms felt strong and comforting, and she told herself that he wasn't warm because it was chilly in the kitchen. It wasn't really true, but that helped.

"I wouldn't hurt you," he murmured. "But I've got to admit, I want to. I spent all my life hating vampires, and now—now look at me."

"You had to," Claire said. "You didn't have a choice."

She felt his sigh go through both of them. "Not true," he said. "Shane's right—I did have a choice. But this is the choice I made, and now I have to live with it."

He let go when she stepped back. Neither of them knew what to say, so Claire busied herself by opening kitchen cabinets to get down the four mismatched cups they used in the morning. Michael's was plain chunky stoneware, oversized, like a diner cup on steroids. Eve's was a petite black thing with a yawning cartoon vampire on it. Shane's had a happy face with a bloody bullet hole in the center of its forehead. Claire had taken one with Goofy and Mickey on it.

"How's school?" Michael asked. Neutral subjects. He didn't want to talk it out; he wanted to keep it inside. She wasn't too surprised. Michael had always been too self-contained for his own good, as far as she could tell.

"Too easy," she sighed, and poured coffee.

They were sitting down and sipping from their mugs when the kitchen door opened, and Shane—wearing pajama bottoms and a ratty old faded T-shirt—came into the kitchen. He avoided Michael, picked up his cup off the counter, and filled it to the brim. He left without a word.

Michael watched him go, face set and hard.

Claire felt the need to apologize. "He's just—"

"I know," Michael said. "Believe me. I know exactly how Shane is. Doesn't mean I have to like it right now."

I really need to stop being the Glass Goodwill Ambassador, Claire thought, but she knew she'd keep on doing it. Somebody had to, after all. So after she'd finished her coffee, she went to talk to Shane.

Shane's door was unlocked and slightly open. Claire pushed it and stepped inside, then stopped short. All her carefully prepared speeches flew right out of her head, because Shane was getting dressed.

The sight of him short-circuited her thought processes and completely grounded her better judgment. He'd already hauled on his blue jeans, and his back was to her. No shirt yet. She was spellbound by the ripples of muscles on his back, the gorgeous smoothness of his skin, the way his shaggy hair brushed the tops of his shoulders and begged to be smoothed back. . . .

The sound of his zipper being pulled up snapped her back to sanity. She stepped hastily back, out into the hall, and pulled the door almost shut, then knocked.

"What?" It wasn't a friendly response.

"It's me," she said. "Can I come in?"

She heard something halfway between a grunt and a sigh, and opened the door to find him dragging a dark gray, form-fitting shirt over his head. It looked very good on him. Not as good as the no-shirt thing, but she was trying hard not to think about that. It had made her warm and fluttery inside.

"Is that a new shirt?" she asked, desperate to get her mind off the vivid mental pictures that kept bubbling up. That got another indefinite grunt. "It looks nice."

Shane gave her an ironic look. "We're talking clothes now? Wait. Let me get my *Fashion for Dummies* book."

"I—never mind. About Michael—"

"Stop." Shane stepped forward and kissed her on the forehead. "I know, you don't want me ripping him, but I can't help it. Give me some time, okay? I need to figure some things out."

Claire tipped her head back, and this time he found her lips. It was, she thought, supposed to be a fast and sweet little kiss, but somehow it slowed down, got warmer and deeper. His lips were damp and soft as silk, and that was such a contrast to the hard lines of his body pressed against her, the strength of his hands sliding around her waist and pulling her even closer. She heard him growl low in his throat, a wild and hungry sound that made her go weak and faint.

He broke the kiss and leaned against her, breathing hard. "Good morning to you, too. Man, I just can't stay mad when you do that."

"Do what?" she asked innocently. She didn't feel innocent. She also didn't feel sixteen-nearly-seventeen, not at all. Shane always made her feel older. Much older. Ready for anything. It was a good thing Shane wasn't as dumb as her hormones seemed to be.

"Unless you want to stay home and cut class, we don't really have time to talk about it," he said, and waggled his eyebrows. "So. Wanna cut class and make out?"

She socked him on the arm. "No."

"You are such a strange girl. Ow," he said, in the way that meant he hadn't felt it at all. "You riding with Eve?"

"When she passes the snarling-cannibal phase, yeah. Another two cups of coffee, probably."

"You sure you don't want a bodyguard?" He meant it. Shane didn't have a job—she wasn't really sure he could get one, after what his dad had been up to in Morganville recently. Probably better he kept it low profile for a while. The fewer vampires—and vampire loyalists—he came in contact with right now, the better. He was still thought of as an unindicted coconspirator to his dad's revenge rampage, and even though the mayor had officially signed his pardon, nobody had much liked it.

Accidents happened.

"I don't need a bodyguard," Claire said. "Nobody's out to get me. Even Monica's gotten all friends-making with me."

That earned her a too-sharp look, which didn't go well with his reddened, kissable lips. "Yeah. Why is that?"

She shrugged and avoided his eyes. "I don't know."

He tipped her chin up with one finger. "So, are we at the lying part of the relationship already? Usually that comes after the exciting, hot and sexy honeymoon period."

She stuck out her tongue at him, and he leaned forward and—to her horror—licked it. "Ewwww!"

"Then don't stick it out." Shane smiled. "If you're going to hang out in my room and tempt me, there's a penalty. One item of clothing per minute comes off."

"Perv."

He pointed to himself. "Male and eighteen. What's your point?"

"You are so—"

"Say, you got any pleated miniskirts and kneesocks? I really get off on—"

She squealed and dodged his grabby hands, then checked her watch. "Oh, crap—I really do have to go. I'm sorry. Look, you'll be—you're okay, right?"

The smile disappeared, leaving only a trace in his dark, secretive eyes. "Yeah," Shane said. "I'll be okay. Watch your back, Claire."

"You too." Claire started for the door, but she heard his footsteps behind her and turned; he moved her back to the wall, tipped up her chin, and kissed her so thoroughly that she felt her head fill with light and her knees turn to rubber.

When she could breathe again, and he pulled back to give her just an inch or so of space between their lips, she gasped, "Was that a good-bye?"

"That was a come-home-soon," he said, and pushed off from the wall. "Seriously, Claire. Watch yourself. I worry."

"I know," she said, and smiled. Her knees were still weak, and the chorusing light in her head just didn't seem to be fading. "Best kiss so far, by the way."

His eyebrows rose. "You're keeping score?"

"Hey, you raised the bar. I don't grade on a curve."

She left him, reluctantly, to grab her backpack and see if Eve was in the mood to eat brains, or to give her a ride to school.

THREE

Morning classes went pretty well, and Claire spent her breaks hanging at the coffee bar at the University Center, where Eve barista'd her way through the day. Eve was good at it—calm, efficient, seemingly impervious to the pissy demands and bitchiness of a lot of the students. Claire had figured out that the rude ones were mostly Protected, so it was a class thing; Eve had elected not to sign up with a vampire for protection, and those who had looked down on her.

Or else they were just bitchy. Which was equally possible. People didn't have to have a vampire connection to be arrogant jerks.

Eve was working today with another girl, somebody Claire didn't know; she had long, straight brown hair that shimmered like a curtain when she moved. She wore it loose around her shoulders, which Claire guessed was okay because she wasn't working directly with the drinks or anything, just taking orders and cash. Her name tag said AMY, and she looked cheerful and sweet. She and Eve were talking like friends, which was good; Eve needed that. Claire killed time between classes by skimming through her English Lit—boring—and reading a book she'd checked out from the library on advanced string theory—not boring. She liked the whole idea of vibrating strings being the basis of everything, that there were all kinds of surfaces that vibrated. It made the world more . . . exciting. Always in motion.

Her watch beeped to let her know she was going to be late for class if she didn't hurry, so she packed it up, waved to Amy and Eve, and jogged out of the UC and into the warm afternoon sunshine.

As she was blinking in the glare, she ran into Monica. Literally, as Monica was coming up the steps while she was going down. Claire automatically reached out to steady the other girl when she wavered, and then thought, *What am I doing?* Because Monica had once laughed as Claire tumbled down the stairs and cracked her head halfway open.

"Hey, *watch it,* bitch!" Monica snapped, and then did a double take. "Claire? Oh, hi. Cute shirt!"

Claire looked down at herself, mystified. It wasn't. She didn't really own any clothes she'd classify as cute, and even the best of them would never match Monica's standards, which were much higher.

"You on your way to class?" Monica continued brightly. "Too bad, I'd buy you a mocha or something."

"I—uh—yeah, I've got class." Claire edged around and tried to descend the steps, but Monica got in her way. Monica's smile was friendly, but it didn't really warm up her big, pretty eyes. "I'll be late."

"One thing," Monica said, and lowered her voice. It occurred to Claire that it was almost the first time she'd seen Monica alone, not flanked by Gina and Jennifer, not trailing an entourage of the Popular. "I'm having a party on Friday night. Can you come? It's at my parents' house. Here's the address." Before Claire could react, Monica pressed a slip of paper into her hand. "Keep it quiet, all right? I'm asking only the best people. Oh, and wear something nice; it's formal."

And then Monica was gone, breezing by her up the steps, where she fell in with a group of girls and went into the UC's glass atrium, chatting and laughing.

The best people? Claire eyed the slip of paper, thought about throwing it away, and then shoved it in her pocket.

Maybe this was a golden opportunity to convince Monica that she wasn't ever going to be anything like a friend.

She headed out for class, moving quickly, but keeping her eyes peeled. When she spotted the guys she was looking for, she veered off the sidewalk and onto the grass.

Gamers. Nerds. They sat around outside most of the afternoon moving counters around on complicated-looking boards and rolling dice. She'd seen them every day for weeks, and in all that time she'd never seen any kind of girl with them, or even approach them. In fact, when she cleared her throat they stared at her as though she were an alien from one of the planets on their game board.

"Hi," she said, and thrust out the slip of paper. "My name's Monica. I'm having a party on Friday night. If you guys want to come. Tell your friends."

One of them reached out and gingerly took the slip of paper. Another snatched it away from him, read it, and said, "Wow. Really?"

"Really."

"Mind if we invite some other people?"

"Knock yourself out."

Claire headed off to class.

"Claire Danvers?"

Last class of the day, and Claire, startled, looked up from writing the date in her notebook. The professor didn't usually take roll. In fact, he seemed pretty much indifferent to who showed up, which was sometimes next to nobody. Like today—she was one of about twelve people. Showing up was really kind of useless in this particular course, since Professor What's-His-Name lectured from PowerPoint slides, bullet by bullet, and then made them available on his Web site right after the lecture. No wonder most people skipped.

She raised her hand, wondering what was going on. She had a guilty flash of handing over the party invitation to the Nerd Squad, but no, how could they have found out so soon? And besides, who'd care, besides Monica?

The professor—gray, wrinkled, tired, and unenthusiastic—stared at her for a second without recognition, then said, "You're wanted in Administration, room three-seventeen. Go now."

"But—" Claire started to ask what was going on, but he'd already dismissed her and turned back to his PowerPoint, droning on in a monotone. She stuffed books into her bag, wondered again what was going on, and left without much regret.

She'd been in the Administration Building exactly three times—once to register, once to file the official paperwork to move off campus, once to do add/drop. It looked just like any administration building at any school—grubby and utilitarian, with tired, crabby employees and desks piled high with file folders. She avoided the first-floor Registrar's Office and went up the steps. The second floor was quieter, but still full of people talking, keys clicking on computers, printers running.

The third floor was whisper-quiet. Claire started down the hallway, and the silence sank deeper. She couldn't even hear sounds from outside the windows, although she could clearly see people out there walking and talking, and cars tooling around the street below. Room 317 was at the end of the hall. All of the glossy wooden doors were firmly closed.

She knocked on 317, and thought she heard someone say "Come in," so she turned the knob and stepped inside . . . into darkness. Complete, velvety darkness that disoriented her immediately. The knob slipped out of her hand and the door clicked shut, and she couldn't find it again. Her hand moved over what felt like a featureless, smooth wall.

A light bloomed behind her and she turned to see the flare of a match, and a candle wick catching fire. In the glow, Amelie's face shone like perfect ivory.

The elder vampire looked exactly the same as before: cool, queenly, pale, with her white blond hair twisted back in an elegant updo that must have required servants to achieve. She was wearing a white silk suit, and her skin was flawless. If she wore makeup, Claire couldn't tell. Her eyes were eerie in the near-dark . . . luminous and not quite human, and very beautiful.

"My apologies for the dramatics," Amelie said, and smiled at her. It was a very nice smile, cool and polite. Claire's mother had always loved the Hitchcock movie *Rear Window*, and Claire was struck by the thought that if Grace Kelly had ended up a vampire, this was how she'd have looked. Icy and perfect. "Don't bother looking for the door. It's gone until I wish it to be there again."

Claire's heartbeat sped up, and she knew Amelie could tell, though the vampire didn't comment on it; she just shook out the match and dropped it in a silver dish on the table next to the candle. Claire's eyes adjusted gradually to the dimness. She was standing in a fairly small room, some kind of library crammed with books. *Crammed* was an understatement—the books were double-stacked on the shelves, leaning in towers on the top of the bookcases, filling the corners in untidy ziggurats. So many books that the whole room smelled like ancient paper. There wasn't any wall space, except where Claire had come in, that wasn't blocked up by packed, groaning shelves.

"Hi," Claire said awkwardly. She hadn't seen Amelie since signing the Protection papers and putting them, as instructed, in the mailbox outside. She'd expected some kind of visit, but . . . nothing. "Um—what should I call you?"

Amelie's delicate brows rose, pale on pale. "I know that the concept of manners has declined, but I should think you would know at least some polite form of address that would be appropriate."

"Ma'am," Claire stammered. Amelie nodded.

"That will do." She lit another candle. The light strengthened, flickering but casting a warm and welcome glow. Claire spotted another door in the shadows, small and fitted with an antique-style doorknob. There was a big skeleton key in the massive lock.

Nobody else in the room, just she and Amelie.

"I have called you to discuss your studies," Amelie said, and sat down in a chair on the other side of the table. There wasn't any seat on Claire's side, so she stood there, awkwardly. She put her backpack down and folded her hands.

"Yes, ma'am," she said. "Aren't my grades okay?" Because usually a 4.0 GPA was okay by most standards.

Amelie dismissed it with a wave. "I did not say classes; I said studies. No doubt you are finding the local college beneath your abilities. You are said to be quite exceptional."

Claire didn't know what to say to that, so she didn't say anything. She wished she had a chair. She wished she could say something nice and get back to class and never, ever see Amelie again, because as superficially polite and kind as the old vampire was, there was something ice-cold about her. Something unsettlingly *not human*.

"I would like you to study privately with a friend of mine," Amelie said. "For credit, of course." She looked around, smiling very slightly. "This is his library. Mine is far more orderly."

Claire's throat felt tight and uncomfortable. "A . . . uh . . . vampire friend?"

"Is that an issue?" Amelie folded her white hands together on the table. The candlelight flickered in her eyes.

"N-no, ma'am." *Yes.* God, she couldn't imagine what Shane was going to say.

"I believe you will find him most interesting, Claire. He is indeed one of the most brilliant minds I have ever encountered in my long life, and he has learned so much through his lifetime that he could never teach it all. Still, he has much to pass along. I have been seeking the right pupil, one who can quickly grasp the discoveries he has made, and assist him in his research."

"Oh," Claire whispered faintly. *So . . .* an old vampire. Her experience wasn't so good with the older ones. Like Amelie, they were cold and strange, and most of them were cruel, too. Like Oliver. Oh God, she wasn't talking about Oliver, was she? "Who—?"

Amelie looked down. Just for an instant, and then she met Claire's eyes and smiled. "You have not met," she said. "Not formally, at any rate. His name is Myrnin. He is one of my oldest friends and allies. Understand, Claire, that your actions since you came to Morganville, including your agreement with me, have won my trust. I would not grant this honor to any but those I found worthy."

Flattery. Claire recognized it, and knew the slight warmth in Amelie's voice was probably calculated, but it still worked. It made her feel less scared. "Myrnin," she repeated.

"It is an old name," Amelie agreed, in response to the question in

Claire's tone. "Old and forgotten, now. But once he was a great scholar, known and revered. His works should not be forgotten as well."

There was something strange in that, but Claire was too nervous to figure out what Amelie could be trying to say. Or not say. She was working hard to swallow a lump in her throat, but it was about the size of a poisoned apple and seemed to be growing larger. She could only nod.

Amelie smiled. It looked kind of artificial, like an expression she'd practiced in a mirror rather than learned as a child. Smiling was something her face just didn't naturally do, Claire decided. And sure enough, the smile was gone in seconds, without a trace.

"If you're ready . . . ?"

"Now?" Claire cast an involuntary, helpless look at the blank wall behind her. There wasn't a door, and that meant there was no way to retreat. So she didn't really have a choice.

Amelie wasn't waiting for her answer, anyway. The ice queen stood up and walked—oh so very undead Grace Kelly— to another small, low doorway with the key in the lock. She turned the key, withdrew it, and looked down at it for a moment before holding it out to Claire. "Keep it," she said. "Leave your book bag here, please. I shouldn't want you to forget it. You will leave through the same door that brought you."

Claire's fingers closed around the key, registering rough, cold, heavy metal. She shoved it in the pocket of her blue jeans as Amelie swung open the door, and leaned her backpack against a convenient bookcase.

"Myrnin?" Amelie's voice was low and gentle. "Myrnin, I've brought the girl I told you about. Her name is Claire."

Claire knew that tone of voice. You used it with old, sick people, people who didn't really understand what was happening anymore. People you didn't think were really going to be around for long. Coming from Amelie, it was really odd, because she could also hear the love in that low voice. Could vampires love? Well, sure, she guessed; Michael could, right? So why not Amelie, too?

Claire stepped out from behind Amelie at the vampire's imperative gesture, and anxiously scanned the room. It was big, full of the weirdest mixture of equipment and junk she'd ever seen. A brand-new wide-screen laptop computer with a shimmying belly dancer as a screen saver. An abacus. A chemistry set that looked straight out of some old Sherlock Holmes movie. More books, carelessly piled around as trip hazards, leaning in columns on every table. Lamps—some electric, some oil. Candles. Bottles and jars and shadows and angles and . . .

And a man.

Claire blinked, because she was expecting an old, sick person; expecting it so much she looked around again, trying to find him. But the only man in the room sat in a chair, peacefully reading a book. He marked the spot with a finger, closed it, and looked up at Amelie.

He was young, or at least he looked it. Shoulder-length curly brown hair, big, dark puppy-dog eyes, flawless, faintly golden skin. Frozen at the age of maybe twenty-five, just enough for creases to be forming at the corners of his eyes. Also, he was really, really . . . *pretty.*

And he didn't look sick. Not at all.

"Ah, good, I've been waiting for you," he said. He spoke English, but with some kind of accent, nothing that Claire could identify. It sounded a little bit like Irish, a little bit like Scottish, but more . . . liquid, somehow. Welsh? "Claire, is it? Well, come forward, girl, I won't bite." He smiled, and unlike Amelie's cool attempt, it was a warm, genuine expression, full of merriment. Claire took a couple of steps toward him. She sensed Amelie tensing behind her, and wondered why. Myrnin seemed okay. Seemed more okay than any vampire she'd seen so far, except maybe Sam, Michael's grandfather—and Michael, the youngest vampire in Morganville.

"Hello," she said, and got an even wider smile.

"She speaks! Excellent. I have no use for someone without a backbone. Tell me, young Claire, do you like the sciences?"

That was an antique way of saying it . . . *the sciences.* People usually said *science* or mentioned a specific thing, like biology or nuclear studies or chemistry. Still, she knew the right answer. "Yes, sir. I love the sciences."

His dark eyes glittered, full of slightly wicked humor. "So very polite, you are. And philosophy?"

"I—I don't know. We didn't study it in high school. I just got to college."

"Science without philosophy is nonsense," he said, very seriously. "And alchemy? Do you know anything of it?"

She just shook her head to that one. She knew what it meant, but wasn't it all about turning lead into gold or something like that? Sort of con-man science?

Myrnin looked tragically disappointed. She almost wanted to lie to him and tell him that she'd gotten an A in Alchemy 101.

"Don't be difficult, Myrnin," Amelie said. "I told you this age doesn't regard the subject with much respect. You won't find anyone with a working knowledge of the Hermetic arts, so you'll have to use what's available. From all accounts, this girl is quite gifted. She should be able to understand what you have to teach, if you are patient."

Myrnin nodded soberly and put the book aside. He stood up—and up—and up. He was tall, gawky, with long legs and arms—like a human stick bug. He was wearing a weird mixture of clothes, too—not homeless-guy weird, but definitely funky. A vertically striped knit shirt under what looked like some kind of frock coat, and blue jeans, old ones, with holes in the knees. And flip-flops. Claire stared at his exposed toes. Somehow, with that outfit, flip-flops looked almost indecent.

But he had pretty feet.

He extended his hand to Claire, bending over to do it. She carefully took it and shook. Myrnin looked surprised, then delighted. He pumped the handshake enthusiastically enough to make her shoulder ache. "A handshake—is that the correct way to greet these days?" he asked. "Even for such a lovely young woman? I know it's common among men, but among women it seems quite a violent gesture—"

"Yes," Claire said quickly. "It's fine. Everybody does it." God, he wasn't going to try to kiss her hand or anything, was he? No, he was letting go and crossing his arms. Studying her.

"Quickly," he said. "What's the elemental designation for rubidium?"

"Um . . . Rb."

"Atomic number?"

Claire frantically called to mind the periodic table. She'd played with it the same way other kids played with puzzles, back when she was young; she'd known every detail. "Thirty-seven."

"Group number?"

She could see the square on the table now, as real as if it were a card in her hand. "Group one," she said confidently. "Alkali metal. The period number is five."

"And what are the dangers of working with rubidium, young Claire?"

"It spontaneously burns when exposed to air. It also reacts violently to water."

"Solid, liquid, gas, plasma?"

"Solid to forty degrees centigrade. That's the melting point." She waited for the next question, but Myrnin only cocked his head and watched her. "How did I do?"

"Adequately," he said. "You've memorized well. But memorization is not science, and science is not knowledge." Myrnin stalked over to a leaning stack of books, tossed some carelessly to the floor, and found a threadbare volume that he flipped open without much regard for the fragile pages. "Ah! Here. What is this, then?"

He held the book out to her. Claire squinted at the dim illustration. It looked a little like a small square sail, full of wind. She frowned and shook her head. Myrnin snapped the book closed with a sharp clap, making her jump.

"Too much to teach her," he said to Amelie. He began to pace, then got distracted and fiddled with a glass retort full of some noxious green liquid. "I don't have time to coddle infants, Amelie. Bring me someone who at least understands the basics of what I am trying to—"

"I've told you before, there is no one available who would recognize that symbol, and in any case, the field has never attracted the most trustworthy of characters. Give Claire a chance. She's a quick study." Her voice cooled to a measured, icy tone. "Do not force me to make it an order, Myrnin."

He stopped moving, but he didn't raise his head. "I don't want another student." He sounded resentful.

"Nevertheless, you must have one."

"Have you explained the risks?"

"I leave that to you. She is yours, Myrnin. But make no mistake, I will hold you responsible for her performance, and for her safety."

Claire heard the click of metal, and when she looked behind her, Amelie was . . . gone.

She'd left her alone. With *him.*

When Claire turned back to him, Myrnin had raised his head and was staring straight at her. Warm, brown eyes no longer amused. Very serious.

"It seems neither of us has much choice," he said. "We'll just have to make the best of it, then." He fumbled through the stacks of books and came up with one that looked just as threadbare and fragile as the first one he'd mishandled, but this one was much thinner. He thrust it toward her, and Claire took it. The inscription on the cover was in English. *Metals in Egyptian Inscriptions.*

"The symbol I showed you is for copper," Myrnin said. "Know the rest when you come back tomorrow. I will also expect you to read Basil Valentine's *Last Will and Testament.* I have a copy here . . . ." He shoved books around, almost frantic, and located something with a cry of satisfaction. He held that out to her as well. "Pay special attention to the alchemical symbols. You'll be expected to copy them out until you know them by heart."

"But—"

"Take them! Take them and get out! Out! I'm busy!"

Myrnin rushed past her, bowling over stacks of books in his haste, to fling open the door through which Amelie had disappeared. He was at least a foot taller than the door itself, like a human in a hobbit house. He stood there, jittering his foot in impatience, the flip-flop making plastic slaps between flesh and floor.

"Did you hear me?" he snapped. "Go. No time now. Get out. Come tomorrow."

"But—I don't know how to get home. Or back here."

He stared for a second, and then he laughed. "Someone will have to bring you. I can't configure the system just for you!"

Configure the system? Claire stopped, staring back. "What system?

These—doorways?" The implications were dizzying. If Myrnin under-stood the doorways, controlled the doorways, the ones that appeared and disappeared out of nowhere in Morganville . . . *I need to know. I need to know how that works.*

"Yes, I am responsible for that, among many other things, though it's hardly the most important thing right now," he said. "Later, Claire. Go now. Talk tomorrow."

He took hold of her, bodily shoved her through the doorway, and slammed it behind her. She heard his hand hit the wood with stunning force.

"Lock it!" he shouted. Claire dug the key out of her pocket. She could barely get it in the lock; the light was bad here, and her hands were shaking. But she managed, and heard the solid click as the tumblers fell. "Take the key!" Myrnin yelled.

"But—"

"You're responsible for me now, Claire. You must keep me safe." Myr-nin's voice had fallen lower now, as if he'd gotten tired. "Keep me safe from everyone."

And then he started . . . crying.

"Myrnin?" Claire said, bending closer to the door. "Are you okay? Should I come in and—"

The whole door vibrated with the force of his blow. Claire scrambled backward, shocked.

And the crying continued. Lost-little-boy crying.

Claire hesitated for a few seconds, then turned to see that Amelie hadn't left after all. She was standing quietly by the desk, in the glow of the single candle, and her expression was composed, but sad.

"Myrnin's mind is not what it once was. He has periods of lucidity, however. And at all costs, you must take full advantage of these to learn what he has to teach. It can't be lost, Claire. It *must not* be lost. There are things he does that—" Amelie shook her head. "There are projects in motion that must continue."

Claire's heart was racing, her whole body shaking. "He's crazy, he's a vampire, and you want me to be his student."

"No," Amelie said. "I *require* you to be his student. You will comply, Claire, by the rules of the contract you signed of your own free will. This is valuable work. I would not risk you unnecessarily."

Have you explained to her the risks? Myrnin had asked that. "What are the risks?" Claire demanded.

Amelie merely pointed to the bookcase, where her backpack still leaned. Claire grabbed it and hauled it to her shoulder—and paused, because a doorway had formed in the blank area of the wall. A solid wooden door, with a plain knob. Identical to those at the university. "Open it," Amelie said.

"But—"

"Open the door, Claire."

Claire did, and the glare of fluorescent lights and the dead, air-conditioned smell of the Administration Building swept over her in a rush.

Amelie blew out the light. In the darkness, Claire couldn't see her anymore.

"Be ready at four o'clock tomorrow in the University Center," Amelie said. "Sam will fetch you. I suggest you do the reading Myrnin requires of you. And Claire—tell no one what you're doing here. Absolutely no one."

It wasn't until Claire was in the hall, with the door shut, that she realized Amelie hadn't answered her question. She opened the door again, but—there was just a room piled with discarded, broken furniture. Something moved furtively in the corner. There was a window with crooked blinds, but no Amelie. No cave of books. No Myrnin.

"He's sick," Claire said aloud, to whatever was rustling in the corner behind a three-legged desk. "That's why she talked to him like that. He's old, and he's sick. Maybe even dying." Vampires could get sick. Vampires could *die?* Somehow she'd never even considered that.

She shut the door gently, adjusted the weight of her backpack, and looked down at the two ancient books in her hand.

Last Will and Testament.

She hoped that wasn't a sign of her future.

Eve chattered on about her day on the drive back, talking about some boy who had totally tried to ask her out, and Amy's boyfriend, Chad, who'd come by to help clean up and was a total sweetheart, and how her boss was a toerag, but at least he'd given her a twenty-cent-an-hour raise. "I think that's just for not quitting in the first couple of weeks," Eve said, but she sounded pretty jacked about it, and Claire was pleased for her. "Yeah, it's only a couple more dollars a week, but—"

"But it's something." Claire nodded. "Congratulations, Eve. You deserve it. You're really good at this. I'll bet you could run the whole thing if you wanted."

"Me? Manager?" Eve laughed so hard she snorted. "Yeah, like I want to become Tinpot Dictator of the coffee bar. Get serious."

"No, I mean it. You're nice. People like you. You know what you're doing. You could. You'd be good at it."

Eve shot her a sideways look that was almost a frown. "You're serious."

"Yep."

"I don't know if I'm ready for management. Don't you have to wear a tie for that?"

"You've got one," Claire said solemnly.

"Only one with the Grim Reaper on it. Hey, wait. That could be my management style! Screw up and I'll kill you, maggot." Eve grinned. "They ought to teach that in business school."

"They probably do here," Claire sighed.

"What's up with you, CB?" CB stood for Claire Bear, which was Eve's funny nickname for her. Claire didn't think she much resembled a bear, not even the stuffed Gund variety. "You seem really—I don't know—thoughtful."

"Yeah, well—" She couldn't talk to Eve about Myrnin. "Homework and stuff." Yeah, it was just that she'd never had quite *this* kind of pass/fail pressure before. She'd flipped through the book on Egyptian inscriptions. That was pretty straightforward, though she wasn't sure how actually Egyptian it all was. Interesting, though. The other one, *Last Will and Testament,* was lots tougher. Tons of symbols in some weird notation she didn't understand. She'd be up all night trying to make sure she remembered even the basics. "Eve . . . has anybody ever broken their contract in Morganville? I mean, and lived?"

"Contract?" Eve shot her yet another look, this one definitely coming with a side order of frowning. "You're talking about a vamp contract? Sure. People have tried everything, at one time or another. But not very successfully."

"What happened?"

"Back in the old days, they got hanged. These days, I think they just throw 'em in jail until they rot, if the vampires don't eat 'em. But hey, not like you and me have to worry about it, right? Live free or die!" Eve held up her hand. "High five!"

Claire slapped it, without much enthusiasm. She was thinking about the way the pen had felt in her hand, moving across that stiff paper. Signing her life away. And she felt ashamed.

"Why?" Eve asked.

"Huh?"

"Why are you asking?" Eve made the turn onto Lot Street, and the glow of the windows of the Glass House—home—spilled out into the street. "C'mon, Claire. Someone you know thinking about it?"

"Um . . . there's this guy at school. I just heard him say—I wondered, that's all."

"Well, quit wondering. His problem, not yours. Ready for the fire drill? Quick like a bunny. Go!" Eve braked the black Caddy hard, Claire threw open her passenger-side door and jogged around the back of the car, banged open the white picket gate, and raced up the walk to the steps with her house keys in her hand. She heard the engine die, and the noisy clatter of Eve's shoes behind her.

Eve's steps stopped. Stopped dead. Claire whirled, scared and expecting to see a vampire on the prowl, but Eve was just checking the mailbox, grabbing a small handful of stuff, and then hurrying up the steps as she sorted through it. Claire stepped over the threshold, and Eve followed, hip-bumping the door shut behind them and shooting the bolt with her elbow, a feat Claire would never have tried—or been able to accomplish with half that grace.

"Electric bill, water bill—Internet bill. Oh, and something for you." Eve pulled out a small bubble-padded mailer from the pile and handed it over. "No return address."

Who'd send her anything? Well, Mom and Dad, sure, and the occasional card from another relative. Her former BFF Elizabeth had sent a postcard from Texas A&M, but only the one. Claire didn't recognize the neat handwriting on the outside of the envelope. Eve left her to it and walked down the hallway, yelling to let Shane and Michael know they were back, to which Michael yelled back, "Get in here and make me some dinner— Now, woman."

"News flash, Michael: You're supposed to have turned evil, not redneck!"

Claire ripped open the package and upended it, and a small jewelry box slid into her hand. A nice one—red velvet, with some kind of gold crest embossed into it. She felt the skin tighten up on the back of her neck. *Oh no.*

Her suspicions were confirmed as she flipped up the lid and saw the gold bracelet nestled on bloodred velvet. It was pretty, and it wasn't too big; delicate enough to circle one of her small wrists.

The Founder's Symbol was embossed discreetly in a small gold cartouche.

Oh no.

Claire bit her lip and stared at the bracelet for a long time, then snapped the lid shut, put it back in the envelope, and went to join Eve and Michael in the kitchen.

"So?" Eve was getting down pots, and Michael was rummaging in the refrigerator. "Spaghetti okay with you?"

"Fine," Claire said. She wondered if she looked spooked. She hoped not, but even if she did, Eve was looking at Michael, and he was looking back, and she was safe from any kind of major inspection while they were making eyes at each other.

Until she turned, and ran into Shane, who'd come in the kitchen door behind her. The package felt hot and heavy in her right hand, and she took an involuntary step back.

Which hurt him. She saw the flash of it in his eyes. "Hey," he said. "You all right?"

She nodded, unable to speak, because if she said anything, it would have to be a lie. Shane stepped closer and put a warm hand on her face; it felt good, so very good that she leaned into it, then further, into his arms. He made her feel small and loved, and for just a second, what was in the package in her hand didn't matter.

"You're working too hard," he said. "You look pale. School okay?"

"School's fine," she said. That wasn't a lie, school was definitely not what scared her anymore. "I guess I need more sleep."

"Just a few more days until the weekend." He kissed the top of her head, bent closer, and whispered, "My room. I need to talk to you."

She blinked, but he was already stepping back and heading out the door. She looked over her shoulder at Eve and Michael, but they were happily talking as Eve adjusted the flame under the pots, and they hadn't noticed anything.

Claire shoved the package into her backpack, zipped it up, and followed Shane upstairs.

Shane's room was very utilitarian—his bed was never made, though he made an attempt as she came in to straighten out the sheets and toss the blanket over it. A couple of posters on the wall, nothing special. No photos, no mementos. He didn't spend a lot of time here, except to sleep. Most of his stuff was crammed into the closet.

Claire leaned her backpack against the wall and sat down next to him on the bed. "What?" she asked. If she'd expected a wild predinner make-out session, she was disappointed. He didn't even put his arm around her.

"I'm thinking of leaving," he said.

"Leaving? But Eve's making dinner—"

He turned and made eye contact. "Leaving Morganville."

She felt a surge of utter panic. "No. You can't!"

"Done it before. Look, this place, it's—I didn't come back here because I missed it. I came back because my dad sent me, and now that he's been and gone and I'm not doing his dirty work anymore..." Shane's eyes were begging her to understand. "I want a life, Claire. And you don't belong here. You can't stay. They'll kill you. No, worse. They'll make you into one of them, one of the walking dead. I'm not talking about the vampires, either. Nobody who lives here has a pulse, not really."

"Shane—"

He kissed her, and his lips were warm and damp and soft and urgent. "Please," he whispered. "We need to leave this town. It's going to get bad. I can feel it."

God, *why* was he doing this? Why now? "I can't," she said. "I—school, and—I just can't, Shane. I can't leave." Her signature on a piece of paper. Her soul on a platter. It had been the price to keep them safe, but she'd have to keep on paying, right? As apprentice to Myrnin. And she guessed that wouldn't be a long-distance study course.

"Please." It was barely a whisper from him, his lips brushing hers, and honestly, she would have done almost anything for him when he used that tone, but this time...

"What happened?" she asked.

"What?"

"Was it something with Michael? Did he—did you—?" She didn't even know what she was asking, but something had deeply disturbed Shane, and she had no idea what it was.

He looked at her for a long few seconds, then pulled away, stood up, and walked to his window to look down on the backyard they never really used. "My dad called," he said. "He told me that he was coming back, and he wanted me to be prepared to take out some vampires. If I stay, I'm going to have to kill Michael. I don't want to be here, Claire. I can't."

He didn't want to make the choice, not again. Claire bit her lip, hard; she could hear the pain in his voice, although he wasn't going to let her see it in his expression. "You really think your dad will come back?"

"Yeah. Eventually. Maybe not this month, maybe not this year, but . . . someday. And next time, he'll have what he needs to start a real war around here." Shane shivered; she saw the muscles in his back tense up under the tight gray shirt he was wearing. "I need to get you out of here before you get hurt."

Claire got up, walked to him, and put her arms around him from behind. She leaned against him, her head on his back, and sighed. "I'm more worried about you," she said. "You and trouble . . ."

"Yeah." She heard the smile in his voice. "We're like that."

FOUR

The spaghetti was good, and a little pleading got Shane to sit down and eat. He sat across from Michael, but they didn't talk, and they didn't make eye contact. All in all, pretty polite. Claire was just starting to relax when Shane asked, blandly, "You put extra garlic in this, Eve? You know how I like the garlic."

She shot him a dirty look. "Oh, the *neighborhood* knows." And then an apologetic one toward Michael. "It's okay, right? Not too much?" Because garlic wasn't something vampires were especially fond of. That was why Shane tended to use it as garnish on everything he ate.

"It's fine," Michael said, but he was picking at his food, and he looked a little pale. "Monica stopped by today. Looking for you, Claire."

Both Shane and Eve groaned. For once, all three of her housemates were entirely in agreement. And they were all looking at her.

"What?" she asked. "I swear, it's not—I'm not sucking up to her or anything! She's just—crazy, okay? I'm not her friend. I don't know why she's coming around."

"She's probably going to set you up again," Eve said, and scooped more spaghetti into her bowl. "Like she did at the frat dance. Hey, she's throwing a party this Friday, did you hear? Superexclusive, flying in out of towners and everything. I guess it's her birthday, or Daddy-gave-me-money day, or whatever. We should crash."

"I like the sound of that," Shane said. "Crashing Monica's party." He glanced at Michael, then quickly away. "What about you? That break some kind of vampire rules of conduct or something?"

"Blow me, Shane."

"Boys," Eve said primly. "Language. Minor at the table."

"Well," Shane said, "I wasn't actually planning to do it."

Claire rolled her eyes. "Not like it's the first time I've heard it. Or said it."

"You shouldn't say it," Michael said, all seriousness. "No, I mean it. Girls should say 'eat me,' not 'blow me.' Wouldn't recommend 'bite me,' though. Not around here."

Eve choked on her spaghetti. Shane pounded her on the back, but he was laughing, too, and so was Michael, and Claire glared at them for a little bit before giving in and admitting it was funny, after all.

Everything was all right.

"So. Friday night?" Eve asked, wiping her eyes and gasping through her giggles. "Par-tay? Because I could so use a good blowout."

"I'm in," Michael said, and took a manful bite of spaghetti. Claire wondered if it burned him. "I think if I'm with you, there's no way she can keep us out. Vampire VIP status. Might as well be good for something."

Shane looked at him, and for a second there was that warmth that Claire missed so much, but then it was gone again, and the wall was back firmly in place between the two of them.

"Must be nice," he said. "We should all go, if it's going to ruin Monica's night."

They finished the rest of the meal in uncomfortable silence. Claire realized that she kept thinking about that red velvet box sitting upstairs in her room, and struggled not to look guilty. Probably didn't succeed. She caught Michael watching her with a strange intensity; whether he was picking up on her discomfort or still wondering about why she didn't jump at the chance to go to Monica's party.

She ate too fast, cleaned her dishes, and dashed upstairs with a mumbled excuse about homework. Well, it wasn't as though they weren't used to her studying. It was Shane's turn for dishes, so that would keep him busy for a while. . . .

The box was right where she'd left it, sitting on the dresser. She grabbed it, put her back against the wall, and slid down to a cross-legged sitting position as she weighed the box in her hand.

"You're wondering whether or not to wear it," Amelie said, and Claire yelped in surprise. The elegant older vampire, completely at her ease, was seated in the antique old velvet chair in the corner, her hands folded primly in her lap. She looked like a painting, not a person; there was something about her—now more than ever—that seemed antique and cold as marble.

Claire scrambled to her feet, feeling stupid about it, but you just didn't sit like that in Amelie's presence. Amelie acknowledged the courtesy with a graceful nod, but didn't otherwise move.

"I apologize for surprising you, Claire, but I needed to speak with you alone," she said.

"How can you get in here? I mean, this is our house; aren't vampires . . . ?"

"Prevented from entry? Not into another vampire's home, and even were you all human, this house ultimately belongs to me. I built it, as I built all of the Founder Houses. The house knows me, and so I need no permissions to enter." Amelie's eyes glinted in the dark. "Does that disturb you?"

Claire swallowed and didn't answer. "What did you want?"

Amelie raised one long, slender finger and pointed at the velvet box in Claire's hand. "I want you to put that on."

"But—"

"I am not asking. I am instructing."

Claire shivered, because although Amelie's voice stayed level, it sounded . . . hard. She opened the box and shook the bracelet out. It felt heavy and warm in her hand, and she peered at it carefully.

There wasn't a catch, but it was clearly too small to fit over her hand. "I don't know how—"

She saw a flash in her peripheral vision, and by the time she looked up, Amelie was taking the bracelet out of her palm, and cold, strong fingers were holding her arm.

"It's made for you," Amelie said. "*Hold still.* Unlike the bracelets most of the other children wear, yours cannot be removed. The contract you signed gives me this right, do you understand?"

"But—no, I don't want—"

Too late. Amelie moved, and the bracelet seemed to pass *through* Claire's skin and bone, and settle heavily around her wrist. Claire tried to yank free, but there was no way, not as strong as Amelie was. Amelie smiled and held her still for another second, just to make the point, before she let go. Claire turned the bracelet frantically, pressing, looking for the trick.

It looked seamless, and it wasn't coming off.

"It must be done this way, the old way," Amelie said. "This bracelet will save your life, Claire. Mark me. It is a favor I have given rarely in my life. You should be grateful."

Grateful? Claire felt like a dog on a leash, and she hated it. She glared at Amelie, and the vampire's smile intensified. She couldn't really say it brightened—there was something in it that undermined the whole concept of comfort.

"Perhaps you'll be grateful at a later date," Amelie said, and raised her eyebrows. "Very well. I'll leave you now. No doubt you have studies."

"How am I supposed to hide this from my friends?" Claire blurted, as the vampire walked toward the door.

"You aren't," Amelie said, and opened the door without unlocking it. "Don't forget. You should be well prepared for Myrnin tomorrow." She stepped out into the hall and closed it behind her. Claire lunged forward and turned the knob, but it refused to open. By the time she twisted the thumb lock and swung it back, Amelie was gone. The hall was empty. Claire stood there, listening to the clatter of dishes from downstairs, the distant laughter, and wanted to cry.

She scrubbed at her eyes, took a deep breath, and went to her desk to try to study.

· · ·

The next day was a busy whirl of classes, quizzes, and discussion groups, and Claire was grateful for the afternoon break when it finally arrived. She felt stupid, dressed in her long-sleeved T, but it was the only thing she had that could hide the bracelet, and she desperately wanted to hide it. So far, so good. Eve hadn't noticed, Shane hadn't been awake when they'd left for school. No sign of Michael, either. She'd gotten desperate last night and tried a couple of ways to break the gold band—scissors, then a pair of rusty old bolt-cutters from the basement—but she broke the blade on the scissors, and the bolt-cutters were clumsy and slid right off the metal. She couldn't do it alone, and she couldn't ask for help.

Can't hide it forever.

Well, she could try.

Claire headed for the UC and the coffee bar, and she found Eve harassed, pink-cheeked under the rice-powder makeup, all alone behind the counter. "Where's Amy?" Claire asked, and handed over three dollars for a mocha. "I thought she was working all week?"

"Yeah, no kidding. Me too. I called my boss, but he's sick and so's Kim, so it's just me today. Not enough coffee in the world to make this easy." Eve blew hair from her sweaty forehead and zipped over to the espresso machine, where she pulled shots. "Ever have one of those dreams where you're running and everybody else is standing still, but you can't catch up?"

"No," Claire said. "Usually mine are about being naked in class."

Eve grinned. "For that, you get a free caramel shot. Go sit down. I don't need you hovering like the rest of these vultures."

Claire claimed a study desk and spread out her books, got her mocha when Eve called her name, and yawned as she cracked open *Last Will and Testament* again. She'd spent most of the night memorizing the symbols, but they were tricky. She'd gotten all of the Egyptian ones down, but these were a whole lot less straightforward, and she had the sense that Myrnin wouldn't be too forgiving of mistakes.

A shadow fell over her book. She looked up and saw Detective Travis Lowe, and his partner, Joe Hess, standing close behind him. She knew both of them pretty well; they'd helped her during that crazy time when Shane's dad had been skulking around Morganville, trying to kill vampires (and succeeding). They didn't wear bracelets, and they weren't Protected; as she understood it, they'd earned some kind of special status. She wasn't sure how they'd managed that, but it had to be something really brave.

"Morning, Claire," Hess said, and pulled up a chair. Lowe did the same. They weren't all that similar in body types—Hess was tall and kind of wiry, with a long face; Lowe was chubby and balding. But the expressions in their eyes were identical—careful, hidden, wary. "How have you been?"

"Fine," she said, and resisted the nearly overwhelming urge to touch her bracelet, fiddle with it. She looked from one to the other, feeling less secure all the time. "What's going on? Is something wrong?"

"Yeah," Lowe said. "You could say that. Look, Claire, there's—I'm sorry to tell you this, but there was a dead girl out back of your house. She was found this morning by the trash collectors."

A dead girl? Claire swallowed hard. "Who is she?"

"Amy Callum," Hess said. "She's a local girl. Family lives just a few blocks from you. Her people are pretty broken up about it." He shifted his gaze toward the coffee bar. "She worked here."

Amy? Coffee Bar Amy? Oh no . . . "I knew her," Claire said faintly. "She worked with Eve. She was supposed to be here today. Eve was saying—" Eve. Claire looked over and saw that Eve was still chattering away brightly, filling orders, taking cash. They hadn't told her yet. "You're sure it was our house?"

"Claire . . ." The two detectives exchanged a look, not a good one. "Her body was stuffed inside your trash can. We're sure."

Claire felt faint. That close . . . she'd put out trash just two days ago, right? Dumped garbage bags into the can. Amy had been alive then. And now . . .

"Did you see anything last night?" Hess continued.

"No, I was—it was dark when I got home. And then I studied all night."

"Hear anything, maybe some racket out by the garbage cans?"

"No, sir. I had headphones on. I'm sorry."

Shane had been looking out the window, she remembered. Maybe he'd seen someone. But he'd have said, right? He wouldn't hide something like that.

An awful thought struck her, and she looked up into Joe Hess's calm, impartial eyes. "Was it—"Too many people around. She mimed fangs in the neck. He shook his head.

"It's the same as the last one we found," Lowe said. "Can't rule out our toothy friends, but it doesn't fit their style. You know whose style it fits, though?"

"Jason's," Claire said numbly. "Eve's brother. He's still out?"

"Haven't caught him doing anything illegal yet. But we will. He's too crazy to live sane." Lowe studied her. "Haven't seen him, have you?"

"No."

"Good." Like there'd been some signal between them, Hess and Lowe got up from their chairs. "We'd better go tell Eve. Look, you think of anything, you call, all right? And don't go out alone. Protection doesn't cover this." Lowe cast a significant look at her wrist, and she felt herself blush, as though he'd guessed what color panties she had on. "You need to go out, you go with one of your friends, all right? Same goes for Eve. We'll try to keep an eye on you, but caution is your best defense."

Claire watched as the cops walked away. They exchanged nods with a tallish young man who was coming in her direction. For a second she thought it was Michael—he had the same walk, the same basic shape— but then his hair caught the light. Red hair, not blond like Michael's.

Sam. Sam Glass, Michael's grandfather. Amelie had told her that Sam would escort her to see Myrnin; she'd just forgotten about it. Well, that was okay. Claire liked Sam. He was quiet and kind and didn't seem much like a vampire at all, except for the pale skin and the slight weird shine to his eyes. Exactly like Michael, now that she thought of it. But then, they were the two youngest, and—weirdly—related. Maybe the older the vampires got, the further they moved from normal.

"Hey, Claire," Sam said, as if they'd just talked five minutes before, although she hadn't seen him for nearly a week, at least. She supposed that time was different for vampires. "What'd they want?" He was wearing a TPU T-shirt and jeans, and it made him look kind of hot. Hot for a redheaded vampire, anyway. And he had a nice, if absent, smile. She wasn't his type. As far as Claire knew, Sam was still totally in love with Amelie, a concept she found harder to wrap her brain around than curved-surface string theory.

He was still waiting for an answer. She scrambled to put one together. "There's a dead girl. She was found in our garbage cans. Amy. Amy Callum?"

Sam's mobile, earnest face took on a grim look. "Dammit. I know the family. They're good folks. I'll stop by and see them." He sat down and leaned closer, dropping his volume. "She wasn't a vampire kill. I know that much. I'd have heard by now if someone had stepped out of line."

"No," Claire agreed. "It sounded as though she was killed by one of us." She realized, with a rush of horror, that he wasn't *us*, exactly, and blushed. "I mean—one of the—humans."

Sam smiled at her, but his eyes were a little sad. "That's all right, Claire; I'm used to it by now. It's an us-and-them town." He looked down at his hands, loose and relaxed on the tabletop. "I'm supposed to take you to your appointment."

"Yeah." She hastily closed up her books and began loading her backpack. "Sorry, I didn't realize what time it was."

"No rush," he said. Still not looking at her. Very softly, he continued. "Claire. Are you sure you know what you're doing?"

"What?"

His hand flashed out and grabbed her wrist—the one with the bracelet hidden under the long sleeve. It dug painfully into her skin. "You know what."

"Ow," she whispered, and he let go. "I had to. I didn't have a choice. I had to sign if I wanted to keep my friends safe."

Sam didn't say anything to that; he was looking at her now, but she didn't dare meet his eyes. She didn't like him knowing about her agreement with Amelie. What if he told Michael? What if Michael told Shane? *He's going to find out, sooner or later.* Well, she'd much rather it be later.

Sam said, "I know that. I wish you wouldn't do this other thing. With Myrnin. It's—not safe."

"I know. He's sick or something. But he won't hurt me. Amelie—"

"*Amelie* isn't in the business of worrying about individuals." That, for Sam, was surprisingly bitter, especially when it came to Amelie. "She's using you the way she uses all humans. It's not personal, but it's not in your best interest, either."

"Why? What is it you're not telling me?"

Sam looked at her for a long time, clearly trying to decide, and finally said, "Myrnin's had five apprentices in the past few years. Two of them were vampires."

Claire blinked, surprised, as Sam got to his feet. "Five? What happened to them?"

"You're asking the right questions. Now ask the right people."

He walked away. Claire gasped, grabbed her bag, and followed.

Over at the coffee bar, the two detectives were breaking the news to Eve. As Claire looked back, she saw the precise second that Eve realized her friend was dead. Even from across the room, it hurt to see the pain in her face, quickly masked and locked away. In Morganville, losing someone was something you got used to, Claire supposed.

God, this town *sucked* sometimes.

Sam had a car, a sleek dark red sedan with dark-tinted windows. It was parked in the underground garage beneath the UC, in a reserved spot marked SPONSORS ONLY, with a graphic of a sticker that had to appear in the corner of the windshield for the parking to be legal.

A sticker that Sam, of course, had. "So that means what, you donate money or something?"

Sam opened the passenger door for her, a bit of chivalry she wasn't really used to, and Claire climbed inside. "Not exactly," he said. "Amelie gives them to vampires who have campus business."

Once he was in the car, turning the key, Claire said, "You have campus business?"

"I teach night classes," Sam said, and grinned. He looked about twelve, when he did that. She had the feeling it wasn't something vampires were into, looking that endearingly goofy. Maybe if they were, they'd be more popular with the local breathing population. "Sort of an outreach program."

"Cool." The tinting was so dark it was like midnight outside. "You can see through this?"

"Like daylight," Sam said, and she gave up, buckled her seat belt, and let him drive. It wasn't a long trip—nothing in Morganville was—but she had time to notice some things about Sam's car. It was clean. *Really* clean. No trash at all. (Well, he wouldn't be chowing down on burgers in the car, now, would he? Wait. He could . . .) It also didn't smell like most cars. It smelled new and kind of sterile. "How are classes going?"

Oh, Sam was going to do the interested-adult thing now. "Fine," Claire said. Nobody ever wanted to really hear the truth, to a question like that, but *fine* wasn't a lie, either. "They're not very hard." Also not a lie.

Sam shot her a glance, or so she thought, in the dim lights from the dashboard. "Maybe you're not getting all you can out of them," he said. "Ever thought of that?"

She shrugged. "I've always been ahead. It's better than high school, but I was hoping for something harder."

"Like working for Myrnin?" Sam's voice had gone dry. "That's a challenge, all right. Claire—"

"Amelie didn't exactly give me a choice."

"But you still want to do it, don't you?"

She did. She had to admit that. Myrnin had been scary, but there had been something so bright in him, too. She knew that spark. She felt it herself, and she was always looking for someone, something to feed it. "Maybe he just needs someone to talk to," she said.

Sam made a noncommittal noise that somehow sounded amused, too, and pulled the car to a stop. "I have to move fast," he said. "It's the door at the end of the alley; I'll meet you there in the shade."

He opened his door and just . . . vanished. The door slammed shut, but it did it on its own. Claire gaped, unbuckled her seat belt, and got out, but there was no sign of Sam at all on the street, in the brilliant sunlight. The car was parked at the curb of a cul-de-sac, and it took her a second, but then she recognized the house in front of her. A big Gothic ramble of a house, nearly a mirror image of the Glass House where she lived, but this one belonged to a lady named Katherine Day and her granddaughter.

Gramma Day was on her porch, rocking peacefully and stirring the warm air with a paper fan. Claire raised her hand and waved, and Gramma waved back. "You come to see me, girl?" Gramma called. "Come on up; I'll get some lemonade!"

"Maybe later!" Claire called back. "I have to go—"

She realized, with a jolt of horror, where Sam had told her to go. *Into the alley.* The alley where everybody, Gramma Day included, had told her *not* to go. The alley with the trap-door spider vampire who'd tried before to lure her inside.

Gramma pulled herself to her feet. She was a tiny, wrinkled woman who looked as dry and tough as old leather. Had to be tough, to be old in Morganville, Claire thought. "You all right, girl?" she asked.

"Yeah," Claire said. "Thanks. I'll—I'll be back."

She headed off down the alley. Behind her, Gramma Day called out, "Girl, what you playin' at? Ain't you got good sense?"

Probably not.

The alley was narrow, with fences on both sides, and it seemed to get even more narrow the farther she went, like a funnel. She didn't feel any strange attraction, though, or hear voices.

She also didn't see Sam.

"Here," a voice said, as she turned a slight corner. And there he was, leaning back in a patch of black shade next to an overhanging doorway, which was attached to what looked like a shack. Not a really well-made shack, either. Claire wondered if it was supposed to lean like that.

"It's Myrnin," she said. "He's the trap-door spider."

Sam looked thoughtful at that, and then nodded. "Most people know not to come down this way," he said. "He only takes Unprotecteds. He can tell the difference, so he wouldn't try it with you. Not now."

Cheery. Sam opened the door, which didn't look sturdy enough to keep out a cool breeze, and stepped inside. A smell washed out into the still air, something old and bitter. Chemicals. Ancient paper. Unwashed clothes.

Well?

Claire sucked in a breath that tasted of all those things, and stepped into Myrnin's lair.

FIVE

Myrnin was in a mood. A *good* mood.

"Claire!" As she came down the steps—the only thing in the shack itself were the steps leading down—into his main chamber, he flashed across the room in a blur and stopped just an inch away from her, close enough that she flinched back into Sam's broad chest and he steadied her. Myrnin's eyes were wide, blazing with enthusiasm. "I've been waiting! Late, late, late, you're very late, you know. Come on, come on, we haven't got time for nonsense. Did you bring the books? Good. What about *Last Will and Testament*? Are you familiar with the symbols? Here, take this." Chalk, pressed into her hand. Myrnin moved again, fast as a grasshopper, and rolled an ancient stained chalkboard closer. He had to shove over some stacks of books to do it, which he did with cheerful disregard for how much of a mess he was making.

Sam, almost inaudibly, whispered, "Be careful. He's dangerous when he's like this."

Yeah, no kidding. Claire nodded, swallowed, and smiled as Myrnin turned toward her with those crazy, delighted eyes. She wanted to ask what came after the manic phase, but she didn't dare.

"I'll be in the other room," Sam said. Myrnin waved him off impatiently, barely sparing him a glance.

"Yes, yes, fine, go. Here. First let's start with the Egyptian inscription for *asem*. *Asem*. You know what element that represents?"

"Electrum," Claire said, and carefully chalked the symbol. Sort of a bowl, with a big staff through the middle. "How's that?"

"Excellent! Yes, that's it. Now, something difficult. *Chesbet*."

Sapphire. That was a hard one. Claire bit her lip for a second, getting the order in her mind, and then drew it out. Circle above a double-slashed line, next to a leg, next to a thing that looked kind of like a car with no wheels over two separated circles.

"No, no, no," Myrnin said, grabbed an eraser, and rubbed out the car. "Too modern. Look."

He drew it again, this time more roughly, and it still looked like a car to her. She copied it, twice, until he was satisfied.

There were a lot of symbols, and he quizzed her on just about all of them, growing more and more excited. Her arm ached from holding up the chalk to the board, especially when, after she screwed up the symbol for lead, he made her repeat it a hundred times.

"We should do this on computer," she said, chalking it carefully for the eighty-ninth time. "With a drawing pad."

"Nonsense. You're lucky I don't make you inscribe it with a stylus on a wax tablet, like the old days," Myrnin snorted. "Children. Spoiled children, always playing with the shiniest toy."

"Computers are more efficient!"

"I can perform calculations on that abacus faster than you can solve them on your computer," Myrnin sneered.

Okay, now he was pissing her off. "Prove it!"

"What?"

"Prove it." She backed off on her tone, but Myrnin wasn't looking angry; he was looking strangely interested. He stared at her for a second in silence, and then he broke into the biggest, oddest smile she'd ever seen on the face of a vampire.

"All right," he said. "A contest. Computer versus abacus."

She wasn't at all sure now that was a good idea, even if it had been *her* idea, essentially. "Um—what do I win?" *More important, what do I lose?* Making bargains was a way of life in Morganville, and it was a lot like making deals with man-eating fairies. Better be careful what you ask for.

"Your freedom," he said solemnly. His eyes were wide and guileless, his too-young face shining with honesty. "I will tell Amelie you were not suited to the work. She'll let you go about your life, such as it is."

Good prize. *Too* good. Claire swallowed hard. "And if I lose?"

"Then I eat you," Myrnin said.

With absolutely no change in expression.

"You—you can't do that." She pulled up the sleeve on her shirt and held up her wrist so the gold bracelet caught the light.

"Don't be ridiculous," he said. "Of course I can do it. I can do anything I want, child. Without me, there is no future. No one, especially Amelie, begrudges me the occasional tidbit. You're hardly large enough to qualify as a meal in any case, and besides, I'm making it well worth your while."

She took a step back from him. A big one. That crazy smile . . . She glanced toward the door of the other room, where Sam was waiting for her. No wonder Amelie had told him to stay.

Myrnin gave a sad, theatrical sigh. "Mortals simply aren't what they used to be," he said. "A thousand years ago, you would have bartered your immortal soul for a crust of stale bread. Now I can't even get you to gamble at all, even for your freedom. Really, people have become so . . . *boring*. So, no bet? Really?"

She shook her head. His expression fell into utter disappointment. "All right," he said. "Then you will write me an essay for tomorrow on the history of alchemy. I can't expect it to be scholarly, but I do expect you to understand the basis of what it is that I am trying to teach you."

"You're teaching me *alchemy*?"

He seemed surprised, and looked around his laboratory. "Can you not see what I'm doing here?"

"But alchemy—it's crap. I mean, it's like magic, not science."

"Alchemy's accomplishments are sadly forgotten, and yes, magic is an excellent description for things for which you have no basis to understand. As for science . . ." Myrnin made a rude noise. His eyes had taken on that hectic shine again. "Science is a method, not a religion, yet it can be just as close-minded. Open minds here, Claire. Always open minds. Question everything; accept nothing as fact until you prove it for yourself. Yes?"

She nodded hesitantly, more afraid to disagree with him than convinced. Myrnin grinned at her and slapped her back with stinging force.

"That's my girl," he said. "Now. What do you know of this theory of Schrödinger's? The one about the cat?"

Myrnin didn't go weird until the very end of Claire's time with him, when he was—she thought—getting tired. She had to admit, there was something fun about working in his lab; he had so much passion, so much enthusiasm for everything. Even for scaring her silly. He was like a little kid, all nervous energy and fiddling hands, quick to laugh, quick to cut her down if she made a mistake. He liked to mock, not correct. He thought if she had to figure it out for herself, she'd learn it properly.

She checked her watch and found it was almost eight o'clock—late. She was supposed to be home by now. Myrnin was ignoring her, temporarily, as she copied out tables of incomprehensible symbols from a book he said was so rare his was the only copy left. She yawned, stretched, and said, "I need to be going."

He had his eye fixed to what looked like a clunky, ancient microscope. "Already?"

"It's late. I should go home."

Myrnin straightened, stared at her, and she saw the storm forming in his expression. "You are dictating to me now?" he snapped. "Who is the master? Who is the student?"

"I—sorry, but I can't stay here all night!"

Myrnin walked toward her, and she couldn't even recognize him. No more manic energy, no more humor, no more sharp, brilliant anger. He looked troubled and clouded.

"Home," he repeated. "Home is where the heart is. Why don't you leave yours here? I'll take very good care of it."

"M-my—heart?" She dropped the pen and backed up, putting a big lab table full of chemical equipment between them. Myrnin bared his teeth and put down his fangs. *Discovery Channel. King cobra. Oh God, can he spit venom or something?* His eyes flared bright, fueled with something that looked to her like . . . fear.

"Don't run," he said, and sounded annoyed. "I hate it when they run. Now, tell me what you're doing here!" he demanded. "Why do you keep following me? *Who are you?*"

"It's Claire, Myrnin. I'm your apprentice. I'm supposed to be here, remember?"

That was the wrong thing to say, and she had no idea why. Myrnin stopped, and the light in his eyes intensified to insanity. Ugly, and very scary. When he moved, it was a smooth, sinuous glide. "My apprentice," he said. "So I own you, then. I can do as I wish."

King cobra.

"Sam!" Claire yelled, and bolted for the stairs.

She didn't get more than two steps. Myrnin came *over* the table, scattering glass instruments to shatter in glittering sprays on the floor, and she felt his cold, impossibly strong hands close on her ankles and jerk backward. She flailed for something to grab on to, but it was only a tower of books, and it collapsed as she fell.

She hit the floor hard enough to put the world on a sparkling, unsteady hold for a few seconds, and when she blinked away the stars, Myrnin had taken hold of her shoulders and was staring down at her, inches away.

"Don't," she said. "Myrnin, don't. I'm your friend! I won't hurt you!"

She didn't know why she said it, but it must have been the right thing to do. His eyes widened, white showing all around, and then the glitter of crazy was replaced by a flood of tears. He patted her cheek, soft and confused, and the fangs folded up in his mouth. "Dear child," he said. "What are you doing here? Is Amelie making you come here? She shouldn't. You're far too young and kind. You should tell her you won't come back. I don't want to hurt you, but I will." He tapped his forehead. "*This* is betraying me. This stupid, stupid flesh." The tapping became violent slaps to his forehead, and tears broke free to run down his cheeks. "I need to teach someone, but not you. Not you, Claire. Too young. Too small. You bring out the beast."

He stood up and wandered away, *tsk*ing over the broken glass, righting the fallen books. As if she'd ceased to exist. Claire sat up and rolled to her feet, shaky and scared.

Sam was standing just a few feet away. She hadn't seen or heard him approach, and he hadn't acted to save her. His face was tense, his eyes uneasy.

"He's sick," Claire said.

"Sick, sick, sick, yes, I am," Myrnin said. He had his head in his hands now, as if it hurt him. "We're all sick. All doomed."

"What's he talking about?" Claire turned to Sam.

"Nothing." He shook his head. "Don't listen to him."

Myrnin looked up and bared his teeth. His eyes were fierce, but they were sane. Mostly sane, anyway. "They won't tell you the truth, little morsel, but I will. We're dying. Seventy years ago—"

Sam moved Claire out of his way, and for the first time since she'd met him, Sam actually looked threatening. "Myrnin, *shut up!*"

"No," Myrnin sighed. "It's time for talking. I've been shut up enough." He looked up, and his eyes were red-rimmed and full of tears. "Oh, little girl, do you understand? My race is dying. My race is dying and I don't know how to stop it."

Claire's mouth opened and closed, but she couldn't find anything to say. Sam turned toward her, fury still radiating off him like heat. "Ignore him," he said. "He doesn't know what he's saying. We should go, before he remembers what he was about to do. Or forgets what he shouldn't."

Claire cast a look back over her shoulder at Myrnin, who was holding a broken glass pipe in his hands, trying to fit the two pieces back together. When it wouldn't go, he dropped it and covered his face with both hands. She could see his shoulders shaking. "Can't—shouldn't somebody help him?"

"There's no help," Sam said in a voice flat with anger. "There's no cure. And you're not coming back here again if I can do anything about it."

SIX

Claire kept her silence for about half the ride home, and Sam didn't offer anything, either. The pressure of questions finally was too much for her. "He was telling the truth, wasn't he?" she asked. "There's some kind of disease. Amelie tried to make me think that not making more vampires was her choice, but that's not really true, is it? You *can't*. She's the only one who isn't sick."

Sam's face went tight and still in the glow of the dashboard lights. Sitting in the car was like traveling through space; the dark-tinted windows refused even starlight, so it was just the two of them in their own pocket universe. He had the radio on, and it was playing classical music, something light and sweet.

"No use telling you to shut up, is there?"

She said regretfully, "Probably not. And I wouldn't stop trying to find out."

Sam shook his head. "Do you even *have* a sense of self-preservation?"

"Shane asks me that all the time."

That made Sam smile, despite his obvious unease. "All right," he said. "Amelie's sick, too. It's getting harder and harder for her to create new vampires—she was barely able to bring Michael over; I was terrified it would kill her this time. The truth is, we're all sick. Myrnin's been searching for the cause—and the cure—for seventy years now, but it's too late now. He's too far gone, and the chance that anyone else could help him through it is too small. I can't let her sacrifice you like this, Claire. I told you that he's had five assistants. I don't want you to become another statistic."

Oh God. *The vampires were all dying.* Claire felt a rush of pure adrenaline, enough to make her hands tremble with the force of it. She felt a fierce surge of something like . . . satisfaction. And then another one, right on top of it, of guilt. *What about Sam? What about Michael?* Yeah, and what about Oliver and all those scary vamps like him? Wouldn't it be great to see them go?

"What if he doesn't find the cure?" Claire asked. She tried not to give away any of what she was feeling, but she was sure Sam could hear her elevated heartbeat. "How long—?"

"Claire, you need to forget you ever heard any of this. I mean it. There are a lot of secrets in Morganville, but this one could kill you. Say *nothing*, understand? Not to your friends, and not to Amelie. *Do you understand?*"

His intensity was even more terrifying than Myrnin's, because it was so controlled. She nodded.

It didn't stop the questions from swirling in her brain, or the possibilities.

Sam let her out at the curb and watched her until she was inside the house—it was full dark, and there were plenty of hunting vampires out on a clear, cool night like this. Nobody would hurt her—probably—but Sam wasn't in the mood to take chances.

Claire shut the door and locked it, leaned against the wood for a long few seconds, and tried to get her head together. She knew her friends would bombard her with questions—where had she been, was she crazy being out alone in the dark—but she couldn't answer them, not without violating some order from either Amelie or Sam.

They're dying. It seemed impossible; the vampires seemed so strong, so frightening. But she'd seen it. She'd seen the way Myrnin was decaying, and how afraid Sam was. Even Amelie—perfect icy Amelie—was doomed. Wasn't that a good thing? And if it was, why did she feel so sick when she thought about Amelie going slowly mad, like Myrnin?

Claire took a few more deep breaths, willed her mind to shut up for a while, and pushed off to walk down the hall.

She didn't get far. There was stuff piled everywhere. It took her a second, but she recognized it with a shock of horror. "Oh no," she whispered. "Shane's stuff." It was blocking the hallway. Claire shoved a path through the boxes and suitcases piled there. *Oh crap.* There was the PlayStation, unplugged and looking mournful, in a heap with its game controllers.

"Hey? Hey, guys? What's going on?" Claire called, edging around the barricades. "Anybody here?"

"Claire?" Michael's shadow appeared at the end of the hall. "Where the *hell* have you been?"

"I—got held up late at the lab," she said. Which wasn't a lie. "What's happening?"

"Shane says he's moving out," Michael said. He looked deeply angry, but it was covering up hurt, too. "Glad you're here. I was about to come looking for you."

Claire heard the indistinct buzz of voices upstairs. Eve's voice, high and strident. Shane's rumbling low. There was about a sixty-second delay, and then Shane came down the stairs carrying a box. His face was pale but determined, and although he hesitated for a second when he saw Claire was back, he kept coming down.

"Seriously, dumbass, what the *hell* are you doing?" Eve demanded from the top of the stairs. She darted around and got into his path, forcing him to back up and try to get around her. "Yo, village idiot! Talking to you!"

"You want to live here with him, fine," Shane said tightly. "I'm going. I've had enough."

"You're moving *at night*? Do you have a head wound?"

He faked Eve to the right and moved past her to the left.

And ran into Claire, who didn't move. She didn't say anything, and after a few seconds of silence he said, "I'm sorry. Got to do it. I told you."

"Is this about your dad?" she asked. "About this prejudice you've got against Michael now?"

"Prejudice? Jesus, Claire, you act like he's still really Michael. Well, he's not. He's one of them. I'm done with this crap. If I need to I'll go break some laws and get my ass thrown in jail. Better that than living here, looking at him—" Shane stopped dead and shut his eyes for a second. "You don't understand. You just don't understand, Claire. You didn't grow up here."

"But I did," Eve said, stepping up closer. "And I don't get your paranoid bullshit, either. Michael hasn't hurt *anybody*! Especially you, you jerk. So lay off."

"I am," Shane said. "I'm leaving."

Claire didn't move out of his way. "What about us?"

"You want to go with me?"

She slowly shook her head, and saw the pain in his face for a split second before it turned hard again.

"Then we've got nothing to talk about. And sorry to break it to you, but there's no *us*. Get it straight, Claire. It's been fun, but you're not really my type—"

Michael *moved*. He smacked the box out of Shane's hands, and it flew halfway across the room, skidded across the wood floor the rest of the way, and slammed into the baseboard, where it tipped over and spilled things all over the place.

"Don't," he said, and grabbed Shane by the shoulders and flattened him against the nearest convenient wall. "Don't you disrespect her. Be an asshole to me, fine. Be an asshole to Eve if you want to; she can give it right back. But don't you take it out on Claire. I've had enough of your crap, Shane." He stopped and took a breath, but the anger wasn't burning out of him, not yet. "You want to go, get the hell out, but you'd better take a good hard look at yourself, my man. Yeah, your sister died. Your mom died. Your dad's a violent, prejudiced asshole. Your life has *sucked*. But you don't get to be the victim anymore. We keep cutting you breaks, and you keep screwing up, and it's *enough*. I'm not letting you whine anymore about how your life sucks worse than ours."

Shane's face went dead white, then red.

And he socked Michael in the face. It was a solid, painful punch, and Claire winced and covered her mouth in sympathy, moving back.

Michael didn't move. Didn't even react. He just stared into Shane's eyes.

"You're just like your dad," he said. "You want to stake me now? Cut my head off? Bury me out back? That work for you, *friend*?"

"Yes!" Shane screamed, right in his face, and there was something so frightening in his eyes that Claire couldn't move. Couldn't breathe.

Michael let him go, walked over, and picked up a couple of things from the pile that had spilled from the box Shane had been carrying out.

A pointed stake.

A wickedly sharp hunting knife.

"You came prepared," he said, and tossed them to Shane, who caught them out of the air. "Go for it."

Eve screamed and threw herself in front of Michael, who gently but firmly moved her out of the way.

"Go on," he said. "We do this now, or we end up doing it later. You want to move out so you can kill me with a clear conscience. Why wait? Come on, man, do it. I won't fight."

Shane turned the knife in his hand, the edge slashing the light with every agitated move. Claire felt frozen, winter-cold, unable to think of anything to say or do. What had happened? How did things get this bad? What—

Shane took a step toward Michael, a sudden long lunge, and Michael didn't move. His eyes—they weren't cold at all, and they weren't vampire-scary, either. They were human, and they were afraid.

For a long breath, nobody moved, and then Michael said, "I know you feel like I betrayed you, but I didn't. This wasn't about you. It was for me; it was so I didn't have to be trapped here anymore. I was dying here. I was buried alive."

Shane's face twisted, as if that hunting knife had slid into his own guts. "Maybe you should have stayed dead." He raised the stake in his right hand.

"Shane, *no*!" Eve was screaming, trying to get between them, but Michael was holding her off. She turned on him in a fury. "Dammit, stop it! You don't really want to die!"

"No," Michael said. "I don't. He knows I don't."

Shane paused, trembling. Claire watched his face, his eyes, but she couldn't tell what he was thinking. What he was feeling. It was just a face, and she didn't know him at all.

"You were my friend," Shane said. He sounded lost. "You were my best friend. How screwed up is this?"

Michael didn't say anything. He took a step forward, took the knife and stake out of Shane's hands, and pulled him into a hug.

And this time, Shane didn't resist.

"Asshole," Michael sighed, and slapped his back.

"Yeah," Shane muttered, stepped back, and scrubbed at his eyes with the heel of his hand. "Whatever. You started it." He looked around and focused on Claire. "You. You were supposed to be home already."

Crap. She'd hoped they'd forget all about her late arrival, in the explosion of Shane's freak-out. But of course, he'd try to find a way to shift attention away, and there she was, a sitting duck.

"Right," Eve said. "Guess you forgot the number to call and tell us you weren't dead in a ditch."

"I'm fine," Claire said.

"Amy wasn't. She was murdered and stuffed in our trash can, so excuse me if I got a little bit worried that you might be *dead*." Eve crossed her arms, her dark stare getting even more fierce. "I already checked out there for you, before Shane decided to pull this crap."

Oh man. Somehow, in all of the stress of her afternoon with Myrnin, Claire had forgotten about Amy's death. Of *course* Eve was angry; not so much angry, really, as plain terrified.

Claire didn't dare meet Shane's gaze. She looked at Michael instead, helplessly. "I'm sorry," she said. "I got—I was at the lab, and—I should have called, I guess."

"And you walked home? In the dark?" Another question she had to avoid. She just shrugged. "You know what we call pedestrians in Morganville? Mobile blood banks." Michael sounded cold, too. Cold and angry. "You scared the shit out of us. That's not like you, Claire. What happened?"

Shane moved to her side, and she felt a moment of relief that at least *he* wasn't angry at her. But then he yanked her shirt away from her neck on the left, then on the right, an efficient rough search that surprised her too much to fight him. He skinned up her right sleeve all the way to the elbow and turned her arm to inspect it.

As he reached for the left, she felt an electric bolt of alarm. *The bracelet. Oh God.*

She yanked free and shoved him back. "Hey!" she said. "I'm fine, okay? I'm fine! Fang-free!"

"Then show me," Shane said. His eyes were steady and scared, and that broke her heart. "C'mon, Claire. Prove it."

"Why do I have to prove anything to you?" She knew she was wrong, and it made her stupidly angry that he cared so much. "You don't own me, like some vampire! I just *said* I'm fine! Why can't you just trust me?"

She would have done anything to take it back, but it was too late, and it hit him like a punch in the face. *He's been hurt so much. Why did I do that? Why . . .*

Michael stepped in between them. He threw a glance over his shoulder at Shane. "I'll do it." He was blocking Eve and Shane's view. Before Claire could do anything to stop him—as if she *could* do anything—he grabbed her left hand and pulled the sleeve up to her elbow.

He stared at the gold bracelet for a paralyzing second before turning her arm first one way, then the other. Then pulling her sleeve back down over the telltale jewelry evidence.

"She's fine," he said, and met her eyes. "She's telling the truth. I'd know if a vampire had bitten her. I'd feel it."

Shane's mouth opened, then closed. He took another step back, stared at her for a second, then walked away. Eve called, "Hey, how about taking some of your crap back upstairs, if you're planning on staying?"

"Later," Shane snapped, and went upstairs without looking back.

"I'd better go talk to him," Claire said. Michael kept hold of her arm.

"No," he said. "First, you'd better talk to me."

He hustled her toward the kitchen. Behind them, Eve said, "Just another great family dinner. Whatever! I'm taking the last hot dog!"

Even with the kitchen door shut, Michael wasn't taking any chances. He pulled Claire along with him to the pantry, opened the door, and turned on the light. "Inside," he ordered. She stepped in, and he shut the door after her. It was cramped with two people, and it smelled like old spices and vinegar, from where Shane had dropped the bottle a few weeks back. Michael's voice dropped to a fierce hiss. "What the *hell* do you think you're doing?"

"What I had to," she said. She was shaking all over, but she wouldn't let Michael intimidate her. She was tired, and besides, *everybody* seemed to be trying to intimidate her these days. She was small; she wasn't weak. "It was the only way. Amelie—"

"You should have talked to me. Talked to *us*."

"Like *you* came clean with us, when you were a ghost? And did you have a house meeting before you decided to go all the way to vampire?" Claire shot back. "Right. Well, you're not the only one who can make choices, Michael. This was mine; I made it; I'll live with it. And it'll keep all of you safe."

"Who says?" Michael asked bluntly. "Amelie? You're trusting vampires now?"

She didn't look away from his big blue eyes. "I trust you."

He suppressed a smile. "Dumbass."

"Dork." She shoved him, just a little, and he let her do it. He even pretended to stagger, although she didn't imagine vampires got knocked off balance very often, except by other vampires. "Michael, she didn't give me any choice. Shane's dad—even though he left, he did damage. Shane wasn't going to be trusted here, and you know what happens if—"

"If they don't trust him," Michael said somberly. "Yeah. I know. Look, don't worry about Shane. I'll protect him. I told you—"

"You may not be able to. Look, no offense, but you've only been a vampire for a couple of weeks. I have library books that have been out longer. You can't promise—"

Michael reached out and put one cool finger across her lips, stilling them instantly. His blue eyes were intense, narrow, and very focused.

"Shhhh," he whispered, and turned out the light.

Claire heard the kitchen door thump, and then the hard-heeled clonk of Eve's shoes crossing the wood floor. "Hello? Helllloooooooo? Great. Why do all my housemates sulk like little girls or vanish when the dishes are dirty? If you can hear me, Michael Glass, I'm talking to *you!*"

Claire snorted, almost laughed. Michael's hand closed over her mouth, stifling her. He tugged on her arm, and she followed him, moving carefully so as not to knock anything off the shelf. She heard the scrape of the door opening at the rear of the pantry, the tiny little bolt-hole, and bent down to go through it. The other side was pitch-black, with not even the tiny crack of light that the pantry had enjoyed, and Claire felt a flutter of panic. Michael's hand pushed her onward, and she stepped hesitantly into the close, thick dark. Behind her, she heard him close the door with a very soft *click,* and bright electric light flooded over the floor.

"Here," Michael said, and handed her the flashlight. "She might come looking for us here, but not for a while."

It was a secret hidey-hole, one that Claire had been shoved into on her very first morning in the Glass House; no exits, only the one entrance. She'd thought from the beginning it looked like someplace a vampire might stash a couple of handy coffins, but it was empty. And as far as she knew, Michael slept on a Serta.

"I meant to ask you. What is this?"

"Root cellar," he said. "This house was built before refrigerators, and ice deliveries were only so-so. This was where they kept most of their vegetables."

"So . . . not a vampire hideout?"

Michael stretched his long legs out with a sigh and leaned against the wall. God, he was pretty. No wonder Eve was willing to overlook the lack of pulse. "Not so far as I've ever known, but the vampires in Morganville never really had to hide. Only the humans did."

Which wasn't what they were here to talk about, she supposed. She crossed her arms and felt the bracelet bite into the skin of her wrist under the shirt. "Whatever lecture you were going to give me, it's too late. I signed. It's done. I've got the souvenir bracelet." Which made her suddenly, strangely want to cry. "Michael—"

"What's she asking you to do?" Which was so right-on that she felt the pressure of tears behind her eyes and in her nose get even higher.

"Um . . ." She couldn't tell him; Amelie and Sam had both made it clear. "It's just extra schoolwork. She wants me to study some things."

"What things?" Michael's voice got sharp and worried. "Claire—"

"It's nothing. Science stuff. I would have probably been doing it anyway, but it's just—it's a lot more time, and I don't know how I'm going to—" *Keep it from Shane.* Because she had to, right? Bad enough he hated Michael for being a vampire, but what was he going to think about *her*, selling herself to Amelie? "I just don't know how I'm going to do all this."

And suddenly, she was crying. She didn't mean to, but there it was, boiling out of her. She expected Michael to do the Shane thing, come and comfort her, but he didn't. He sat right where he was and watched her. When her sobs died down, and she swiped her hands across her wet cheeks, he said, "Finished?"

She gulped and nodded.

"You made the choice; now you want to have it both ways—the benefits, but not the consequences. You can't, Claire. It's coming home to roost, and you'd better handle it now rather than later." Michael's tone softened, just a little. "Look, I'm not an asshole; I know how scared you are. But you're a player in this town now. You're not the fragile little thing we took in for protection. You're trying to protect *us.* That means you may not be as well liked anymore, and you're going to have to sack up about that."

"What?" She felt dazed. Somehow, this wasn't how she'd expected all this to go. Especially Michael's cool, challenging look, and the lack of hugging.

"Signing the contract isn't the last choice you're going to have to make," he said. "It's the choices you make from now on that show whether you did the right thing or not." He stood up, pale and strong and as gorgeous as an angel in the glow of Claire's flashlight. "And stop lying to me. You ought to get off to a better start."

"I—what?"

"You said what Amelie has you doing is just more studying," he said grimly. "And I can tell when you're lying. No, I'm not going to ask, because I can tell it scares you, but just remember, vampires know, all right?"

He swung the door open and ducked out. Claire stared after him, openmouthed, but by the time she'd scrambled through and switched off the flashlight, Michael was already gone, out of the pantry. In fact, by the time Claire followed, Michael was already sitting on the couch, Eve curled next to him with her head on his chest. They were watching something on TV, and Eve's gaze followed Claire as she hurried past them, mumbling an apology.

She stopped on the stairs and looked back at them. Two people she cared about, wrapped in a moment of warmth and happiness.

Michael was a vampire, and that meant that Michael was *dying.* Like Myrnin. He was going to suffer and lose his mind and hurt people.

He could even hurt Eve, no matter how much he cared about her.

Tears pricked at her eyes, and she felt suddenly short of breath. When it had been just an abstract problem, just Morganville minus vampires equals safety, then that had been one thing, but it wasn't abstract. It was people she knew, liked, even loved. She wouldn't shed any tears over Oliver, but how could she not care about Michael? Or Sam? Or even Amelie?

Claire picked up her book bag and went upstairs.

Shane's door was shut. She knocked. He didn't answer for a long moment, and then said, "If I ignore you, will you go away?"

"No," she said.

"Might as well come in, then."

He was flopped on the bed, staring at the ceiling, hands under his head, and he didn't look at her as she entered and closed the door behind her.

"So is this how it's going to go?" she asked. "I do something dumb like stay out late, you get mad and run away, and then I come and apologize and make everything better?"

Shane, surprised, looked at her, then said, "Well, that kinda works for me, yeah."

Claire thought about Michael, about the suddenly grown-up way he'd treated her. She sat down on the bed next to Shane, staring down at the floor for a few seconds to gather her courage, and then she pulled back her sleeve to expose the bracelet.

Shane didn't make a sound. He slowly sat up, staring at the shiny gold band with its Founder's Symbol.

"We need to talk," she said. She felt sick and terrified, but she knew it was the right choice. The only other thing to do was lie, but she couldn't keep on lying. Michael was right about that.

Shane could have done anything—he could have run away, he could have thrown her out of his room. He could even have hit her.

Instead, he took her hand in his, bent his head, and said, "Tell me."

Eve wasn't so understanding. "Are you *out of your mind*?" She picked up the handiest thing to throw—it happened to be the PlayStation controller— and Shane quickly, carefully de-gamed her. Claire thought he probably wouldn't have moved that fast if Eve had grabbed, oh, say, a book.

"Let's be adults about this," Michael said. They were downstairs again, together, although Shane and Michael were still clearly standing at op- posite poles. It was getting late—eleven already—and Claire was feeling the strain of a very long, hard day. In fact, she yawned, which only made Eve shoot her a look of absolute exasperation.

"Oh, I'm sorry, are we *keeping you awake*? Michael, how the hell do we be adults about this when one of us *isn't an adult*?" Eve leveled a shaking finger at her. "You're a *kid*, Claire. As in, you're still a wet-behind-the-ears dumbass who hasn't even been in this town a couple of months. You have no idea what you're doing!"

"Maybe I don't," Claire agreed. Her voice was almost steady, which pleased and surprised her. She didn't like having Eve angry at her. She didn't like having *anyone* angry at her. "The thing is, it's done. I made the choice; that discussion was over before we had it. I wanted you to know, though. I didn't want to"—her eyes met Michael's briefly—"lie to you."

"Why the hell not? Everybody around here lies. Michael lied about being a ghost. Shane lies about shit all the time. Why not you, too?"

Shane groaned. "Yo, Drama Princess, want to tone it down a little? Somewhere, Sandra Bernhard wants her tantrum back."

"Oh, like *you* don't throw a hissy every time somebody trips your angst switch!"

Claire looked helplessly at Michael, who was having a hard time not smiling. He shrugged and took a step forward. That meant, of course, that Shane backed up. "Eve," Michael said, ignoring Shane for the moment. "Give the girl some credit. At least she told you, instead of letting you figure it out on your own."

"Yeah, and she told me *last!*" Eve glared at the two boys, hands on her hips.

"Boyfriend," Shane said, holding up his hand.

"Landlord," Michael chimed in.

"Crap," Eve sighed. "Right, next time you sell your soul to the devil, *I get first contact!* Girl solidarity, right?"

"Um—okay?"

"Dumbass," Eve sighed, defeated. "I can't believe you did that. I worked so hard to get away from that Protection crap, and here you are, all . . . Protected. I just wanted you to be—safe. And I'm not sure this is."

"Yeah," Claire said. "Me neither. But I swear, it was the best thing I could think of. And at least it's Amelie. She's okay, right?"

They all looked at each other. Shane said, "But you won't tell us what she's got you doing that keeps you out late."

"No. I—I can't do that."

"Then she's not okay," Shane said. "And neither are you."

But none of them had any good suggestions for how to fix it, and Claire fell asleep on the couch with her head in Shane's lap as he and Michael and Eve kept talking, and talking, and talking. It was three a.m. when she woke up. Shane hadn't moved, but she was covered with a blanket, and he was sound asleep, sitting straight up.

Claire yawned, groaned at sore muscles, and rolled to her feet. "Shane. Up. You need to go to bed."

He woke up cute, softened by sleep. "Come with?" He was only half joking. She remembered being curled up with him in her bed the night she'd been so scared; he'd been careful then, but she wasn't sure she could count on that kind of self-restraint at three a.m., when he was half-awake.

"I can't," she said reluctantly. "Not that I don't want to. . . ."

He smiled and stretched out on his side on the couch, leaving a narrow space between his warm, solid body and the cushions. "Stay," he said. "I promise, no clothes will come off. Well, maybe shoes. Do shoes count as clothes?"

She kicked hers off and climbed over him to slip into that small pocket, and sighed in relief as his body pressed against hers. She didn't even need the blanket, but he put it over the two of them, anyway, and then combed her hair back from her neck and kissed her on the soft, vulnerable skin.

"You were leaving," she whispered. He stopped moving. As far as she could tell, he stopped breathing. "You were leaving, and you didn't even know if I was okay."

"No. I was going to go look for you."

"After you packed."

"Claire, I didn't even know you hadn't come home until Eve came upstairs to yell at me. *I was going to look for you.*"

She looked back at him, over her shoulder, and saw the desperation hiding in his eyes.

"Please," he said. "Please believe me."

Against her will, even against her better judgment, she did believe him. She felt safe, anchored against the troubled world by the heat of his body against hers.

His arm went around her waist, and she felt absolutely protected.

"I won't let anything happen to you," he said. It was a promise he probably couldn't keep, but in the night, in the dark, it meant everything to her. "Hey."

"What?"

"Wanna fool around?"

She did.

She must have drifted off to sleep, because she woke up with her heart pounding, and feeling like there was something really, really wrong. For a second, as she came awake, she thought she smelled smoke, and that propelled her upright in a surge of panic. The house had almost burned once already. . . .

No, not fire, but something was definitely wrong. There was something in the whole atmosphere of the house. The smoke had been some kind of signal, from it to her. A *get your butt out of bed* signal.

Shane was still lying next to her on the couch, but he was already awake, too, and in the next second he rolled off to his feet as if he'd also felt it.

"What's happening?" Claire felt a jolt go through her like electricity. "Shane?"

"Something's wrong."

They both froze as they heard the sudden loud blare of a siren. It sounded as though it was right in front of the house.

Claire heard feet on the stairs and saw Eve hurrying down in a satin nightgown and fluffy black robe. Eve's face was bare of any Goth makeup, and she looked flushed and anxious and scared.

"What is it?" Eve called. "What's going on?"

"I don't know," Shane said. "Something bad. Can't you feel it?"

This was an event; they were all up and it was barely six a.m.

Eve plunged down the steps and yanked up the cord to raise the blinds on the window that faced the front yard. They all looked out. A police car was in the middle of the street, siren still wailing, and its headlights cast a hot circle of light on a maroon sedan stopped on the street, its driver's-side door open. Its lights were still on, and there was a body slumped on the road next to it.

The windows were dark-tinted.

It was a vampire's car.

Eve screamed, spun, and looked at them with wide, terrified eyes. "Where's Michael?" she asked, and Claire stupidly looked behind her, as if she were going to find him standing there.

They all looked back at the street, the car, the body.

"It can't be," Claire whispered. Shane was already moving for the door at a flat run, but Eve just stood there staring, frozen. Claire put her arm around her and felt her shaking.

She saw Shane blow through the gate at the fence and run toward the body; the cop who'd just emerged from the patrol car grabbed him, slung him around, and slammed him face-first onto the hood. Shane was yelling something.

"I need to go out there," Claire said. "Stay here."

Eve nodded numbly. Claire hated leaving her there, but Shane was going to get himself arrested if he kept it up, and who knew what could happen to him in jail?

She was only to the porch when another police car turned the corner, lights flashing, siren adding its howl to the chaos. It braked beside the first one, and another policeman got out and moved to where Shane was being restrained.

Claire didn't recognize the cop who had Michael facedown on the hood, but she knew the new arrival. It was Richard Morrell, Monica's big brother. He wasn't a bad guy, although he was definitely from the same icky gene pool. He took over for the other cop, who backed away.

"Shane! Dammit, Shane, calm the hell down. This is a crime scene; I can't let you run out there, do you understand? Calm down!"

Richard was occupied with keeping Shane under control, so the other policeman went to crouch next to the body on the street. *The body.* Claire took a step closer, and the policeman produced a flashlight and focused it on the face of the man lying in the street. Red hair flared in the light.

Not Michael.

Sam.

There was a stake in his chest, and he was still and white and *not moving.*

"Richard!" the cop yelled. "It's Sam Glass! Looks dead to me!"

"Sam," Claire whispered. "No."

Sam had been kind to her, and somebody had dragged him out of his car and put a stake through his chest.

"Shit!" Richard spat. "Shane, sit your ass down. Down, right now. Don't make me handcuff you." He yanked Shane by the collar of his T-shirt and sat him down on the curb, glared at him for a second, then came over to look at the body. "Holy Mother of— Grab his feet."

"What?" The other cop—his name tag said FENTON—looked at him with a frown. "It's a crime scene; we can't—"

"He's still alive, you idiot. Grab his damn feet, Fenton! If he burns, he's dead."

The first rays of sun crept over the horizon and fell on Sam's still form.

And Claire saw him start to smoke.

"What are you waiting for?" Richard shouted. "Pick him up!" The other cop, after a blank hesitation, grabbed Sam by the feet. Richard took him under the arms, and together they bodily threw him into the maroon sedan, the one with tinted windows, and slammed the door shut. Fenton started for the driver's side, but Richard got there first. "I'll drive," Richard said. "The wound's still fresh. He's got a chance if I can get him to Amelie."

Fenton backed off. Richard gunned the engine and slammed the door even as he was peeling rubber toward the end of the street.

Officer Fenton glared at Shane. "You going to give me trouble, boy?" he demanded. Claire sure hoped not. This man was twice the size of Richard Morrell, twice as old, and he looked like a human pit bull.

Shane held up his hands. "No trouble from me, Officer. Sir."

"You two see what happened here?"

"No," Claire said. "I was asleep. We all were."

"All in the same room?" the cop grunted, and looked her over, from her bed-head to the wrinkled clothes. "Didn't take you for the type."

She couldn't figure out what he meant for a few seconds, and then felt a wave of hot embarrassment sweep over her. "No, I mean—Eve was in her own room. We were asleep on the couch."

Shane said, "Yeah, we were all asleep. Woke up when we heard the siren." Which wasn't quite true, was it? They'd woken up, and *then* heard the siren. But Claire wasn't sure why that would be important.

The cop tapped on a handheld device, still frowning. "Ought to be four of you in the house. Where're the other two?"

"Eve's still inside. And Michael—" Where the hell was Michael? "I don't know where he is."

"I'll go see if he's in his room," Shane volunteered, but the cop froze him in place with another thunderous scowl.

"You'll sit your ass down on that curb and be quiet. You, what's your name?"

"Claire Danvers."

"Claire, get in there. Find out if Michael Glass is inside. If he's not, find out if his car is missing."

Claire stared at him, wide-eyed. "You don't think . . . ?"

"I don't think anything until I have facts. I need to know who's here, who isn't, and work from there." The cop transferred his dark stare to Shane, who was starting to get up. "I already told you, sit your ass down, Collins."

"I didn't have anything to do with this!"

"If I had to put together a list of prime suspects out to stake some vampires, you'd be right at the top, so yeah, you do. *Sit down.*"

Shane sat, looking furious. Claire silently begged him not to do anything stupid, and hurried back into the house. Eve was upstairs dressing— black baby-doll T with a bling-enhanced cartoon Elmer Fudd on the front, and black jeans with clunky Doc Martens.

"It wasn't—"

"I know. I saw," Eve said. Her voice sounded stuffy, as though she'd been crying, or was about to. "It was Sam, right? Is he alive? Or—whatever?"

"I don't know. Richard said something like he could still be okay." Claire gripped the doorknob tightly, and glanced down the hall. Michael's door was closed. It was always closed. "Did you look—?"

"No." Eve took a deep breath and stood up. "I'll go with you."

Michael's door was unlocked, and it was completely dark inside. Claire flipped on the lights. Michael's bed was empty, neatly made, and the room looked absolutely normal. Eve checked the closets, under the bed, even the master bathroom.

"No sign of him," she said breathlessly. "Let's check the garage."

The garage was a shed in the back, not attached to the house; the two of them went out the back kitchen door and crossed the rutted driveway. The shed's doors were closed.

Eve opened one side, Claire the other.

Michael's car was gone.

"What about work? Could he be at work?"

"TJ's doesn't open until ten," Eve said. "Why would he be in there at six?"

"Inventory?"

"You think they're going to call a vampire in at six a.m. to do *inventory*?" Eve slammed the shed door and kicked it for good measure. "Where the hell is he? And why the *hell* don't I have a working cell phone? Why don't you?"

Hers had been lost, Eve's had been smashed; both of them miserably looked at each other for a few seconds, then, without a word, walked to the front yard where Shane was still sitting on the curb. If anybody could sit rebelliously, he was doing it.

"Give me your phone," Eve demanded and held out her hand. Shane looked at her with a frown. "Now, dumbass. Michael's not inside, and his car's gone."

"Michael's got a car? Since when?"

"Since the vampires issued him one. He didn't tell you?"

Shane just shook his head. A muscle jumped in his jaw. "He doesn't tell me shit, Eve. Not since—"

"Not since you started treating him like the Evil Dead? Yeah. Imagine that."

He silently handed over his cell phone and looked away, staring at the street where Sam's body had been tossed. Claire wondered if he was thinking about his dad's crusade, about how *the only good vampire is a dead vampire.*

Claire wondered if he really, deep down, still agreed.

Eve dialed and put the phone to her ear. For a tense few seconds nothing happened, and then Claire saw relief melt the tension out of Eve's face and body. "Michael! Where the hell are you?" Pause. *"Where?"* Pause. "Oh. Okay. I need to tell you—" Pause. "You know." Pause. "Yeah, we'll . . . talk later."

Eve closed the phone and handed it back. Shane slipped it in his pocket again, eyebrows up and signaling questions.

"He's okay," she said. Her eyes had gone dark and narrow.

"And?"

"And nothing. He's fine. End of story."

"Bullshit," Shane said, and tugged her down to sit next to him on the curb. "Spill it, Eve. Now."

Claire sat, too, on Eve's other side. The curb felt cold and hard, but the good thing was that the patrol car blocked Fenton's view of them. He was talking to the occupants of another car, vampire-tinted, who had pulled up behind the cruiser.

"He was downtown," Eve said. "At the Elders' Council. They pulled him in there early this morning."

"Who did?"

"The Big Three." Oliver, Amelie, and the mayor, Richard and Monica's dad. "Amelie just got word about Sam. But Michael's not hurt or anything." An unspoken *for now* was at the end of that. Eve was worried. She bent her head closer to Shane's, lowered her voice even further, and said, "You didn't have anything to do with what happened to Sam, right?"

"Jesus, Eve!"

"I'm only asking because—"

"I know why you're asking," he whispered back fiercely. "Hell no. If I were going to go after some vampire, it wouldn't have been *Sam*. I'd be staking somebody like Oliver, make it worth my time. Speaking of Oliver, he'd be my number one suspect."

"Vampires don't kill their own."

"He arranged for Brandon to die," Claire offered. "I think Oliver's capable of anything. And he'd love to see Amelie even more isolated." She swallowed hard. "She told me once that Sam was safer if she didn't keep him close. I guess she was right."

"Doesn't matter. Oliver keeps his hands clean, no matter what. Some broke-ass human is going to burn for this, and you know it," Shane said. "And it happened in front of our house, and nobody's forgotten what happened with my dad. You don't think we're being set up?"

Crap. Shane was right. The fact that Michael was safe was good, but it was also a double-edged sword; it meant that Michael had been gone when Sam had been attacked.

And Michael was the only one of them whose word might be worth anything to the vampires.

Sure enough, Fenton came back around the cruiser and stared at the three of them for a few seconds, then said, "You're being taken in for questioning. All three of you. Get in the backseat."

Shane didn't move. "I'm not going anywhere."

The policeman sighed and leaned against the quarter panel. "Son, you've got a lot of attitude, and I respect that. But get it straight: either you get in my car, or you get in *their* car." He pointed toward the silent dark sedan, the one with vampires inside. "And I promise you, that won't end so well. You get me?"

Shane nodded, stood, and gave Eve a hand up.

Claire stayed seated. She pulled up the sleeve on her left arm. The bracelet glittered and glimmered in the morning light, and she held it up for Fenton's clear view.

His eyes widened. "Is that . . . ?"

"I want to see my Patron," Claire said. "Please."

He went off to talk on his radio, then came back and jerked his head at Shane and Eve. "In the backseat," he said. "You're going to the station. You, kid . . ." He nodded toward the other sedan. "They'll take you to Amelie."

Claire swallowed hard and exchanged a look with Shane, then Eve. That hadn't been her plan. She wanted them all to stay together. How could she keep them safe if they got separated?

"Don't," Shane said. "Come with us."

Truthfully, that was starting to sound like a better idea. The vampires weren't going to be happy, and her shiny gold bracelet didn't exempt her from suspicion. Amelie could still order her hurt, or killed.

"Okay," Claire said. Shane looked massively relieved as he ducked his head and entered the backseat of the cruiser. Eve followed him in.

The cop slammed the door after Eve, before Claire could get in the patrol car.

"Hey!" Shane yelled, and hit the car window. He and Eve were both trying to get out, but the doors weren't opening.

Fenton grabbed her by the arm and hustled her over to the other sedan, opened the door, and put her in the backseat before she could protest. Claire heard the faint click of locks engaging, and sat very still, trying to see through the gloom.

One of the vampires flicked on the overhead light. *Oh crap.* It was two of her not-favorite people. The woman was pale as snow, with white-blond hair and eyes of palest silver. Gretchen. Her partner, Hans, was a hard man made of angles, with graying short hair, and a stony expression.

"I wish we'd gotten the boy instead," Gretchen said, clearly disappointed. Her voice was low-pitched, throaty, with a heavy foreign accent. Not quite German, but not quite anything else, either. An old accent, Claire thought. "He was so rude to us when last we spoke. And surely his father deserves a lesson, even if the boy does not."

"Amelie says just bring this one," Hans said, and put the car in gear. He looked at Claire in the rearview mirror. "Seat belt, please."

She had trouble wrapping her head around that—why did he care?— but she clicked the safety restraint shut and sat back. Like the ride in Sam's car the day before, she couldn't see a thing outside the windows except a faint gray dot where the sun was rising.

"Where are you taking me?" she asked. Gretchen laughed. Claire caught the flash of fangs, but Gretchen didn't really need them to be scary. Not at all.

"To the Elders' Council," she said. "You remember it, Claire. You had such a good time there when last we visited."

SEVEN

There was Morganville—the dry, dusty, run-down town that was all most people ever saw—and then there was Founder's Square, a lush little piece of Europe where people with a pulse weren't welcome. Claire had been inside once, and it wasn't a fond memory; no matter how cute the little cafés were, or how nice the shops, she could see only the center of the square in the park, with the cage where they'd locked up Shane.

Where they'd been meaning to burn him alive as punishment for something he hadn't even done.

For some reason, Claire had expected to be parked in the same place as last time—outside of the square, at the police checkpoint—but of course that wasn't possible, was it? A few of the older vampires might be able to stand the sun, but they wouldn't willingly stroll around in it. Morganville was built for the convenience of vampires, not humans, and when Claire's door opened, and Gretchen impatiently gestured for her to get out, they were in an underground parking garage. It was full of cars, all nice ones, with darkened windows. Like a Beverly Hills mall or something.

There were armed guards. One of them started toward them as Gretchen pulled Claire out of the car, but Hans flashed him a badge, and the other guy—vampire, presumably—backed off.

"Let's go," Hans said. "Your Patron is waiting."

Gretchen chuckled. Not a happy sound. Claire stumbled over her own feet trying to keep up as the two vampires set off at a brisk walk, Gretchen's iron-hard grip on her upper arm setting in with bruising force. Claire was short of breath by the time they got to a long double flight of stairs, which the vampires took at a jog. At the top of the stairs was some kind of fire door, with a code panel. Claire didn't dare try to sneak a look at what Hans entered; knowing the vampires' paranoia, it wouldn't do her any good. The machines were probably calibrated to exclude anybody with a heartbeat.

Which made her wonder: was Myrnin behind the town's security, too? Was that something else she was supposed to learn? It could really come in handy if she could persuade him to show her. . . .

She was obsessing on technicalities to avoid feeling the terror, but as soon as the door lock released, she had nothing else to focus on except fear, and it washed over her in a sticky, cold wave. Gretchen seemed to sense it. She looked down at Claire with those cool, mirror gray eyes, and smiled. "Worried, little one?" she asked sweetly. "Worried for yourself, or for your friends?"

"Worried for Sam," Claire said. Gretchen lost her smile, and for just an instant, she seemed honestly off balance and surprised. "Is he alive?"

"Alive?" Gretchen's armor slid firmly back in place, and she raised a slender arched eyebrow. "He may yet be saved, if that is what you mean. I suppose your friend Shane will have to try again."

"Shane didn't do anything!"

This time, Gretchen's smile got positively cruel. "Perhaps not," she said. "Perhaps not *yet*. But be patient. He will. It's in his nature, as much as killing is in ours."

Claire had to save her breath, because they were walking again, big strides across thick maroon carpet. Claire's first impression of the Elders' Council building had been that it was a funeral home; it still felt like that to her, all hushed and quiet and elegant. They'd had roses in the last time, when the vampire they'd thought Shane killed had been lying in state. She didn't see any flowers this time.

Gretchen led her down a hallway and through thick double doors, into the round entry hall. There were four armed vampire guards in the room, and Gretchen and Hans had to stop and show ID, and surrender their weapons. Claire got searched—quick, competent pats from cold hands that made her shiver.

And then the doors opened, and she was pulled into a big round room with a high ceiling, chandeliers like falls of ice, and dim, expensive paintings on the walls. She hadn't imagined the smell of roses. In the center of the room stood a massive round conference table, surrounded by chairs, and in the center was a vase filled with red, red blooms.

Nobody was at the table. Instead, a group of at least ten was standing at the other side of the room, looking down.

Some of them turned, and Claire's gaze fixed irresistibly on Oliver. She hadn't seen him since he'd threatened her life, trying to lure Shane out of hiding, and as he stood up, now she had a flash of that again, how icy and hard his hands had been around her throat. How scared she'd been.

Oliver snarled, low in his throat but loud enough to be heard, and his eyes were like a wolf's. Not human at all.

"I see you brought us a criminal for punishment," he said, and moved toward them.

Gretchen looked at Hans, and then shoved Claire behind her. "Stop," she said. Oliver did, mostly in surprise. "The girl asked to come, to see her Patron. We have no proof she is guilty."

"If she lives in that house, then she's guilty," Oliver said. "You surprise me, Gretchen. When did you begin taking the side of the breathers?"

She laughed, but it had a bright, false sound to it. She said something in a language that Claire didn't recognize; Oliver spat something back, and Hans put a big hand on Claire's shoulder.

"She's our responsibility," he said. "And she's Amelie's property. Nothing to do with you, Oliver. Move."

Oliver, smiling, raised his hands and backed away. Hans moved Claire forward, past him, and she felt his stare on the back of her neck, as sharp as knives.

The circle of people parted as Hans approached. It was mostly

(Claire guessed) vampires; they didn't wear tags or anything, but most of them had the same cool, pale skin, the same whip-snake quickness when they moved. In fact, the only two humans—breathers?—she saw were Mayor Morrell, looking miserably uncomfortable as he stood near the edge of the group, and his son Richard. Richard's uniform was damp in places, and it took Claire a few seconds to realize that it was wet with blood.

Sam's blood.

Sam was lying on his back on the carpet, with his head cradled in Amelie's lap. The elder vampire was kneeling, and her hands were stroking gently through Sam's bright copper hair. He looked pale and dead, and the stake was still in his chest.

Amelie's eyes were closed, but opened as Hans pushed Claire toward her. For a long second the older vampire didn't seem to recognize Claire at all, and then weariness flashed through her expression; she looked down at Sam, her fingers trailing across his cheek.

"Claire, assist me," she said, as if they were continuing a conversation Claire hadn't even been in on. "Give her room, please."

Hans let go, and Claire felt a wild urge to run, run out of this room, get Shane and just *go*, anywhere but here. There was something too big to understand in Amelie's eyes, something she didn't want to know. She started to take a step back, but Amelie's hand flashed out and grabbed her wrist and pulled, and Claire fell to her knees on the other side of Sam's body.

He looked dead.

Really, really dead.

"When I tell you, take hold of the wood and pull," Amelie said, her voice low and steady. "Not until I tell you."

"But—I'm not very strong. . . ." Why wasn't she asking Richard? Asking one of the vampires? Oliver, even?

"You are strong enough. When I tell you, Claire." Amelie closed her eyes again, and Claire scrubbed her damp palms nervously over her blue jeans. The wooden stake in Sam's chest was round, polished wood, like a spike, and she couldn't tell how deep it was in his body. Was it in his heart? Wouldn't that kill him, once and for all? She remembered they'd talked about other vampires who'd gotten staked, and they'd died. . . .

Amelie's expression suddenly twisted in pain, and she said, "Now, Claire!"

Claire didn't even think. She fastened her hands around the stake and pulled, one massive yank, and for a terrifying second she thought it wouldn't work, but then she felt it sliding free, scraping against bone as it went.

Sam's whole body arched, as though he'd been shocked with one of those heart machines, and the circle of vampires moved back. Amelie kept hold of him, her fingers white as bone where they pressed on the sides of his head. Her eyes flew open, and they were pure blazing silver.

Claire scrambled backward, clutching the stake in both hands. Someone plucked it out of her grip—Richard Morrell, looking grim and tired. He put it into a plastic bag and zipped it shut.

Evidence.

Sam went limp again. The wound in his chest was bleeding a steady, slow trickle, and Amelie took off her jacket—white silk—and folded it into a pad to press it against the flow. Nobody spoke, not even Amelie. Claire sat there feeling helpless, watching Sam. He wasn't moving, not at all.

He still looked dead.

"Samuel," Amelie said, and her voice was low and quiet and warm. She bent closer to him. "Samuel. Come back to me."

His eyes opened, and they were all pupil. Scary owl eyes. Claire bit her lip and thought again about running, but Hans and Gretchen were at her back and she knew she didn't have a chance, anyway.

Sam blinked, and his pupils began to shrink slowly to a more normal size. His lips moved, but no sound came out.

"Breathe in," Amelie said, in that same quiet, warm tone. "I'm here, Samuel. I won't leave you." She stroked fingers gently over his forehead, and he blinked again and slowly focused on her.

It was as though there was nobody else in all the world, just the two of them. *Amelie was wrong,* Claire thought. *It isn't just that Sam loves her. She loves him just as much.*

Sam looked from Amelie to the circle of people, searching it for someone. When he didn't find the right one, he looked at Amelie again. His lips formed a name. *Michael.*

"Michael is safe," Amelie said. "Hans. Fetch him here."

Hans nodded and left, walking quickly. *Michael.* Claire realized with a jolt that she'd forgotten he'd be here, forgotten all about him in the shock of all that had happened. Sam was, at least, looking better with every passing second, but Amelie continued to press the makeshift bandage to the wound in his chest.

Sam's hand crept up, clumsy and slow, to cover hers, and for a long few seconds they looked at each other silently, and then Amelie nodded and let go.

Sam held the bandage in place and, with Amelie's help, pulled himself to a sitting position. She helped him lean against the wall.

"Can you tell us what happened?" she asked him. Sam nodded, and Claire looked up to see Richard Morrell crouching down, notebook and pen at the ready.

Sam's voice, when it finally came, was soft and thin, and it was clearly an effort for him to speak at all. "Went to see Michael," he said.

"But Michael was here, with us," Amelie said. "We summoned him during the night."

Sam's hand—the one not occupied holding the jacket to his chest—rose and fell helplessly. "Sensed he wasn't home, so I backed out of the drive. Someone pulled open the car door—Taser, couldn't fight back. Staked me while I was down."

"Who?" Richard asked. Sam's eyes closed briefly, then opened.

"Didn't see. Human. Heard the heartbeat." He swallowed. "Thirsty."

"You must heal first," Amelie said. "A few more moments. Is there anything at all you can tell us about this human who attacked you?"

Sam's eyes opened again, with an effort. "He called me Michael."

Michael arrived just in time to hear that last part. He looked at Claire, wide-eyed, then crouched down beside Sam. "Who did? The one who did this?"

Sam shook his head. "I don't know who. Male, that's all I know. He used your name. I think he thought I was you." Sam's lips curled in the pale ghost of a smile. "Guess he didn't see the hair before he staked me."

The article in the newspaper. *Captain Obvious.* Somebody had decided to take out the newest vampire in town, and it was sheer luck that they'd gotten Sam instead. It could have been Michael lying in the street.

And from the look on Michael's face, he was thinking the exact same thing.

Amelie was agitated. It wasn't really obvious, but Claire had seen her enough to know the difference. She moved more swiftly, and there was something less calm than usual in her eyes. Claire shivered a little when Amelie summoned her into a side room. It was small and empty, probably some kind of meeting room. Amelie didn't come alone; a tall blond vampire guy followed along and stood with his back to the door, a flesh-and-blood dead bolt. No getting out quickly, or at all, really.

"What happened?" Amelie demanded.

"I don't know," Claire said. "I was asleep. I woke up when—" *When I heard the sirens,* she'd been about to say, but again, that wasn't really true. She'd felt something, a flash of alarm that had come out of nowhere. And Shane and Eve had felt it, too. It normally would take a nuclear explosion to blast Shane out of sleep in the predawn hours, but he'd been wide-awake. "It was like some alarm went off in the house."

Amelie's face went very still and smooth. "Indeed."

"Why? Is that important?"

"Maybe. What else?"

"Nothing—we went downstairs. The sirens were going outside, and by the time we got down there it was all over, I guess. Sam was down on the road, and the cop was already there."

"You saw no one else?"

Claire shook her head.

"And your friends?" Amelie asked. "Where were they?"

It wasn't a casual question. Claire felt her pulse speed up, and tried to stay calm. If Amelie didn't believe her . . . "Asleep," she said firmly.

"Shane was with me, and I saw Eve come out of her own room. They couldn't have done it."

Amelie shot her a look. Not one that made her feel any too secure. "I know how much you value their lives. But understand, Claire, if you lie for them, I will not forgive it."

"I'm not lying. They were in their rooms when I came out. The only one missing was Michael, and he was here with you."

Amelie turned away from her and paced the length of the room in slow, graceful steps. She looked so perfect, so . . . *together.* Unable to help it, Claire blurted out, "Aren't you worried about Sam?"

"I am more concerned about whoever attacked him not receiving another chance to do such harm," Amelie said. "Sam was old enough to survive such a thing—but only barely. If the stake had remained in his chest much longer, or the sun had burned him, he could not have survived. Had the assassin succeeded in attacking Michael, he would have died almost instantly. It would take decades for him to build up an immunity."

Claire's mouth opened, shut, and opened again when she found the words. "You mean—vampires *don't* die from stakes in the heart?"

"I mean that it takes quite a lot to kill one of us," Amelie said. "More every year we survive. You could put a stake through *my* heart, and I would simply pull it out and be very annoyed with you for ruining my wardrobe. If I failed to remove it within a few hours, it would damage me, perhaps seriously, but it would not destroy me in the way you're thinking. We are not so fragile, little Claire." Her teeth gleamed for a second like pearls as she smiled. "You would do well to tell your friends. Especially Shane."

"But—Brandon—"

Amelie's smile faded. "He was tortured," she said. "Burned with sunlight to reduce his resistance. By the time he was murdered, he had no more strength than a newborn. Shane's father understands us too well, you see."

And now, so did Claire. Which probably wasn't good. "The cops took Shane and Eve to the police station. I don't want anything to happen to them."

"I'm sure you don't. As I did not want anything to happen to my dear Samuel, who would willingly die for the rights of breathers in this town." Amelie's tone had gone cold and dark, and it gave Claire a deep-down trembling in her stomach. "I wonder if I have been too lenient. Allowed too much freedom."

"You don't own us," Claire whispered, and it seemed like the bracelet around her wrist tightened all of a sudden, pinching. She grabbed at it, wincing.

"Do I not?" Amelie asked coolly. She exchanged a glance with the vampire at the door. "Let her leave. I am done with her."

He bowed slightly and stepped out of the way. Claire resisted the urge to lunge for the exit. Being in the same room with Amelie, never mind her guard, was scary and intense, but she needed to at least try. "About Shane and Eve—"

"I don't interfere in human justice," Amelie said. "If they are innocent, then they will be released. Go now. I shall expect you to attend to Myrnin today, and I have arranged for some additional classes at university for you to attend. A list has been provided to you at your home this morning."

Claire hesitated.

"Sam was supposed to take me to Myrnin—who's going to—"

Amelie spun on her, and there was something wild and terrible in her eyes. "Little fool, don't bother me with trivia! Go *now!*"

Claire ran.

The house was empty when she arrived. No Shane, no Eve, and she hadn't seen Michael again at the Elders' Council building before Hans and Gretchen had bundled her off. Claire felt very alone, and she locked all the doors and made sure of all the windows.

The house felt . . . warm, somehow. Not in the hot-air sense, but cozy. Welcoming. Claire put her hand flat on the wall in the living room. "Can you hear me?" she asked, and then felt stupid. It was just a house, right? Just wood and bricks and concrete and wiring and pipes. How could it hear her?

But she couldn't shake the feeling that the *house* had jabbed her awake this morning, her and Shane and Eve. That it had been trying to warn them. The house had saved Michael, after all, when he'd been killed by Oliver; it had given him what life it could, as a ghost. It *wanted* to help.

"I wish you could talk," she said. "I wish you could tell me who tried to kill Sam."

But it couldn't, and she was talking to a dumbass *wall*. Claire sighed, turned away, and caught a glimpse of a piece of paper stirring in a breeze.

A breeze that wasn't there.

The paper was lying on the table, on top of Michael's guitar case. Claire grabbed it and read it, barely daring to believe—

What was she thinking? That the house was going to provide her with the name of Sam's would-be Van Helsing? Of course not. It wasn't an answer to her question.

It was a class schedule printout, stamped AMENDED in big red letters. Her core classes were mostly gone; the notation next to them showed that she'd tested out.

What caught her attention, though, was what had been scheduled in their place. *Advanced Biochem. Philosophical Studies. Quantum Mechanics. Honors Myth and Legend.*

Wow. Was it wrong that she felt her heart skip a beat over that? Claire checked the times, then her watch. She barely had an hour until the first new class, but she couldn't go yet. Not until she'd heard from Shane and Eve.

Thirty minutes later she was on the phone, trying to get somebody to answer her questions at the police station, when she heard the locks rattle on the door and Eve's voice saying, "—dumbass," and the knot of fear in Claire's chest began to loosen. "Yo, Claire! You here?"

"Here," she said, and hung up to come down the hall toward them.

Eve had her arm around Shane, half supporting him. Claire blinked and focused on his face. At the swelling and bruises. "Oh God," she said, and hurried to his side to help Eve. "What happened?"

"Well, Big Man here decided to get a little shirty with Officer Fenton. You ever see *Bambi Versus Godzilla?* It was like that, only with more punches," Eve said. She sounded false and bright, like tinsel. "I tried to take him to the hospital and get checked out, but—"

"I'm fine," Shane gritted out. "I've had worse."

Probably true, but Claire still felt painfully helpless. She wanted to *do* something. Anything. She and Eve got Shane to the couch, where he collapsed against the cushions and closed his eyes. He looked pale, under the bruises. Claire stroked his matted hair anxiously, silently asking Eve what to do; Eve shrugged and mouthed, *Just let him rest.* She looked scared, though.

"Shane," Eve said aloud. "Seriously, I don't want to leave you here alone. You need to go to the hospital."

"Thanks, *Mom,*" he said. "It's bruises. I think I'll live. Go on, get out of here." He reached up and captured Claire's hand, and his dark eyes opened. Well, one of them. The other was swelling shut. "What happened to you? You okay?"

"Nothing happened. I'm fine. I talked to Amelie." Claire pulled in a deep breath. "Sam's going to be okay, I think."

"And Michael? Michael was all right?" Eve asked.

"Yeah, he was all right. I'm sorry I couldn't get you out any earlier. Amelie—" Probably best not to get into how not-bothered Amelie had been by the idea of Eve and Shane behind bars. "She was busy with Sam."

Eve shrugged and shot Shane an exasperated look. "We probably would've been out of there in ten minutes if he'd behaved himself," she said. "Look, Shane, I know you're a hard-ass, but do you have to pick a fight with *every* jerk in the world? Can't you just choose half or something?"

"The scary thing? I *do* only pick fights with half of them. That's how many there are." He groaned and adjusted himself to a more comfortable position on the couch. "Crap. Officer Asshole can really hit."

"Shane," Claire said, "really. Are you okay? I can take you to the hospital if you're not."

"They'd just give me an ice pack and send me home, minus a hundred bucks I don't have." He caught her hand in his. His knuckles were scraped. "What about you? Nothing bitten or broken, right?"

"No," she said softly. "Nothing bitten or broken. They're angry, and they're worried, but nobody tried to hurt me." She checked her watch, and her heart skipped and hammered faster. "Um . . . I have to go. I have class. You're sure you're—"

"If you ask me if I'm okay again, I'm going to smack myself in the face just to punish you," he said. "Go on. Eve, make sure she doesn't go wandering off by herself, okay?"

Eve already had her keys in her hand, and she was jingling them impatiently. "I'll do my best," Eve said. "Hey. This came special delivery for you." She tossed Claire a package with her name neatly lettered on it. Same handwriting, Claire thought, as the package that had held her bracelet.

This one held a sleek new cell phone, complete with MP3 player and a tiny little flip-open keypad for texting. It was on, and it was fully charged.

The note said, simply, *For safety.* The signature, of course, was Amelie's. Eve saw it, and raised her eyebrows. Claire quickly crumpled it up.

"Do I even want to know what that is?" Shane asked.

"Probably not," Eve said. "Claire, little girls who take candy from strangers in Morganville get hurt. Or worse."

"She's not a stranger," Claire said. "And I really need a phone."

The classes were nothing like Claire had experienced before. It was as if she'd finally come to school. From the first moment of the first class, the professors seemed bright, engaged; they seemed to *see* her. Even better, they *challenged* her. She fumbled her way nervously through Advanced Biochem, made notes of the books she needed, and did the same in Philosophy. There was a lot of talking in Philosophy, and she didn't understand half of it, but it sounded a lot more interesting than the droning voices of her core class instructors.

She felt exhilarated by the time her late lunch break rolled around . . . she felt, in fact, *alive.* She was happy as she hunted for used copies of the textbooks she needed, and even happier when she discovered that, mysteriously, she had a scholarship account set up to cover the costs. It even came with its own cash card.

She bought a new long-sleeve T-shirt, too. And some disposable razors. And some shampoo.

Scary, how good it felt having money in her pocket.

By the time three p.m. rolled around, she was starting to wonder if she was expected to head out for Myrnin's house on her own, but she decided to wait. Nobody had told her of a change of plan, so she headed over to the UC to get in some study time while she waited. The big main study room was packed, and somebody was playing guitar in the corner of the room—quite a big crowd over there, clapping between songs. Whoever it was played well—something complicated and classical, then a pop song right after. Claire was spreading out her books on the table when she heard a song that sounded familiar, and stood up on her chair to get a better look over the heads of the people gathered in the corner.

As she'd suspected, it was Michael. He was sitting down to play, but she could see his head and shoulders. He looked up and met her eyes, nodded, then went back to focus on the music. Claire jumped down, wiped her dusty footprints off the wooden chair, and sat. Her brain was racing. *Michael* was here. Why? Was it just a coincidence? Or was it something else?

She sat down and tried to concentrate on the properties of low frequency wave modes in magnetized plasma, which was frankly pretty cool. The physics of stars. She couldn't wait for the lab demonstrations ... the reading was slow going, but interesting. It linked to another thing about plasma physics that had caught her attention: confinement and transport. It might have been coincidence, but somehow she felt there was something there she ought to understand. Something that related to what Myrnin had been telling her about recomposition, which was a key element in alchemy. Was it possible there really was a link between the two?

Plasma is charged particles. It can be controlled and influenced by shaped magnetic fields. Plasma was the raw state between matter and energy ... between one form and another.

Reconstitution.

It hit her, suddenly, what Myrnin had discovered. *The doorways.* They were shaped magnetic fields, holding a tiny, pliable field of plasma held in a steady state. But how did he make them into portable wormholes? Because that was what they had to be, to bend space like that . . . and the plasma couldn't be regular plasma, could it? Low-heat plasma? Was that even possible?

Claire was so absorbed that she didn't even hear the chair scrape back across from her, didn't know someone had sat down, until a hand grabbed the book propped in front of her and pushed it down.

"Hey, Claire," said Jason, Eve's nutty brother. He looked weasely and pale—not Goth-pale, sick-pale. Anemic. There were crusty sores on his neck, and his eyes were wide and red-veined, and he looked high. Really, crazy high. He also hadn't had a bath or been near a Laundromat in a few days or weeks; he smelled filthy and rotten. Ugh. "How you doing?"

She couldn't quite think what the right move would be. Scream? She closed the book and held on to it—it was pretty heavy, and would make a decent blunt object—and darted a look around. The UC was filled with people. Granted, Michael's playing was the center of attention at the moment, but there were plenty of others walking around, talking, studying. From where she sat, Claire could see Eve at the coffee bar, smiling and pulling espresso shots.

It was as though Jason were invisible or something. Nobody was paying him the slightest bit of attention.

"Hi," she said. "What do you want?"

"World peace," he said. "You're pretty."

You're really not. She didn't, and couldn't, say it. She just waited. *I'm perfectly safe here. There are a lot of people, Michael's right over there, and Eve . . .*

"Did you hear me?" Jason asked. "I said, you're pretty."

"Thank you." Her mouth felt dry. She was scared, and she couldn't even think why, really, except what Eve had told her about Jason. He did look dangerous. Those scabs on his throat—had he been bitten? "I have to go."

"I'll walk you to class," Jason said. Somehow, he made that sound filthy, like some porn movie come-on. "I always wanted to carry some hot college girl's books."

"No," she said. "I can't. I mean—I'm not going to class. But I have to go." And why couldn't she just tell him to leave her alone? *Why?*

Jason blew her a kiss. "Go on. But don't blame me when the next dead girl shows up in the trash because you wouldn't do me a simple favor."

She was in the act of standing up when he said it, and she just . . . stopped. Stopped moving, and stared. "What?" she asked, stupidly. Her brain, which had been moving at light speed while skipping from one physics problem to the next, felt sluggish now. "What did you say?"

"Not that I did anything. But if I had, I'd be planning another one. Unless somebody talked to me and convinced me to stop, for instance. Or I made a deal."

Claire felt cold. Worse, she felt *alone.* Jason wasn't doing anything—he was just sitting there, talking. But she felt violated, and horribly exposed. *Michael's right over there. You can hear him playing. He's right there. You're safe.*

"All right," she said, and swallowed a mouthful of what felt like dust and tacks. She sank slowly back into her chair. "I'm listening."

Jason leaned forward, rested his arms on the table, and lowered his voice. "See, it's like this, Claire. I want my big sister to understand what she did to me when she sent me to that place. You know what a jail is like in Morganville? It's as though some third-world country threw it out for prisoner abuse. *Eve put me there.* And she didn't even try to save me."

Claire's fingers felt numb, she was holding her book so tightly. She forced herself to relax. "I'm sorry," she said. "That must have been bad."

"Bad? Bitch, are you even *listening?*" He kept on staring at her, and, as though he were dead, he never blinked. "I was supposed to be his, you know. Brandon's. He was going to make me a vampire someday, but now he's dead, and I'm screwed. Now I'm just waiting around for somebody to put me back in jail, and guess what, Claire? I'm not going. Not without a little fun first."

He grabbed her wrist, and she opened her mouth to scream. . . .

All of a sudden he had a knife, and he was pressing it to her wrist. "Hold still," he said. "I'm not done talking. You move, you bleed."

She was going to yell anyway, but when it made it to her lips it died into a weak little yelp. Jason smiled, and he tossed a filthy-looking handkerchief on top of her wrist and the knife, covering it up. "There," he said. "Now nobody's going to notice, not that they'd care. Not in Morganville. But just in case there are any dumbass heroes, let's keep this between just us."

She was shaking now. "Let me go." Somehow, her voice stayed low and steady. "I won't say anything."

"Oh, come *on*. You'll run to your friends, and then you'll run to the cops. Probably those two dicks Hess and Lowe. They've been out to get me since I was a kid, did you know that? Sons of bitches." He was sweating. A milky drop ran down the side of his pale face and splashed on his camouflage jacket. "I hear you're in good with the vamps. That true?"

"What?" The knife pressed harder against her wrist, hot and painful, and she thought about how easy it would be for him to cut right through her veins. Her whole arm was shaking, but somehow, she managed to hold still against an overwhelming urge to try to yank her wrist away. It would only do the job for him. "I'm—yes. I'm Protected. You'll get in trouble for this, Jason."

He had a truly creepy smile, a rubbery snarl that didn't affect his hot, strange eyes at all. "I was born in trouble," he said. "Bring it on. You tell whatever vamp put the mark on you that I know something. Something that could blow this town in half. And I'll sell it for two things: rights to do whatever I want to my sister, and a ticket out of Morganville."

Oh God oh God oh God. He wants to bargain. For Eve's life.

"I'm not making any deals," she said, and knew it was probably a death sentence. "I'm not going to let you hurt Eve."

He actually blinked. It made him look almost human, for a second, and Claire remembered that he wasn't much older than she. "How you going to stop me, cupcake? Hit me with your book bag?"

"If I have to."

He sat back, staring at her, and then he laughed. Loudly. It was a harsh, metallic clatter of a laugh, and she thought, *Oh God, he's going to kill me,* but then he lifted up the handkerchief covering her wrist and like a magic trick, the knife was gone. There was a trickle of blood dripping from the shallow cut in her skin, and she was starting to feel the burn.

"You know what, Claire?" Jason asked. He got up, stuck his hands in his jacket pockets, and smiled at her again. "I'm going to like you a lot. You're a scream."

He strolled off, and Claire tried to get up and see where he was going, but she couldn't. Her knees wouldn't cooperate. He was out of sight in seconds.

Claire looked at the coffee bar. Eve was standing there, motionless, staring right at her with huge dark eyes, and even without the Goth rice powder she'd have been pale as death.

Eve mouthed, *You okay?*

Claire nodded.

She really wasn't, though, and the cut on her wrist wouldn't stop bleeding. She dug in her backpack and found an adhesive bandage—she always kept them, just in case she got blisters on her feet from all the walking. That seemed to do the trick.

She was smoothing it in place when she felt someone standing over her, and jumped, expecting the return of Jason, complete with psycho stabbing attack.

But it was Michael. He had his guitar case in his hand, and he looked— great. Relaxed, somehow, in a way that she'd never really seen him. There was even a slight flush of color in his face, and his eyes were shining.

But that quickly faded, and he frowned. "You're bleeding," he said. "What happened?"

Claire sighed and held up her wrist to show him the bandage. "Man, you would be so embarrassed if I said it was something else." Michael looked blank. "I'm a girl, Michael. It could have been all natural, you know. Tampons?"

Vampire or not, he was *such* a guy, and his expression was priceless— a combination of embarrassment and nausea. "Oh crap, I hadn't really thought that through. Sorry. Not really used to this yet. So—what happened?"

"Paper cut," she said.

"Claire."

She sighed. "Don't freak, okay? It was Eve's brother, Jason. I think he just wanted to scare me."

Michael's eyes widened, and his head turned fast, searching the coffee bar for Eve. When he saw her, the relief that spread over his face was painful—and it didn't last long before it curdled into something grim. "I can't believe he'd come here. Why can't they catch this jerk?"

"Maybe somebody doesn't want to," she said. "He's only killing human girls. *If* he's the one doing it." Although he'd pretty much confessed, hadn't he? And the knife was a big clue. "We can talk about it later. I need to get—" She remembered, just in time, that she couldn't talk to Michael about Myrnin. "Get to class," she said. She hadn't really thought Amelie would make her go alone, and she wasn't sure she could do it. Myrnin was fascinating, most of the time, but then when he turned . . . no, she couldn't go alone. What if something happened? Sam wouldn't be there to help get him off her.

Michael didn't move. "I know where you're going," he said. "I'm your ride."

She blinked. "You're my—what?"

He lowered his voice, even though nobody was paying attention. "I'll take you where you're supposed to go. And I'll wait for you."

Amelie had told him, Claire found out on the way to Michael's new car. She'd needed to, apparently; she hadn't trusted any vampire but Sam with the information and access to Myrnin, but Michael had an investment in Claire's well-being, and Sam was going to be out of action for a couple of days at least. "But he's okay?" Claire asked.

Michael opened the door to the parking garage for her, an automatic gesture that he'd probably learned from his grandfather, once upon a time. He had some of Sam's mannerisms, and they had the same walk. "Yeah," Michael said. "He nearly died, though. People—vampires—are pretty wired right now. They want the one who staked him, and they don't really care how it happens. I made Shane promise to keep his ass inside, and not to go out alone."

"You really think he'll keep his word?"

Michael shrugged and opened the door of a standard-issue, dark vampire-tinted sedan, exactly the same as the one Sam had driven. A Ford, as it happened. Nice to know the vamps were buying American. "I tried," he said. "Shane doesn't listen to much of anything I have to say. Not anymore."

Claire got into the car and buckled in. As Michael climbed in the driver's side, she said, "It's not your fault. He's just not dealing with it very well. I don't know what we can do about that."

"Nothing," Michael said, and started the car. "We can't do anything about it at all."

It was a short drive, of course, and as far as Claire could tell from the dimly seen streets outside, Michael took the same route Sam had to the alley, and Myrnin's cave. Michael parked the car at the curb. When she got out, though, Claire realized something, and bent to look into the dim interior of the car, then ducked back inside.

"Crap," she said. "You can't come inside, can you? You can't go out in the sun!"

Michael shook his head. "I'm supposed to wait out here for you until the sun goes down; then I'll come in. Amelie said she'd make sure you were safe until then."

"But—" Claire bit her lip. It wasn't Michael's fault. There were about three hours of sun left, so she was just going to have to watch her own back for a while. "Okay. See you after dark."

She closed the car door. When she straightened she saw that Gramma Katherine Day was on the porch of her big Founder House, rocking and sipping what looked like iced tea. Claire waved. Gramma Day nodded.

"You bein' careful?" she called.

"Yes, ma'am!"

"I told the queen, I don't like her putting you down there with that thing. I told her," Gramma Day said, with a fierce stab of her finger for emphasis. "You come on up here and have some iced tea with me, girl. That thing down there—he'll wait. He don't know where he is half the time, anyway."

Claire smiled and shook her head. "I can't, ma'am. I'm supposed to be there on time. Thank you, though." She turned toward the alley, then had a thought. "Oh—who's the queen?"

Gramma made an impatient fly-waving gesture. "*Her*, of course. The White Queen. You're just like Alice, you know. Down the rabbit hole with the Mad Hatter."

Claire didn't dare think about that too much, because the phrase *Off with her head!* loomed way too close. She gave Gramma Day another polite smile and wave, hitched her backpack higher on her shoulder, and went to night school.

EIGHT

Amelie had made sure she was safe, all right. She'd done it by locking Myrnin up.

Claire dropped her backpack at the bottom of the stairs—where it was easy to grab in midrun—and spotted a new addition to the lab: a cage. And Myrnin was inside it.

"Oh my God——" She took a few steps toward him, navigating around the usual haphazard stacks of books, and bit her lip. It was, as far as she could tell, the same cage that the vampires had used to lock up Shane in Founder's Square—heavy black bars, and the whole thing was on wheels. Vampire-proof, hopefully. Whoever had locked Myrnin in had been nice enough to give him a whole pile of books, and a comfy (if threadbare) tangle of blankets and faded pillows. He was lounging in the corner on the cushions, with a pair of old-fashioned, Benjamin Franklin–style glasses perched on the end of his hooked nose. He was reading.

"You're late," he said, as he turned a page. Claire's mouth opened and closed, but she couldn't think of a thing to say. "Oh, don't fret about the cage. It's for your precaution, of course. Since Samuel isn't here to watch over you." He turned another page, but his eyes weren't moving to follow text. He was pretending to read, and somehow that was worse than heartbreaking. "Amelie's idea. I can't say that I really approve."

She finally was able to say, "I'm sorry."

Myrnin shrugged and closed the book, which he dropped with a bang on the pile next to him. "I've been in cages before this," he said. "And no doubt I will be let out once your appointed guardian is here to chaperone. In the meantime, let's continue with our instruction. Pull a chair close. You'll excuse me if I don't get up, but I'm a bit taller than—" He reached up and rapped the bars overhead. "Amelie tells me you have enrolled in advanced placement classes."

Claire gratefully took that as an opportunity not to think about how disturbingly reassuring this was, seeing him locked up like an animal in a cage, because of *her*. She read off her class schedule, and answered his questions, which were sharply worded and a strange mix of expert knowledge and complete ignorance. He understood philosophy and biochem; he didn't know anything at all about quantum mechanics, until she explained the basics, and then he nodded.

"Myth and Legend?" he echoed, baffled, when she read off the class title. "Why would Amelie feel it necessary . . . ah, no matter. I'm sure she has reason. Your essay?" He held out his hand. Claire dug the stapled computer printout from her bag and handed it over. Six pages, single spaced. The best she could do on the history of a subject she was only just now starting to understand. "I'll read it later. And the books I gave you?"

Claire went to her backpack and pulled them out, then came back to her chair. "I read through *Aureus* and *The Golden Chain of Homer.*"

"Did you understand them?"

"Not—really."

"That's because alchemy is a very secretive field of study. Rather like being a Mason—are there still Masons?" When she nodded, Myrnin looked oddly relieved. "Well, that's good. The consequences would be quite terrible, you know, if there weren't. As to alchemy, I can teach you how to translate the codes that were spoken and written, but I'm more concerned that you learn the mechanics than the philosophy. You do understand the methods outlined in the texts for constructing a calcining furnace, yes?"

"I think so. But why can't we just order what we need? Or buy it?"

Myrnin flicked the silver ring on his right hand into the bars of his cell, setting up a metallic ringing. "None of that. Modern children are fools, slaves to the work of others, dependent for everything. Not you. You will learn how to build your tools as well as use them."

"You want me to be an *engineer*?"

"Is it not a useful thing for one who studies physics to understand such practical applications?"

She stared at him doubtfully. "You're not going to make me get an anvil and make my own screwdrivers or anything, are you?"

Myrnin smiled slowly. "What a good idea! I'll consider it. Now. I have an experiment I'd like to try. Are you ready?"

Probably not. "Yes, sir."

"Move that bookcase—" He pointed to a leaning monstrosity of shelves that looked ready to collapse. It was groaning with volumes, of course. "Push it out of the way."

Claire wasn't at all sure the thing would hold together to *be* pushed, but she did as he said. It was better built than it looked, and to her surprise, when she'd pushed it aside, she found a small arched doorway. It was secured with a big heart-shaped iron lock.

"Open it," he said, and picked up the book he'd dropped upon her entrance, leafing randomly through the pages.

"Where's the key?"

"No idea." He flipped faster, frowning at the words. "Look around."

Claire looked around the lab in complete frustration. "In *here*?" Where was she supposed to start? It was all piles and stacks and half-open drawers, nothing in any order at all that she'd been able to determine so far. "Can you give me a hint, at least?"

"If I remembered, I would." Myrnin's voice was dry, but just a little sad, too. She shot him a glance out of the corner of her eye. He folded the book closed again and stared out of the cage—not at her, or at anything, really. There was a careful blankness to his face. "Claire?"

"Yeah?" She pulled open the first drawer near the door. It was full of bottles of what looked like dust, none of them labeled. A spider scuttled frantically out of sight into the darker recesses, and she made a face and slammed it shut.

"Can you tell me why I'm in this cage?" He sounded odd now, strangely calm with something underneath. Claire pulled in a deep breath and kept looking in the drawers. She didn't look directly at him. "I don't like cages. Bad things have happened to me in cages."

"Amelie says you have to stay in there for a while," she said. "Remember? It's to help us."

"I don't remember." His voice was warm and soft and regretful. "I'd like to get out of here. Could you open it, please?"

"No," she said. "I don't have the—"

Keys, except that she did. There was a ring of them sitting right there in front of her, half-hidden by a leaning tower of loose yellowing pages. Three keys. One was a great big iron skeleton key, and she was instantly almost sure that it fit the big heart-shaped lock on the door behind the bookcase. The other one was newer, still big and clunky, and it had to be the key to Myrnin's cage.

The third was a tiny, delicate silver key, like the kind that opened diaries and suitcases.

Claire reached out for the key ring and pulled it toward her, trying to do it silently. He heard, of course. He got up from the corner of the cage and came to the front, where he held on to the bars. "Ah, excellent," he said. "Claire, please open the door. I can't show you what you need to do if I'm locked in this cage."

God, she couldn't look at him, she just couldn't. "I'm not supposed to do that," she said, and sorted out the big iron skeleton key. It felt cold and rough to her fingers, and old. Really old. "You wanted me to open this door, right?"

"Claire. Look at me." He sounded so *sad*. She heard the soft ringing chime of his ring on the bars when he gripped them again. "Claire, *please*."

She turned away from him and put the key into the heart-shaped lock.

"Claire, *don't open that!*"

"You told me to!"

"*Don't!*" Myrnin rattled the bars of his cage, and even though they were solid iron, she heard them rattle. "It's *my* door! *My* escape! Come here and release me! *Now!*"

She checked her watch. Not enough time, not nearly enough; it was still at least an hour to sunset, maybe more. Michael was still stuck in the car. "I can't," she said. "I'm sorry."

The sound Myrnin made then was enough to make her glad that she was across the room. She'd never heard a lion roar, not in person, but somehow she imagined that it would sound like that, all wild animal rage. It shredded her confidence. She closed her eyes and tried not to listen, but he was talking; she couldn't understand what he was saying now, but it was a constant, vicious stream in a language she didn't know. The tone, though—you couldn't *not* get the evil undercurrents.

He'd kill her if he got hold of her now. Thank God, the cage was strong enough to . . .

He snarled something low and guttural, and she heard something metal snap with a high, vibrating sound.

The cage wasn't strong enough.

Myrnin was bending the bars away from the lock.

Claire spun, key still in her hand, and saw him rip at a weak point in the cage as though it were wet paper. How could he do that? How could he be that strong? Wasn't he hurting himself?

He was. She could see blood on his hands.

It came to her with a jolt that if he got out of that cage, he could do the same thing to *her.*

She needed to get out.

Claire moved around the lab table, squeezed past two towering stacks of volumes, and tripped over a broken three-legged stool. She hit the floor painfully, on top of a pile of assorted junk—pieces of old leather, some bricks, a couple of withered old plants she guessed Myrnin was saving for botanical salvage. Man, that hurt. She rolled over on her side, gasping, and climbed to her feet.

She heard a long, slow creak of metal, and stopped for a fatal second to look over her shoulder.

The cage door was open, and Myrnin was out. He was still wearing his little Ben Franklin glasses, but what was in his eyes looked like something that had crawled straight out of hell.

"Oh crap," she whispered, and looked desperately toward the stairs.

Too far. *Way* too far, too many obstacles between her and safety, and he could move like a snake. He'd get there first.

She was closer to the door with the lock on it than the stairs, and the key was still clutched tightly in her hand. She'd have to abandon her book bag; no way to get to it now.

She didn't have time to think about it. The cut Jason had put on her wrist was still fresh; Myrnin could still smell it, and it was ringing the dinner bell loud and clear.

She kicked stacks of books out of the way, jumped over the pile of junk, and, with the key outstretched, raced for the locked door. Her hands were shaking, and it took two tries to get the oversized key into the hole; when she started to turn it there was a terrible moment of utter panic because *it wouldn't turn. . . .*

And then it did, a smooth metallic slide of levers and pins, and the door swung open.

On the other side was her own living room, and Shane was sitting on the couch with his back to her, playing a video game.

Claire paused, utterly off balance. That couldn't be real, could it? She couldn't be seeing him, right there, but she could hear all of the computerized grunts and punches and wet bloody sounds from whatever fight game he had on. She could *smell* the house. Chili. He'd made chili. He still hadn't taken some of his boxes back upstairs. They were piled in the corner.

"Shane," she whispered, and reached out, through the doorway. She could feel something there, like a slight pressure, and the hair on her arm shivered and prickled.

Shane put the game on pause, and slowly stood up. "Claire?" He was looking in the wrong place; he was looking up, at the staircase.

But he'd heard her. And that meant she could just step right through and she'd be safe.

She never got the chance.

Myrnin's hand landed on her shoulder, dragged her back, and as Shane started to turn toward them, Myrnin slammed the door and turned the key in the lock.

She didn't dare move. He was crazy; she could see it. There was nothing in him that recognized her at all. Amelie's warnings screamed through her head, and Sam's. She'd underestimated Myrnin, and that was what had gotten all the other would-be apprentices killed.

Myrnin was shaking, and his broken hands were crunched into fists. His blood was dripping on an open copy of an old chemistry textbook that lay by his feet.

"Who are you?" he whispered. The accent she'd noted the first time she'd met him was back, and strong. Really strong. "Child, what brings you here? Do you not understand your danger? Who is your Patron? Were you sent as a gift?"

She closed her eyes for a second, then opened them and looked right into his eyes and said, "You're Myrnin, and I'm Claire; I'm your friend. I'm your friend, okay? You should let me help you. You hurt yourself."

She pointed to his injured fingers. Myrnin looked down, and he seemed surprised, as if he hadn't felt it at all. Which maybe he hadn't.

He took two steps backward, ran into a lab table, and knocked over a stand that held empty glass test tubes. They fell and shattered on the dirty stone floor.

Myrnin staggered, then sank down to sit against the wall, his face covered by bloody hands, and began to rock back and forth. "It's wrong," he moaned. "There was something important, something I had to do. I can't remember what it was."

Claire watched him, still scared to death, and then sank down to a crouch across from him. "Myrnin," she said. "The door. The one I opened. Where does it go?"

"Door? Doorways. Moments in time, just moments, none of it stays; it flows like blood, you know, just like blood. I tried to bottle it, but it doesn't stay fresh. Time, I mean. Blood turns, and so does time. What's your name?"

"Claire, sir. My name's Claire."

He let his head fall back against the wall, and there were bloody tears running down his cheeks. "Don't trust me, Claire. Don't ever trust me." He bounced the back of his head off the wall with enough force to make Claire wince.

"I—no, sir. I won't."

"How long have I been your friend?"

"Not that long."

"I don't have friends," he said hollowly. "You don't, you know, when you're as old as I am. You have competitors, and you have allies, but not friends, never. You're too young—far too young—to understand that." He closed his eyes for a moment, and when he opened them, he looked mostly sane. Mostly. "Amelie wants you to learn from me, yes? So you are my student?"

This time, Claire just nodded. Whatever the fit was, it was leaving him, and he was empty and tired and sad again. He took off his glasses, folded them, and put them in the pocket of his coat.

"You won't be able to do it," he said. "You can't possiby learn quickly enough. I nearly killed you tonight, and next time I won't be able to stop. The others—" He stopped, looked briefly sick, and cleared his throat. "I'm not—I wasn't always like this, Claire. Please understand. Unlike many of my kind, I never wanted to be a monster. I only wanted to learn, and this was a way to learn forever."

Claire bit her lip. "I can understand that," she said. "I—Amelie wants me to help you, and learn from you. Do you think I'm smart enough?"

"Oh, you're smart enough. Could you master the skills, given enough time? Perhaps. And you'll have no choice in the matter; she'll keep you coming until you learn, or I destroy you." Myrnin slowly lifted his head and looked at her. Rational again, and very steady. "Did I remind you not to trust me?"

"Yes, sir."

"It's good advice, but just this once, ignore it and allow me to help you."

"Help . . . ?"

Myrnin stood up, in that eerie boneless way that he seemed to have, and rummaged around through the glass jars and beakers and test tubes until he found something that looked like red salt. He shook the container—it was about the size of a spice jar—and opened it to extract one red crystal. He touched it to his tongue, shut his eyes for a second, and smiled.

"Yes," he said. "I thought so." He recapped it and held it out to her. "Take it."

She did. It felt surprisingly heavy. "What is it?"

"I have no idea what to call it," he said. "But it'll work."

"What do I do with it?"

"Shake a small amount into your palm, like so." He reached out for her hand. She pulled away, curling her fingers closed, and Myrnin looked briefly wounded. "No, you're right. You do it. I apologize." He handed her the shaker and made an encouraging gesture. She hesitantly turned the shaker upside down over her palm. A few red chunky crystals poured out. He wanted her to keep going, so she did, making quick jerks with the container until there was maybe half a teaspoon of the stuff piled up.

Myrnin took the shaker from her, set it back where he'd found it, and nodded at her. "Go on," he said. "Take it."

"Excuse me?"

He mimed popping it into his mouth.

"I—um—what is it, again?"

This time, Myrnin rolled his eyes in frustration. "Take it, Claire! We don't have much time. My periods of lucidity are shorter now. I can't guarantee I won't slip again. Soon. This will help."

"I don't understand. How is this stuff supposed to help?"

He didn't tell her again; he just pleaded silently with her, his whole expression open and hopeful, and she finally put her hand to her mouth and tentatively tasted one of the crystals.

It tasted like strawberry salt, with a bitter after-flavor. She felt an instant, tiny burst of ice-cold clarity, like a strobe light going off in a darkened room full of beautiful, glittering things.

"Yes," Myrnin breathed. "Now you see."

This time, she licked up more of the crystals. Four or five of them. The bitterness was stronger, barely offset by the strawberries, and the reaction was even faster. It was as though she'd been asleep, and all of a sudden she was awake. Gloriously, dizzyingly awake. The world was so sharp she felt as though even the dull battered wood of the table could cut her.

Myrnin picked up a book at random and opened it. He held it up in front of her, and it was like another burst of light in the darkness, brilliant and beautiful, *oh, so pretty*, the way the words curved themselves around each other and cut into her brain. It was painful and perfect, and she read as fast as she could.

> *The essence of gold is the essence of Sun, and the essence of silver is the essence of Moon. You must work with each of these according to its properties, gold in the daylight, silver in the night . . .*

It all made sense to her. Total sense. Alchemy was nothing but a poet's explanation of the way matter and energy interacted, the way different surfaces vibrated at different speeds; it was physics, nothing but physics, and she could understand how to use it now.

And then . . . then it was as though the bulbs all dimmed again.

"Go on, take it," Myrnin said. "The dose in your hand will last for an hour or so. In that time, I can teach you a great deal. Enough, perhaps, for us to understand where we should be going."

This time, Claire didn't hesitate licking up every last bit of the red crystals.

Myrnin was right; the crystals lasted for a little more than an hour. He took some as well, one at a time, carefully measuring them out and making them last until finally even a red crystal couldn't drive the growing confusion out of his eyes. He was getting anxious by the end. Claire started closing the books and stacking them up on the table—the two of them were sitting cross-legged on the floor, practically buried in volumes. Myrnin had jumped her from one book to another, pulling out a paragraph here, a chapter there, a chart from physics, and a page from something so old he had to teach her the language before she could understand.

I learned languages. I learned . . . I learned so much. He'd shown her a diagram, and it hadn't been just a diagram—it had been three-dimensional and as intricate as a snowflake. Morganville hadn't just happened; it had been planned. Planned around the vampires. Planned *by* the vampires, carried out by Myrnin and Amelie. The Founder Houses, they were part of it—thirteen bright, hard nodes of power in the web, holding together a complex pattern of energy. It could move people from one place to another, via the doorways, although Claire didn't yet understand how to control them. But the web could do more. It could change memories. It could even keep people away, if Amelie wanted it to do that.

Myrnin had shown her the journals, too, with all his research conducted over the last seventy years into the vampire's sickness. It was chilling, the way his notes degenerated from meticulous to scrawls at the end, and sometimes into nonsense.

Some part of her still wondered if she shouldn't just stand by and let it happen, but Myrnin . . . what he knew, what he'd accomplished—and she'd never learned so much, never, not from anyone.

Maybe just a little. *Maybe I could help him just a little.*

The influence of the crystals was dimming now, and Claire felt horribly tired. There was a steady ache in her muscles, a feverish throb that told her this stuff wasn't exactly kind to the human body. She could feel every heartbeat pounding through her head, and everything looked so *dark.* So . . . so confusing.

She felt a breath of air stir against her cheek, and she turned toward the stairs. Michael was descending, moving faster than she'd ever seen him, and he came to a fast halt when he saw her sitting beside Myrnin.

"He's supposed to be—"

"Locked up in a cage? Yeah, I know." Claire knew she sounded bitter. She didn't care. "He's sick, Michael. He's not an animal. And anyway, even if you lock him up, he'll get out."

Michael looked young to her, all of a sudden, although he was older than she was. And a vampire, on top of that. "Claire, get up and come to me. Please."

"Why? He's not going to hurt me."

"He can't help what he does. Look, Sam told me how many people he's killed—"

"He's a *vamp*, Michael. Of course he's—"

"How many he's killed *in the last two years*. It's more than all the other vampires in Morganville combined. *You're not safe*. Now, get up and walk over here."

"He's right," Myrnin said. He was losing it, Claire could see that, but he was desperately hanging on to being the man who'd been with her for the last hour. The gentle, funny, sweet one, ablaze with excitement and passion for showing her his world. "It's time for you to go." He smiled, showing teeth—not vampire teeth. It was a very human kind of expression. "I do all right on my own, Claire, or at least there's rarely anyone for me to harm. Amelie will send someone to look after me. And I usually can't leave here, once I—forget things. It's too difficult for me to find the keys, and I can't remember how to use them once I have them. But I never forget how to kill. Your friend is right. You should go, please. Now. Continue your studies."

It was stupid, but she hated leaving him like this, with all the light going out in his eyes and the clouds of fear and confusion rolling in.

She didn't mean to do it; it just happened.

She hugged him.

It was like hugging a tree; he was so surprised, he was as stiff as a block of wood. She wasn't actually sure how long it had been since anybody had touched him like this. For a second he resisted her, and then his arms went around her, and she felt him heave a great sigh. Still not a hug, not really, but it was as close as he was likely to get.

"Go away, little bird," he whispered. "Hurry."

She backed away. His eyes were strange again, and she knew they were out of time. *Someday, he won't come back. He'll just be the beast.*

Michael was beside her. She hadn't heard him cross the room, but his hand closed around hers, and there was real compassion in his face. Not for Myrnin, though. For her.

"You heard him," Michael said. "Hurry."

She bumped into the table, and the small jar of red crystals shuddered a little, nearly tipping over. She grabbed it to put it back upright, and then thought, *What if he loses this? He loses stuff all the time.*

She would only be keeping it safe, that was all. It helped him, right? So she ought to make sure he didn't knock it over or throw it away or something.

She slipped it into her pocket. She didn't think Myrnin saw, and she knew Michael didn't. Claire felt a hot burst of something—shame? Embarrassment? Excitement? *I should put it back.* But really, she'd never find it again if he moved it around. Myrnin wouldn't remember. He wouldn't even know it was gone.

She kept looking back, all the way up the stairs. By the time they were halfway out, Myrnin had already forgotten them, and he was restlessly flipping through a pile of books, muttering anxiously to himself.

Gone already.

He looked up at them and snarled, and she saw the hard glint of fangs.

She hurried to the door at the top of the stairs.

NINE

Michael wasn't talking to her, and that was bad. He wasn't sullen, like Shane got from time to time; he was just thoughtful. That made the drive uneasily quiet. It was fully dark out, not that she could see through the window tinting, anyway.

The world didn't seem real to her anymore, and her head ached.

"This is the deal you made with Amelie," Michael said. "To work for him."

"No. I made the deal with Amelie; *then* she told me to work for him. Or learn from him."

"Is there a difference?"

Claire smiled. "Yeah. I don't get paid."

"Brilliant plan, genius. Is *anybody* paying you?"

Actually, she had no idea. The thought hadn't occurred to her, to ask Amelie for money. Was that normal, to get paid for a thing like this? She supposed it was, if she was supposed to risk her life with Myrnin on a regular basis. "I'll ask," she offered.

"No," Michael said grimly. "*I'll* ask. I want to talk to Amelie about this whole thing, anyway."

"Don't get all older-brother on me, Michael. It's not safe. You may be one of them now, but you're not—"

"One of them? Yeah, I know that. But you're way too young for this, Claire, and you don't know what you're doing. You didn't grow up in this town; you don't understand the risks."

"What, death? I understand that one pretty well already." She was feeling tired and achy, but also strangely annoyed with Michael's protectiveness. "Look, I'm fine, okay? Besides, I learned a lot today. She'll be happy, trust me."

"Amelie's mood isn't what bothers me," Michael said. "It's you. You're changing, Claire."

She looked straight at him. "Like you haven't?"

"Cheap shot. Look, I'm sick of having to tiptoe around Shane. Don't make me do it with you, too." Ah, now Michael was annoyed, too. Great.

"Tell you what? I'll stop nagging you about your life if you'll stay out of mine. You're not my brother, you're not my dad—"

"No," he interrupted. "I'm the guy who says if you get to stay in the house."

He wouldn't. He *wouldn't*. "Michael—"

"You made a deal with Amelie without talking to anyone, and then you covered it up. Look, the only reason you even came clean was because I saw the bracelet. If I hadn't, you'd still be lying to us. That doesn't exactly make you the ideal housemate." Michael paused for a second. "And then there's Shane."

"How am I to blame for *Shane*?"

"You're not. But I can't deal with both of you, not now. So just straighten up, Claire. No more lying, and no more risk-taking, all right? I'll convince Amelie to let you out of these sessions with Myrnin. You're too young to be doing this; she ought to know that."

No more lying. No more risk-taking. Claire shifted and felt the bottle in her pocket, and had a flash of that perfect clarity again. She wondered what Michael would have to say about her letting Myrnin give her the crystals. Probably nothing. He was talking about throwing her out of the house, right? So he probably didn't care at all.

The car slowed and turned, then bumped down a rutted drive. Home.

Claire bolted before Michael could say anything else to her.

Shane was in the kitchen, pouring himself a beer. He toasted her silently, took a sip, and nodded toward a pot on the stove. "Chili," he said. "Extra garlic."

Michael was closing the kitchen door, and he sighed. "When is this going to stop?"

"When you quit sucking blood?"

"Shane—"

"Don't get pissy. I made yours garlic-free." Shane looked at her again, and frowned a little. "You okay?"

"Sure. Why wouldn't I be?"

"Just—I don't know. Whatever." He slung an arm over her shoulders and kissed her on the forehead. "Bad day, probably."

Let's see, she'd been threatened by Eve's brother, had her wrist cut, and then played keep-away with Myrnin for hours. Did that qualify as a bad day in Morganville? Probably not. No body count.

Not yet, anyway.

Michael pushed past them and through the door into the living room. Claire pulled free of Shane's arm and went to the stove to ladle herself a bowl of chili. It smelled hot and delicious. But mostly hot. She tasted a drop and nearly choked; was it usually this molten-lava wicked spicy? Everything felt raw to her right now. She supposed that was a side effect of the crystals.

"I thought I heard you," Shane said. "Weirdest thing: I heard your voice today. Right out of the air. I thought you—I kept thinking about Michael, how he used to be during the daytime. . . ."

When he was a ghost. "You thought I was—?"

"I thought maybe something happened," he said. "I called your cell number, the new one."

She'd left it in her backpack. Claire reached down and unzipped the pocket, then checked the phone. Three calls, all from Shane. With voice mails. "Sorry," she said. "I didn't hear it. Guess I need to turn the ringer up."

He looked at her very steadily, and she felt the cold spot in her center, the place that had chilled while she'd been with Myrnin, slowly warm. "You worry me," he said, and put his hand on her cheek. "You know that, right?"

She nodded, and hugged him. Unlike Myrnin, he was warm and solid, and his body just molded right into hers, perfect and sweet. When he kissed her she tasted beer and chili, but only for a second. After that, it was pure Shane, and she forgot all about Myrnin, and any kind of physics except friction. Shane backed her up against the stove. She felt the low heat of the burner at her back, but she was too preoccupied to worry much about bursting into flames from outside sources. Shane just had that effect on her.

"I missed you," he whispered, brushing her damp lips with his. "Want to go upstairs?"

"What about my chili?"

"Get it to go."

There were good things about the way she felt tonight, she decided; her nerves might be raw, but that only made his touch all the sweeter. She would have felt awkward, usually, and uncertain, and scared, but it seemed like the afternoon that had started with Jason and ended with Myrnin's snarl had burned all that out of her.

"Not hungry," she said breathlessly. "Come on."

She felt as wild and free as a little kid, running up the steps with Shane in hot pursuit, and when he grabbed her around the waist, spun her around into his room, and kicked the door shut, she squealed in delight. And wiggled to fit herself against his warm, hard body as she kissed him again, breathless and flying.

He kissed as though their lives depended on it. As though it were an Olympic event and he intended to earn a medal. Somewhere in the back of her head she was chattering to herself, warning that this was going to go too far, that she was just making things worse for both of them, but she couldn't help it. Before long they were stretched out together on Shane's bed, and his big, warm hands were teasing under the hem of her shirt, stroking the fluttering skin of her stomach and stealing her breath. She lost it all when he spread his fingers out, pressing his palm flat against her, and she felt an almost irresistible impulse to feel those hands all over. Everywhere. Her heart was hammering hard enough to make her dizzy, and it was all just so . . .

Perfect.

She reached down and pulled up her shirt. Slowly, feeling the cool air slip over tender skin.

Up, to the bottom line of her bra. Then up.

Shane stopped.

"I want to," she whispered against his mouth. "Please, Shane. I want to." She sat up and reached for the clasp on her bra, and unhooked it. "Please."

He pulled back from her and sat up, head down. When he looked up he licked his lips, and his eyes were wide and dark, and she could fall into them, fall forever.

"I know," he said. "Me too. But I made promises, and I'm going to keep them. Especially the one to your parents, because your dad said he'd hunt me down like a dog." Shane gave her a wild, bitter smile. "Sucks to be me."

"But—" She felt her bra slipping, and quickly grabbed to hold it in place. She felt ridiculous now, and wounded.

He sighed. "Don't, Claire. It's not like I'm a saint or anything; I'm not, and trust me, for you, a saint would buy a condom and go to confession. But it's not about that. It's about keeping my word, and around here, my word is all I've got."

She wanted him with a red fury that was all out of character for her, but somehow, the way he said it, the way he looked her straight in the eyes, she felt all that fall away and the fury turn into something pure, hot, and silver.

"Besides," Shane said, "I'm all out of condoms, and I hate confession."

He put his arms around her and hooked her bra with an ease that showed he had plenty of practice.

She threw a pillow at him.

· · ·

Somebody was rummaging around outside the house.

Claire woke up with a start, instantly tense, as she heard the distant rattle of metal. She rolled out of bed and peeked out of the blinds. Her bedroom window looked out on the back, a glorious corner vantage point, and she had a clear view of the fence, and the trash cans on the other side.

Somebody was definitely out there, a black shape in the moonlight. Claire could see him moving around but couldn't tell what he was doing. She reached for her cell phone and dialed 911, and told the operator she needed either Joe Hess or Travis Lowe. Detective Lowe picked up the call, sounding wide-awake even at three in the morning; Claire described what she was seeing in a whisper, as if whoever was across the yard might hear her.

"It's probably Jason," she said. She heard the scratch of pen on paper on the other end of the phone.

"Why Jason? Can you see his face?"

"No," she admitted, "but Jason told me—he practically admitted it. About the dead girl. I think it's Jason, honest."

"Did he threaten you, Claire?"

The cut on her wrist was still throbbing. "I guess you could say so," she said. "I was going to tell you about it, but I—I had things to do."

"More important than keeping us in the loop? Never mind. What happened?"

"Shouldn't I tell you when you get here?"

"Patrol car's already en route. Where did you see him today?"

"At the university," she said, and told the story. He didn't interrupt her, just let her talk, and she could hear him continuing to take notes.

When she paused for breath, Lowe said, "You know that was stupid, right? Look, next time you see him, you start screaming bloody murder. And put me and Hess on speed dial. Jason's nobody to play around with."

"But—we were in public. He wouldn't have—"

"Ask Eve about why he ended up in jail in the first place, Claire. Next time, don't hesitate. This isn't about you being strong; this about you living through the day, all right? Trust me."

She swallowed hard. "I do."

"Is he still there?"

"I don't know. I can't see him. He might've gone."

"The patrol car ought to be there in just a couple of seconds; they're doing a silent approach. You see them yet?"

"No, but my room faces the alley." Something moved in the yard, and she felt a lurch of pure adrenaline. "I think—I think he's in the yard now. Coming to the house. To the back."

"Go wake up Michael and Shane. Make sure Eve's okay. Go now, Claire."

She wasn't dressed, but she supposed it didn't really matter; the oversized T-shirt she was wearing came to her knees, anyway. She unlocked her door and swung it open, and yelled in shock.

Tried to, anyway. She couldn't quite get the sound out, because Oliver's hand clapped over her mouth, spun her around, and dragged her backward over the threshold. She screamed, but it was barely a buzz in her throat. Her bare heels scraped on the wood as she tried to get her feet under her, but he had her helpless and off balance. She dropped the phone.

She could hear Lowe's voice distantly whispering her name, but it was blotted out by Oliver's soft voice in her ear as he bent close and said, "I only want to talk. Don't make me hurt you, girl. You know I will if you force me."

She went still, breathing hard. Had *he* been out there in the yard? How had he gotten up here so fast? Didn't the protections on the house keep him out?

No. They only work against uninvited humans now, because Michael's—Michael's a vampire. Oliver had some way in and out. Easy access. *God.*

"Good girl. Stay quiet," Oliver whispered. He looked up and down the hall, moved the painting next to the doorway, and pressed the hidden switch. The secret doorway across from Eve's room opened with a soft sigh, and he dragged her inside, then shut it. No knob on the inside. The release switch was up a flight of stairs, and he'd never let her get there if she tried to run. When he let her go, Claire stayed where she was.

He let his voice return to normal levels. Not afraid of being over-heard, not here. "I thought it was time we had a talk. You signed an agreement with Amelie. That hurts me, Claire. I thought we had a special friendship, and after all, I did offer first." Oliver smiled at her, that cold and oddly kind smile that had suckered her in the first few times she'd met him. "You turned me down. So why, I wonder, did you decide that Amelie would be a better choice?"

He might know about Myrnin, but not what Myrnin did. Amelie had been pretty specific: he could *never* know that.

"She smells better," Claire said. "And she made me cookies." Some-how, after the day she'd had, Oliver just didn't seem all that terrifying anymore.

Until he bared his fangs, and his eyes went a strange, wide black. "No games," he said. "The room's soundproofed. Amelie used to play with her victims here, you know. It's a killing jar, and you're inside. So perhaps you should be more polite, if you intend to see morning."

Claire held up her left wrist. The golden bracelet glinted in the light. "Bite it, Oliver. You can't touch me. You can't touch anybody in this house. I don't know how you got in, but—"

He grabbed her right wrist and ripped away the bandage covering the cut Jason had made. It broke open, and a red trickle ran from it down the interior of her arm.

Oliver licked it off.

"Okay, that's just *gross*," Claire said faintly. "Let go. *Let go!*"

"You belong to Amelie," he said, and let her go. "I can taste it. Smell it on you. You're right, I can't touch you, not anymore. But the others, you're wrong about them. While they're in the house they're safe, but not out there, not in *my* town. Not for long."

"I made a deal!"

"Did you? Did you see in writing that your friends would be protected from all attacks? Because I very much doubt that, little Claire. We've been writing agreements for thousands of years, and you're only sixteen years old. You have no idea what kind of deal you've made." Oliver actually sounded a little sorry for her, and that *was* scary. He folded his arms and leaned against the door. He was in his usual good-guy disguise tonight: a tie-dyed T-shirt, battered cargo pants, his graying, curling hair pulled back in a ponytail. He'd probably just closed up Common Grounds, she figured. He smelled like coffee. She wondered what Oliver wore on his days off, if he wasn't trying to intimidate. Pajamas? Fuzzy slippers? One thing she'd figured out about the vampires in Morganville, they were never exactly what they seemed to be, even the bad ones.

"Fine," she said, and backed away from him until her heels hit the first step. She sat down. "You tell me what I've done."

"You've upset the balance of power in the town, and that's a terrible thing, little Claire. You see, Amelie intended to be queen of this little kingdom. She thought I was safely dead when she did so. When I came here a year ago, many people decided that they'd rather listen to me than to her. Not all, of course, and not even a majority. But she's won no real friends during her long existence, and it isn't only the humans who are trapped here, you know. It's the vampires as well."

This was a new idea to her. "What are you talking about?"

"We can't leave," he said. "Not without her permission. As I said, she fancies herself the cold White Queen, and most are content to let her. Not all. I was working to come to some . . . arrangements with her, to let a number of us leave Morganville and set up a community outside of her influence. Things had been static here for fifty years, you see, since she made the last vampire. Now Amelie feels the need to protect her position. She's blocked me. She won't allow me to make a move without her permission." He lowered his chin and stared at her, and it chilled her deep inside. "I don't like to be controlled. I tend to get . . . unhappy."

"Why are you talking to me? What can I do?"

"*You*, stupid little child, are her pet. When you want something, she indulges you. I want to know why."

Amelie hadn't exactly indulged her the last time they'd talked, although the cell phone sitting abandoned in her room might argue otherwise. "I don't *know!*"

"She thinks you have something she needs, or she'd hardly bother.

She's seen whole cities die without shedding a tear or lifting a finger. It's not altruism."

Myrnin. It's about Myrnin. If I weren't learning from him . . . She couldn't say that, didn't even dare to really think it through. Oliver was unnerving, and sometimes he seemed downright psychic. "Maybe she's lonely."

He laughed, a harsh bark of sound with no amusement in it. "She certainly deserves to be." He took a step forward. "Tell me why she needs you, Claire. Tell me what she's hiding, and I'll make a deal, a perfectly straightforward one: I'll give your friends my direct Protection. No one will hurt them."

She didn't say anything this time; she just looked back at him. She didn't dare *not* look at him; even when she was watching him she had the eerie feeling that somehow he was creeping up behind her, ready to do something awful to her when she least expected it.

Oliver made a sound of deep frustration. "You stupid, stupid girl." He shoved past her, going up the stairs so lightly the wood hardly even creaked. After a second, the hidden, knobless door sighed open. Claire got up, steadied herself for a second, and then stepped out into the hallway. Nobody else had heard a thing, apparently. It was quiet as the grave.

Oliver's hands closed around her shoulders, and he moved her out of his way by simply picking her up and putting her down, as if she weighed nothing. He didn't let go once he'd done it; he stepped up behind her, bent down, and whispered, "Not a sound, Claire. If you wake your friends and they come against me, I'll destroy you all. Understand?"

She nodded.

She felt the cold pressure of his hands go away, but not his presence, and she was surprised when she looked back and saw that he was gone.

As if he'd never been there at all.

She pressed the button behind the painting, and the hidden door sealed itself. Then she picked up her phone from the floor of her bedroom. The call had ended; Travis Lowe was probably on his way over, burning sirens all the way.

She sat down to wait for the panic to start.

·   ·   ·

There just had to be something out there in the alley, given the response. It wasn't only a couple of cops, some yellow tape, and a write-up in Captain Obvious's underground newspaper; it looked, from Claire's window, like a full-blown *CSI*-style investigation, with people in white jumpsuits collecting evidence and everything. There was a big blocky van with heavily tinted windows that she guessed housed vampire detectives or forensics people or something, with the emblem of the Morganville police on the side, and she guessed the majority of people roaming around in Michael's backyard this morning were, in fact, the undead.

Crime-solving undead. That was new.

She wasn't sure what she was feeling anymore. Light-headed, disconnected, looped. Last night had felt like a dream, and it had passed in a blur from the time she and Shane had come upstairs until she'd heard the rattle of trash cans in the alley.

Someone was ringing the doorbell downstairs. She didn't move away from the window—couldn't seem to convince herself to move at all, in fact. It was probably the cops. Travis Lowe had, as she'd thought, already come racing to the rescue, but on finding her unfanged and still alive, he'd called in the full-on police assault. So those were probably the detectives, Gretchen and Hans, or maybe Richard Morrell coming to take her statement.

Claire looked down at herself. *I should probably get dressed.* Her wrist was a mess, smeared with slow-leaking blood, and she pressed her T-shirt against it before she could think about what she was doing. Great, now she wasn't only undressed, she was undressed in bloody nightclothes.

It took ten minutes to shower, change, and bandage up her arm, and then she padded down the stairs in bare feet to face the music.

Her housemates were all standing in the living room, and they all looked at her with identical expressions, blank enough that she came to a stop on the steps. "What?" Claire asked. "What'd I do now?"

Michael stepped aside so Claire could see who was sitting cross-legged in the chair, flipping through a bubble-gum pink edition of *Teen People*.

Monica Morrell.

She was dressed in a tight-fitting pink top with diamonds that spelled out BITCH/PRINCESS, and white short-shorts that even Daisy Duke would have thrown out as too trashy. Her tan was deep and dark, and she was lazily dangling a pink flip-flop with a yellow flower on top from her perfectly manicured toes.

"Hey, Claire!" she said, and stood up. "I thought we could grab some breakfast."

"I—what?"

"Break . . . fast," Monica said, drawing out the word. "Most important meal of the day? Do you even *have* parents?"

Claire felt ridiculously off balance. "I don't understand. Why are you here?"

Shane leaned against the wall, glaring at Monica. He had a serious bed-head thing going on, and Claire wanted to run her hands through his thick, soft hair and return it to its usual shaggy mess. "What a good question. The second-best one being, who let her inside? And we're going to have to throw out that chair. The smell's never coming out."

"I let her in," Michael said quietly, and that got him a stare from Shane. "Lay off the daggers. It was better to let her in than have her pitch a fit on the porch with all the cops around. We've already got enough trouble."

"What's this *we*, paleface? I mean that in the vampire sense, not—"

"Shut up, man."

Claire rubbed her forehead, feeling her headache blooming back to hot, throbbing life. She ignored Michael and Shane with an effort and focused on Monica, who had a malicious smile curving her lips. "You're enjoying this," Claire said. Monica shrugged.

"Of course. They're jackasses to me most of the time; it's nice to see them take it out on each other for a change. Not that I care." Monica arched one perfectly groomed eyebrow. "So? I know you like coffee. I've seen you drinking it."

Eve stepped in between them, and for a second Claire thought her friend honestly looked . . . dangerous. "You're not taking Claire anywhere. And you're *sure* not taking her anywhere near that son of a bitch," she said.

"Which son of a bitch would that be, exactly? Because hey, she lives *here*. It's not like she's choosy about who she hangs out with."

Eve bunched up a fist, and for a second Claire thought she was going to haul off and slug Monica right in her perfect, pouty mouth. But Eve checked herself. Barely.

"You *so* need to leave our house," Eve said. "Now. Before something bad happens that I won't really regret."

Monica gave her a look. "I'm sorry, were you talking? Because I think I dropped off. Claire? I'm not here to banter with the mentally challenged. I'm just trying to be friendly. If you don't want to go, just say so."

Claire felt ridiculously like laughing, it was so weird. Why was this happening to her?

"What do you really want?" she asked, and Monica's lovely, crazy eyes widened. Just a little.

"I want to talk to you without the Losers Club hanging over my shoulder. I figured we could have breakfast, but if you're allergic to caffeine and pastry . . ."

"Anything you can say to me, you can say in front of my friends," Claire said. That brought *both* of Monica's eyebrows up.

"Oooookay. Your funeral," she said, and glanced at Shane. "So where was your boyfriend last night after midnight?"

"Who? *Shane?*" What time had she left his room, anyway? Late. But . . . not after midnight.

"None of your damn business where I was," Shane said to Monica. "Eve told you to get out. The next step is I throw your skanky ass and see if you bounce when you hit the porch. I don't care whose pet you are; you don't come here and—"

"Shane," Monica interrupted with elaborate calm, "shut the hell up. I saw you, idiot."

Claire waited for Shane to give her a biting comeback, but he just sat there. Waiting. His eyes had gone very dark.

"They don't know, do they?" Monica continued, and tapped her rolled-up copy of *Teen People* against her hip. "Wow. Shocker. Bad boy keeps secrets. That *never* happens."

"Shut up, Monica."

"Or you'll *what?* Kill me?" She smiled. "There wouldn't even be DNA left when they got done with you, Shane. And the rest of you, too. *And your families.*"

"What's she talking about?" Eve asked. "Shane?"

"Nothing."

"*Nothing,*" Monica mocked. "Deny everything. That's a brilliant plan. Then again, it's what I'd expect from someone like you."

Michael was frowning at Shane now, and Claire couldn't resist, either. Shane's dark eyes darted to each of them in turn, Claire last.

"The cops aren't going to find any bodies out there in the alley. And they're not going to find one anywhere else in your house," Monica said, "because Shane moved a body last night, out the back door."

Shane *still* wasn't saying anything. Claire covered her mouth with her hand. "No," she said. "You're lying."

Monica folded her arms. "Why exactly would I do that? Why would I admit to hanging around watching your house unless I had to? Embarrassing! Look, if I'm lying, all it takes is for him to deny it. Ask him. Go on." She was staring right at Shane.

Shane's eyes narrowed, but he didn't say anything. For a frozen second or two, nobody moved, and then Michael said, "*Christ,* Shane, what the hell?"

"Shut up!" Shane snapped. "I had to! I thought I heard something down in the basement last night, when I was getting some water in the kitchen. So I went to check it out. And—" He stopped, and Claire saw his Adam's apple bob as he swallowed, hard. "She was dead down there. At the bottom of the stairs, as if somebody had just . . . thrown her. For a second I thought it was"—he glanced at Eve, then away—"I thought it was you. I thought you'd tripped and fallen down the stairs or something. But when I got down there, it wasn't you. And she was dead, not just knocked out."

Eve sank down on the arm of the sofa, looking as stunned as Claire felt. "Who? Who was it?"

"I didn't recognize her. Some college girl, I guess. She didn't look local and she wasn't wearing a bracelet." Shane took in an audible deep breath.

"Look, we've been in enough trouble as it is. I had to get rid of her. So I wrapped her up in one of the blankets out of the boxes down there and carried her out. I put her in the trunk of your car—"

"You *what?*" Michael snapped.

"And I drove her to the church. I left her there, inside. I didn't want to just—dump her. I thought"—Shane shook his head—"I thought it was the right thing to do."

Monica sighed. She was checking out her fingernails with exaggerated boredom. "Yeah, yeah, touching. The point is, when I saw you, you were hauling a dead chick into the trunk of *his* car. And I just can't *wait* to tell my brother. You know my brother, right? The cop?"

Unbelievable. "What do you *want?*" Claire practically yelled it at her.

"I told you. Breakfast." Monica gave her a sunny movie-star smile. "Please. If you say yes, I just could forget all about what I saw. Especially since I was, you know, out after curfew, and I don't want to get asked about why. Think of it as mutually assured destruction."

It sounded like a deal, but it wasn't, not really. Monica had all the cards, and they had none. None at all.

"There's no body in the alley," Claire said. "The police aren't going to find anything. You're sure?"

"Don't think so, but wouldn't that suck for you if they did?" Monica shrugged, puckered her lips, and blew Shane a mocking kiss. "You've got guts, Shane. No brains, but a whole lot of guts. You thought it out, right? Now that Michael's one of the chosen undead, humans can't get in this house without an invitation. So you have to either blame it on a vampire, or face up to the fact that one of you killed her. Either way, it's not going to be pretty, and somebody's going down." She held up her hand. "I vote for Shane. Anybody else?"

"Leave him alone!" Claire said sharply. "You want to go out, fine. We'll go. No, don't you even start!" Eve hadn't even had a chance to do more than open her mouth, and now she shut it, fast. "You guys work it out between the three of you. I won't be long. Believe me, I probably won't be able to keep anything down, whatever I manage to eat."

Monica nodded, as if she'd known it would happen all along, and did a runway model's walk down the hall toward the front door. From the back, her shorts were barely legal.

And however much they hated her, Shane and Michael were watching her go.

"Guys," Claire muttered, and grabbed her backpack.

Claire hadn't been inside Common Grounds in a while, but it hadn't changed. It was bohemian, warm, packed to the gills with college types grabbing their morning venti-whatever, and if Claire hadn't known better—known very well—she'd never have believed that the nice, smiling hippie type behind the counter was a vampire.

Oliver locked gazes with her and nodded slightly. His face stayed pleasant. "Nice to see you back," he said. "What'll it be?"

Much as she hated to admit it, he made the best drinks in town. Better than Eve, actually. "White mocha," she said. "With whip." She managed to hold back from adding anything more, because she didn't like being nice to him. God, he'd been licking blood off her wrist two hours ago! The least she could do was not say *please* and *thank you.*

"No charge," he said, and waved away the five-dollar bill she dug out of her jeans pocket. "A welcome-back present, Claire. Ah, Monica. Your usual?"

"Half-caf no foam double pump latte, with pink sugar," she said. "In a real cup, not that foam stuff."

"A simple yes would suffice," he said. As Monica started to turn away, he reached out and grabbed her wrist. He did it in such a way that nobody but Claire would notice, but it was unmistakably threatening. "She doesn't pay. You do, Monica. You may think of yourself as a princess, but trust me, I've met them, and you don't qualify." He grinned just a little, but there was no humor in his eyes. "Well, perhaps *met* isn't quite the right word."

"Eaten?" Claire supplied acidly. His smile turned darker.

"Oh, the charm and eloquence of the younger generation. It does warm my heart." Oliver let go of Monica's arm and stepped away to make the drinks. Monica backed away, looking flushed. She threw a dirty look at Claire—*Yeah, like it's my fault,* Claire thought—and stalked to the table in the corner. The one the deceased vampire Brandon had once staked out—pun intended—as his own. There were two young college girls sitting there, with books and papers piled up. Monica folded her arms and took up a belligerent pose.

"You're in my chair," she said. "Move."

The two girls—shorter and pudgier than Monica—stared up with saucer-huge eyes. One of them stammered, "Which one of us?"

"Both," Monica snapped. "I like my space. Get out."

They gathered up papers and books and hurried away, nearly dumping coffee all over Claire in their haste to go. "Did you have to do that?" Claire asked.

"No. It was just fun." Monica sat, crossed her smooth tanned legs, and patted the table. "Come on, Claire. Have a seat. We have so much to talk about."

She didn't want to, but it was stupid to stand there, looking obvious. So she sat, dumped her backpack on the floor next to her feet, and concentrated on the scarred wood of the tabletop. She could see Monica's flip-flop living up to its name as the other girl casually jiggled her foot. Ridiculously, it reminded her of Myrnin.

"That's better." Monica sounded way too pleased with herself. Not cool. "So. Tell me all about it."

"About what?"

"Whatever Amelie's got you doing," Monica said. "Your supersecret stuff. I mean, she picked you for a reason, and it's not for your charm and good looks, right? Obviously. It's for your brains. You don't have any family here; you've got nothing anybody wants other than that."

Monica was smarter than she looked. "Amelie's not asking me to do anything," Claire lied. "Maybe she will later, I don't know. But she hasn't yet." She nervously twisted the gold bracelet circling her left wrist. It was starting to remind her of those bands biologists put on endangered species.

And lab animals.

Monica's eyes were half-closed when Claire risked a glance upward. "Huh," she said. "Really. Well, that's disappointing. I really thought you'd have something good I could use. Oh well. Then let's talk about making a deal."

"A deal?" First Jason, now Monica. How had Claire stepped into the role of negotiator?

"I want to talk to Amelie about Protection. You can give me an introduction. And a recommendation."

Claire nearly laughed. "Ask her yourself!"

"I would, but she won't let me near her. She doesn't like me."

"I'm shocked," Claire muttered under her breath.

Monica gave her a long look, one strangely missing the usual hip, ironic, contemptuous features. It looked almost . . . earnest. "Since Brandon died, Oliver took over his contracts. The thing is, he's not keeping most of them. He's trading them for favors with other vampires. If I don't make a better deal, there's no telling what could happen to me." Monica pointed at Claire's bracelet. "Might as well start at the top."

Claire drummed her short fingernails on the table, glaring at the bar where it seemed like Oliver was taking forever to deliver their drinks. It occurred to her to wonder if it was really safe to drink something prepared by a vampire who'd been threatening her just a couple of hours before, but honestly, if Oliver wanted to get her, it wasn't as though it would be hard for him.

And she really wanted the white mocha.

"Oliver's your Patron now?"

"For now. Until he finds something he wants more than holding on to my contract, anyway."

"Is he behind your asking about why Amelie signed me up?"

"Do I look like I run somebody else's errands?"

Claire glanced back again at the bar. "Maybe."

Monica went quiet. It wasn't the comfortable kind of silence, and Claire was glad when Oliver called out their orders. She jumped up to get hers, hesitated, and then picked up Monica's as well. She managed to do it without making eye contact with Oliver. He was just a dark shape at the corner of her eye, and she turned her back on him as soon as she could.

Monica had gotten up, and she looked honestly surprised when Claire handed her the drink. "What?" Claire asked. "It's called being polite; they probably didn't teach you that at home. Doesn't mean I like you or anything."

Monica seemed to have to think hard about what to say to that, and finally came up with a simple "Thanks." Which, Claire had to admit, might have been the nicest thing Monica had ever managed to say to her. Claire gave her a nod and sat down again. *Peace in our time*, she thought wryly. And promptly blew it by asking again, "Did Oliver put you up to it?"

Monica didn't even glance in his direction. "No." But somehow, Claire didn't believe her.

"Do you have to do everything he says?" she asked, as if Monica hadn't just lied. And Monica lifted one shoulder in a half shrug. No other answer. "So you don't really want to talk to me, do you? You've just been told to do it."

"Not exactly. I thought it was a good chance to get my name in front of Amelie, too." Monica smiled slightly, and very bitterly. "Besides, check it out: you're a star. Everybody wants to know about you, vampires and humans. They're looking into your history, your family's history. If you farted in grade school, somebody in Morganville knows it now."

Claire almost choked on her first mouthful of white mocha. "*What?*"

"The Founder isn't what you might call accessible. And most of the vamps don't understand her any better than we do. They're always looking for clues about who she is, what she's doing here, with this town. This isn't normal, you know. The way they live here." Monica's gaze flicked to Oliver, then away. "*He's* old enough to know more than most, but he still needs inside information. And the word is, you could be the way to get it. If I can't get Protection from Amelie, at least I can get in good with him if I have something new and valuable to tell him."

Claire rolled her eyes. "I'm nobody. And if she cared about me at all—which she doesn't—she'd never let anybody know it. I mean, look how she treats—" She stopped herself cold, heart suddenly hammering fast. She'd almost said *Myrnin*, and that would have been bad. "Sam," she finished lamely. Which was also true, but Monica had to have noticed her stumble.

Which Monica emphasized by waiting for a full ten seconds of silence before she continued. "Whatever. The point is, you're sort of famous, and by hanging with you, I get seen by the right people doing the right thing, and I do what Oliver wants. Which is all I care about. You're right, I don't care if we're BFFs. We're not going to trade clothes and get matching tattoos. I've got friends. I need allies." She sipped her complicated drink, her eyes steady on Claire. "Oliver wants what you know, yeah. And this"— she tapped her own bracelet—"this says that I do what he says, or else."

"Or else what?"

Monica looked down. "You've met him. Best case, it means he hurts me. Bad. Worst case . . . he trades me down."

"That's *worse?*"

"Yeah. That means I get handed to the bottom-of-the-barrel vamps, the ones too lame to get the good earners and the pretty people. That means I'm a loser." She looked down and fidgeted with her ceramic coffee cup, frowning at it. "Sounds shallow, maybe, but around here, it's survival. If Oliver blackballs me, I can't get anything but the freaks and the skanks, the ones who get their fix the hard way. They'll kill me, if I'm lucky. If not, I end up some strung-out junkie fang-banger."

She said it with such dry, matter-of-fact intensity that Claire could tell she'd spent a lot of time thinking about it. It was a long way to fall, from the darling daughter of the mayor to some addict trying to please a kinky freak for protection.

"You could be neutral," Claire blurted. She felt oddly sympathetic, even after everything Monica had done. She *had* been born here, after all. Not like she'd ever had a real choice in what she was going to be, or do. "Some people are, right? They're left alone?"

Monica sneered, and the second or two of humanity Claire had imagined she'd seen in that pretty face vanished. "They're left alone until

they're not. Look, officially, they're untouchable because they've done favors, big favors, and their Patrons let them out of contracts. By big favors,
I mean the kind they were lucky to live through, get it? I'm not interested
in that kind of hero crap."

Claire shrugged. "Then go without a contract."

"Yeah, *right.* That works. I'm really looking forward to a future as second assistant fry wrangler at the Dairy Queen, and decomposing in some
ditch before I'm thirty." Monica rested her elbows on the table, coffee cup
cradled in both hands. "I thought about leaving. I actually went to Austin
for a semester, you know? But . . . it wasn't the same."

"Meaning you flunked out of school."

That earned Claire a filthy look. "Shut up, bitch. I'm here only because I need to be, and you're here only because you have to be. Let's not
get too touchy-feely."

Claire swallowed a mouthful of sweet, rich mocha. If it was poisoned,
she'd die happy, at least. "Fine by me. Look, I can't help you get to Amelie. I don't even know how to get to her myself. And even if I did, I don't
think she'd take your contract."

"Then just shut up and smile. If I don't get anything else out of this
wasted morning, at least Oliver can see that I tried."

"How long do I have to do this?"

Monica checked her watch. "Ten minutes. Suck it up that long, and I
won't call my brother about your boyfriend's little indiscretion."

"How can I be sure?"

Monica slapped both hands to her cheeks and looked overdramati-
cally horrified. "Oh no! You don't trust me! I'm crushed." She dropped
the act. "I don't care if Shane has opened his own corpse taxi service; I
care only about what I can get out of it."

"Maybe you want revenge," Claire said.

Monica smiled. "If I'd wanted that, I'd have already turned him in.
Besides, I hear it's best served cold."

Claire pulled out a book. "All right. Ten minutes. I need to study,
anyway." Monica sat back and began a running, acidly accurate mono-
logue on the outfits of the girls standing in line for coffee, which Claire

tried earnestly not to find funny. Which she was able to do, until Monica pointed out a girl wearing a truly horrible polka-dot-leggings-undershorts ensemble. "And somewhere in heaven, Versace sheds a single, perfect tear."

Claire couldn't control a snort of laughter, and hated herself for it. Monica cocked an eyebrow.

"See?" she said. "I'm so good I can even charm a hard case like you. It's a waste of my talent, but I need to keep myself sharp." She finished her coffee and picked up her little pink purse with the *Teen People* magazine sticking out of it. "Gotta fly, loser. Tell your boyfriend as far as I'm concerned, we're even. Well, okay, I'm a little bit more than even, and that's the way I like it. Consider this his restraining order: if I see him within fifty feet of me, I'll not only tell my brother about Shane's midnight adventure, but I'll get some football types to pay his kneecaps a visit."

She walked out, hips swaying dangerously. People got out of her way, and they watched her go. Fear and attraction, in just about equal measure.

Claire sighed. She supposed people always did like that sort of girl, and always would. And secretly? She envied Monica's confidence. Maybe just a little, traitorous bit.

TEN

The dead girl that Shane had taken to the church was Jeanne Jackson, a sophomore who'd gone missing from a sorority party two nights before. The papers said that she'd been raped and strangled, but nothing about suspects, and no cops showed up to interrogate Shane, much to Claire's relief. He'd done a dumbass thing, but she could understand his paranoia. In Morganville, he was one suspicion away from taking up residence in Jason's old cell, whether he'd actually done anything or not.

That was if the vampires didn't decide to hold their own brand of frontier justice.

Captain Obvious's *Fang Report* had a much more detailed article on the killings, linking the other two that Claire knew about with this one, and speculating that instead of a vampire menace, they might be dealing with a human one this time. He didn't seem as enthusiastic about forming vigilante parties for someone with a pulse, Claire noticed. Not that it mattered to the dead girls which type of monster had killed them.

She got a note from Amelie giving her time off from working with Myrnin for the rest of the week, so she devoted herself to keeping up with classes. They were tougher than she was used to, which was kind of a relief. She loved a good challenge, and the professors seemed to actually care whether or not their students had a clue. Myth and Legend wasn't what she'd expected, not at all; it wasn't Greek gods, or even Native American Trickster stories. No, it was about . . . vampires. Comparative vampires, actually, examining the literature and folklore from earliest recorded history to the latest vampire-as-hero in pop culture. (Which, now that Claire thought about it, kind of was the modern-day version of myth and legend.) Oddly, for Morganville, the professor wasn't skipping the parts about vampire-killing methods, but Claire guessed that she was one of the few in the class who'd ever know the score about the town, anyway. The rest would bumble cluelessly through their one or two years, transfer out to bigger schools, and never know they'd rubbed elbows at parties with real monsters.

She kept her mouth shut about anything that might get her in trouble, because the professor had a bracelet, too. She was trying to match up glyphs with vampires, and she thought he probably belonged to a female vamp named Susan, who seemed to be into finance. Susan owned a lot of property, anyway, and was some kind of bigwig at the Morganville Bank and Trust.

Claire began keeping notes in a special book about glyphs, vampires, who owned what. Not because she had any agenda, but just because it was interesting, and could be useful someday. She supposed if she'd asked, Amelie would have told her all about it, but it was more challenging to figure it out herself—and this way, Amelie couldn't be really sure how much Claire knew, which couldn't be a bad thing. *She's nice when it suits her. That doesn't mean she's nice.*

And on Friday, Eve left a note stuck to the bathroom mirror for Claire to find when she got up.

> *CB—Don't forget tonight is the party. Objective: look hotter than Monica and make everybody totally forget who threw the party in the first place. Outfit on back of door. Pay me back.—E.*

The outfit was nothing Claire would ever, ever, *ever* have bought for herself. For one thing, the black leather skirt was . . . short. Like, really short. There were some kind of patterned panty hose and a sheer red shirt with big red roses woven into the fabric in flocked material. And a black cami to go under it.

There was another sticky note attached to the skirt. *Shoes under the cabinet.* Claire looked. They were thick clunky platforms, in her size, in shiny patent leather.

She took it all back into her bedroom and put it down, backed off, and stared at it for a few seconds. *I can't wear that. It's not me.*

Eve would totally mock her if she wore her blue jeans to the party. And she'd gone to a lot of trouble, because all of this stuff was Claire's size, not Eve's. Even the shoes.

And . . . it really *would* burn Monica if Claire looked hot. (She'd never be hotter than Monica; that was a fantasy, but still.) Imagining the expression on Monica's face, Claire slowly stroked her fingers down the soft leather of the skirt. *No. I can't.*

And then she imagined Shane's face when he saw her.

Well. Maybe she could, after all.

She hadn't gotten his expression quite right in her imagination, because the stunned, vacant expression on Shane's face when she started down the stairs was even better than fantasy. His mouth actually *dropped open.* Next to him, Michael turned around, and although she hadn't counted on it, there was a warm fuzzy feeling to making a hot golden-angel vampire blink and give her a quick, involuntary once-over.

Claire stopped on the steps above them and did a tentative hip shimmy. "Okay?" she asked. Shane's mouth shut with a snap, and Michael actually cleared his throat.

"Fine," Michael said.

"Fine?" That was Eve, coming down the stairs behind Claire. She moved around the roadblock and punched Michael in the arm. "She looks amazing. I'm not half-gay, and I think she's hot."

Shane wasn't saying *anything.* Claire felt warm and a little dizzy, the way he was looking at her. She resisted the urge to check to see if her skirt was straight—she'd done it a dozen times already—and forced herself to meet his gaze and smile.

"You sure this is smart?" Shane asked, which was not what she'd expected, not at all. "You look fantastic."

"Thanks—"

He interrupted her. "*Fantastic* in this town pops you to the top of the take-out menu."

She held up her left hand and pointed to her wrist. The gold bracelet was clearly visible. "I'll be okay," she said. "The vamps won't bother me."

"Not even talking about the vamps. You're going to be drawing every guy there who's looking to get off."

Eve rolled her eyes. "Oh, *God*, Shane, buzz kill? She looks great, and you don't have to get all jealous and overprotective about it! She'll be with us; we'll all look out for her. And you've got to admit, girlfriend looks good all cleaned up. I did her hair, too. Smokin', right?" The hair, Claire felt, was just almost over the top. It was mostly gel and sprays and stuff, but it did have that carefully tousled look that models always seemed to wear.

Eve wasn't exactly wallflower quality tonight, either; she was wearing a dramatic, floor-sweeping black dress that left her pale arms bare, plunged a neckline halfway to China, and had a slit in the side that went all the way to her hip. Fishnet hose, even. It was outrageously sexy, and if Michael had noticed Claire's transformation, he was completely focused on Eve now.

Eve winked at him and spun around to show him the back. Of which there wasn't any. It was just her skin, and a crimson rose tattoo at the small of her back.

"Man," Shane said. "That's just—yeah."

It wasn't until she'd gotten past their reactions—which were pretty fun—that Claire realized that Eve must have done a number on the boys, too . . . because they looked amazingly fine. Michael was wearing black pants and a black leather coat, and a dark blue silk shirt. It made him just . . . blaze, like white gold against velvet.

Shane looked good enough to drag back to her room. Eve must have forced him to get the worst of his shag evened up, which brought out his strong cheekbones and chin. He was wearing black, too, with a dark maroon knit shirt. Claire had never seen him in a jacket. She decided he needed to never take it off.

Michael shook his head and offered Eve his arm. She took it, smiling with her red, red lips, and winked at Claire. Claire winked back, suddenly feeling *very* wicked, and slid her arm through Shane's.

"I can't believe we're doing this," Shane said.

This was going to be fun.

Claire hadn't forgotten the address, even though she'd given away the invitation, and Michael knew Morganville like the back of—Eve's back, the way he kept looking at her exposed skin, especially the tattoo. And besides, if you were within a couple of blocks of the party, you couldn't possibly miss it. Between the glow of the lights and the low-pitched rumble of the music, there was no sleeping through it if you lived nearby.

Michael cruised around the block, looking for parking, and finally located a narrow few feet of curb. As he pulled in, he said, "Ground rules. We don't split up. Eve and Claire, you two especially. It's not just because of the vampires; it's because of Jason. Got it?"

They nodded.

"Besides," Shane said, and playfully tugged at Claire's overgelled hair, "I want to see Monica's face when she catches sight of the two of you. Kodak moment."

Eve fumbled in her tiny little coffin-shaped purse and held up a brand-new cell phone, with camera. "I'm ready."

"Me too," Claire said, and pulled out the fancy phone that Amelie had given her. She felt a blast of shame as Shane glanced at it, but controlled it. She couldn't be ashamed all the time, and besides, it wasn't so bad, right? What she was doing? It wasn't any worse than having a day job. Just . . . different.

"Be careful what you eat and drink," Michael continued. "Monica's party is probably roofie heaven. I can smell what they put in the drinks; you guys can't. And if you get into any trouble, step back; let me handle it. If you're going to have a freak vamp friend, you might as well get your money's worth out of it."

Shane didn't answer, but Claire could see there was some smart-ass remark burning a hole in his tongue. She was glad he didn't let it loose. It was nice to feel like four friends again, instead of four people all about to spin apart in different directions.

"Anything else, Dad?" Eve asked. Michael kissed her, very lightly, sparing her lipstick.

"Yeah," he said. "You look good enough to eat. Promise me you'll remember that."

Claire was caught between a smile and a shiver, and saw that Eve was, too.

The Morrell home looked like Tara from *Gone With the Wind*, post–Sherman's march. Claire watched, blinking, as a mob of drunken frat boys stumbled down the walk, roaring something she couldn't make out, and carrying a *couch*.

The couch they deposited in the giant European-style fountain in front of the house. Apparently they were relocating most of the living room out there. Some partyers were already sitting in chairs, soaking in the fountain's spray, and now three or four of them piled giggling onto the wet couch.

"Now this," Shane said with respect, "is out of bounds. I like it."

It was totally out of control. The four of them stood together by Michael's shiny vampire-tinted car, watching in admiration. The house was blazing with lights, there were lit tiki torches tilting drunkenly all over the lawn, and partyers were *everywhere*. Making out under the trees, in full glare of the security lights. Doing shots on the big, white-columned front steps. A girl ran by, dressed in half a bikini. The top half.

"Damn," Michael said. "Monica does know how to throw it."

No kidding. Claire watched as a big bobtail truck inched its way through a knot of people toward the back of the house. It had the logo of BOB'S FINE LIQUORS. Apparently, Monica had called in liquid reinforcements already, and the night was young.

"Well?" Eve said. "Are we standing out here all night? Because I'm ready to knock somebody dead."

The four of them strolled up the walkway, keeping an eye out for frat boys and wandering furniture. They went as a group up the front steps, where about ten people were playing some complicated game that involved drinking shots, spray cans of fluorescent paint, and giggling hysterically. Even the drunkest turned to look at the four of them and whistle.

The frat boys, the drunks in the fountain, and the even drunker people on the porch were all wearing standard college casual dress, mostly shorts and T-shirts. "Um," Claire said, "maybe we should have come a little less formal."

"No way," Eve replied. "If you're going, go big."

"Remind me to play poker with you later," Michael said. "I love a girl who'll go all in."

She hip-bumped him. "*That's* what you want to do with me later? Dude. Respect the dress, at least."

Michael trailed his pale fingers down her back, following the line of her spine, all the way to the red rose. Eve shivered, and her eyes went half-closed. Whatever Michael whispered in her ear, Claire thought it was probably way too personal to hear.

Not that she could have, because right then the front door banged open and the noise flowed out in a syrup-thick wave of pounding techno and yelled conversations. Two people stumbled out of the door, arms around each other. Claire blinked and recognized two of the gamers whom she'd given Monica's invitation to that afternoon on campus.

"Freakin' awesome party!" one of them screamed, and fell flat on his face.

"Apparently." Eve stepped over him and swept into the party, with Michael right behind her. Claire started to follow, but Shane's grip on her arm had tightened, and he was holding her back.

"What?" she asked, and turned to face him. God, he looked amazing. He needed to let Eve dress him all the time.

"Before we go in," he said, and bent and kissed her. Claire distantly heard the whistles and catcalls of the shot drinkers—distantly, because the kiss was sweet and hot and wild, and there was something crazy in it that made her just quiver inside.

He pulled away way too soon. "Stay with me," he said, with his lips near her ear, and she nodded. *Like I'd let you out of my sight.*

And then they followed Michael and Eve into the party of the century.

It was the second big party of Claire's life—not counting birthday parties and ones where there were as many chaperones as kids. The first one, the Dead Girls' Dance thrown by the EEK fraternity, hadn't exactly come out well, what with Shane's dad going on a rampage through the place looking for vampires to stake. This one looked, if possible, even crazier.

She was grateful to be with her friends. She couldn't imagine how scary it would be if she'd stepped into this by herself. The main hall was wide and tall, but it was jam-packed with people talking, dancing, kissing, groping—it was like the hottest dance club with all the lights up full. Claire brushed up against a couple who were—what *were* they doing? She looked away before she could be sure, but the guy's hand was in places that she couldn't imagine a porn actress allowing in public.

Michael and Eve pushed through the crowd into the next room, and Claire and Shane followed, staying close. There were a few people in the big living area who were dressed fancy, but most had on standard-issue college wear, and somehow, Claire had the distinct impression the casual-dress crowd had *not* come invited.

Monica was standing at the top of the stairs, arms folded, looking right at them.

"Oooh, that *is* a Kodak moment," Eve said, and held up her cell phone to snap a photo of Monica's scowl. "Yep. We're good."

She high-fived Shane, who seemed to be expecting it. Monica cleared the annoyance out of her expression with an effort and started down the steps. She was dressed in a pink, clinging sheath dress with huge lime-outlined flowers climbing the fabric, and her shoes were prissy-perfect in matching pink. Very fancy.

"Claire, you brought strays," Monica said. "How nice." And then she looked strangely sorry. "Michael, I didn't mean you. You're always welcome."

He raised his pale eyebrows. "I am?"

"Of course."

Claire elbowed him. "Because you're a VIP. Vampire Important Person."

Two more of the gamers Claire had gifted with the invitation stumbled by; one grabbed Claire's arm and planted a sloppy, wet kiss on her cheek. "We passed out copies," he said, and giggled. "Hope that was okay. Great party!"

Shane sighed and moved him off with one hand on his shoulder. "Yeah, yeah, whatever. Naked Vulcan chick in the next room. Better hurry."

The gamers sobered up fast, and moved on. Monica's glossy, perfect lips were open, her eyes wide.

"You?" she said. "*You* did this? These idiots made flyers! They put them all over campus! *This was supposed to be the best people!*"

"Don't worry," Eve said sweetly. "We're here." She smiled, which in that lipstick was Wicked-Witch-of-the-West evil. "Air kiss!" She *mwahed* the air somewhere near Monica's cheek. "Lovely party. Shame about the furniture. Ta!" She sashayed on, Michael on her arm, as if she were the Queen of Everything, never mind Morganville. Claire got out her camera and captured a picture of the murderous fury on Monica's face as she watched her go.

"You treacherous little *bitch!*" Monica snarled.

Claire lowered the phone and met her eyes for a long second. She wasn't scared, not anymore. "You got your friends to roofie me and told them I wanted it rough. All I did was recycle your invitation. Let's call it even."

"Let's call it *not!*"

Shane leaned forward, dropped his voice so that Monica had to work to hear it, and said, "Calm down. You get blotchy when you're angry. And if you call my girlfriend a bitch one more time, I won't be so nice about it."

Monica's eyes were fierce and fiery, but she didn't move, and after a second she turned and ran up the steps to the second floor, where her formally dressed friends were huddled together like the cast of *Survivor: Abercrombie & Fitch Island*.

"Score one for the little guys," Shane said. He stared at a bunch of guys wearing football shirts who rumbled past, carrying a bed. Claire blinked. Yes, that was a bed. "Okay, I don't really think I want to know. So. Drinks?"

In the kitchen, a group was making punch in a trash can. Claire hoped it was a new trash can, but as blitzed as the guys were who were pouring stuff in, she really couldn't be sure of that.

"I'd avoid that," Shane said, his mouth close to her ear. "See anybody you know?"

She wasn't sure. There was barely room to move in here, with people crowding up to the counters, and streaming in and out with red plastic cups in their hands. . . .

A shock zipped down her spine. "Yeah," she said. "I see somebody."

How the hell had Eve's brother gotten into the party? He was standing in a corner, slouching and sneering. Lank hair dripped toward his shoulders, and he wore the same filthy, dangerous-boy clothes that he'd had on when he'd threatened Claire at the UC. He had a drink, but he wasn't drunk; there was too much hot contempt in his eyes as he surveyed the crowd. Crazy eyes. *Oh God, that's how they look, those guys who shoot up rooms full of people.*

His eyes locked with Claire's, and he gave her a bent smile. Claire anxiously looked at Eve, but her back was to her brother and she was talking to Michael; she clearly hadn't seen the potential trouble at all.

"What?" Shane asked.

Claire turned back and pointed.

Jason was gone.

Shane shook his head when she told him, and moved away to talk to Michael. Michael nodded, then handed Eve off to Shane. Claire saw his lips move: *Watch her.*

And then Michael angled off through the crowd.

So much for staying together.

Shane draped his arms over both of their shoulders and said, "Now this is the life. Want to get a room, girls?"

Eve rolled her thickly mascaraed eyes. "Like you'd know what to do with one of us, never mind two. Where's he going?"

"Bathroom," Shane said blandly. "Even vamps gotta pee."

Which, for all Claire knew, might be true, but she was sure that wasn't why Michael had cut out on them. Shane steered them up to the counter and snagged a sealed bottled water for Claire and two sealed beers, which he opened himself. *Not taking any chances,* Claire thought, and cracked the top on the bottle to take several gulps of the cool, sweet water. She hadn't realized how hot it was until then, but she could feel sweat sticking her flocked mesh shirt to her exposed skin.

Somebody grabbed her ass. Claire yelped and jumped, then turned and saw a drunk-off-his-butt frat boy leaning in next to her. "Oh baby, me like!" he yelled in her ear. "You, me, outside, okay?" He did a drunken pantomime of what he was thinking of doing outside, and she felt a hot roll of embarrassed shame.

"Get lost," she said, and shoved him off. His buddies tossed him back toward her, and this time, he crashed into her off balance and pushed her up against the bar. He took advantage of it, too, hands all over her, hips grinding her right into the counter.

Shane grabbed him by the collar of his TPU golf shirt, spun him around, and punched him right in the face.

Great, Claire thought in shaken disgust. *That's always the answer around here. Punch somebody.* Then again, she didn't think reasoned discourse was going to be big tonight.

And of course, the guy's friends piled on. Eve grabbed Claire's hand and pulled her out of the way; a tight circle formed around the combat, with people whooping and clapping. "We have to stop him!" Claire yelled. Eve patted her on the shoulder.

"This is Shane's idea of a good time," she said. "Trust me. You do *not* want to try to stop him right now. Let him do his thing. He'll be fine."

Claire hated it. She hated seeing Shane get hit, and she didn't much like the way his eyes lit up when he was knee-deep in conflict, either. Stupid to be upset by it, she guessed, considering this was part of why she was so attracted to Shane in the first place—the way he would unhesitatingly throw himself into things, especially when it came to protecting others.

Eve was practically reading her mind. "Let him be who he is," she said. "I know it's hard, because in general, guys are clueless, and you just want to fix it, but just—let him be. You don't want him trying to change you, right?"

Right. She didn't, although he *was* changing her, whether he knew it or not. *Not in bad ways,* she thought. *Just . . . change.* A year ago she'd have been paralyzed with terror at the idea of coming to a party like this, and even more terrified to imagine being groped by a stranger like that.

Now, she was mostly just annoyed, and felt like she needed a shower.

Eve whirled. "Hey! I know my ass is fine, but look, don't touch!" An eruption of drunken laughter. She took Claire's hand. "We need a wall behind us. Less chance of getting the stealth feel-up."

"But—" She gave up as somebody else patted her rear. "Yeah. Okay."

That put them half a room away from Shane, who was now somehow at the center of a knot of maybe ten guys, all whaling away at each other (mostly without connecting; they were all too drunk to really do damage). Claire leaned gratefully against the wall and sipped water. Somehow, she'd ended up holding Shane's beer, and with a quick sideways glance at Eve, she took a sip of that, too. Ugh. Nasty.

"Acquired taste," Eve said, laughing at her expression. "Shane buys like a college boy. If it's cheap and the ad has a girl in a bikini, it must be great."

"That's disgusting," Claire said, and took another long drink of water to wash her tongue clean. Even the water tasted bitter, after that.

"Well, in fairness, beer is mostly about the buzz, not the taste," Eve said. "You want taste *and* buzz, you get something like rum and Coke, or White Russians." She seemed to remember, suddenly, how old Claire was. "Not that I'm going to let you have any of that, by the way. We promised your parents." She managed to look almost righteous when she said it, and she took Shane's beer out of Claire's hand. "I'll keep this." Eve raised her normally soft voice to a parade-ground bellow. "Yo, Shane! Quit screwing around or I'm drinking this!"

A ripple of laughter through the room. The fight was mostly over, anyway, and Shane shoved away the last stumbling frat boy who'd tried to take a swing at him, wiped blood from his mouth with the back of his hand, and left the field of battle. He looked rumpled and flushed and a little bit savage, and Claire felt something in her just *growl* in response.

She stared at him, wide-eyed. *I'm not ready for this.*

Parts of her clearly were.

"Have a drink, Galahad," Eve said, and handed him his bottle. They clinked glass. "Our hero. Here. Fix your hair." She picked at it with her black-manicured nails, twitching it this way and that, until it had that glamour-boy, carefully careless look again. "God, you're hot. Get felt up yet?"

"Couple of times," he said, and smiled at Claire. "Don't hurt them. They just couldn't help themselves."

Eve snorted and looked around. "Where's Michael?"

"Probably in line at the bathroom." Shane shrugged. It was probably true, but Claire didn't think that was the reason. Shane did that thing where he looked at Eve too long and didn't blink. She thought she could tell when he was lying, and that definitely was a flashing neon sign. "Ladies? Let's wander."

It wasn't so much *wander* as *wriggle*, like salmon heading upstream. What Claire could see of the house was amazing—fine art on the walls, gorgeous old furniture (mostly being splashed with drinks or shoved against the walls to make room for dancing), big, expensive Turkish rugs (Claire hoped they were dry-cleanable), and huge plasma TVs that were all playing the same music channel, blasting at ear-piercing volume. Nine Inch Nails' "Closer" was on now, and despite her best intentions Claire found herself moving to the rhythm. Eve was dancing, too, and then they were dancing together, which should have seemed weird but didn't, really. Shane formed the third point on their triangle, but Claire could see that he wasn't really giving in to the festive atmosphere; he was scanning the crowd, looking for trouble. Or Michael.

Somebody tried to pass her something—a shot glass with a hit of something clear. She shook her head and passed it right back. Not that she wasn't tempted, but after what had almost happened to her at the last party, she wasn't going to be stupid.

Well, not any stupider than she already was to come here in the first place.

The drinks and drugs kept coming. Liquid E, poppers, shots, even something that she was almost sure was a crack pipe. Morganville liked its drugs, but she guessed that made sense. There was a hell of a lot to escape from around here.

She kept on dancing. Shane and Eve didn't take anything, either—not that Claire saw, anyway. Shane was looking less into the party and more worried all the time.

Michael didn't come back. Two songs later—two long songs—Eve finally got Shane to look for him, and the three of them moved out through the bottom floor, checking out the rooms (all packed) and not finding Michael anywhere. In the hall bathroom a line of people was waiting for the toilet, but no sign of a tall, blond vampire.

When they went up the big, sweeping steps toward the second floor, Claire couldn't help but think about *Gone With the Wind*, and Rhett Butler carrying Scarlett. Her mom loved that movie. She'd always thought it was boring, but that scene stayed with her, and she could almost see it in this house. But instead of Scarlett, Monica Morrell was still standing at the top of the steps, surrounded by her protective circle of toadies. Gina and Jennifer were back, each wearing a dress that was plainer than what Monica had on, but in complementary colors. Her very own backup group. There were a couple of other girls in the crowd, but mostly it was guys—good-looking, polished types. The entitled of Morganville, and every one of them was wearing a bracelet.

"Well," Monica said. "Look who's coming up in the world." Her crowd laughed. Monica's eyes were vicious. If she'd been sort of human when they'd been alone in the coffee shop, she'd gotten over it. "Scrubs stay downstairs. We're going to have to have the place gutted and rebuilt anyway, after this."

"Yeah, I'll bet Daddy's going to be furious when he gets home," Eve said. "I meant to ask, is that dress vintage? Because I could swear I saw it on my mother once." She swept up, heading straight for one of Monica's big strong linebacker types; he looked confused, and edged out of her way. Shane and Claire followed. Monica was dangerously silent, probably realizing that any comeback she could try would sound cheap.

"We're going to have trouble getting out of here," Shane said. It was quieter upstairs, although the continuing clamor downstairs throbbed through the floor and walls. The hallway was deserted, and all the doors were closed. It was lined with expensive portraits and framed formal photographs of the Morrell family. Not surprisingly, Monica took a lovely picture. Claire had never seen Mrs. Mayor, but there she was in the family photos—a wispy, half-ethereal woman always looking somewhere other than her family. Unhappy, somehow. Richard Morrell seemed grounded and adapted to this town, and of course, so did the mayor; Monica might not be stable, but she was definitely Morganville material.

Her mom, maybe not so much.

"Wonder where her parents are?" Claire said aloud.

"Out of town," Eve said. "So I heard, anyway. Bet they'll just love getting back to find somebody did an *Extreme Home Makeover: Crackhead Edition.*" She tested the doorknob of the first room on the left. Locked. Shane tried the one on the right, opened it, and leaned in. He leaned out again, eyebrows arched.

"Well, that's new," he said. Claire tried to look. He put his big hand over her eyes. "Trust me, you're not old enough. *I'm* not old enough." He carefully shut the door. "Moving on."

Claire opened the next room, and for a second she couldn't figure out what she was seeing. Once she did, she couldn't speak. She backed up and touched Shane wordlessly on the shoulder and pointed.

There were three guys in the room, and a girl on the bed, and she was passed out. They were taking off her panty hose.

"Shit," Shane said, and moved Claire back. "Eve, call the cops. Now. Time to shut this crap down before somebody gets really hurt."

Eve got out her cell phone and dialed, and Shane went into the room and closed the door. He came back after about a minute with the unconscious girl in his arms. "Anybody know who she is?"

Claire shook her head. "What about those guys?"

"They're sorry," Shane said. "Eve? You recognize her?"

"Um . . . maybe. I think I've seen her around the UC—couldn't swear to a name or anything. But she's definitely gown, not town. No bracelet."

"Yeah, I figured." Shane adjusted her to a more comfortable angle in his arms. The girl—petite, brunette, pretty—snuggled into his embrace with a sleepy moan. "Damn it. I can't just leave her."

"What about Michael? We need to find him!"

"Yeah, I know. Look, I'll carry her. Check the other rooms."

Claire was having trouble controlling her breathing. She'd almost been that girl, not so long ago. Only she'd been a little more alert, a little more able to take care of herself. . . .

Get it together, she told herself, and opened the next door. She gasped and covered her mouth with both hands, because there was a vampire in the room, and he was bending over a girl lying limp on the floor.

He looked up, and she saw the hard gleam of fangs before his face came into focus and became shockingly familiar.

Michael.

There were two raw holes in the girl's neck, and her open, dry eyes had gone gray. Her skin was the color of old, wet paper, more blue than white.

"Oh," Claire whispered, and stumbled backward out of the room. "Oh no, no, no—"

Michael shot to his feet. "Claire, *wait!* I didn't—"

Eve was in the doorway now, and Shane. Eve took one look at the dead girl, one at Michael, and turned and ran. Shane just stood there, staring at him, then said quietly, "Claire. Go after her. Now. The two of you, stay together. I'll come find you."

Michael took a step toward them. "Shane, I know you're looking for reasons to hate me, but you know I wouldn't—"

Shane backed up, fast, keeping distance between them. His eyes had gone very dark, his face flushed and set with anger. "Claire," he said again. "Get the hell away from him. *Now.*"

"Shit!" Michael looked furious, but he also looked scared and hurt. "You *know me*, Shane. You know I wouldn't do this. Think!"

"You come near me or the girls, I will kill you," Shane said flatly, and then turned and yelled at Claire, full volume. "*Go!*"

She backed out of the room and ran after Eve. Her heavy platform shoes felt awkward, and her cool outfit was nothing but a cheap dress-up costume. She wasn't cool. She wasn't sexy. She was a stupid jerk to be here, and now Michael . . . God, he couldn't have, could he? But there was a flush to his skin, as though he'd fed. . . .

Eve was heading down a set of back stairs. Claire caught sight of the sweep of her long black dress around the spiral. She followed as fast as she dared, with the treacherous shoes. As she neared ground level, the volume of the party swelled and broke into a roar.

When she got to the bottom of the steps, there was no sign of Eve anywhere. It was a sea of moving, swaying bodies, a drunken orgy of dancing (and maybe, in the corners, just an orgy), but she didn't see anybody in formal wear.

"Eve!" she yelled, but even she couldn't hear it. She looked back up the stairs but she didn't see Shane, either.

She was alone.

When she craned her neck, she caught a flash of black velvet heading out of a door, and threw herself into the crowd to follow. If drunks groped on her way by, she barely noticed; she wanted out of here, badly, and she couldn't let anything happen to Eve. Her dignity was the least of her worries.

A hand slipped under her skirt. She turned, instinctively furious, and slapped the guy, hard. Didn't even register his face, or anything about him. He held up his hands in surrender, and she turned and plunged on.

The next room was nearly empty for some reason that Claire didn't understand, until she saw (and smelled) some guy throwing up in the corner. She hurried faster. *Was* that Eve she was following? She couldn't be sure. It looked like her, but the glimpses were too short, the angles all wrong. Claire had to move quicker.

She wasn't sure how it happened, but she ended up in the vast, gleaming kitchen. A bunch of burly guys were carrying in boxes of liquor. Claire pushed past two frat guys who were high-fiving each other. "Liquid panty remover's here!" one of them yelled, and there was a cheer in the other room.

Claire made it outside and gulped the cool, clear night air. She was shaking, sweating, and she felt utterly filthy, inside and out. That was *fun*? Yeah, she supposed if she were drinking and didn't care, it'd be fun, but then again, this was Morganville. Fun like that, you could end up passed out on a bed with strangers . . . or in a morgue drawer.

Eve was leaning against a tree in the glare of a security light, gasping for breath. She looked glamorous, like some lost Hollywood starlet from the days of black and white, except for the red blaze of her lipstick.

"Oh God," she moaned, and as Claire came toward her she realized she was crying. "Oh God, he's done it; he's really done it—"

"We don't know that," Claire heard herself say. "Maybe he just found her. Was trying to help her."

Eve glared at her. "He's a *vampire*! There's a *dead girl with holes in her neck*! I'm not stupid!"

"I can't believe he'd do it," Claire said. "Come on, Eve, do you? Really? You know him. Is he a killer? Especially when he doesn't have to be?"

Eve shook her head, but that wasn't really an answer. She was shaking off the question.

Shane came out of the kitchen door with the brunette still held in his arms. "Let's go."

"We came in Michael's car," Eve said numbly. "He has the keys. I could—"

"No. Nobody goes up there, and you guys stay the hell away from Michael until we know what's going on." Shane thought for a second, then pulled in a breath. "We walk."

"Walk!" Claire and Eve both blurted. Eve improved it by squeaking, "Are you freaking *mental*?"

"Claire's got Protection, and I'm in the mood to beat the hell out of the first vamp to look at me sideways, and it's safer than getting the three"—he glanced down at the nameless girl in his arms—"four of us in the car with Michael right now. I want room to run if I have to. And fight."

"Shane—"

"We walk," he interrupted. "University first, we can drop this one off with the campus cops."

Claire cleared her throat. "Can't we wait for the police here?"

"Trust me, no," Eve said. "They're going to roust everybody that isn't tagged, and that includes me and Shane. And once they find a drained dead girl, it'll be a free-for-all. We can't take the chance. We need to go. Now."

Claire was half hoping that Michael would show up, but he didn't come out after them. She wondered why. She wondered where he'd been, while they'd been searching the house for him.

Shane started walking toward the street, with the drugged girl murmuring and giggling in his arms. He'd saved one victim, but lost another. And he was taking that second part very personally.

Claire looked at Eve, put her arm around her, and hurried the both of them after Shane.

It was a quiet walk to the university campus. They didn't see anybody. The few cars that passed didn't stop, and although they heard sirens converging on the party, none of the police cars cruised their way.

The night was just cool enough to be pleasant, and the air felt dry and crisp. No clouds. It would have been pretty and romantic, except for the general crappiness of the evening. Eve had stopped crying, but that was almost worse; she'd been so happy before, and now she'd sunk into a gloom so deep she really did seem like a true Goth.

Claire's feet hurt. She was glad when they turned the corner and caught sight of the big, well-lit campus behind the wrought-iron fencing. They'd have to go to one of the four entrances to get through. She'd never really thought about it before, but the place looked unnatural, like a wildlife park.

Or a zoo.

Shane was getting tired, and put the girl down on the first bench they came to once they were inside the fence, while Eve flagged down a passing campus cop car. The Q&A went pretty well, but then, the campus cops weren't especially sharp. It took about half an hour, and then the girl was whisked off to the clinic for detox and checkups, and the three of them looked at one another in the glow of the cop car's headlights as it backed up and pulled away.

"Right," Shane said. "Probably ought to get moving."

Eve got out her phone.

"What are you doing?" he asked.

"Calling a cab."

He snorted. "In Morganville? At night? Right. Eddie doesn't even like picking people up during the daytime. No way is he risking his ass out here for us at night. He probably took his phone off the hook, anyway. He hates frat parties."

"What about Detective Hess?" Claire offered. "I'm sure he'd give us a ride."

"Light it up."

Claire tried. The number rang, but nobody picked up. Same thing with Travis Lowe. She looked at Shane with a sinking feeling and shrugged helplessly. Eve stood up, shivered, and crossed her bare arms for warmth. Shane took his black jacket off and draped it around her shoulders.

"Guess we're on foot," he said, and took Claire's hand, then Eve's. "Don't slow down, and don't stop for anything. If I tell you guys run, you run. Got it?"

He didn't give them a chance to argue. They walked down the path to the exit from the university grounds. Outside, the streetlights were few and far between, and Claire could just feel eyes on her in the shadows. Whether that was real or not, she didn't know, but it made her shake all over with fear. *Come on, Claire, get it together. There are three of us, and Shane can kick enough ass for all of us.*

They crossed the street and headed over a couple of blocks, then down. It was the straightest shot to the house, and the best lit, but it also was going to take them right by Common Grounds. Somehow, Claire felt even more uncomfortable at the idea that Oliver was going to see them trailing by, in all their not-too-smart glory. They'd had a rough enough night without that.

Although, it was a cheering thought that Monica almost certainly was having a worse one, trying to explain to the cops about why there were more drugs in her house than the Rite Aid Pharmacy, not to mention the underage drunken orgies and the dead girl in the bedroom.

By contrast, walking home in darkness in Vampire U.S.A. seemed a little bit mild.

At least until Eve whispered, "Somebody's following."

Claire almost faltered, but kept walking when Shane's hand tightened around hers. "Who?" he asked. Eve didn't turn her head.

"Don't know; I just caught a glimpse. Somebody in dark clothes."

Since only Amelie seemed to like colors in the pale winter hues, Claire figured that didn't narrow it down much. She walked faster, tripped over a crack in the sidewalk, and nearly went down, if it hadn't been for Shane's steadying grip. But it slowed them all down, and they couldn't afford for it to happen again.

"Crap," Shane breathed. They were still at least a block from the next burning streetlight, and now Claire could hear slow, steady footsteps behind them. Up ahead, a single open storefront spilled warm yellow light onto the street. Common Grounds. Neutral territory, at least theoretically. "Right. We're not going to make it all the way home. We go into Common Grounds, and—"

"No way, I'm not going in there!" Eve blurted. "I can't!"

"Yes you can; you have to. Neutral ground. Nobody will hurt you there. We can make some kind of deal with Oliver if we have to, temporary protection or something. Promise me—"

Shane didn't have time for anything else, because all hell broke loose. The footsteps behind them suddenly accelerated to a run, Shane swung around and pushed the two girls behind him, and there was a flash of movement Claire couldn't really see. Something hit Shane in the head. Hard. He stumbled and went down to one knee.

Claire screamed and reached for him, but Eve grabbed her and hauled her by force toward the glow of Common Grounds.

"Get up!"

Claire twisted out of Eve's grip and whirled to see that the yell had come from the jerk from the party, the one who'd felt her up and then gotten his ass kicked by Shane. He'd followed them, and he had a baseball bat. He'd hit Shane in the head *with the baseball bat* and he was getting ready to do it again.

"No!" Claire cried, and lunged back toward them, but Eve grabbed her tightly and swung her around toward the coffee shop again.

"Get inside!" she screamed.

"Let go—"

They stopped fighting each other as a shadow stepped out of the alley, right in front of them, blocking the way.

A long silver line glinted in the starlight. A knife.

It was Eve's brother Jason, looking as greasy and starved and fevered as he had at the party.

"Hey, sis," he said, and the knife turned, and turned, and turned. "I knew you'd be coming this way. Soon as I heard you left the party without your bloodsucking bodyguard, I knew the time was right."

"Jason"—Eve let go of Claire and stepped in between the two of them—"this isn't her problem. Let her go."

Claire was torn—watch Jason, who was terrifying, or pay attention to what was happening behind her, because Shane was fighting now, fighting for his life, and he was already hurt. She risked a glance back and saw Shane grab the baseball bat from his attacker, hit a home run to the guy's shoulder, and send him spinning into the brick wall. The frat guy went down, screaming, but Shane was clearly not doing well, either—he lurched, off balance, and went down to his hands and knees. The bat rolled away.

"Oh God," Claire whispered. There was blood running down his face, dripping in a wet thread to the pavement. "*Shane!*"

Shane shook his head, and the blood flew in a spray, splattering the concrete around him. He looked up, saw her, and blinked.

Then he saw Eve, and behind her, with the knife, Jason.

Shane fumbled for the bat, found it, and climbed to his feet. He stumbled forward, grabbed Claire, and pushed her behind him, then yanked Eve away from Jason, as well. He set his feet wide apart and took up a batting stance.

He looked pale and shaken and half-dead, but Claire knew he wasn't backing down.

"Leave them alone," he said. Not a yell, not a threat, just a low, quiet voice with absolute control. "Walk away, Jason."

Jason lost his smile. He put the knife in his pocket and held up his hands. "Sure. Sorry, man. Don't go all Sammy Sosa on me." He lowered his hands again and stuffed them in his coat pockets, looking casual, but there was an avid glitter to his eyes, and a cruel twist to his thin lips. "I heard you found a present in your basement. Something girl-shaped."

Eve groaned, and Claire reached out to steady her when she swayed. "Jason," Eve whispered, and she looked awful, as though she was going to throw up. "Oh God, *why*?"

Shane took a step forward, bat raised and ready, and Jason backed up again. "Doing it there, that was just fun," he said. "But it's not about the girls. I had to show them I was ready."

"Ready?" Eve echoed. "Oh God, Jase, is that what this is about? You're just some pathetic wannabe vampire making his bones?" Eve sounded so freaked it made Claire's guts knot up. "You're trying to *impress* them? By killing?"

"Sure." Jason shrugged. He looked thin and weedy, almost lost inside that black leather jacket. "How else do you get attention around here? And I'm going to get *lots* of attention. Starting with you, Claire."

Shane yelled—it wasn't even words, just a yell of pure fury—and swung at him. Jason jumped back, faster than Claire would have expected, and the bat missed him. Then he lunged forward. Shane was off balance, not really steady on his feet, but that wouldn't matter; if Jason was crazy enough to want to go hand to hand with Shane, it was all over.

Wasn't it?

Jason punched Shane low in the stomach, and Shane made a surprised sound and took a step back from him.

Shane was *backing away.* . . .

And then Claire saw the knife in Jason's hand, glittering silver and red, and for a second she didn't understand, she didn't understand at all.

It wasn't until Shane's hand opened and the baseball bat hit the pavement with a noisy rattle, and Shane collapsed to his knees, that she realized that he'd been stabbed.

Shane didn't seem to understand it, either. He was panting, trying to say something, but he couldn't get the words out. His eyes were wide and confused. He tried to get up, but couldn't.

Jason pointed the knife at him, slung it in an arc that spattered them all with blood drops, and turned and walked away. He put the blade back in his pocket. People were coming out of Common Grounds, looking puzzled and alarmed, and at the forefront was Oliver. Oliver's head turned quickly to stare at Jason's departing form, and then he focused on them.

Claire dropped to her knees next to Shane. He looked desperately into her face, and slowly collapsed to his side.

His hands were clutching his stomach, and there was so much blood. . . .

Eve hadn't moved. She was just—standing there, in her lovely black dress, staring blindly after her brother.

Oliver grabbed her and shook her. Her black hair flew wildly, and when he let go, Eve sank down in a defeated slump against the building's brick wall. Oliver shook his head impatiently and turned to Claire, and Shane.

Claire looked up, mute with misery, and saw Oliver staring down at them.

For just a second, she thought she saw something in him. Maybe just a tiny glimmer of empathy.

"Someone is calling the ambulance," he said. "You should put pressure on the wound. He's losing a lot of blood. It's a waste." The blood, he meant. Not Shane.

"Help me," Claire said. Oliver shook his head. *"Help me!"*

"You'll find that vampires aren't particularly good with the wounded," he said. "I'm doing you a favor by staying away. And don't try to order me, little girl. That gold bracelet of yours means almost nothing to me, except that I shouldn't leave witnesses behind."

Shane coughed, wet and hard, and blood trickled out of his mouth. He looked as pale as Michael. Vampire pale.

Claire cradled him in her arms. Oliver glanced at Eve, frowned, and went away. People were coming closer, murmuring, asking questions, but Claire couldn't make any sense out of it. She pressed down on the wet bloody mess of Shane's shirt, felt him tense and try to squirm away, and didn't let him. *Pressure on the wound.* It seemed to take forever until she heard the distant sound of sirens approaching.

Shane was still breathing when they loaded him inside the ambulance, but he wasn't moving, and he wasn't talking.

Claire went to Eve, got her on her feet, and put an arm around her shoulders. "Come on," she said. "We should ride with Shane."

Oliver was staring at the wet, dark smears of blood on the concrete, and as Claire helped Eve up into the back of the ambulance, he looked at one of his coffee shop employees and nodded toward the mess.

"Clean it up," he said. "Use bleach. I don't want to smell it all night."

ELEVEN

Shane survived the trip, and they rushed him right into surgery. Eve sat silent in her black velvet dress, looking more Goth than ever, and wildly out of place in the soothing neutral waiting room. Claire kept getting up and washing her hands, because she kept finding more of Shane's blood on her clothes and skin.

Eve was crying quietly, almost hopelessly. For some reason Claire didn't cry at all. Not at all. She wasn't even sure she could. Did that make her sick? Screwed up? She wasn't sure whom she could ask. She couldn't seem to feel anything right now except a vague sense of dread.

Richard Morrell came to take their statements. It was simple enough, and Claire had no hesitation in turning in Jason for the stabbing. "And he confessed," Claire added. "To killing those girls."

"Confessed how?" Richard asked. He sat down in the chair across from her in the lounge area, and Claire thought he looked tired. Older, too. She guessed it wasn't easy being the semisane one in the family. "What exactly did he tell you?"

"That he left one for us," she said, and glanced at Eve, who hadn't said a word. Hadn't, as far as Claire could tell, actually blinked. "He called them presents."

"Did he mention any of them by name?"

"No," she whispered. She felt very, very tired all of a sudden, as if she could sleep for a week. Cold, too. She was shivering. Richard noticed, got up, and came back with a big gray fleece blanket that he tucked around her. He'd brought a second one for Eve, who was still wrapped in Shane's black coat.

"Is it possible that Jason just said that because he knew about the bodies being found near your house?" Richard asked. "Did he talk about anything more specific that wasn't in the papers?"

Claire almost said yes to that, but she stopped in time. The police didn't know about the girl being found in their basement. They thought she'd been taken to the church by her killer.

She had no choice. She just shook her head.

"It's possible Jason's all talk, then," Richard said. "We've been watching him. We haven't seen anything to prove that he's got any involvement with these dead girls." He hesitated, then said, very gently, "Look. I don't want to make this about Shane, but he did have a bat, right?"

Eve raised her head, very slowly. "What?"

"Shane had a bat."

"He took it from another guy," Claire said, nearly tripping over the words in her hurry to get them out. "A guy from Monica's party. Shane got jumped; he was just defending himself! And he was trying to get Jason to back off—"

"We have witnesses who say that Shane swung the bat at Jason after Jason had put away his knife."

Claire couldn't find the words. She just sat there, lips parted, staring into Richard's weary, hard eyes.

"So that's it," Eve said. Her voice started out soft, but hardened quickly. "It's all going to be Shane's fault, because he's Shane. Never mind that some frat ass tried to knock his head off, or that Jason *stabbed him*. It's still Shane's fault!" She stood up, stripped away the blanket, and threw it at him. Richard grabbed it before it hit his face, but just barely. "Here, you'll need it for your cover-up!" She stalked away, slender and pale as a lily in all that black.

"Eve—" Richard sighed. "Dammit. Look, Claire, I have to have the facts, okay? And the facts are that during the confrontation, Jason put his knife away, Shane had a bat, and Shane threatened him. Then Jason stabbed him in self-defense Is that right?"

She didn't answer. She sat for a few seconds, just staring at him, and then stood up, stripped off the blanket, and handed it to him.

"You're going to need a bigger cover-up," she said. "See if there's a circus in town. Maybe you can borrow a tent."

She walked down the hall to see if Shane was out of surgery.

He wasn't.

Eve was pacing the hallway, stiff with rage, hands clenched into fists barely visible as knots in the too-long sleeves of the coat. "Those sons of bitches," she said. "Those *bastards!* They're going to put Shane down; I can feel it."

"Put him down?" Claire repeated. "What do you mean, put him down? Like, a dog?"

Eve glared at her. Her eyes were rimmed with red, and wet with tears. "I mean even if he makes it through the surgery, they're not going to let him get out of this. Richard practically told us; don't you get it? It's the perfect frame. Shane took the swing, Jason acted in self-defense, and nobody's even going to *look* at Jason for these murders. They'll just bury it, like they bury the bodies."

She stopped talking, and her eyes refocused over Claire's shoulder. Claire turned.

Michael was striding toward them, lean and powerful and tall, and he headed straight for Eve. No hesitation, as if nothing had happened. As if they hadn't seen him bending over a dead girl at the party.

He stopped just inches away from Eve, and held out his hands.

"I went looking for you guys. I finally tracked you to Common Grounds. How is he?" he asked. His voice was hoarse.

"Not so good," Eve whispered, and flowed into his arms like water through a broken dam. "Oh God. Oh God, Michael, it all went wrong. It's all wrong—"

He sighed and wrapped his arms around her, and rested his golden head next to her dark one. "I should have come with you. I should have

made you get in the damn car. I was going to, but—things happened;
I had to take care of it at the party. I never thought you'd try to walk
home." He paused, and when he finally went on, his voice was thick with
pain. "It's my fault."

"It's nobody's fault," Claire said. "You know you can't make Shane do
something he doesn't want to do. Or Eve, for that matter. Or me." She put
a hand hesitantly on Michael's arm. "You didn't kill that girl, did you?"

"No," he said. "I found her when I was searching for Jason. I was trying to find him and get him out of the party. He was probably already
gone by then."

"Then who—"

Michael looked up, and his blue eyes were fiercely bright. "That's
what I had to take care of. There were vampires there, hunting. I had to
stop it."

One of the nurses passing by slowed, watching Michael and Eve. Her
eyes narrowed, and she stopped to stare. She muttered something, then
walked on.

Michael turned to the nurse, who was already halfway down the hall.
"Excuse me," he said. "What did you say?"

The nurse stopped dead in her tracks and turned to face him. "I
didn't say anything. *Sir.*" That last word sounded sharp enough to cut.

"I think you did," Michael said. "You called her a fang-banger."

The nurse smiled coldly. "If I muttered something under my breath,
sir, that shouldn't concern you. You and your—*girlfriend*—ought to do
your business in the waiting room. Or the blood bank."

Michael's hands curled into fists, and his face went tight with rage.
"It's not like that."

The nurse—her name tag said her name was Christine Fenton, RN—
outright sneered at him. "Yeah, it never is. It's always different, right?
You're just *misunderstood.* You want to hurt me, go ahead and try. I'm not
afraid of you. Any of you."

"Good," Michael said. "You shouldn't be afraid of me because I'm
a vampire. You ought to be scared because you just trash-talked my girlfriend *to her face.*"

Nurse Fenton flipped him off and kept walking.

"Wow," Eve said. She almost sounded like herself again, as if having somebody diss her had helped, like a slap in the face. "And people treated me bad when I dated Bobby Fee. At least he was breathing. Mouth-breathing, yeah, but—"

Michael put his arm around her, still staring after the nurse. He had a frown on his face, but he forced it off to smile at Eve and plant a kiss on her forehead.

"You need some rest. Let's go back to the waiting room," he said. "I promise not to embarrass you anymore." He guided her in that direction, and threw a look back. "Claire? You coming?"

She nodded absently, but her mind was somewhere else, trying to sort through data. *Fenton.* She'd seen that name before, hadn't she? Not the nurse, though; she'd never met her before and now really didn't look forward to ever seeing her again.

Claire realized she was standing alone in the hallway, and shivered. While this was a modern building, not nearly as nasty as the old, falling-to-ruins abandoned hospital where she and Shane had been chased for their lives, it still gave her the creeps. She threw one last, aching glance at the frosted-glass doors that read SURGICAL AREA—ADMITTANCE TO AUTHO-RIZED PERSONNEL ONLY. She couldn't see anything beyond except vague moving shadows.

She followed Michael back to the waiting room. Richard Morrell was gone, which was good, and Claire sat in silence, rubbing her hands together, still feeling the phantom slickness of Shane's blood on her skin.

"Hey," Michael said. She didn't know how much time had passed, just that she was stiff and sore and tense. She looked up into his crystal blue eyes, and saw strength and kindness, but also just a little bit of a glitter that didn't seem . . . natural. "Rest. I can almost hear the gears grinding in your head." Eve was asleep in his lap, curled up like a cat. He was strok-ing her dark hair. "Here," he said. "Lean in." And he put his arm around Claire, and she leaned, and despite everything that had happened, she felt warm and safe.

It all fell in on her then, all the fear and the pain and the fact that

Shane had gotten stabbed, right in front of her, and she didn't know how to deal with that, didn't know how to feel or what to say or do, and it was all just . . .

She turned her face into Michael's blue silk shirt and cried, silent heaving sobs that tore up out of her guts in painful jerks. Michael's hand cradled her head, and he let her cry.

She felt him press his cool lips to her temple when she finally relaxed against him, and then she just slid away, into the dark.

Claire fought her way, panicked, out of a nightmare, and into another one. *Hospital. Shane. Surgery.*

Eve was shaking her with both hands on her shoulders, babbling at her, and she couldn't follow the words, but the words didn't matter at first.

Eve was smiling.

"He's okay," Claire said in a whisper, then louder. "He's okay!"

"Yeah," Eve said, the words tumbling out in a confusing bright flood, way too fast. "He's out of surgery. It was touch and go. He had a lot of internal bleeding. He's going to be in ICU for a few days before they let him come home, and he'll have a temporary bracelet, you know, the plastic kind?"

Claire tried to literally shake the sleepy fog out of her head. "Plastic— Wait. Don't you always get one of those in the hospital? Like an ID tag?"

"Do you? Really? How weird. Oh. Well, in Morganville you leave it on when you leave, and it protects you for up to a month after surgery. Kind of like a temporary vampire restraining order." Eve actually bounced up and down. "He's going to be okay, oh my God, he's going to be okay!"

Claire scrambled out of her seat, grabbed Eve's arms, and the two of them bounced together up and down, then fell into a hug and squealed.

"I'll just—let you guys do that," Michael said. He was sitting in the chairs watching, but he was smiling. He looked tired.

"What time is it?" Claire asked.

"Late. Early." Eve checked her skull watch. "About six in the morning. Michael, you should get home; it'll be dawn soon. I'll stay here with Claire."

"We should all go home," Michael said. "He's not going to wake up for hours yet. You could change clothes."

Claire looked down at herself, and grimaced tiredly. "Yeah, I could," she admitted. Shane's blood had soaked into her patterned tights, and she thought Michael could probably smell it. *She* could even smell it, a musty, rotten odor that made her gag. "Eve? You want to go, too?"

Eve nodded. The three of them walked out of the waiting room and down the long, empty hallway toward the elevators. They passed the front desk, where Nurse Fenton glared at them. When Claire looked back, as they waited for the elevator, Nurse Fenton was dialing the phone.

"Why do I know that name?" she asked, and then realized, *duh*, she was with two Morganville natives. "Fenton? You guys know anything about her?"

The elevator arrived. Eve stepped in and pushed the button for the lobby, and she and Michael looked at each other for a second.

"The family's been here for generations," Michael said. "Nurse Charming out there's a new arrival. She came to TPU for school, married into the family."

"You met her husband," Eve said. "Officer Fenton, Brad Fenton. He's the one who—"

"The one who showed up when Sam was attacked," Claire blurted. "Of course! I forgot his name." Why did that still leave her vaguely uneasy? She couldn't remember anything that Officer Fenton had done that had made her think he was antivamp; he'd acted quickly enough when Sam was in trouble. Not like his wife, who clearly wasn't as open-minded.

She worried about it for a while, but couldn't see any real connection, and there were other things to think about. After all, Shane was okay, and that was all that mattered.

A shower helped, but it didn't banish the dull ache between Claire's eyes, or the strange gray cast the world had taken on. Exhaustion, she guessed, and stress. Nothing looked quite right. She changed clothes, grabbed her backpack, and went back to the hospital—this time, taking a cab, despite it being broad daylight—to wait for visiting hours to start in ICU. No sign of Jason, but then, she hadn't expected him to be that obvious. Or that stupid. He'd managed to get away with it this long.

But then again . . . He really hadn't struck her as all that far-thinking, either. More of a want-take-have kind of guy. So what did that mean? Was Eve right? Was this a giant official cover-up, and Jason had been given free rein to run around town raping and killing and stabbing as the mood moved him? She shuddered just thinking of it.

Nurse Fenton was, mercifully, off duty when Claire arrived. She checked in with the younger, nicer lady at the desk, whose name was Helen Porter, and went to find the least uncomfortable chair in the waiting area. The building wasn't completely lame; there were laptop connections and desks, and she set herself up there. The wireless was crap, but there was a LAN connection, and that worked fine.

Of course, the filters restricted where she could go on the Internet, and she quickly grew frustrated trying to find out what was happening in the world outside of Morganville . . . more of the same, she guessed. War, crime, death, atrocity. Sometimes it hardly seemed that vampires were the bad guys, given the things people did to each other without the excuse of needing a pint of O neg to get through the day.

She wondered if the vampires had made any headway tracking down who could have staked Sam. Surely they'd found out something. Then again, they hadn't had a lot of luck cornering Shane's dad, either. . . .

Her laptop connection stopped working, right in the middle of an e-mail to her parents. She'd been avoiding making the call, because there was this dangerous temptation to start spilling out her hurt and fear and look for comfort—after all, wasn't that what parents were for?—but if she did, they'd either come running to town, which would be bad, or they'd try to pull her out of school again, which would definitely be worse. Worse in every way.

Still, she knew she was overdue to talk to her mom, and the longer she put it off, the more stress it was going to be for both of them.

Claire logged off the laptop, packed it, and opened up her new cool phone. It glowed with a pale blue light when she dialed the number, and she heard faint clicking. That probably meant the call was being recorded, or at least monitored. More reason to be careful about what she said . . .

Mom answered the phone on the third ring. "Hello?"

"Hi!" Claire winced at the artificial cheeriness of her tone. Why couldn't she sound natural? "Mom, it's Claire."

"Claire! Honey, I've been worried. You should have called days ago."

"I know, Mom, I'm sorry. I got busy. I got transferred into some advanced classes; they're really great, but there's been a lot of homework and reading. I just forgot."

"Well," her mother said, "I'm glad to hear those teachers are recognizing that you need special attention. I was a little worried when you told me the classes were so easy. You like challenges, I know that."

Oh, I'm challenged now, Claire thought. Between the classes and Myrnin, being stalked by Jason, and being terrified for Shane . . . "Yeah, I do," she said. "So I guess this is all good."

"What else? How are your friends? That nice Michael, is he still playing his guitar?" Mom asked it as if it was a silly little hobby that he'd give up eventually.

"Yes, Mom, he's a musician. He's still playing. In fact, he was playing in the University Center the other day. He got quite a crowd."

"Well, fine. I hope he's not playing in some of those clubs, though. That gets dangerous."

There was more of that, the danger talk, and Claire worried that her mother was, if not remembering exactly, at least remembering *something.* Why would she be so fixated on how dangerous things could be?

"Mom, you're overreacting," Claire finally said. "Honest, everything's fine here."

"Well, you started out this semester in the emergency room, Claire; you can't really blame me for worrying. You're very young to be out on your own, and not even in the dorm. . . ."

"I told you about the problems with the dorm," Claire said.

"Yes, I know; the girls weren't very nice—"

"Not very nice? Mom! They threw me down the stairs!"

"I'm sure that was an accident."

It hadn't been, but there was something about her mother that wasn't going to accept that, not really. For all her fluttering and worrying, she didn't want to believe that something really could be badly wrong.

"Yeah," Claire sighed. "Probably. Anyway, the house is great. I really like it there."

"And Michael has our numbers? In case there's any problem?"

"Yes, Mom, everybody's got the numbers. Oh, speaking of that, here's my new cell phone—" She rattled off the digits, twice, and made her mother read them back. "It's got better reception than the old one, so you can get me a lot more easily, okay?"

"Claire," her mother said, "are you sure you're all right?"

"Yes. I'm fine."

"I don't want to pry, but that boy, the one in the house—not Michael, but—"

"Shane."

"Yes, Shane. I think you should keep your distance from him, honey. He's old for you, and he seems pretty sure of himself."

She did *not* want to get into the subject of Shane. She'd nearly stumbled over saying his name, it hurt so bad. She wanted to talk to her mother the way she'd used to. They'd talked about everything, once, but there was no way she could really talk about Morganville with her family.

And that meant that there was no way she could talk about anything at all.

"I'll be careful," she managed to say, and her attention was caught by the young nurse standing in the doorway of the waiting area, waving for her attention. "Oh—Mom, I have to go. Sorry. Somebody's waiting for me."

"All right, honey. We love you."

"Love you, too." She hung up, slid the phone into her pocket, and grabbed her backpack.

The nurse led her through another set of glass double doors into an area labeled ICU. "He's awake," she said. "You can't stay long; we want him to rest as much as possible, and I can already tell he's going to be a difficult patient." She smiled at Claire, and winked. "See if you can sweeten him up a little for me. Make my life easier."

Claire nodded. She felt nervous and a little sick with the force of her need to see him, touch him . . . and at the same time, she dreaded it. She hated the thought of seeing him like this, and she didn't know what she was going to say. What did people say when they were this scared of losing someone?

He looked worse than she'd imagined, and she must have let it show. Shane grunted and closed his eyes for a few seconds. "Yeah, well, I'm not dead; that's something. One of those in the house is enough." He looked awful—pale as, well, Michael. The baseball bat had left him with Technicolor bruising, and he seemed fragile in ways Claire hadn't even thought about. There were so many tubes and things. She sat down in the chair next to his raised bed and reached over the railing to touch him lightly on his scraped, bruised hand.

He turned it to twine their fingers together. "You're all right?"

"Yeah," she said. "Jason ran away, after." Walked, really, but she wasn't going to say that. "Eve's okay, too. She was here while you were in surgery; she just went home to change clothes. She'll be back."

"Yeah, I guess the diva dress might have been a little much around here." He opened his eyes and looked at her directly. "Claire. Really. You're okay?"

"I'm fine," she said. "Except that I'm scared for you."

"I'm okay."

"Except for the stab wound and all the internal bleeding? Yeah, sure, tough guy." She heard her voice quiver, and knew she was about to cry. She didn't want to. He wanted to laugh it off, wanted to be tough, and she ought to let him, right?

He tried to shrug, but it must have hurt, from the spasm that went across his face. One of the machines near Claire beeped, and he let out a slow sigh. "That's better. Man, they give you the good stuff in ICU. Remind me to always get seriously wounded from now on. That minor injury stuff isn't as much fun."

It was wearing him out to talk. Claire got up and leaned over to stroke her fingertips lightly over his lips. "Shhhh," she said. "Rest, okay? Save it for somebody who isn't me. It's okay to be scared. It's okay to be hurt, Shane. With me, it's okay."

For a second his eyes glittered with tears, and then the tears spilled over, threading wet trails into his hair. "Damn," he whispered. "Sorry. I just—I felt it all going away, I felt you going away, I tried—I thought he was going to hurt you and there was nothing I could do about it—"

"I know." She leaned forward and kissed him very lightly, careful of the bruises. "I know."

He cried a little, and she stayed right where she was, his shield against the world, until it was over. Finally, he fell into a light sleep, and she felt a tap on her shoulder. The nurse motioned for her to step out, and Claire carefully pulled her hand free of Shane's and followed.

"Sorry," Helen said. "I'd like for him to sleep a while before we start with the poking and prodding. You can come back this afternoon, all right?"

"Sure. What time?"

Four o'clock. That left her the entire day to kill, and not the slightest idea what she ought to be doing with it. She didn't have to see Myrnin; Amelie hadn't given her any other instructions to follow. It was Saturday, so she wasn't cutting any classes, and she didn't want to go back to the Glass House and just . . . worry.

Claire was still trying to decide what to do when she spotted a familiar well-groomed figure standing outside the hospital doors.

What was Jennifer, one of Monica's regular clique, doing hanging around here?

Waiting for Claire, apparently, because she hurried to catch up as Claire strode by, heading for the taxi stand. "Hey," she said, and tucked her glossy hair behind her ear. "So. How's Shane doing?"

"Like you care," Claire said.

"Well, yeah. I don't. But Monica wants to know."

"He's alive." That was no more than Monica could learn without her help, so it didn't really matter, and Claire didn't like having Jennifer this close. Monica was creepy, but at least she was Alpha Creepy. There was something pathetic and extra-weird about her two groupies.

Jennifer kept pace with her. Claire stopped and turned to face her. They were halfway down the sidewalk, in the full glare of early-fall sunlight, which at least meant it wasn't too likely some vampire would be sneaking up on her while Jennifer kept her distracted. "Look," Claire said, "I don't want anything to do with you, or Monica, okay? I don't want to be friends. I don't want you sucking up to me just because I'm . . . somebody, or something."

Jennifer didn't look like she wanted to be sucking up, either. In fact, she looked as bitter and resentful as a glossy, entitled rich girl could look—which was a lot. "Dream on, loser. I don't care who your Patron is; you're never going to be anything more than jumped-up trailer trash with delusions. Friends? I wouldn't be friends with you if you were the last person breathing in this town."

"Unless Monica said so," Claire said spitefully. "Fine, you don't want to exchange friendship rings. So why are you bothering me?"

Jennifer glared at her for a few seconds, stubborn and angry, and then looked away. "You're smart, right? Like, freak smart?"

"What does that have to do with anything?"

"You placed out of the two classes we were in together. You must have aced the tests."

Claire nearly laughed out loud. "You want *tutoring*?"

"No, idiot. I want test answers. Look, I can't bring home anything under a C; that's the rule, or my Patron cuts off my college. And I *want* my full four years, even if I never do anything with it in this lame-ass town." A muscle fluttered in Jennifer's jawline. "I don't get this economics crap. It's all math, Adam Smith, blah blah blah. What am I ever going to use it for, anyway?"

She was asking for help. Not in so many words, maybe, but that was what it was, and Claire was off balance for a few heartbeats. First Monica, now Jennifer? What next, a cookie bouquet from Oliver?

"I can't give you test answers," she said. "I wouldn't even if I could." Claire took in a deep breath. "Look, I'm going to regret this, but if you really want help, I'll go over the notes with you. *Once.* And you pay me, too. Fifty dollars." Which was wildly out of line, but she didn't really care if Jennifer said no.

Which Jennifer clearly thought about, hard, before giving her a single, abrupt nod.

"Common Grounds," she said. "Tomorrow, two o'clock." Which was pretty much the safest time to be out and about, providing they didn't stay too long. Claire wasn't wild about visiting Oliver's shop again, but she didn't suppose there were too many places in town that Jennifer would agree to go. Besides, it wasn't far from Claire's house.

"Two o'clock," Claire echoed, and wondered if they were supposed to shake hands or something. Not, obviously, because Jennifer flipped her hair and walked away, clearly glad to have it over with. She jumped into a black convertible and pulled away from the curb with a screech of tires.

Leaving Claire to contemplate the afternoon sunlight and the odds of walking home through a Morganville where Jason was still on the loose.

She took out her cell phone and called the town's lone taxi driver, who told her he was off duty, and hung up on her.

So she called Travis Lowe.

Detective Lowe wasn't really happy to be the Claire Taxi Service. She could tell because he wasn't his usual self, not at all—he'd always been kind to her, and a little bit funny, but there wasn't any of that in the way he pulled his blue Ford to the curb and snapped, "Get in." He was accelerating away even before she got strapped in. "You do know I've got a real job, right?"

"Sorry, sir," she said. The *sir* was automatic, a habit she couldn't seem to break no matter how hard she tried. "I just didn't think I should be walking home, with Jason—"

"Right thought, just wrong timing," he said, and his tone softened some. He looked tired and sallow, and there were dark bags under his eyes as though he hadn't slept in days. He needed a shave and a shower. Probably the shower more than the shave. "How's Shane?"

"Better," she said. "The nurse told me he was going to be okay; it's just going to take some time."

"Good news. Could've gone the other way. Why'd you try to walk home like that?"

She fidgeted a little in the seat. In contrast to the vampire cars, with their dark tinting, the glare inside Lowe's car seemed way too bright. "Well, we tried getting a ride," she said. In retrospect, none of the explanations seemed all that good, really. She didn't mention that she'd tried both Lowe's phone and Joe Hess's. No point in making him feel guilty. Guiltier. "We thought with the three of us together . . ."

"Yeah, good plan, if it had been any other kids. You guys, you're just trouble to the power of three. And I'm no math whiz, but I'm betting that's a lot." His eyes were cold and distant, and she had the distinct feeling he wasn't really thinking about her at all. "Listen, I've got to make a stop. I'm running late as it is. You stay in the car, okay? Just stay in the car. Do *not* get out."

She nodded. He turned some corners, into a residential area of Morganville she didn't recognize. It was run-down and faded, with leaning fences that were marked with sun-bleached gang signs. The houses weren't much better. Most of them just had sheets tacked up in the windows instead of real curtains.

He parked in front of one, got out, and said, "Windows up. Lock the doors."

She followed his orders and watched him go up the narrow, cracked sidewalk to the front door. It opened on the second knock, but she couldn't see who was inside, and Lowe closed the door behind him.

Claire frowned and waited, wondering what he was doing—cop stuff, she guessed, but in Morganville that could be anything, from running errands for vampires to dog-catching.

He didn't come back. She checked her watch and found that more than ten minutes had passed. He'd ordered her to stay put, but for how long? She could have been home already if she'd been able to get the taxi, or even if she'd walked.

And it was getting hot in the car.

Ten more minutes, and she started to feel anxious. The neighborhood seemed deserted—no people on the street, even in the bright sunlight. Even for Morganville, that didn't seem . . . normal. She didn't know this area, hadn't been through it before, and she wondered what went on around here.

Before Claire could decide to do something really stupid, like investigating on her own, Detective Lowe came out of the house and, after rapping on the window for her to unlock the door, got back in the car. He looked, if possible, even more tired. Depressed, almost.

"What's wrong?" she asked. The sheets tacked up as curtains twitched in the window of the house, as if somebody was peering out at them. "Sir?"

"Quit calling me sir," Lowe snapped, and put the car in gear. "And it's none of your affair. Stay out of it."

There was blood on his hand. His knuckles were scraped. Claire pulled in a fast breath, her eyes widening as she noticed, and he sent her a narrow glance as the car accelerated away down the deserted street. "Were you in a fight?" she asked.

"What did I just tell you?" Detective Lowe had never been angry before, not with her, but she could tell he was being pushed pretty far. She nodded and turned face forward, trying too keep herself still. It wasn't easy. She wanted to ask questions, a dozen of them. She wanted to ask him where Detective Hess had gone. She wanted to find out who lived in that house, and why Lowe had gone there. And whom he'd hit, to scrape up his knuckles like that.

And why he was so desperately angry that he'd snap at her.

Lowe didn't enlighten her about any of it. He pulled the car to a stop with an abrupt jerk of brakes, and Claire blinked and realized that she was home. "You need another ride, call a taxi," Lowe said. "I'm on police business the rest of the day."

She climbed out and tried to thank him, but he wasn't listening. He was already flipping open his cell phone and dialing one-handed as he put the car in gear with the other. She barely got the door shut before he pulled away from the curb.

"Bye," she said softly, to the empty air, and then shrugged and went inside.

Michael was sitting in the living room, playing guitar. He looked up and nodded at her when she came in. "Eve went to the hospital," he said. "She must have just missed you."

Claire sighed and slumped down on the couch. "They won't let her in. Visiting hours are over." She yawned and curled up, tucking her feet under her. She ached all over, and everything seemed too bright, and not quite right. "Michael?"

"Yeah?" He was working out a chord progression and was focused on the music; his response didn't mean he was listening, really.

"Shouldn't you be asleep? I mean, don't vampires——?"

He was listening after all. "Sleep during the day? Yeah, mostly. But I—couldn't. I keep thinking . . ." The chord progression turned minor, then wrong, and he grimaced. "I keep thinking that I should have fixed this crap with Shane by now. I don't know if he's going to get over it, not really. Not in the ways that count. And I hate it. I can't stop thinking—I don't want him doing this stuff. Not without me watching his back."

Claire leaned her head against the battered black pillow on the corner of the couch. It smelled like spilled Coke, a little, but mostly it smelled like Shane, and she gladly turned her face into it and took a deep breath. It made it seem like he was here, at least for a second.

"He wouldn't hate you so bad if he didn't love you, at least a little bit," she said. "We'll be okay. We're going to stay together, right? The four of us?"

Michael looked up, and for a second she wasn't sure what he was going to say; but then he said, "Yeah. We'll stay together. No matter what."

It felt like a lie, and she wished he hadn't said it.

She fell asleep, listening to him compose a new song, and dreamed about vibrating strings and doorways that led nowhere, and everywhere. Someone was watching her; she could feel it, and it wasn't Michael. It wasn't warm and kind; it wasn't safe. She wasn't safe, and there was something wrong, wrong, *wrong.* . . .

She nearly fell off the couch, she jerked so hard. Michael wasn't there, and his guitar was in the case on the table. Claire squinted at the clock. It was nearly two o'clock, and she'd slept through lunch, but it wasn't hunger that had woken her up. She'd heard something.

It came again, a thumping knock on the front door. She yawned and pushed back the blanket that Michael had draped over her, and, still trying to rub the sleep out of her eyes, padded to the door.

She had to stand on tiptoes at the peephole to see out. Some guy, nobody that clicked any immediate recognition—not Jason, at least. That was good. Claire looked over her shoulder, but there was no sign Michael had heard. She had no idea where he'd gone.

She opened the door. The guy standing outside looked up and held out a padded mailer with stickers on it; she took it and read her own name on it. "Oh," she said, preoccupied. "Thanks."

"No problem, Claire," he said. "Be seeing you."

There was something way too familiar about the way he said it. She jerked her head up, staring at him, but she still didn't know him. He was just . . . normal. Average height, average weight, average everything. There was a silver bracelet on his wrist, so he was human, not vampire.

"Do I know you?" she asked. He tilted his head a little, but didn't answer. He just turned and walked away down the sidewalk, toward the street. "Hey, wait! Who are you?"

He waved and kept walking. She went a couple of steps outside into the early-afternoon heat, frowning, but she'd left her shoes off, and the concrete was blazing hot. No way could she run after him in bare feet; she'd fry like bacon.

She retreated back into the cool darkness of the house and sighed in relief at the feeling of cool wood under her soles. She looked down at the envelope in her hand and suddenly wanted to drop it and step away. She didn't know who this guy was, and it was really strange that he wouldn't answer her. And strange, in Morganville, was rarely going to be a good thing.

She closed and locked the door, took a deep breath, and tore open the top of the envelope. No smell of blood or disgusting rotting things, which was a plus. She carefully squeezed the sides to open it up, and saw nothing in it but a note. She shook it out into her hand, and recognized the paper immediately—heavy, expensive paper, cream-colored, embossed with the same logo that was on her gold bracelet.

It was a note from Amelie. Which meant the guy who'd dropped it off had to be somebody she trusted, at least that far.

"Everything okay?" Michael's voice came from the end of the hall. Claire gasped, stuffed the paper back into the envelope, and turned to face him.

"Sure," she said. "Just mail."

"Good stuff?"

"Don't know yet; I haven't read it. Probably junk."

"Enjoy the fact that you don't have electricity, water, cable, Internet, and garbage to pay for," he said. "Look, I'm going upstairs. Yell if you need anything. There's stuff in the fridge if you're hungry." A brief pause. "Don't open the pitcher in the back on the top shelf."

"Michael, *tell* me you're not putting blood in our refrigerator."

"I told you not to open it. So you'll never know."

"You *suck!*" Of course he did; he was a vampire. "I mean, not in a good way, either!"

"Eat something! I'm sleeping." And she heard his door shut, so she was effectively alone.

Claire fumbled out the letter and unfolded it. A smell of faint, dusty roses came from the paper, as though it had been stored in a trunk with dried flowers. She wondered how old it was.

It was a short, simple note, but it made her whole body turn cold.

It read:

> *I am displeased with your progress in your advanced studies. I suggest you spend additional time learning all you can. Time is growing short. I do not care how you arrange this, but you will be expected to demonstrate within the next two days at least a journeyman understanding of what you are being taught. You cannot involve Michael. He is not to be risked.*

Nothing else. Claire stared at the perfect handwriting for a few seconds, then folded the note up and put it back in the envelope. She still felt tired and hungry, but more than anything else, now she felt scared.

Amelie wasn't happy.

That wasn't good.

Two days. And Michael could go with her only in the evenings. . . .

She couldn't wait.

Claire checked in her backpack. The red crystal shaker was still inside, safely zipped into a pocket.

If she took Michael's car—no, she couldn't. She'd never be able to see through the tinting, even if she felt confident in her ability to drive it. And Detective Lowe wasn't going to give her a ride. She could try Detective Hess, but Lowe's attitude had made her gun-shy.

Still, she couldn't just go out alone.

With a sigh, she called Eddie, the taxi driver.

"What?" he snapped. "Don't I get a day off? What is it with you?"

"Eddie, I'm sorry. I'm really sorry. I need a favor." Claire hastily checked her wallet. "Um, it's a short trip. I'll pay you double, okay? Please?"

"Double? I don't take checks."

"I know that. Cash."

"I don't wait. I pick up, I drop off, I leave."

"Eddie! Double! Do you want it or not?"

"Keep your panties on. What's the address?"

"Michael Glass's house."

Eddie heaved a sigh so heavy it sounded like a temporary hurricane. "You again. Okay, I come. But I swear, last time. No more Saturdays, yes?"

"Yes! Yes, okay. Just this time."

Eddie hung up on her. Claire bit her lip, slipped the note from Amelie into her bag, and hoped Michael had been serious about going to bed. Because if he'd eavesdropped on her, even by accident, she was going to have a lot of explaining to do.

It took five minutes for Eddie to arrive. She waited on the sidewalk, and jumped in the back of the battered old cab—barely yellow, after so much sun exposure—and handed Eddie all the cash she had. He counted it. Twice.

Then he grunted and flipped the handle on the taxi meter. "Address?"

"Katherine Day's house." One thing Claire had learned about riding with Eddie—you didn't need numbers, only names. He knew everybody, and he knew where everybody lived. All the natives, anyway. The students, he just dropped on campus and forgot.

Eddie threw an arm over the back of his seat and frowned at her. He was a big guy, with a lot of wild dark hair, including a beard. She could barely see his eyes when he frowned, which was pretty much always. "The Day House. You're sure."

"I'm sure."

"Told you I'm not staying, right?"

"Eddie, *please!*"

"Your funeral," he said, and hit the gas hard enough to press her back into the cushions.

TWELVE

Myrnin's shack was easy enough to get into—the trick, after all, wasn't getting in. It was getting out. Light slashed in thin ribbons through the darkness where the boards didn't quite meet, but it wasn't exactly easy to see, and she didn't much like roaming around in Myrnin's lair in the dark. Or even half dark. She found a flashlight on the shelf near the door and thumbed it on. A pure white circle of light brushed across the dusty floor and showed her the narrow steps at the back that led down.

She went very slowly. Very carefully. "Myrnin?" She said it quietly, because he'd hear her; he'd told her that his ears were sensitive because of the silence and his lack of company.

He didn't answer.

"Myrnin?" Claire could see the hard edge of light at the bottom of the steps. He had everything on, it looked like—the light had a funny color, a mixture of fluorescent bulbs and oil lamps, candles and incandescents. "Myrnin, it's Claire. Where are you?"

She almost missed him, because he was so still. Myrnin was usually in motion of some kind—moving fast, like a hummingbird, from one bright attraction to the next. But what was standing in the center of the room looked like Myrnin—only completely still. Vampires did breathe, a little; the blood they took from humans needed oxygen, Claire had figured out, although a lot less than in a normal person. But his chest was still, his eyes were open and staring, and he wasn't moving at all. Not even to look at her. His attention was focused somewhere off to the side.

"Myrnin?" She put her bag down slowly. "It's Claire. Can you hear me?"

His chest rose just a fraction, and he whispered, "Get out. Go."

And tears slid out of his wide, staring eyes to run down his pale cheeks.

"What is it? What's wrong?" She forgot about caution, and moved toward him. "Myrnin, please tell me what's wrong!"

"You," he said. "This is wrong."

And then he just—collapsed. Dropped like his knees had given out, and the rest of him followed. It wasn't a graceful fall, and it would have hurt a normal human, maybe badly. Myrnin's head hit the floor with a solid crack, and Claire crouched down next to him and put her hand on his chest—not sure what she was doing, what she was supposed to be feeling for. Not his pulse—vampires didn't have one, at least not that humans could detect. She knew that from leaning against Michael.

"I can't do this," Myrnin said. His cold hand flashed out and grabbed hold of her arm, hard enough to bruise. "Why are you here? You weren't supposed to come!"

"What are you talking about?" Claire tried to pull free, but she might as well have been pulling against a bridge cable. Myrnin could snap her bones, if he wanted. Or even if he got careless. "Myrnin, you're hurting me. Please—"

"*Why?*" He shook her, and she could see the panic in his eyes. That made her take a deep breath and forget the ache where he was holding her. "You weren't supposed to come back!"

"Amelie sent me a note. She said I had only two days to learn—"

Myrnin groaned and let her go. He covered his eyes with his hands, dry-scrubbed his face, and said, "Help me up." Claire put a hand under his arm and managed to get him upright, leaning against a solid lab cabinet that seemed like it was bolted to the floor. "Let me see the note."

She went back to the stairs, grabbed her backpack, and produced the note. Myrnin unfolded it in shaking hands and looked at it intently.

"What? Is it a fake?"

"No," he said slowly. "She sent you to me." He dropped the note in his lap, as if it had gotten unbearably heavy, and rested his head against the hard surface of the lab cabinet. "She's lost hope, then. She's acting out of fear and panic. That isn't like her."

"I don't understand!"

"That's exactly the problem," Myrnin said. "You don't. And you won't, child. I explained this to her before—even the brightest human can't learn this quickly. And you are so very young." He sounded tired and very sad. "Now we come to the last of it, Claire. Think it through: Amelie sent you to me, knowing that I do not believe you are the solution to my problems. *Why would she do that?* You know what I am, what I do, what I crave. Why would she put you in front of me if she didn't want me to—to—" He seemed to be begging her to understand, but he wasn't making any sense. "You don't know what she is capable of doing, child. *You don't know!*"

There was so much fear in his voice, and in his face, that she felt a real sense of dread. "If she didn't want you to teach me, why did she send me?"

"The question is, why—after being so careful to provide you with escorts—would she send you to me *alone*?"

"I—" She stopped, remembering. "Sam said to ask you about the others. The other apprentices. He said I wasn't the first—"

"Samuel is quite intelligent," Myrnin said, and squeezed his eyes tightly shut. "You glow, you glow like the finest lamp. So much possibility in you. Yes, there have been others Amelie sent to learn. Vampires and humans. I killed the first one almost by accident, you must understand, but the effect—you see, the more intelligent the mind, the longer my clarity lasts, or so we thought at first. The first bought me almost a year without attacks. The second . . . mere months, and so on, in ever-decreasing cycles as my disease grew worse."

"She sent me here to die," Claire said. "She wants you to kill me."

"Yes," Myrnin said. "Clever, isn't she? She understands my desperation so well. And you do glow so brightly, Claire. The temptation is al-most—" He shook his head violently, as if trying to throw something out of his mind. "Listen to me. She seeks to fend off the inevitable, but I can't accept this trade. Your life is so fragile, just beginning; I can't steal it away for half a day, or an hour. It's no use."

"But—I thought you said I could learn—"

He sighed. "I wanted to believe, but it isn't possible. Yes, I could teach you—but you'd be nothing more than a gifted mimic, a mechanic, not an engineer. There are things you cannot do, Claire, not for years at best. I'm sorry."

Myrnin was saying that she was stupid, and Claire felt a hot, strange spark of anger. "Let go of my arm!" she snapped, and he was surprised enough that some of the blankness in his dark eyes went away, replaced with concern. He slowly relaxed his fingers. "Explain it to me. You're not all-knowing; maybe you forgot something."

Myrnin smiled, but it was a shadow of his usual manic grin. "I assure you, I probably have," he agreed. "But, Claire, attend: already, my muscles disobey me. Soon I won't be able to walk, and then my voice will lock in my throat. And then blindness, and madness, and I will end my days locked in a black, dark place, screaming silently as I starve. If there were any shred of hope that I could avoid that fate, don't you think I would seize it?"

He said it so . . . calmly. As if it had already happened. "No," Claire said. She couldn't help it. "No, that isn't going to happen." She'd some-how thought that he'd just . . . fade away. Without pain. But this kind of torture—he didn't deserve it. Not even Oliver deserved to have this creeping up on him. "How— Do you know what causes it?"

Myrnin smiled, but the smile looked bitter. "I thought I did, once. Amelie knows much of what I've forgotten, but you may find your clues in the notebooks. I was cautious, of course, but if you look closely, you may find my theories. In any case, it no longer matters. I can feel myself slipping into the black. There's no return."

"How do you *know*?"

"I've seen it happen. It's always the same. Amelie will lock me away because she'll have no choice; she must try to keep the secret, and it will take me a very long time to die, because I am so very old." He shook his head. "Doesn't matter. Not now. All that matters is that you go home, child, and never come back. I can't imagine I would have the unexpected strength of will to refuse such a lovely warm gift twice."

It was stupid. She didn't like Myrnin, she *couldn't*. He was scary and strange and he'd tried to kill her not just once, but at least twice.

So why did she feel like she wanted to cry?

"What if we use the crystals?" she blurted. Myrnin's eyes narrowed. "I learned, when you had me take them. What if we use them now? Both of us? Would that help?"

He was already shaking his head. "Claire, it's a fool's quest. Even if we continue research on the cure, there's not enough time—"

"The cure to your disease!" She felt a sudden surge of hope as she dug through her backpack and came up with the shaker of crystals. "Isn't this what you've done so far?"

"It is. Clever of you to discover that. But the point is, it's taken years to develop it, and it's at best only a temporary measure. Even a large dose will wear off in a few hours for either one of us, and the consequences for you . . ."

"But if we can come up with a cure, a real cure?"

"It's naive to think that we could perfect such a thing in mere hours. No, I think you had better go. I have been quite noble today. You really should let me enjoy it while I can." He looked at the shaker in her hands, and for a second she thought she saw a spark of that quick interest that had driven him so hard in earlier meetings. "Perhaps—if I show you the research, you could carry that part of it onward. For the others."

"Sam said you were all sick. Even Amelie."

Myrnin nodded. "As I am, so shall they all be. Every vampire who lives will suffer this in the next ten years, unless it is stopped."

Ten years! No. Not Michael.

She couldn't stand by without trying to stop it, at least for him.

"Amelie brought us to Morganville to buy us time, to find a way to ensure our survival. She believed—she believed that humans might hold the keys to this plague, and she also believed that we could no longer afford to live as we had, preying in the night or hiding. She thought that humans and vampires could live in cooperation, and find the solution to our illness together. That quickly became impossible, of course; she realized, after telling the first few vampires, that they would go mad knowing what was to come, that they would kill indiscriminately. So it became a secret, a terrible secret. She told them part of the truth, that she was seeking a cure to what makes us sterile. Never the rest."

"So—Morganville's a kind of lab. She's trying to find a cure, and protect all of you at the same time."

"Exactly so." Myrnin rubbed his hands over his face again. "I'm getting tired, Claire. Best give me the crystals."

She poured out a few in his hand. He met her eyes. "More," he said. "The disease has advanced. I will need a large dose to stay with you, even for a while."

She poured about a teaspoon out. Myrnin popped it into his mouth, made a face at the bitterness, and swallowed. A shudder went through him, and she actually saw the weariness and confusion fade. "Excellent. That really was an amazing discovery. Too bad about the doctor; really, he was very bright." Oh dear. Myrnin was swinging toward the manic now, thanks to the drugs. That was dangerous. "You're very bright. Perhaps you could read through the notes."

"I—I'm just *now* starting advanced biochemistry—"

"Nonsense, your native ability is clear." He pointed toward the shaker of crystals in her hand. "Take it."

"No. It's your medicine, not mine."

"And it will help you keep up with me, because we have very little time, Claire, very little." His eyes were bright and clear, like a bird's, and with about as much affection. "There are two ways you can assist me. You can take the crystals, or you can help me extend this period of clarity in other ways."

She sat back on her heels. "You said you wouldn't."

"Indeed. But you see, the disease makes me a sentimental fool. If I am to find an heir to my knowledge, *and* find a cure for my people, then

I can't be burdened with such considerations." His gaze brushed over her, abstract and hungry. "You burn so very brightly, you know."

"Yeah," she muttered. "You said." She hated this. She hated that Myrnin could change like this, go from friend to enemy in the space of a minute. Which one was real? Or was any of it?

Claire shook half a teaspoon of the crystals into her palm.

"More," Myrnin said. She added a couple, and he reached out, took the shaker, and poured a heaping mound of it into her hand. "You have a great deal to learn, and you are operating from such a disadvantage. Better safe than sorry."

She didn't want to take it—well, she did, a little, because the strawberry smell of the crystals brought back flashes of the way the world had looked: diamond clear, uncomplicated, *simple.*

Hard not to want that.

Myrnin said, "Take it, or I will have to take you, Claire. We have no more moves on our chessboard."

She poured the crystals onto her tongue and almost gagged from the bitterness. The strawberry flavor was overwhelmed by it, and the aftertaste was rotten and cold on her tongue, and she thought for a second she might throw up. . . .

And then everything snapped into hot, sharp, *perfect* focus.

Myrnin no longer looked strange and pathetic; he was a burning pillar of energy barely contained by skin. She could see that he was sick, somehow; there was a darkness in him, like rot at the heart of a tree. The room took on a fey glitter. *Neurotransmitters,* she thought. Her brain was rushing a million miles an hour, making her giddy and breathless. *My reaction time must be ten times faster.*

Myrnin bounded up to his feet, grabbed her hand, and dragged her to the shelves, where he began frantically pulling down books. Notebooks, textbooks, scraps of handwritten paper. Two black-bound composition books, the same kind Claire used in lab class. Even a couple of the cheap blue books she used for essay tests. Everything was crammed with fine, perfect handwriting.

"Read," he said. "Hurry."

All she had to do was flip pages. Her eyes captured things, like cameras, and her brain was so fast and efficient that she translated and comprehended the text almost instantly. Nearly two hundred pages, and she paged through as fast as her fingers could go.

"Well?" Myrnin demanded.

"This is wrong," she said, and flipped back to the first third of the notebook. "Right here. See? The formula's wrong. The variable doesn't match up with the prior version, and the error gets replicated going forward—"

Myrnin gave out a fierce, sharp cry, like a hunting hawk, and snatched the book away from her. "Yes! Yes, I see it! That fool. No wonder he sustained me only for a few days. But you, Claire, oh, you are different."

She knew she ought to be afraid of the slow, predatory smile he gave her, but she couldn't help it.

She smiled back.

"Give me the next one," she said. "And let's start making crystals."

When it wore off, it hit Myrnin first. He took more, but she could see it wasn't really working this time. Diminishing returns. That was why he'd only taken a few crystals last time, to prolong the effects even if the change hadn't been as dramatic.

This crash was like hitting a brick wall at ninety miles an hour.

It started when he lost his balance, caught himself, and knocked a tray off the lab table; he tried to catch it in midair, a feat he'd been more than capable of an hour before, and missed it completely. He stared at his hands in frustration and viciously kicked the tray. It sailed across the room and hit the far wall with a spectacular clatter.

Claire straightened up from spreading the crystals out on the drying tray. She could feel the effects, too—her brain was slowing down, her body aching. It had to be worse for Myrnin, because of the disease. *It was wrong to do this,* she thought. Wrong, because his manic phase always led to dementia, and he'd wanted so badly to be himself again.

But the crystals drying on the tray could change that, or at least, she hoped they could. It wasn't that Myrnin had been wrong, but that his last assistant had made mistakes; whether deliberate or not, Claire couldn't tell. But the crystals in the tray would be more effective, and longer lasting.

Myrnin could stabilize again.

"It isn't a cure," Myrnin said, as if he were reading her thoughts.

"No, but it buys you time," Claire said. "Look, I can come tomorrow. Promise me you'll leave these here, all right? Don't try to take them yet; they're not ready. And they're more powerful, so you'll have to start with a small dose and work up."

"Don't tell me what to do!" Myrnin barked. "Who is the master here? Who is the student?"

This was familiar, and dangerous. She lowered her head. "You're the master," she said. "I have to go now. I'm sorry. I'll come back tomorrow, okay?"

He didn't answer. His dark eyes were fixed on her, and she couldn't tell what he was thinking. Or even *if* he was thinking. He was right on the edge.

Claire took the shaker of the less effective crystals and stuffed it in her backpack—there wasn't that much left, but enough for one more dose for them both, and if he did something to the crystals during his manic phase, they might need it. She needed to ask Amelie for some kind of strongbox where she could store things. . . .

"Why?" Myrnin asked. She looked up at him, frowning. "Why are you helping us? Isn't it better for humans if we waste away and die? By helping me, you help all vampires."

Claire knew what Shane would have done. He'd have walked away, considered it a win all around. Eve might have done the same thing, except for Michael.

And she . . . she was helping. *Helping.* She couldn't even really explain why, except that it seemed wrong to turn away. They weren't all bad, and she couldn't sacrifice people like Sam and Michael for the greater good.

"I know," Claire said. "Believe me, I'm not happy about it."

"You do it because you're afraid," he said.

"No. I do it because you need it."

He just stared at her, as if he couldn't figure out what she was saying. Time to go. She shivered, shouldered her backpack, and hurried for the stairs. She kept looking behind, but she never saw Myrnin move. . . . Even so, he was in a different place, closer, every time she looked. It was like a child's game, only deadly serious. He wouldn't move while she was looking at him.

Claire turned and walked backward, staring at him. Myrnin chuckled, and the sound echoed through the room like the rustle of bat wings.

When her heels hit the steps, she turned and ran.

He could have caught her, but he didn't. She burst through the doors of the shack into the alley, breathing hard, sweating, shaking.

He didn't follow. She didn't think he could, past the steps. She wasn't sure why—maybe the same way that Morganville itself kept people in town, or wiped their memories, kept Myrnin confined in his bottle.

She felt the hair on the back of her neck stir, and then she heard a voice. Whispering and indistinct. Shane? What was Shane doing here?

He was inside. He was inside and he was in trouble; she had to go to him. . . .

Claire found herself reaching for the door to the shack before she knew what she was doing.

"Myrnin, stop it!" she gasped and pulled away. She turned and ran down the alley toward the relative safety of the street.

It was only when she got there that she saw it was already nightfall.

Eddie wouldn't come for her after dark, and she was a long way from home. Too far to walk.

Claire was about to dial Michael at home when she spotted a police car cruising slowly down the cul-de-sac. Not a vampire squad car—this one had only light tinting on the front windows, although the back was blacked out. Claire squinted against the harsh brightness and waved. The effects of the crystals were ebbing fast, and she felt clumsy, strange, and exhausted. All she wanted to do was sleep. She'd have taken a ride with Satan in his big red handbasket if it had helped her get off her feet for a few minutes.

The cruiser pulled to a stop, and the passenger-side window rolled down. Claire bent over to look inside.

Officer Fenton. "You shouldn't be out by yourself," he said. "You know better. Everybody's looking for you. Your friends called you in as missing."

"Oh," she said. That hadn't even occurred to her. She hadn't realized how long she'd been away. "I just—can I get a ride home? Please?"

He shrugged. "Hop in." She did, gratefully, and buckled herself in. Everything ached now—her head, her eyes, every muscle in her body. And she had the feeling it was going to get worse before it got better. "Speaking of your friends, how are they? Heard about that thing with Shane. Damn shame."

"He'll be okay," she said.

"And the other one? Michael?"

"Yeah, he's fine," she said. "Why?"

"Just checking. Probably good to keep an eye on him, since he was the target of the hit in the first place," Fenton said. He turned the patrol car in a slow, crunching circle and headed back out, away from the alley. "Since the guy was looking for him, specifically."

Claire's head hurt too much for conversation. "I guess," she agreed faintly. And then some last flash of cognitive clarity put together strings of chemicals, and she felt her heartbeat jump and hammer harder. "How did you know that?"

"What?"

"I mean, about Sam not being the real target? He was unconscious when you found him. He couldn't have said anything."

"Unconscious, crap. He was dead."

"But anyway, he couldn't have said—" Things clicked into place, and the pattern looked bad. Very bad. "You were there before the sirens."

"What are you talking about?"

"When we first looked out, we saw you parked behind Sam's car and we just thought you'd found him there. But you didn't just find him lying in the street—"

Officer Fenton pressed the gas pedal, and the cruiser shot forward at a high rate of speed. He turned on the lights. She heard the harsh clicking sound they made, and the night was flooded with flashes of blue and red strobes.

"Where are you taking me?"

"Shut up."

Claire put her hand on the door handle, but they were going so fast she knew she couldn't jump. She'd be badly hurt, at the very least. "If you hurt me, the Founder—"

"That's what we're counting on," Fenton sneered. "Shut up."

Shane would have totally gotten off on the whole vampire-killer-secret-society thing. Claire just wanted to go home. Badly.

In addition to Officer Fenton, the group that gathered in the shed behind the photo processing store included Fenton's wife, the unpleasant nurse who treated Claire as though she were carrying some totally disgusting disease. She even wore latex gloves to tie Claire to the chair.

Claire barely recognized the others. One was a maintenance worker from the university; she'd seen him a few times. One was a bank teller. One was the smooth-faced, unremarkable guy who'd delivered Amelie's note to her that afternoon. He'd killed her courier, Claire found out. He spent a lot of time tracking down who worked for Amelie and trying to find out where she stayed.

He was the one who leaned over into her space, hands braced on the arms of the chair, and said, "We don't much care for collaborators. Even little underage ones."

Claire's mouth felt foul and dry, and she was shaking now with the aftereffects of the crystals. Myrnin had been right: the consequences weren't going to be pleasant. "Captain Obvious, I presume," she said.

He laughed. He had nice, white teeth, no sign of vampire fangs. "Aren't you the clever one? Living up to your reputation, I see." He tapped a finger on her gold bracelet. "Not too many breathers have ever seen the Founder, much less become her pet. Sam Glass was the last one, before you. Did you know that? This is his bracelet you're wearing. Probably sized down a little, though."

She squirmed a little, but the ropes were too tight. "What do you want with me?"

"Leverage," said Officer Fenton. "Vamps seem to like you."

"Not all of them," Claire said. If they asked Oliver to come running to her rescue, it wasn't too likely he'd so much as yawn. "And if you think Amelie's going to sacrifice herself for me, you're crazy." Amelie had already sold her down the river, by sending her to Myrnin with the clear expectation that Myrnin would . . . eat her. The fact that he hadn't was just Claire's good luck. "In fact, I don't think any of them would raise a finger—"

"Michael Glass would," Captain Obvious said. "And he's the one we want. She knows that, of course. She's done everything she could to keep him away from us." He flipped open the phone and pressed something on speed dial. "Tell him where you are."

Claire glared. "No." She clamped her lips shut as she heard Michael's distant *hello* on the other end. *I'm not going to talk; I'm not going to make a sound. . . .*

The door at the back of the shed opened, and someone came in. Thin, greasy, dressed in a black leather jacket with a hole in the pocket. Crazy eyes. Fang marks on his neck.

Jason.

He took the phone from Captain Obvious. "Hey, Mikey. It's Jason. Just shut up and listen. I've got Claire, and I'm thinking about all the things I can do with her until you get here. Better hurry."

"No!" Claire blurted, and realized it was a mistake. She'd just confirmed that she was there, and now Michael wouldn't have any choice, would he? "Michael, *don't!*"

She could hear the sound of Michael's voice, but not what he was saying. Jason put the phone back to his ear and listened. "Yeah, that's right. You've got half an hour to show, or I'll bring her home in pieces. Oh, and it's not a trap; it's a business proposition. You walk in alone, you both walk out alive." Pause. "Where? Oh, come on, man. You know where. The captain's waiting."

He snapped the phone shut, tossed it in the air, and caught it, smiling. His eyes never left Claire.

Michael wouldn't do it. He just wouldn't be that stupid, right? But Shane was in the hospital. He didn't have anybody he could turn to for help except the other vampires, and they wouldn't lift a finger to save

Claire. She wasn't sure anymore that Amelie would bother, unless she was just saving her as Myrnin's midnight snack.

The door to the shed opened again, and both Captain Obvious and Jason turned to look.

Detective Travis Lowe stepped inside and closed the door, and for a second Claire felt a wild jolt of relief and satisfaction, but it faded just as quickly. Lowe looked at Jason and Captain Obvious as though he was expecting to find them there, and when his gaze moved to Claire, he didn't react except to seem angry and harassed.

Oh God. He was one of them. Whoever *them* might be.

"Could you screw this up any more?" he asked, low and vicious. "I told you, Glass isn't important. We don't need to do this."

"He's the youngest. He's a symbol, man," Captain Obvious said. "And he was one of us. He's a traitor."

One of us? Did he mean—no, he couldn't mean that. He couldn't mean that Michael *knew* these people, that he'd been part of this skanky little conspiracy . . . but Jason had acted as though Michael knew where they were.

Nurse Fenton destroyed that hope by saying, "We've already been over this. Michael knows too much. If he decides to talk, we're all dead. We can't take the risk. Not anymore." She shot her husband a dark look. "If you hadn't screwed up—"

"Don't blame me! Vampire car pulling out of the vampire's house, how was I supposed to know it wasn't him?"

Of course. No wonder that had bothered her all along—the house had woken all of them up not because of the threat to Sam, but the threat to Michael, its owner. Even though Michael wasn't there, it was reacting to intent.

Officer Fenton hadn't been the first man on the scene; he'd been the one who staked Sam and left him to die, then pretended to be Johnny-on-the-spot. If Richard Morrell hadn't shown up to scoop and run, he would have succeeded.

Claire swallowed hard and focused on Detective Lowe. "I thought you were a good guy."

Something weary and painful passed across his face. "Claire——" He shook his head. "It's not as simple as that. Not in Morganville. You don't just get to be one thing around here."

"It's not his fault," Jason said, and grinned like a wolf. "If he wants his partner back, he's not going to do anything stupid."

Detective Hess. They had him. No wonder she hadn't seen him for days—and no wonder Lowe had been acting weird. She looked more closely at Officer Fenton, and found he had a dark bruise on his left cheek that matched the scrapes on Detective Lowe's knuckles. He'd been in the house, maybe with Detective Hess, and Lowe had taken a swing at him.

Lowe's eyes were dark and full of misery, and he looked away from Claire. "The kid has nothing to do with this," he said.

"The *kid* hangs with the top-shelf vampires," Nurse Fenton shot back. "How many humans do you know with access to the Founder? She doesn't even let her own kind get close! Of *course* she's got something to do with this. Probably a lot more than you know."

Truer than Nurse Fenton knew. Claire thought about what she'd learned from Myrnin—the vampire sickness, the wormhole doorways through town, the network of Founder Houses—and realized that she knew enough to destroy Morganville.

She did her best to look scared and clueless. The first part, at least, wasn't much of a stretch.

When Jason sauntered over and put his hand on Claire's shoulder, she flinched. He smelled like a garbage heap in the summer, and she caught a lingering hint of blood from his coat. *He stabbed Shane.* And he'd smiled about it, too.

"Get your hands off me," she said, and turned to stare right at him. "I'm not afraid of you."

Lowe grabbed Jason by the arm, swung him around, and slammed him face-first into the rough wooden wall of the shed. "Me neither," he growled. "And I'm not tied to a chair. Leave her alone."

"Big hero," Nurse Fenton said bitterly. "You and Hess, you're both pathetic."

"Am I?" Lowe twisted Jason's arm painfully high. "I'm not the one raping and killing girls for fun."

"Jason's not the one doing it, either," Fenton said. "He just likes to talk about it."

Claire said, "Then how'd he know about the one in our basement?"

They all looked at her. "I never saw a report about any body in your house," Lowe said. "Just the one in the alley."

Jason laughed, a dry crack of sound. "They moved it. Hey, Claire, you ever think that maybe it wasn't me? Maybe it was one of your two boyfriends *inside* the house. Shane, he ain't too stable, you know. And who knows about Michael these days?"

She wanted to scream at him, but she saved her strength. She had thin wrists, and Captain Obvious hadn't done a very good job of tying her; she could feel a little give in the ropes, and she wouldn't need much slack to slip at least one hand free. The rough surface of the rope sawed at her skin, but she kept pulling, trying not to make it too obvious, and felt a sudden sharp pain in her wrist as the cut Jason had given her broke open again, sending a slow trickle of blood down her wrist.

It helped, along with the sweat running down her arms. She coughed, and at the same time pulled, and her right hand slipped free of the ropes with a fiery scrape. She kept it behind her back and started working on the knot holding her left hand to the crossbar of the chair.

"So what are you?" she asked, to fill the silence and keep them from noticing what she was doing. "Vampire hunters?"

"Something like that," Officer Fenton said.

"Not that I've noticed," Claire sniffed. "Shane's dad blew into town and killed all the vampires that I know about. What have *you* done?"

"Shut up," Nurse Fenton said flatly. "You've been here months, if that. You have no idea what this town is like to live in. When we're ready, we'll act. Frank Collins had the right idea, but he wasn't much of a planner."

"So you're planning a revolution," Claire said. "Not just random attacks."

"Would you *stop* telling the prisoner our plans?" Captain Obvious snapped. "Jesus, don't you watch movies? Just shut up!"

"She's not going to tell anybody," Officer Fenton said, in such an off-hand way that Claire's heart sank.

They didn't intend to keep any promises to Michael. No way were they letting Michael, or her, walk out of here alive.

Don't do it, Michael. Don't come for me.

But fifteen minutes later, the door burst open and a vampire rushed in, wrapped in a heavy blanket. The greasy smell of cooking flesh filled the shed, and then the vampire kicked the door closed and collapsed against it, gasping. Smoke rose up from him in a thick, choking cloud. In a few places, Claire could see blackened skin beneath the covering.

"About time," Fenton growled. Then he picked up a black stick from a crate next to him and drove it into the vampire's chest. For a second Claire thought that it was a stake, but then she saw sparks, and the vampire went down in a tangle of blankets and smoke.

He'd been Tasered.

Captain Obvious brought out a wooden stake and rolled the vampire over. Claire screamed. Somehow, she'd been avoiding thinking of him as *Michael,* but the flash of golden hair and the pale shape of his face were unmistakable.

His blue eyes were open, but he couldn't move. There were burned patches on his hands and arms, but he was alive. . . .

Captain Obvious positioned the stake.

Claire lurched to her feet and spun to her right. Her left hand was still tied to the crossbar of the chair, but the momentum helped her swing it with bone-breaking force right into Captain Obvious's back. He crumpled against the wall. Claire grabbed the chair in both hands and used it as a shield as Officer Fenton jabbed the Taser at her, knocking it aside, and managed to hit him in the gut with at least one of the chair's legs as she screamed for help. He stumbled backward.

Travis Lowe cursed and flicked handcuffs onto Jason's wrists. "Sit," he ordered, and pulled his gun. He looked strained and grim, but determined. "Back up, Fenton. You too, Christine. Turn and face the wall."

"You can't do this," Officer Fenton said. "Trav, if you cross us—"

"I know. You'll get me. I'll try not to pee all over myself in terror."

Lowe nodded to Claire, who was undoing the last of the knots holding the chair to her left hand. "Put the cuffs on them. I'll cover you." He tossed her an extra two sets, and she fumbled the unfamiliar weight in her numbed fingers. As she bent to pick them up, Captain Obvious—down, not out—reached over Michael's still body, grabbed her foot, and yanked. Claire cried out and fell, and Captain Obvious dragged her backward.

Lowe spun, aiming his gun, but it was too late. Captain Obvious had a knife, a big, wicked thing, and he put it to Claire's throat, right under her chin. It felt cold, then hot as it pressed into the tender skin. "Put it down, Jeff," Lowe barked. He took a threatening step forward. "I mean it; I will put you down."

He got Tasered in the back. Claire watched him convulse and fall, and felt panic well up inside. *They'll kill us now. All three of us.* Four, counting Joe Hess, who was being held prisoner somewhere else.

She heard a sharp, loud crack, and a pale strong hand exploded through the boards beside Captain Obvious's head, grabbed him, and pulled. The entire section of boards broke away, and Captain Obvious was yanked backward. Claire felt the knife slide along her neck, but it didn't have any force behind it. He dropped it, flailing for balance, and then he was outside in the bright, dusty sunlight, and there was a dry snapping sound.

Dressed in a black leather trench coat, a black broad-brimmed hat, and black gloves, Oliver stepped into the shed. He gave them all a vampire smile.

"Well, that was refreshing," he said. He reached down and pulled Michael up to a sitting position next to Claire, then stepped in front of them.

"Could've come sooner," Michael whispered. He was shaking all over, but he was coming out of his paralysis. Claire hugged him. He fumbled in his pocket, came up with a handkerchief, and pressed it to Claire's neck. She hadn't even realized she was bleeding.

Oliver ignored them and walked toward the Fentons, who tried to get to the door. He flashed ahead of them with that easy snakelike speed vampires could display when they wanted, and Claire shuddered at the looks on their faces.

They knew what was going to happen to them.

"Don't worry," Oliver said. "There'll be a fair trial. Since Samuel didn't die, and you didn't succeed today, you won't burn for what you've done." He reached for Christine Fenton's wrist, ripped her sleeve, and exposed her silver bracelet. It fit tightly around her wrist, but he slid a finger underneath the metal and it split along an invisible seam. He dropped the bracelet in his pocket, then did the same to Officer Fenton.

The places where their bracelets had been were sickly pale, and Christine kept rubbing hers, as if the shock of open air on the skin was painful.

"Congratulations," Oliver said. "I release you from your contracts."

And then he grabbed Christine. Claire had a glimpse of his fangs flashing down, silvery and sharp, and then he slammed the woman against the wall of the shed and bit.

Claire hid her face against Michael's chest. He put his hand on her hair and held her there, turned away from the sight of Christine Fenton dying.

She heard the woman's body hit the floor and then Oliver, his voice thick and dark, say, "Your turn now."

A sharp, snapping sound, and another body hit the floor.

When Michael let her go, Claire didn't look at the bodies. She couldn't.

She looked at Oliver, who was staring down at Travis Lowe. The detective was just starting to stir. "What about this one?" he asked. "Friend or foe?"

He wasn't waiting for an answer. He grabbed Lowe by the collar and lifted him off the ground.

"Friend! Friend!" Claire blurted frantically, and saw Lowe's eyes close in relief. "His partner's missing. I think they were holding him somewhere."

Oliver shrugged, clearly not interested. He dropped Lowe back to the ground and turned a slow circle. "There was another one," he said. "Where is he?" He pulled in a deep breath, then let it out with a disgusted cough. "Jason. Well, well."

Sometime while Oliver had been busy killing the Fentons, Jason had escaped out the door, and Michael hadn't stopped him. Maybe too weak, maybe just worried for Claire. But anyway, Jason was long gone.

"I'll find him," Oliver said. "I've been tolerant, so long as he didn't threaten our interests, but enough." He glanced down at Michael and Claire. "Go home." He stalked away, out into the sun, without a backward glance. Three dead bodies, and he didn't even pause.

Travis Lowe managed to pull himself to a sitting position, groaning, and rested his head in his hands. "I hate Tasers." He looked up and fixed his bloodshot gaze on Claire. "You're okay? Let me see your throat."

She moved the handkerchief. There was just a thin smear on the cloth. Her wrist was worse; she tied the cloth around it as a makeshift bandage and thought, *I'm going to have to buy Michael some new ones.* Though why she thought of that now, she had no idea. Maybe she just wanted to imagine normal life.

Because this definitely wasn't normal.

Michael stood up and helped Claire to her feet, then Lowe. He pulled keys from his pocket and tossed them to Lowe. "Pull the car in with the trunk facing the door," he said. "Open it and honk when you're ready."

Lowe nodded and went outside, into the blinding sun. Michael put both hands on Claire's shoulders and looked down at her, then cupped her cheeks in his palms.

"Don't do that again," he said.

"I didn't do *anything.* I got a ride from a cop, that was all—"

"Not that," he said. "Myrnin. Don't do it again. You can't go back. He'll kill you next time."

He knew where she'd been. Well, she supposed it hadn't been hard to figure out.

"You shouldn't have come," she said. "You knew it was a trap; what are you, crazy?"

"I called Oliver," Michael said.

"You didn't!"

"It worked, didn't it?"

She looked around at the dead people in the shed. "Yeah."

He looked ill for a second and started to say something, but then the horn honked outside, and he changed it to, "Ride's here."

She nodded, and walked out into the dazzling glare. Something brushed by her, moving fast, and then the trunk of the sedan slammed closed before she'd taken more than two steps.

Claire trudged to the passenger side of the car. Exhausted and aching, and feeling a stupid need to cry, she said nothing at all on the ride home.

THIRTEEN

Joe Hess was in the run-down house on Spring Street, locked in a closet, filthy, with a broken arm and two broken ribs—Lowe had called with the news of his rescue two hours later. Claire tried to be happy, but the crash that had started for her before she left Myrnin's just kept driving her down. She felt sick and weak and hollow, and she couldn't even summon the energy to go to the hospital to see Shane. Michael told Eve that she was sick, which wasn't much of a lie; Claire stayed in bed, shivering, wrapped in layers of blankets even though the room was warm. Everything kept shifting in her head, from dull gray fog to glittering icy clarity, and she didn't know how long it was going to last. She developed a knife-sharp headache sometime during the night, and by the time she finally slept, it was nearly morning.

Her cell phone rang at two p.m. on Sunday. She'd gotten up to visit the bathroom and grab a bottle of water, but no food, and her whole body felt weak and abused. "Where are you?" the voice on the other end demanded. Claire squinted at the clock and scrubbed a hand through her matted, oily hair.

"Who is it?"

A sigh rattled the speaker. "It's Jennifer, idiot. I'm waiting at Common Grounds. Are you going to show or what?"

"No," she said, and then tried again. "I'm sick."

"Look, I don't care if you're dying; I've got a midterm tomorrow for half my grade! Get your ass down here *now!*"

Jennifer hung up. Claire threw the phone down on the nightstand with a clatter and sat—or fell—onto the bed. *I can't. I just want to sleep, that's all.*

Someone rapped gently on the door, and then it creaked open. Eve was standing there, with a cracked, much-abused plastic tray in her hands. On it was a frosty glass of Coke, still fizzing, a sandwich, and a cookie.

And a red rose.

"Eat," she said, and slid the trap onto Claire's lap. "Man, that's one hell of a hangover."

"Hangover?" Claire looked at her oddly, and sipped the Coke. It went down sweet and cool, and that helped. "I'm not hungover."

Eve just shook her head. "Been there, CB. Trust me on this. Eat, shower, you'll feel better."

Claire nodded. She did feel a spark of hunger, distant as it was, and managed to take two bites of the sandwich before weariness overtook her again. She tried the cookie in between.

The shower felt like heaven, and Eve was right about that, too; when she finally got dressed and finished half the sandwich she felt almost alive.

Her cell phone rang again. Jennifer. Claire didn't even let her get started yelling and threatening. "Ten minutes," she said, and hung up. She didn't want to go, but staying in bed didn't seem to be doing much for her. She took the tray downstairs, washed up, and grabbed her backpack on the way out.

"Where the *hell* do you think you're going?"

Michael. He was standing in the hallway, blocking the door, looking like he was guarding the gates of heaven itself. His hands looked raw and pink—still healing from the burns. She thought about that, about how important his hands were to him, because of the music, and felt a sharp stab of guilt.

"I'm meeting Jennifer at Common Grounds," she said. "Tutoring. For money."

"Well, you're not walking, and I can't take you until dark."

"I can," Eve offered. She joined Claire in the hall. "I need to go into work, anyway. Kim didn't show again; they called a little while ago. Hey, overtime pay. Gotta love it. Maybe we can afford tacos."

Michael looked exasperated, but it wasn't as though there were a lot of choices. He nodded and stepped out of the way. Eve stretched up on her toes to kiss him, and that went on for a while before Claire cleared her throat, checked her watch, and got her moving to the car.

It was a short ride to Common Grounds, but not exactly a comfortable one, because the first thing Eve said was, "Is it true? Oliver killed the Fentons and Captain Obvious?"

Claire didn't want to talk about it, but she nodded.

"And Michael? Michael was there?"

Again, the nod. Claire looked out the window.

"He got hurt. I saw the burns." This time she didn't even try to answer. Eve let the silence stretch for a few seconds, then said, "Don't shut me out, Claire. The four of us, we're all we've got."

Except that what Claire had couldn't be shared. Not with Michael, not with Eve, and certainly not with Shane.

She was alone, carrying an ugly weight of knowledge she didn't want and couldn't use. And every time she thought about Oliver's icy smile, about him ripping out Christine Fenton's throat, she felt sick. *I'm helping him, if I keep working for Myrnin and Amelie.* But she was also helping Michael. Sam. Myrnin.

Eve seemed to sense it wasn't time to push; she pulled to a stop in front of the coffee shop and said, "Stay inside until dark; Michael will come get you."

"I'm going to see Shane," Claire said. "But I'll get a ride home."

"Claire, dammit—" Eve sighed. "I can't stop you. But if you wait, you and Michael can go together. I'll see you guys tonight. Tacos for dinner, right?"

Nothing sounded very exciting to her right now, but Claire nodded. She got out and walked into Common Grounds, which was a sea of noise and conversation—packed, as always, with college students and a few locals. She was getting used to picking out the gleam of ID bracelets.

Jennifer was sitting at the same table Monica favored, sipping a drink that Claire bet was the same thing Monica always had, wearing an outfit that was probably Monica's hand-me-downs, or at least copied from the same designers. She looked angry and scowled at Claire as Claire dropped her backpack on the floor and slid into her chair. "You look like crap," Jennifer said. "Sick sick, or hungover?"

"Does it matter?"

"Hungover," Jennifer said, and grinned. "And here I thought you were all underage Goody Two-shoes."

The smell of coffee was making her feel queasy, but Claire went to the counter and ordered a mocha anyway. Oliver wasn't on duty, and she didn't know the two working as baristas.

When she turned around, somebody else was sitting at Jennifer's table in the previously empty third chair.

Monica.

Crap. I can't deal with her. Not now. She felt horrible, and the last thing she wanted to do was match wits with the witch queen.

Monica gave her the X-ray scan, looked at Jennifer, and did an over-the-top hand to the forehead. "I thought the homeless look died in the nineties."

"Shut up." Claire slid into her chair, mocha in hand. "I'm tutoring Jennifer, not you."

"Bitch, I wouldn't *let* you tutor me. You'd probably give me all the wrong answers."

Which was a totally good idea, and Claire saw the fear flash into Jennifer's expression. She sighed. "I wouldn't," she said.

"Why not?"

"Because—because this matters. School." They both looked at Claire as though she were a lunatic. "Never mind. I just wouldn't. You want my help or not?"

Jennifer nodded. Claire reached for her notebook and flipped to the notes she'd taken in Economics, and started explaining. Jennifer was trying, at least; Monica kept sighing and fidgeting, but Jennifer seemed to be kind of following along. She even got a couple of the formulas right, when Claire pop-quizzed her. It took about an hour to get her to the level of a solid B, but that was good enough. Jennifer wasn't interested in A's, and Monica couldn't have cared less.

Claire's mocha was making her nauseated. She tossed the half-full cup and went to the bathroom. She picked up her backpack and brought it along; half out of an entirely reasonable expectation that Monica and/or Jennifer would do something mean if she left it at their mercy.

She was standing at the mirror staring at her sallow face with its raccoon-bruise eyes and pale lips when the second of clarity hit again, a flicker of unforgiving beauty in a world that seemed drowning in gray.

Maybe a little. Just to get through the day. There wasn't that much left, anyway.

She didn't let herself think. Her head was pounding, her mouth dry, her muscles aching, and she needed to feel better. Because right now, she didn't know if she could make it through the day.

She shook about ten measly crystals out into her palm. The strawberry scent teased her, and she shifted them around, watching the light glint on the sharp edges. It looked like candy.

It's a drug. She was finally admitting it to herself. *It's not even for you. It's for Myrnin. What are you doing? It's making you sick.*

But it would also make her well.

She was in the process of dumping the crystals in her mouth when Monica shoved open the bathroom door.

Claire swallowed and choked and quickly wiped her hand on her pants. She knew she looked guilty. Monica, who'd been heading for the stall, stopped and looked at her.

"What was that?" Monica asked.

"What was what?" Wrong answer, Claire knew it as soon as she said it. Why not, *aspirin for my hangover?* Or, *breath mints?* She was a terrible liar.

She couldn't help but drag in a shocked breath as the crystals raced their chemical message through her nerve endings, ice in every vein, and the whole world turned sharp and bright and—for the moment—painless.

And Monica was way too savvy. She looked at the hand Claire was convulsively rubbing against her blue jeans, then gave her the X-ray stare again, and slowly smiled. "Man, that must be good stuff. Your pupils just dilated like crazy." Monica edged up next to her and checked her makeup. "Where'd you get it?"

Claire said nothing. She reached for the shaker, which was sitting on the edge of the sink, but Monica got there first. She looked it over and shook a crystal out in her hand. "Cool. What is it?"

"Nothing. It's not for you."

Monica pulled the shaker back when she reached for it. "Oh, I think it is. Especially if you want it so bad."

Claire didn't think; she just acted. Her brain worked so fast that she moved in a blur, slamming Monica back against the wall, then twisting the silver can out of her hand. Monica didn't even have time to yell.

Monica straightened her clothes and tossed back her hair. There was a crazy light in her eyes, and a glow in her cheeks. She *liked* this.

"Oh, you stupid bitch," Monica breathed. "That was such a bad idea. So, it makes you faster. And I'm betting it's something from the vamps. That makes it *mine.*"

"No," Claire said. She'd screwed up, she knew that, but talking was only going to make it worse. She put the shaker in her backpack and zipped it up, shouldered the load, and turned to go.

Her hand was on the doorknob when Monica said, "Shane's still in ICU." There was something about the way she said it. . . . Claire turned slowly to face her. "That means he's not out of the woods yet. Funny thing, people can have all kinds of setbacks. Maybe he gets the wrong meds or something. That can kill you. They did a story about it on the news." Monica's smile was vicious. "I'd hate to see that happen."

Claire felt the wildest, coldest impulse that had ever come over her— she wanted to lunge for Monica, knock her head into the wall, rip her apart. She could *visualize* it. That was terrifying, and she pulled herself back with a snap into sanity.

"What do you want?" she said. Her voice wasn't quite steady.

Monica just held out her finely manicured hand, raised an eyebrow, and waited.

Claire put down her backpack, pulled out the shaker, and handed it over. "When that's gone, I don't have any more," she said. "I hope you choke on it."

Monica poured some of the red crystals into her palm. "How much? And don't be stupid. You OD me, and it's your neck, not mine."

"Don't do more than half of that," Claire said. Monica scraped half of the crystals off her palm, back into the container. It looked about right. Claire nodded.

Monica dumped it into her mouth, licked the residue from her palm, and Claire could tell the exact second that the chemicals hit her—her eyes went wide, and her pupils began to grow. And grow. It was eerie, and Claire felt her skin crawl as Monica began to shake. *This is what it looks like.* It looked awful.

"You're pretty." Monica sounded surprised. "It's all so clear now—"

And then her eyes rolled back in her head, and she fell down and started to convulse.

Claire screamed for help, jammed her backpack under Monica's head to keep her from knocking it against the tile floor, and tried to hold her down. Jennifer ran in and screamed, too, then came at Claire, swinging. Claire moved out of the way of the punch—it seemed slow to her—and shoved Jennifer out of the way. "I didn't do it!" she yelled. "She took something!"

Jennifer called 911.

This wasn't how Claire had intended to end up at the hospital. Worse, by the time they'd gotten there, Monica had stopped breathing, and the paramedics had to put a tube down her throat. They were hooking her up to machines now, and the mayor was coming, and half the cops in town were converging on it.

"I need to know what she took," the doctor was saying. Claire tried to look over his shoulder; she saw Richard Morrell coming through the parking lot doors. The doctor snapped his fingers in front of her face to get her attention. "Your pupils are dilated. You took something, too. What is it?"

Claire silently handed over the shaker. The doctor looked at the red crystals, frowned, and said, "Where did you get these?" He was wearing a bracelet, silver, with a symbol she didn't recognize. "Look, I'm not kidding. That girl is dying, and I need to know—"

"I can't tell you," she said. "Ask Amelie." She held up the bracelet. She felt numb. Even though she'd wanted to kill Monica, she hadn't really meant to *kill* her. Why had this happened? It was the same dose Claire had taken, and she knew the crystals weren't contaminated. . . .

The doctor gave her a look of cold contempt, and handed it to an orderly. "Lab," he said. "I need to know what this stuff is, right now. Tell them it's priority one."

The orderly left at a run.

"I want you in the lab, too," the doctor said, and grabbed a passing nurse. He rattled off tests, talking faster than even Claire's heightened brain could process, though the nurse just nodded. *Blood tests,* she thought. Claire went without complaint. It was better than waiting for Richard Morrell to hear that she'd poisoned his sister.

As soon as the nurse was finished drawing her blood, Claire went to ICU. Shane was awake, reading a book. He looked better, and his smile was warm and relieved. "Eve said you were sick," he said. "I figured maybe you were just sick of seeing me here."

Claire wanted to cry. She wanted to crawl into the bed with him and be wrapped in his arms and not have all this guilt and horror bearing down on her shoulders, just for a minute.

"What's wrong?" he asked. "Your eyes—"

"I made a mistake," she blurted. "I made a terrible mistake, and I don't know how to fix it. She's dying and I don't know how—"

"Dying?" Shane struggled to sit up. "Who? God, not Eve—"

"Monica. I gave her something, and she took it and she's dying." There were tears sliding cold down her cheeks, and she could feel every icy pinprick. "I have to do something. But I don't know what I can do."

Shane's eyes narrowed. "Claire, are you talking about drugs? You gave her drugs? Christ, what are you thinking?" He grabbed her hand. "Did you take something, too?"

She nodded miserably. "It doesn't hurt me, but it's killing her."

"You have to tell them. Tell them what you took. Do it now."

"I can't—it's—" She knew what it would mean, saying this. She already knew how it would change things between them. "I can't tell because it's something to do with Amelie. I can't, Shane."

His hand tightened, then released. He let go and looked away. "You're going to let a human die because Amelie told you not to say anything. Not even Monica ranks that low. If you don't do something—" He paused and took in a long, slow breath. His voice wasn't quite steady when he went on. "If you don't do something, that means that you put the vampires first, and I can't deal with that, Claire. I'm sorry, but I can't."

She knew that. Tears continued to burn in her eyes, but she didn't try to talk him out of it. He was right, she was wrong, and she had to find a way out of this; she had to. Enough people were dying in Morganville, and some of them had died because of her.

The notes. The notes I left at Myrnin's. Those could tell the doctor exactly what the crystals were, and how to counteract them. She could start reconstructing them now, since her brain was still working at high speed, but she could already feel things starting to fade at the edges.

"Shane," she said. He didn't look at her. "I love you." She wasn't going to say it, but she knew that she might not come back. Ever. And as if he knew that, he grabbed her hand and squeezed it. When he did finally look at her she said, "I can't tell them anything, but I think I can help her. And I'm going to."

His brown eyes were tired and anxious and understood way too much. "You're going to do something crazy."

Well," she said, "not as crazy as what you'd do, but . . . yeah." She kissed him, and it felt terrifyingly good, the perfect way his lips fit to hers, the way time seemed to stop when they touched. "I'll see you," she whispered, and stroked her fingers down his cheek.

And then she escaped before he could try to talk her out of it.

"Wait!" he called after her. She didn't.

Claire left the hospital at a run, moving faster than anyone could react to stop her, and headed for the last place on earth she wanted to go.

. . .

It was deathly silent inside Myrnin's lab. Claire came down the steps very slowly, very carefully, listening for any hint of his presence. All the lights were burning, oil lamps flickering, and a couple of Bunsen burners hissed under bubbling flasks. The whole place smelled of strawberry and rot, and it felt strangely cold.

If I hurry . . . Myrnin had a bedroom somewhere down here, right? Maybe he was asleep. Or reading. Or doing something normal.

And maybe he's not.

Claire picked her way across the room, moving very slowly and taking care not to tip over any of the leaning books, or crunch on any broken glass. At the back of the lab she saw that the tray where she'd put out the red crystals for drying was empty. There was no sign of the crystals themselves, but the notebooks were stacked neatly on one corner.

As she picked them up, Myrnin's voice came from right behind her shoulder. She felt his breath cool on the back of her neck. "Those don't belong to you."

She whirled, backed up, and overturned a stack of books that slithered into another, like stacks of dominos crashing.

"Now look what you've done," Myrnin said. He seemed very quiet, but there was something wrong in his eyes.

Badly wrong.

Claire backed up, glancing behind her to be sure the way was clear; in that instant, Myrnin was on her. She shoved the notebooks between them, and his claws tore into them, shredding them. "No! Myrnin, *no!*"

She threw him off, mainly because his knees slipped on fallen books, and she scrambled away, panting. Somehow, she remembered to hold on to the damaged notebooks. Myrnin snarled and tried to follow, but the debris made for uncertain footing, and his jump went wrong. He crashed into a bookcase, and it toppled over on him, raining volumes.

Claire tried to get to the stairs, but there was no way she was going to make it. He was already flanking her, angling to cut her off from any hope of rescue or escape.

She was going to die, and Monica would die, too. And so would

Myrnin, because he was too far gone now. She hadn't seen any flicker of recognition left, not even for an instant.

She backed up, and her shoulders hit the hard stone wall. She slid, trying to put herself in a corner, but there was a leaning bookcase in the way. When she fell against it, it slid sideways, revealing the door that Myrnin had shown her before.

The heart-shaped lock was hanging open.

Unlocked.

Claire gasped and grabbed it, ripped it away, and swung open the door.

She felt Myrnin's claws catch in her hair, but she pulled free and fell forward . . . into the dark.

No, no, this showed me my house; it led to the living room. . . .

It didn't now. Myrnin had changed the destination, and this was no place she recognized at all. It was dark, damp, and it smelled like a combination of sewer and garbage dump. She blinked, and her eyes adjusted much more quickly to the darkness than they should have—the crystals, still doing their job. She was feeling an ache in her extremities now, working its way in. Once it reached her core, she'd be into withdrawal again.

She had no idea how bad it would be this time, but she couldn't afford to wait.

Claire whirled, and the doorway was still there, right where it had been.

Myrnin was framed in it, staring at her.

She couldn't go that way. She had to find another path.

Claire ran into the dark. There was just enough light filtering in from very narrow, very tall windows, that as her eyes adjusted, she realized she was inside a prison—a filthy, horrible prison, with very little light.

And some of the cells were full.

It took her a while to realize it, because they were all so *quiet*—pale, quiet things, one to a cell, that flashed to the bars like ghosts as she ran past. That changed, the farther she went. A sound went up—a whisper at first, rising to a howl. She heard metal rattling.

They were trying to get out.

Claire was gasping, and she was getting tired, and Myrnin was behind her.

This is where she keeps them. The ones who can't be fixed.

It was where all the vampires would end up, one after another. Left to die in the dark, alone, trapped, and starving.

Amelie let that happen.

It got quiet suddenly, and that was worse than the howling and rattling. Claire glanced over her shoulder and saw that Myrnin was slowing down, then stopping. There was only the sound of her feet hitting the stone floor, until she skidded to a stop, too.

"Claire," Myrnin whispered. "What are you doing here?" He sounded confused, but at least he knew her name. He fumbled at his pockets, found some kind of small silver box, and opened it. Red crystals spilled out into his palm, mounded up, and, choking and retching, he forced them into his mouth.

The effects sent him staggering. He braced himself with one shoulder against the wall of the hallway and moaned. It sounded like it hurt. A lot.

"Not much time," he said. His voice was barely there at all, but in the cold silence, she heard every word. "The notebooks. You need them?"

"I—I made a mistake. Somebody else took the crystals. I need to give them to the doctors."

"Someone else took the crystals?"

"Yes."

"Most die," he said, as if it didn't matter. "Maybe you can find a way from what you wrote; I don't know. I never tried."

That meant that when he'd given her the crystals that first time, he hadn't even known if they would kill her.

God. And she'd thought he actually cared.

He sounded very tired. "You understand how to use the doors now?"

"No."

"All you have to do is find a doorway, then concentrate on your destination. Mind you, it's the rare human who has the mind to manage it even once, never mind on a regular basis—and the doors have a subtle go-away to anyone not invited to use them. You can go to any Founder House, or to seven other doorways in town, but you must have a mental picture of where you are going first. If you fail to do so, you end up"—he raised a hand with effort, and gestured feebly—"here. Where she keeps the monsters." Myrnin smiled faintly, but his smile looked broken. "After all, I ended up here, didn't I?"

Claire fought to still her heartbeat. "How do I get back? Back to your lab?"

"That way." Myrnin looked down at his hand, as if it seemed odd to him. He turned it this way and that, examining it, and then pointed. "Stay to the right; you'll find it. Don't go near the bars. If they grab you, you must not let them pull you close enough to bite. And, Claire . . ."

She clutched the notebooks tight to her chest as he met her eyes. He still seemed rational, but even that massive dose of crystals hadn't driven the beast completely back.

"I need you to do me two services," he said. "First—promise me that you'll continue to work to find the cure. I'm no longer able to carry it forward."

She swallowed hard, and nodded. She'd have tried, anyway. "I can't do it alone," she said. "I'll need help. Doctors. I'm going to give them the notes and see if we can find something."

Myrnin nodded. "Just don't explain what it does." He looked around. On the far side of the wall was an empty cell, with its door standing open. There was a decaying bunk, but nothing else.

He took a breath, let it out, and walked into the cell. Then he turned and firmly closed the door behind him. Claire heard the lock engage with a thick, metallic *clank*.

"Second thing," Myrnin said, "do bring me some books, when you visit. And perhaps more crystals, if you're able to produce more. It's so nice to think clearly again, even for a few moments."

She felt as though he'd punched into her chest and ripped out her heart. She felt hollow, light, and empty.

And very, very sad.

"I will," she said. "I'll be back."

When she looked back, Myrnin had settled himself on the edge of the bunk, staring at the floor.

He didn't look up when she said, "I won't just leave you here. I promise. I'll come see you."

She hesitated, and thought she heard something whispering to her. A voice.

Her mother's voice.

"You should go," Myrnin said tonelessly. "Before we both have cause to regret it."

She ran.

Nothing got her on the way back to the door, although a lot of the sick vampires reached out mutely to her, or screamed; she covered her ears and ran, heart pounding, feeling sicker and more terrified all the time. The relief of seeing the open door ahead was like a warm blanket after the cold. The doorway was black, just black; she couldn't see Myrnin's lab on the other side. Couldn't see anything.

Think! Myrnin had said she had to focus, visualize where she wanted to go. Of course, he'd also said that she probably wouldn't be able to do it. *No, don't think about that. If you want out of here, you have to focus. Hard!*

Nothing. Nothing at all.

She closed her eyes, even though it was terrifying to do it here, in this place, and slowed her breathing. She thought about the lab, about the confusion of clutter, the books, the bottles, the new and the old. She *smelled* it, like a breath of home, and when she opened her eyes she could see it on the other side of the door.

Claire took a deep breath, stepped over the threshold through a slight tug of resistance, and turned to close the door as soon as she was through.

When she turned back, Amelie was waiting.

She stood in the center of the room, hands folded. Her ancient, smooth face was untroubled by any kind of expression, but there was something bitter in her eyes.

"He's gone," Amelie said. "Where is he?"

"I—the prison."

"You took him below." Amelie frowned slightly. "*You* took him below."

"I think he wanted to go there. He—put himself in a cage." Claire struggled to keep her voice steady. "How—how can you leave them like that?"

"I have no choice." It would never occur to Amelie to explain, of course, and it would probably get Claire nowhere to demand it. "If he is truly lost, then it's over. The experiment is ended, and there is no cure. No way to save my people." She sat down in one of the threadbare armchairs, shoving books out of the way as she did. It was the first ungraceful thing Claire had ever seen her do. "I thought—I never thought we would fail."

Claire came a step or two closer. "I have the notebooks," she said. "And—Myrnin must have left more stuff here I can read. You haven't failed yet."

Amelie shook her head, and a wisp of hair broke free from the coronet. It made her look young and very fragile. "I must have someone trusted to maintain the machines, or it will all fail, anyway. And only Myrnin could do that. I had hoped that you—but he told me only a vampire could. And there is no one else."

"Sam?"

"Not old enough, and nowhere near powerful enough. It would have to be someone near my own age, and that would mean—" Amelie looked at her sharply. "I can't give such power to my enemy."

Claire didn't like the thought, either. "What else can you do?"

"End it." Amelie's voice was so soft Claire barely understood the words. "Let it all go. Destroy it."

"You mean—let everybody go?"

Amelie's gaze locked with hers, and held. "No," she said. "That is not what I mean at all."

Claire shuddered. "Then—why not let Oliver in? You've been fighting so hard to keep him out. Why not try this first? What do you really have to lose?"

Amelie's pale eyebrows slowly rose. "Nothing. And everything, of course. But you should fear that we would succeed, Claire. Because if we do, if the vampire race is not doomed to die, where does that leave you? An interesting question, for another day, perhaps." She nodded at the note-books in Claire's hands. "If you intend to save the Morrell girl, you should hurry," she said. "Use the portal. I will send you directly to the hospital."

There was a portal to the hospital? Claire blinked and looked back at the closed and locked door. "Um—are you sure it won't open to—"

"To below?" Amelie shook her head. "I have no intention it should. If you do not, then it will do as we say. Myrnin could only make the doorway work to below, never back here. So only you and I have such abilities, for now."

Claire thought about something, with a sickening wrench. "Are you sure?"

"What do you mean?" Amelie looked up, slowly, her eyes fierce and bright.

A rush of images flitted through Claire's mind: Oliver, grabbing her in her own house. The dead girl in the basement. Jason appearing and disap-pearing from Monica's party, and reappearing near Common Grounds.

Oh no.

"Can you tell?" Claire asked. "If somebody's using the portal?"

"Myrnin could, I suspect, but I cannot. Why?" Amelie stood up, and this time the frown was definite. "What do you know?"

"I think you've got a traitor," Claire said. "Somebody showed Oliver, and Oliver showed Jason. And Captain Obvious and his friends probably knew, too. Jason must have shown them—"

"Impossible," Amelie interrupted with a flash of impatience. "My people are beyond suspicion."

"Then how did Jason bring a dead girl into Michael's house with-out permission? Because you said he'd have to be invited in. And he wasn't."

Amelie froze, and her eyes went cold and flat. "I see," she said, and then whirled toward the small door that led into the narrow, overstuffed library, and the door that Claire had once used to come in from the uni-versity. "You seem to be proven right. Someone's coming in. Go, take the doorway. *Hurry.*"

Claire opened the door. Beyond it, air rippled, and shifted . . . her living room. A stranger's house. A quiet white room with a stained-glass window.

"Now!" Amelie said sharply. "That's the hospital."

Claire stepped through. As she looked back, she saw Oliver walk into Myrnin's lab, look around, and focus on Amelie. Jason was right behind him, grinning, clearly Oliver's new pet. Or maybe, Oliver's pet all along.

"Interesting," Oliver said, and then turned his head to look at the open doorway, and Claire. "And unexpected."

She slammed the door between them, heart pounding, and it vanished on her side. That didn't mean it couldn't reappear, but at least she was safe for the moment. She didn't think Amelie would let Oliver follow her.

She hoped.

She flipped pages in the notebooks. Myrnin had clawed them, but only the last one, and only at the back. The rest were intact.

She left the white room and found that she was standing in the hospital's nondenominational chapel—more of a meditation room than anything else. It was empty, except for one person kneeling near the front.

Jennifer. She scrambled to her feet when she saw Claire, and blurted, "What are you doing here?" Her eyes were red, and she sniffled and swiped angrily at her eyes, smearing mascara and ruining what was left of her makeup. She had freckles. Claire had never known that.

"Saving your friend," Claire said. "I hope."

It took three days for the lab to work out a counteragent, but once they did, Monica came off the ventilator within hours. Or so Claire heard from Richard Morrell, who dropped by on Wednesday night, as the four of them—Shane being finally released from the hospital—were sitting down to dinner.

"I'm glad she's going to be okay," Claire said. "Richard—I'm sorry. If I'd known—"

"You're lucky that stuff didn't fry you, too," he said, but without any real heat. "Look, my sister isn't the best person I've ever met, but I love her. Thanks for helping."

Claire nodded. Michael was nearby, seeming to be just lounging but, she knew, ready to step in if Richard went postal. Not that Richard would. So far, he was the best-adjusted Morrell she'd met.

"Don't come by the hospital," Richard continued. "I'm trying to convince her you weren't out to kill her. If you show up, I may not be able to keep a lid on things. As it is—" He shifted uncomfortably and looked away. "Just watch your back, Claire."

"She doesn't need to," Eve said, and put her arm around Claire's shoulders. "Tell your sister, if she messes with Claire, she messes with all of us."

Richard's expression went deliberately bland. "I'm sure that'll terrify her," he said. "Night, Claire. Eve." He nodded to Michael. Shane hadn't gotten up from the table, partly because hey, gut wound, but also he wasn't about to put himself out for any Morrell, even Richard. Claire had the impression Richard was just as happy not to have to make nice.

Claire saw Richard out the door, locked it, and came back to fight over who would get the last taco. Which, of course, turned out to be Shane. "Wounded!" was his new comeback, and it was one they couldn't really argue with, at least for a couple of weeks. He happily loaded up his plate, and Claire sat back and felt, for the first time in days, a little of the tension relax. Shane was even being civil to Michael again, especially after she'd explained to him how Michael had raced to her rescue. That mattered to Shane, in ways that other things didn't.

When the knock came on the front door, the four of them froze, and Michael sighed. "Right. My turn to play doorman, I guess."

Claire nabbed some meat off Shane's plate. He pretend-stabbed her hand, and ended up licking Claire's fingers for her, one at a time.

"Okay, that's either gross or hot, but I'm thinking gross, so quit it," Eve said. "If you're going to be licking each other, get a room."

"Good idea," Shane whispered.

"Wounded!" Claire shot back mockingly. "And anyway, I thought you wanted to play it safe."

"Dude, I live in Morganville. How exactly is that playing it safe?"

Michael came back down the hall with a very odd expression. "Claire," he said. "I think you should come."

She pushed away from the table and went after him. He opened the door and stepped aside.

Her parents were standing on the step.

"Mom! Dad!" Claire threw herself into their arms. It was stupid to be so cheered by the sight of them, but for a second she enjoyed being stupid, through and through.

And then the dread hit her, and she backed up and said, "What are you doing here?" *Please say you're dropping something off. Please.*

Her mother—dressed in pressed blue jeans and a starched blue work shirt and a Coldwater Creek jacket, even in the heat of summer—looked taken aback. "We wanted to surprise you," she said. "Isn't that all right? Claire, you *are* only sixteen—"

"Nearly seventeen," Claire sighed, under her breath.

"And really, we ought to be able to come see you when we want to, to be sure you're safe and happy." Claire's mom gave Michael a distracted, nervous smile. "All right, then, I'll tell you the truth. We've been very worried about you, honey. First you had that trouble in the dorm; then you were attacked and ended up in the hospital—and someone told us about that party."

"What?" She sent Michael a look, but he looked just as surprised as she felt. "Who told you?"

"I don't know. An e-mail. You know I can never figure those things out; anyway, it was some friend of yours."

"Oh," Claire breathed, "I really don't think it was. Mom, look, it was—"

"Don't tell us it was nothing, honey," her dad cut in. "I read all about it. Drinking, drugs, fighting, destruction of property. Kids having sex. And you were at this party, weren't you?"

"I—no, Dad, not like—" She couldn't lie about it. "I was there. We were all there. But Shane wasn't stabbed at the party; it was after, on the way home." She realized as soon as she said it that neither one of them had mentioned anything about Shane. And it was too late to take it back.

"Stabbed?" her mother echoed blankly, and covered her mouth with her hand. "Oh, that is just *it*. That's the last straw!"

"Let's talk about all this inside," her father said. He looked so grim now. "We've decided we had to make a change."

"A change?" Claire echoed.

"We're moving," he said. "We bought a nice house on the other side of town. Looks kind of like this one, maybe a little smaller. Even has the same layout to the place, I think. Good thing we did. Clearly, things are much worse than we thought."

"You're—" She could *not* have heard that right. "Moving *here*? To *this* town? You can't! You can't move here!"

"Oh, Claire, I was so hoping you'd be happy," her mom said, in that tone that Claire dreaded. The *I'm-so-disappointed-in-you* tone. "We've already sold our old house. The truck with the furniture should get here tomorrow. Oh"—she turned to Claire's father—"did we remember to—"

"Oh, for heaven's sake—yes," he rumbled. "Whatever it is, yes, we remembered."

"Well, you don't have to be—"

"Mom!" Claire interrupted desperately. "*You can't move here!*"

Michael put his hand on her shoulder. "Just a second," he said to her parents, and pulled Claire a few feet back. "Claire, don't. It's already too late. If the Council hadn't wanted them here, they wouldn't be here, and they wouldn't have a Founder House. If it looks like this house and has the same layout, that's what it is, a Founder House. That means Amelie wants it to happen. She probably made it happen."

That didn't exactly make her feel any better. She was shaking all over now. "But they're my *parents!*" she whispered fiercely. "Can't you do something?"

He looked grim and shook his head. "I don't know. I'll try. But for now we'd better just make nice, okay?"

She didn't want to. She wanted to drag her parents out to their car and *make* them go.

How could Amelie do this to her? No, that was obvious: it was easy. Her parents were just another way to force Claire to do whatever the vampires needed. And now that she knew so much, now that she was their only hope of working with Myrnin on a cure, they'd never let her go.

"Hello?" Claire's mom called. "Can we come in?"

Michael kept his expression blank and friendly. "Sure. Everybody inside." Because it was getting dark.

Claire's mom and dad stepped over the threshold. As Michael started to swing the door shut, a third person stopped the door from closing with an open hand and stepped through. Claire had no idea who he was. She'd never seen him before, and she was sure she'd have remembered. He had thick gray hair, a big gray mustache, and huge green eyes behind thick, fifties-style eyeglasses.

Michael froze, and Claire knew instantly that something was very, very wrong.

"Oh," Claire's mother said, as if she'd forgotten all about him. "This is Mr. Bishop. We met him on our way into town; his car was broken down."

Mr. Bishop smiled and tipped an invisible hat. "Thank you for the kind invitation to enter your home," he said. His voice was incredibly deep and smooth, with an inflection that sounded like Russian. "Although I really didn't require one."

Because he was a vampire.

Claire backed slowly away. Michael looked like he couldn't move at all as Bishop walked into the house.

"I don't want to upset your nice family," Bishop said in a lower tone, focusing on Claire, "but if Amelie isn't here to talk to me in half an hour, I'll kill everyone breathing in this house."

Claire involuntarily looked after her parents, but they were already moving down the hall. They hadn't heard.

"No," Michael said. "You won't touch anyone. This is my house. Get out now, or I'll have to hurt you."

Bishop looked him up and down. "Nice bark, puppy, but you don't have the teeth. Get Amelie."

"Who are you?" Claire whispered. There was menace boiling off this old man like fog. She could almost see it.

"Tell her that her father's come to visit," he said, and smiled. "Aren't family reunions nice?"

FEAST OF FOOLS

To the Time Turners, who keep me moving forward . . .
And to P. N. Elrod, who knows why.

ACKNOWLEDGMENTS

Couldn't have happened without Sondra Lehman, Josefine Corsten, Sharon Sams, and my friends at LSG Sky Chefs.

Thanks also to Lucienne Diver and Anne Bohner, without whom... well, you know!

THE STORY SO FAR...

Claire Danvers was going to Caltech. Or maybe MIT. She had her pick of great schools... but her parents were a little worried about sending a wide-eyed sixteen-year-old into such a high-pressure world. So they compromised and sent her to a safe place for a year—Texas Prairie University, a small school located in Morganville, Texas, just an hour or so from their home.

One problem: Morganville isn't what it seems. It's the last safe place for *vampires*, and that makes it not very safe at all for the humans who venture in for work or school. The vampires rule the town... and everyone who lives in it.

Claire's second problem is that she's gathered enemies, major ones, human and vampire. Now she lives with housemates Michael Glass (newly made a vampire), Eve Rosser (always been Goth), and Shane Collins (whose absentee dad is a vampire killer). Claire's the normal one... or she would be, except that she's deep into the secrets of Morganville. She's become an employee of the Founder, Amelie, and befriended one of the most dangerous, yet most vulnerable, vampires of them all—Myrnin.

And just when she thinks things can't get any worse... they have.

Amelie's vampire father has come to town, and he's not happy.

When Daddy's not happy... nobody's happy.

ONE

It was hard to imagine how Claire's day—even by Morganville standards—could get any worse . . . and then the vampires holding her hostage wanted breakfast.

"Breakfast?" Claire repeated blankly. She took a look at the living room window, just to prove to herself that, yes, it was still dark outside. Getting darker all the time.

The three vampires all looked at her. It was bad enough having that kind of attention from the two she hadn't properly met yet—man and woman, eerily pretty—but when the cold, old Mr. Bishop's eyes focused her way, it made her want to curl up in a corner and hide.

She held his stare for a full five seconds, then looked down. She could almost feel him smiling.

"Breakfast," he said softly, "is something to be eaten in the mornings. Mornings for vampires are not controlled by sunrise. And I like eggs."

"Scrambled or over easy?" Claire asked, trying not to sound as nervous as she felt. *Don't say* over easy. *I don't know how to make eggs over easy. I don't even know why I mentioned it. Don't say* over easy. . . .

"Scrambled," he said, and Claire's breath rushed out in relief. Mr. Bishop was sitting in the comfortable chair in the living room that her housemate Michael normally occupied while he was playing his guitar.

Unlike Michael, Mr. Bishop made it look like a throne. Part of it was that everybody else stayed standing—Claire, with her boyfriend, Shane, hovering protectively by her side; Eve and Michael a little distance away, holding hands. Claire risked a glance at Michael. He looked . . . contained. Angry, sure, but under control, at least.

Claire was more scared about Shane. He had a pretty well-documented history of acting before thinking, at least when it came to the personal safety of those he cared about. She took his hand, and he sent her a quick, dark, unreadable glance.

No, she wasn't sure about him at all.

Mr. Bishop's voice pulled her attention back to him with a cold snap. "Have you told Amelie that I've arrived, girl?"

That had been Bishop's first command—to let his daughter know he'd come to town. *His daughter?* Amelie—the head vampire of Morganville—didn't seem human enough to have family, not even family as scary as Mr. Bishop. Ice and crystal, that was Amelie.

He was waiting for an answer, and Claire hastily got one together. "I called. I got her voice mail," Claire said. She tried not to sound defensive. Bishop's eyebrows drew together in a scowl.

"I suppose that means you left some sort of a message." She nodded mutely. He drummed his fingers impatiently on the arm of the chair. "Very well. We'll eat while we wait. Eggs, scrambled, as I said. We shall also have bacon, coffee—"

"Biscuits," drawled the woman leaning on the arm of his chair. "I love biscuits. And honey." The vampire had a molasses-slow accent, something that wasn't quite Southern and wasn't quite not, either. Mr. Bishop gave her a tolerant look, the kind a human would give a favorite pet. She had the icy glitter in her eyes, and moved so smoothly and quietly that there was no way she was regular-flavored human. Not hiding it, either, the way some of the vampires of Morganville tried to do.

The woman kept smiling, dark eyes fixed on Shane. Claire didn't like the way she was looking at him. It looked—greedy.

"Biscuits," Mr. Bishop agreed, with a quirk of a smile. "And I'll indulge you further by agreeing to gravy, child." The smile vanished when he turned back to the four standing in front of him. "Go about your business, then. Now."

Shane grabbed Claire's hand and practically dragged her toward the kitchen. However fast he was moving, Michael was there first, pushing Eve through the door. "Hey!" Eve protested. "I'm walking here!"

"And the faster, the better," Michael said. His normally angelic face looked stark, all sharp edges, and he closed the kitchen door once they were safely inside. "Right. We don't have a lot of choices. Let's do exactly what he says and hope Amelie can sort all this out when she gets here."

"I thought *you* were all Big Bad Bloodsucker these days," Shane said. "It's your house. How come you can't just throw them out?" That was a reasonable question, and Shane managed to say it without making it seem like a challenge. Well, much of one. The kitchen felt cold, Claire noticed—as if the temperature of the whole house was steadily dropping. She shivered.

"It's complicated," Michael said. He yanked open cabinets and began assembling the makings of fresh coffee. "Yeah, it's our house"— emphasis, Claire noted, on the *our*—"but if I revoke Bishop's invitation, he will still kick our asses, I guarantee you."

Shane leaned his butt against the stove and crossed his arms. "I just thought you were supposed to be stronger than them on home ground—"

"Supposed to be. I'm not." Michael spooned coffee into the filter. "Don't be an asshole right now—we don't have time for it."

"Dude, I wasn't trying to be." And Claire could tell he actually meant it this time. Michael seemed to hear it, too, and sent Shane an apologetic glance. "I'm trying to figure out how big a pile of crap we're in. Not blaming you, man." He hesitated a second, then continued. "How do you know? Whether or not you have a chance?"

"Any other vampire I meet, I know where I stand with them. Who's stronger, who's weaker, whether or not I could take them in a straight-up fight if it came to that." Michael poured water into the machine and switched it on to brew. "These guys, I know I haven't got a chance in hell. Not against one of them, much less all three, not even with the house itself backing me up. They're badass, man. Truly black hat. It's going to take Amelie or Oliver to handle this."

"So," Shane said, "landfill-sized pile of crap. Good to know."

Eve pushed him out of the way and began getting pots and pans out of the cabinets, clattering everything noisily. "Since we're not fighting, we'd better get breakfast ready," she said. "Claire, you get the eggs, since you volunteered us for short-order cooks."

"Better than volunteering us for breakfast," Shane pointed out, and Eve snorted.

"You," she said, and pressed a finger into the center of his well-worn T-shirt. "You, mister. You're making gravy."

"You do want us all to die, don't you?"

"Shut up. I'll do the biscuits and bacon. Michael—" She turned, looking at him with big dark eyes, made almost anime-wide by the Goth eyeliner. "Coffee. And I think you have to be the private eye here. Sorry."

He nodded. "I'll go make sure I know what they're doing when I finish here."

Assigning Michael the barista and spy duties made sense, but it left the three of them the majority of the work, and none of them were exactly future chefs in training. Claire struggled with the scrambled eggs. Eve cursed the bacon grease in a fierce whisper, and whatever Shane was making, it didn't really look that much like gravy.

"Can I help?"

They all jumped at the voice, and Claire whirled toward the kitchen door. "Mom!" She knew she sounded panicked. She *was* panicked. She'd forgotten all about her parents—they'd come in with Mr. Bishop, and Bishop's friends had moved them into the not-much-used parlor at the front of the house. In the great scheme of scary things, Bishop had taken the forefront.

But there was her mother, standing in the kitchen doorway, smiling a fragile, confused smile and looking . . . vulnerable. Tired.

"Mrs. Danvers!" Eve jumped in, hurried over, and guided her to the kitchen table. "No, no, we're just—ah—making some food. You haven't eaten, right? What about Mr. Danvers?"

Her mother—looking every year of the forty-two she claimed not to be—seemed tired, vague, kind of out of focus. Worried, too. There were lines around her eyes and mouth that Claire couldn't remember seeing before, and it scared her.

"He's—" Claire's mom frowned, then leaned her forehead on the palm of her hand. "Oh, my head hurts. I'm sorry. What did you say?"

"Your husband, where is he?"

"I'll find him," Michael said quietly. He slipped out of the kitchen with the grace and quickness of a vampire—but at least he was *their* vampire. Eve settled Claire's mom at the table, exchanged a helpless look with Claire, and chattered on nervously about what a long drive it must have been to Morganville, what a nice surprise it was that they were moving to town, how much Claire was going to enjoy having them here. Etc., etc., etc.

Claire numbly continued to rake eggs back and forth in the skillet. *This can't happen. My parents can't be here.* Not now. Not with Bishop. It was a nightmare, in every way.

"I could help you cook," Mom said, and made a feeble effort to get up. Eve glared at Claire and mouthed, *Say something!* Claire swallowed a cold bubble of panic and tried to make her voice sound at least partly under control.

"No, Mom," Claire said. "It's fine. We've got it covered. Look, we're making extra in case you and Dad are hungry. You just sit and relax."

Her mom, who was usually a control freak deluxe in the kitchen, prone to take command of something as error free as boiling water, looked relieved. "All right, honey. You let me know if I can help."

Michael opened the kitchen door, and ushered in Claire's father. If her mom looked tired, her dad just looked . . . blank. Puzzled. He frowned at Michael, like he was trying to work out exactly what was happening but couldn't put his finger on it.

"What's going on around here?" he barked at Michael. "Those people out there—"

"Relatives," Michael said. "From Europe. Look, I'm sorry. I know you wanted to spend some time with Claire, but maybe you should just go on home, and we'll—"

He paused, then turned, because someone was standing in the kitchen door behind him. Following him.

"Nobody's going anywhere," said the other one of Bishop's vampire companions—the guy. He was smiling. "One big happy family, eh, Michael? It's Michael, isn't it?"

"What, we're on a first-name basis now?" Michael got Claire's dad inside the kitchen and closed the door in the other vampire's face.

"Right. Let's get you guys out of here," he said to Claire's parents, and opened the back door, the one that led out into the backyard. "Where's your car? Out on the street?"

Outside the night looked black and empty, not even a moon showing. Claire's dad frowned at Michael again, then took a seat at the kitchen table with his wife.

"Close the door, son," he said. "We're not going anywhere."

"Sir—"

Claire tried, too. "Dad—"

"No, honey, there's something strange going on here, and I'm not leaving. Not until I know you're all okay." Her father transferred the frown back to Michael again. "Just who are these . . . relatives?"

"The kind nobody wants to claim," Michael said. "Every family's got them. But they're just here for a little while. They'll be leaving soon."

"Then we'll stay until they do," Dad said.

Claire tried to focus on the scrambled eggs she was making.

Her hands were shaking.

"Hey," Shane whispered, leaning close. "It's okay. We'll all be okay." He was a big, solid, warm presence next to her, stirring what could not possibly *really* be gravy. She knew this mainly because Shane's sole culinary ability came in the genre of chili. But at least he was trying, which was new and different, and probably showed just how seriously he was taking all this.

"I know," Claire said, and swallowed. Shane's arm pressed against hers, a deliberate kind of thing, and she knew if his hands weren't full, he'd have put his arms around her. "Michael won't let them hurt us."

"Weren't you listening?" Eve joined them at the stove, whispering fiercely. She scowled at the frying bacon. "He can't stop them. Best he can do is get himself really hurt in the process. So maybe you ought to call Amelie again and tell her to get her all-powerful ass over here *now*."

"Yeah, good idea, piss off the only vampire who *can* help. Look, if they were going to kill us, I don't think they'd ask for eggs first," Shane said. "Not to mention biscuits. If you ask for biscuits, clearly, you think you're some kind of a guest."

He had a point. It didn't really stop the trembling in Claire's hands, though.

"Claire, honey?" Her mom's voice, again. Claire jumped and nearly flipped a spatula full of eggs out onto the stove top. "Those people. What are they really doing here?"

"Mr. Bishop—he's, uh, waiting for his daughter to come pick him up." That wasn't a lie. Not at all.

Claire's father got up from the table and went to the coffeepot, which had wheezed itself full; he poured two mugs and took them back to the table. "Have some coffee, Kathy. You look tired," he said, and there was a gentle note in his voice that made Claire look at him sharply. Her dad wasn't the most emotional of guys, but he looked worried now, almost as worried as Mom.

Dad drained his coffee like it was water after a hot afternoon of lawn mowing. Mom listlessly creamed and sugared, then sipped. Neither of them spoke again.

Michael slipped out the kitchen door, taking mugs of coffee out to the others. When he came back, he closed the door and leaned against it for a minute. He looked bone white, strained, worse than he had in the months since he'd been transformed fully into a vampire. Claire tried to imagine what they'd said to him to make him look like that, and couldn't even begin to guess. Something bad. No, something *horrible*.

"Michael," Eve said tensely. She nodded toward Claire's parents. "More coffee?"

He nodded and moved away from the door to pick up the coffeepot, but he never made it to the breakfast table. The kitchen door opened again, and Mr. Bishop and his entourage entered the room.

Tall and haughty as nineteenth-century royalty, the three vampires surveyed the kitchen. The other two vampires were pretty, young, and frightening, but Mr. Bishop was the one in charge; there was no mistaking it. When his gaze fell on her, Claire flinched and turned back to the sizzling eggs.

The female vampire strolled over and dipped her finger in the gravy Shane was stirring, then lifted the finger slowly to her lips to suck it clean. She stared at Shane the whole time. And Shane, Claire realized with a helpless, unpleasant shock, stared right back.

"We'll sit for the meal now," Bishop said to Michael. "You will have the pleasure of serving us, Michael. And if your little friends decide to try to poison me, I'll have your guts out, and believe me, a vampire can suffer a very, very long time when I want him to."

Michael swallowed and nodded once. Claire sent an involuntary look toward her folks, who could not *possibly* have missed that.

And they hadn't. "Excuse me?" Claire's father asked, and began to rise out of his chair. "Are you threatening these kids?"

Bishop turned those cold eyes toward them, and Claire desperately thought about whether a hot iron skillet with a panful of frying eggs might be a useful weapon against a vampire. Her dad froze, halfway up.

She felt a wave of something go through the room, and her parents' eyes went blank and vague. Her dad sank down again heavily in his chair.

"No more questions," Bishop said to them. "I tire of your chatter."

Claire felt a surge of utter black fury. She wanted to leap on that evil old man and claw his eyes out. The only thing holding her back, in those two long seconds, was the fact that if she tried, they'd all end up dead.

Even Michael.

"Coffee?" Eve broke the silence with a desperate, brittle brightness in her tone. She grabbed the coffeepot from Michael and bore down on Claire's mom and dad like the avenging dark angel of caffeine. Claire wondered what her parents made of Eve, with her rice-powder makeup and black lipstick and raccoon eyeliner, and her dyed-black hair teased into fierce spikes.

Then again, she had coffee, and she was smiling.

"Sure," Claire's mom said, and tried a tentative smile in return. "Thank you, dear. So—did you say that man is a relative of yours?" She cast a look toward Bishop, who was exiting the kitchen and heading for the dining table in the living area. The handsome younger male vamp caught Claire's look and winked, and she hastily focused back on Eve and her parents.

"Nope," Eve said, with fear-fueled cheer. "Distant relative of Michael's. From Europe, you know. Cream?"

"Eggs are done," Claire said, and turned down the burner. "Eve—"

"I hope we have enough plates," Eve interrupted, more than a little frantic. "Jeez, I never thought I'd say this, but where's the good china? *Is* there good china?"

"Meaning plates without chips in the edges? Yeah. Over there." Shane pointed to a cabinet about four feet higher than Eve's head. She gave him a stare. "Don't look at me—I'm not reaching for it. Still wounded, you know." He was. Claire had forgotten that, too, in the press of all the other stuff—he was doing better, but he'd been out of the hospital only a short while. Hardly enough time to really heal up from the stab wound that had nearly killed him.

That was another good reason not to make waves unless they absolutely had to—without Shane, their ability to fight back was seriously compromised.

Eve climbed up on the counter, found the plates, and handed them down to Claire. Once that was done, Claire took Shane's place at the stove, stirring the lumpy stuff that was supposed to be gravy. It looked like something an alien would barf.

"That girl," Claire said to Shane.

"What girl?"

"The—you know. Out there."

"You mean the bloodsucker? Yeah, what about her?"

"She was staring at you."

"What can I say? Irresistible."

"Shane, it's not funny. I just—you should be careful."

"Always am." Which was an absolute lie. Shane's eyes fixed on hers, and she felt a burst of heat inside that crept up to burn in her cheeks. He smiled slowly. "Jealous?"

"Maybe."

"No reason. I like my ladies with a pulse." He took her hand and pressed his fingers gently against her wrist. "Yep, you've got one. It's beating pretty fast, too."

"I'm not kidding, Shane."

"Neither am I." He stepped closer, and they were barely a breath apart. "No vamp's going to come between us. You believe me?"

She nodded wordlessly. For the life of her, she couldn't have forced out a single word just then. His eyes were dark, the color of rich brown velvet, with a thin rim of gold. She'd looked into his eyes a lot recently, but she'd never noticed just how *beautiful* they were.

Shane stepped back as the door opened again. Michael turned first toward them, offering up a mute apology, then faced Claire's parents.

"Mr. and Mrs. Danvers, Mr. Bishop would like for you to join him for dinner," he said. "But if you have to go home—"

If Michael was hoping they'd changed their minds, Claire could have told him that wasn't going to happen. As long as her dad had the idea something funny was going on, he wasn't about to do the sensible thing. Sure enough, he got to his feet, holding his coffee cup. "I could do with some breakfast. Never tasted Claire's eggs before. Kathy? You coming?"

Clueless, Claire thought in despair, but then again, she'd been just as bad when she'd first come to Morganville. She hadn't taken the strong hints, or even the outright instructions, seriously. Maybe she'd gotten that from her parents, along with the fair skin and slightly curly hair. In their defense, though, Mr. Bishop was playing with their heads.

And they were scared for *her*.

She watched as her parents followed Michael into the other room, and then helped Eve get the eggs and bacon and biscuits onto serving dishes—nice ones at that. The lumpy gravy couldn't be helped. They poured it into a gravy bowl and hoped for the best, then silently carried it out into the dining area, which was really a corner of the living room.

Claire was struck again, as she was at the oddest times, how the mood of the house could change at a moment's notice. Not just the mood of the people in it—the house itself. Right now, it felt dark, cold, foreboding. Almost hostile. And yet all that dark emotion seemed directed at the intruding vampires.

The house was worried, and on guard. The solid Victorian furniture crouched hunched and deformed, nothing warm or welcoming about it. Even the lights seemed dimmed, and Claire could feel something, almost a *presence*—the way she'd been able to sometimes sense Michael when he'd been trapped in the house as a ghost. The fine hair on her arms stood on end, and her skin pebbled into gooseflesh.

Claire set the eggs and bacon down on the wooden table and backed away. Nobody had asked her, Eve, and Shane to take seats, although there were empty places at the table; she caught Eve's eye and retreated back to the kitchen, grateful to escape. Michael stayed by the table, putting food on plates. Serving. There was a tight, pale set to his face and a cold fear in his eyes, and God, if Michael was panicking, there was definitely reason for a total freak-out.

As soon as the kitchen door closed again, Shane grabbed her and Eve and hustled them to the farthest corner of the room. "Right," he whispered. "It's official—this is getting way more than creepy. Did you feel that?"

"Yeah," Eve breathed. "Wow. I think if the house had teeth, it'd be chomping down right now. You have to admit, that's cool."

"Cool isn't getting us anywhere. Claire?"

"What?" She stared at him blankly for a few long seconds, then said, "Oh. Right. Yeah. I'll call Amelie again." She dug the cell phone out of her pocket. It was new, and came with a few important numbers preloaded on it. One of them—the first on speed dial, in fact—was a contact number for Amelie, the Founder of Morganville.

The head vampire. Claire's boss, sort of. In Morganville, the technical term was *Patron*, but Claire had known from the beginning that it was just a more polite word for *owner*.

It rang—again—to voice mail. Claire left another hurried, half-desperate message to *"come to the house, please, we need your help,"* and hung up. She looked mutely at Eve, who sighed and took the phone, then dialed another number.

"Yeah, hi," she said when she got someone on the line. "Let me talk to the boss." A longish pause, and Eve looked like she was steeling herself for something really unpleasant. "Oliver. It's Eve. Don't bother to tell me how nice it is to hear from me, because it's not, and this is business, so save the BS. Hold on."

Eve handed over the phone to Claire. Frowning, Claire mouthed, *Are you sure?* Eve made an emphatic thumb-and-little-finger phone gesture at her ear.

Claire reluctantly took the call.

"Oliver?" she asked. On the other end of the line, she heard a low, lazy chuckle.

"Well," he said. The owner of Common Grounds, the local coffee shop, had a warm voice—the kind that had made her think he was just an all-around nice guy when she'd first met him. "If it isn't little Claire. Eve didn't want to hear it, but I'll tell it to you—it's nice that you turn to me in your moment of need. It *is* a moment of need, I assume? And not an invitation to socialize?"

"Someone's here," she said as softly as she could. "In the house."

The warmth drained out of Oliver's voice, leaving a sharp annoyance. "Then call the police if you have a prowler. I'm not your security service. It's Michael's house. Michael can—"

"Michael can't do anything about it, and I don't think we should call the cops. This man, he says his name is Mr. Bishop. He wants to talk to Amelie, but I can't get her on the—"

Oliver cut her off. "Stay away from him," he said, and his voice had grown edges. "Do nothing. Say *nothing*. Tell your friends the same, especially Michael, yes? This is far beyond any of you. I will find Amelie. Do as he says—*whatever* he says—until we arrive."

And Oliver hung up on her. Claire blinked at the dead phone, shrugged, and looked at her friends. "He says do what we're doing," she said. "Take orders and wait for help."

"Fantastic advice," Shane said. "Remind me to stock a handy vampire-killing kit under the sink for times like these."

"We'll be okay," Eve said. "Claire's got the bracelet." She grabbed Claire's wrist and lifted it to show the delicate glitter of the ID bracelet circling it—a bracelet that had Amelie's symbol on it, instead of a name. It identified her as property, someone who'd signed over life and limb and soul to a vampire in return for certain protections and considerations. She hadn't wanted to do it, but it had seemed like the only way, at the time, to ensure the safety of her friends. Especially Shane, who was already on the bad side of the vamps.

She knew that the bracelet could bring its own brand of hazard, but at least it obligated Amelie (and maybe even Oliver) to come to her defense against other vampires.

In theory.

Claire slipped the phone into her pocket. Shane took her hands in his and rubbed lightly over her knuckles, a gentle, soothing kind of motion that made her feel at least a little safe, just for a moment.

"We'll get through this," he said. When he tried to kiss her, though, he winced. She put a hand lightly on his stomach.

"You're hurting," she said.

"Only when I bend over. When did you get so short, anyway?"

"Five minutes ago." She rolled her eyes, playing along, but she was worried. According to the rules of Morganville, he was off-limits to vampires during his convalescence; the hospital bracelet still around his wrist, glowing white plastic with a big red cross on it, ensured that any passing bloodsucker would know he wasn't fair game.

If their visitors played by the rules. Which Mr. Bishop might not. He wasn't a Morganville vampire. He was something else.

Something worse.

"Shane, I'm serious. How bad is it?" she asked in a low whisper, just for Shane's ears. He ruffled her short hair, then kissed it.

"I'm cool," he said. "Takes more than a punk with a switchblade to put a Collins down. Count on it."

Unspoken was the fact that they were up against a hell of a lot more than that, and he knew it.

"Don't do anything dumb," she said. "Or I'll kill you myself."

"Ouch, girl. Whatever happened to unconditional love around here?"

"It got tired of visiting you in the hospital." She held his eyes for a long few seconds. "Whatever you're thinking about doing, don't. We have to wait. We have to."

"Yeah, all the *vampires* say so. Must be true." She hated hearing him say the word quite that way, with so much loathing; when he said it, she always thought of Michael, of the way that he suffered when Shane's hatred boiled out. Michael hadn't *wanted* to be a vampire, and he was trying as best he could to live with it.

Shane wasn't making that any easier.

"Look." Shane put his hands around her face and stared earnestly into her eyes. "What if you take Eve and get out of here? They're not watching you. I'll cover for you."

"No. I'm not leaving my parents. I'm not leaving *you.*"

And they didn't have time to talk about it, because there was a tremendous crash from the living room. The kitchen door flew open, and Michael stumbled backward through it, held by the throat by the handsome young vamp who'd come in with Bishop. He slammed Michael up against the wall. Michael was fighting, but it didn't seem to be doing him a lot of good.

The other vampire opened his mouth in a snarl, and his big, sharp vampire teeth flashed down like switchblades.

So did Michael's, and Claire involuntarily backed up against Shane.

Shane yelled, "Hey! Let him go!"

Michael choked out, "Don't!" but of course Shane wasn't listening, and Claire's grip on his arm wasn't going to stop him, either.

What did stop him was Eve, holding a big, nasty-looking knife. She gave Shane a wild warning look, then spun around and leveled the knife at the vampire holding Michael. "You! *Let him go!*"

"Not until this one apologizes," the vampire said, and emphasized it by banging Michael against the wall again, hard enough that every piece of glass in the room rattled. No—it wasn't the impact; it was a low-level vibration coming from the room itself. The walls, the floor . . . the house. Like a warning growl.

"You'd better let him go," Claire said. "Can't you feel that?"

The vampire frowned at her, and his pretty green eyes narrowed even as the pupils expanded. "What are you doing?"

"Nothing," Eve said, and gestured with the knife. "*You're* doing it. The house doesn't like it when you play dirty with Michael. Now step away from him before something bad happens."

He thought they were bluffing—Claire could see it in his eyes—but he also didn't see much of a reason to push his luck. He let Michael go, his full lips curling in contempt. "Put that away, silly girl," he told Eve, and before any of them could even blink, he slapped it out of her hand—slapped it so hard it flew across the room and stuck in the wall. Eve grabbed her hand and cradled it close, backing away from him.

"Apologize," he told her. "Beg my forgiveness for threatening me."

"Bite me!" she snapped.

The vampire's eyes flared like hot crystal, and he lunged for Eve. Michael moved faster than Claire had ever seen him, just a confusing blur, and then the stranger was hurtling into the stove. He caught himself with both hands out, and she heard the sizzle as his palms hit the burners, followed by an enraged cry of pain.

This was going to get really bad, and there was nothing, *nothing*, they could do.

Shane grabbed Eve by the shoulder, Claire by the arm, and he hustled them into the corner by the breakfast table, where they had at least partial cover. But that left Michael on his own, fighting out of his weight class against something more like a wildcat than a man.

It didn't take long, maybe a few seconds, before Michael's strength failed. The stranger threw Michael to the kitchen floor and straddled him, fangs down and gleaming. The temperature in the kitchen plummeted to icy chill, cold enough that Claire could see her own breath as she panted in fear. That low-frequency rumble began again, jittering plates and glasses and pans.

Eve screamed and fought to get free of Shane's hold, not that she could do anything, anything at all—

The back door shuddered and crashed open under a single, overpowering blow. Wood splinters flew across the room, and Claire heard the locks snap like ice breaking.

Oliver, the second-scariest vampire in town (the first, some days), stood at the back door, staring inside. He was a tall man, built like a runner, all wiry muscles and angles. Tonight, he'd dispensed with his usual nice-guy disguise; he was in black, and his hair was pulled back in a ponytail. His face looked like carved bone in the moonlight.

He slapped an open palm against the empty air of the doorway, and it smacked into a solid barrier. "Fools!" he shouted. "Let me in!"

The stranger laughed, and yanked Michael up to a sitting position, fangs poised just over his neck. "Do it and I'll drain him," he said. "You know what that will do. He's too young."

Claire didn't know, but she knew it couldn't be anything good. Maybe not even survivable.

"Invite me in," Oliver repeated, in a deadly soft voice. "Claire. Do it now."

She opened her mouth, but she was interrupted.

"No need for that," said a cool female voice. The cavalry had finally arrived.

Amelie moved Oliver aside and walked through the invisible barrier like it wasn't there—which, to her, it wasn't, as Amelie was technically the creator and owner of the house. She was without her usual attendants and bodyguards, but there was no mistaking that she, not Oliver, was in charge by the way she swept across the threshold.

As always, Claire thought of her as a queen. Amelie was wearing a perfectly tailored yellow silk suit, and her pale hair was piled in a glossy crown on top of her head and secured with gold and diamond pins. She wasn't especially tall, but the aura she gave off was as powerful as an unexploded bomb. Her eyes were cold and very wide, and focused completely on the intruding vampire threatening Michael.

"Leave the boy alone," she said. Claire had never heard her use that tone, not ever, and she shuddered even though it wasn't directed toward her. "I rarely kill our own, but if you test me, François, I'll destroy you. I only give one warning."

The other vampire hesitated only for a second, then let go of Michael, who collapsed back full length on the floor. François rose to his feet in a single smooth, graceful motion, facing Amelie.

And then he bowed. Claire didn't have a lot of experience with seeing men bow, but she didn't think that one looked exactly respectful.

"Mistress Amelie," he said, and the vampire teeth folded back into his mouth, discreetly hidden. "We've been waiting for you."

"And amusing yourself at my expense while you do," she said. Claire didn't think she'd blinked at all. "Come. I wish to talk with Master Bishop."

François smirked. "I'm sure he wishes to speak with you, as well," he said. "This way."

She swept in front of him. "I know my own home, François—I don't require a guide." A quick glance over her shoulder, to where Oliver still stood silently at the door. "Come inside, Oliver. I will replace the Protections against you later, on behalf of our young friends."

He raised his eyebrows and crossed the threshold. Michael was just sitting up. Oliver extended a hand to him, but Michael didn't take it. They exchanged a look that made Claire shiver.

Oliver shrugged, stepped over him, and followed Amelie and François into the other room.

When the kitchen door swung shut, Claire let out a long, relieved breath, and heard Eve and Shane do the same. Michael rolled painfully to his feet and braced himself against the wall, shaking his head.

Shane put a hand on his shoulder. "Okay, man?" Michael gave him a thumbs-up answer, too shaken to do anything more, and Shane slapped his back and grabbed the collar of Claire's shirt as she rushed past him, heading for the door of the kitchen. "Whoa, whoa, Flash, where do you think you're going?"

"My parents are in there!"

"Amelie's not going to let anything happen to them," Shane said. "Get your breath. This isn't our fight, and you know it."

Now *Shane* was talking sense? Wow. Was it opposite day? "But—"

"Your parents are okay, but I don't want you rushing in. Got it?"

She nodded shakily. "But—"

"Michael. Help me out here. Tell her."

Michael was doing the vampire equivalent of gasping for air, but he nodded, eyes unfocused and vague. "Yeah," he said weakly. "They're okay. That's why François came after me, because I got between him and your mom."

"He went after my *mom*?" Claire flung herself toward the door of the kitchen, and this time Shane barely managed to hold on.

"Dude, that was not the kind of help I was looking for," Shane said to Michael, and wrapped both arms around Claire to hold her in place. "Easy. Easy, Amelie's in there, and you know she'll keep things under control—"

Claire did. After a second's thought, it made her struggle harder, because Amelie was perfectly capable of seeing Claire's parents as expendable if it served her needs. She saw *Claire* as expendable, off and on. But Shane didn't let go until she jabbed an elbow back and felt him stagger and release his grip. She didn't realize what she'd done . . . until she saw a thin line of red on his T-shirt, and Shane thumped himself down hard in the nearest available chair.

She'd hit him where he'd been stabbed.

"Dammit!" Eve hissed, and yanked Shane's shirt up to expose his chest and stomach—still bruised—and the white bandages, which were staining fresh with blood. Claire could even smell it . . .

. . . and as if she were in a dream, or a nightmare, she turned to look at Michael.

His eyes weren't vague and unfocused anymore. No, they were wide and intent and very, very scary. His face was still and white, and he wasn't breathing at all.

"Get the bleeding stopped," he whispered. "Hurry."

Michael was right. Shane was bait in a shark tank, and Michael was one of the sharks.

Shane was staring back at him as Eve poked and probed at his bandages, making sure they were tight. "I think it's okay, but you need to be careful," she said. "These bandages need to be changed. You might have popped a stitch or something."

She put her shoulder under Shane's and helped him to his feet. Shane was still watching Michael, and Michael didn't seem to be able to physically look away from the bloody slash of bandage on Shane's stomach.

"Want some?" Shane asked. "Come and get it, bat boy." He was almost as pale as Michael, and his expression was tight and furious.

Michael somehow managed to smile. "You're not my blood type, bro."

"Rejected again." But some of the wildness in Shane's eyes eased. "Sorry."

"No problem." Michael turned toward the closed kitchen door for a moment. "They're talking. Look, I'm going to go in and get your parents, Claire. I want everybody together who's still—"

"Breathing?" Shane asked.

"In danger," Michael said. "Back in a second." He hesitated just a breath, then added, "See if you can fix him up while I'm gone."

And then he was out the door, moving unnaturally fast, as if it was a relief to get away from the smell of Shane's blood. Claire swallowed and exchanged a look with Eve. Eve looked just as shaken as she felt, but she moved quickly on with priorities. "Okay. Where's the first-aid kit?"

"Upstairs," Claire said. "In the bathroom."

"Nope, it's down here," Shane said. "I moved it."

"You did? When?"

"Couple of days ago," he said. "Figured it would be better where I could get to it, since I'm the one who's usually getting bandaged. Look under the sink."

Eve did, and hauled out a big white metal box marked with a red cross. She opened it up and pulled out supplies. "Shirt off."

"You only love me for my abs."

"Shut up, loser. Shirt off."

With a glance toward Claire, Shane pulled it over his head and tossed it on the breakfast table next to him. Claire took the shirt to the sink, where she rinsed it in cold water, watching as Shane's blood tinted the water light pink. She didn't like to watch what Eve was doing; seeing the damage that Shane put himself through made her feel sick and frail, because he'd done it—as always—for other people. For her, and Eve.

"Done," Eve pronounced a few minutes later. "You'd *better* not bleed all over my nice clean bandages, or I'll stick a sale price on you and put you on the corner for the next neck-muncher."

"You're such a bitch," Shane said. "Thanks."

She gave him an air kiss and a wink. "Like most girls wouldn't line up to play nurse with you. Right."

Claire felt an unwelcome, completely surprising surge of jealousy. *Eve?* No, it was just Eve's usual teasing. Nothing else, right? She wasn't—she wouldn't. She just wouldn't.

Claire wrung out the shirt until her hands ached, then pressed it between two towels to try to get it as dry as possible. She handed it to Shane while Eve was busy putting the unused supplies back in the box, and helped him drag the damp fabric over his head and down his chest. She couldn't help but let her fingers brush down his skin, and to be honest, she didn't really try. In fact, she might have moved a little more slowly than she should have.

"Feels good," Shane said, very quietly, in her ear. "You okay?"

Claire nodded. He touched her lightly under the chin to lift it, and studied her face closely.

"Yeah," he said. "You're okay." He brushed her lips with his and looked past her at the kitchen door as it opened.

Michael, with Claire's parents in tow. The knot in Claire's chest, the one tied tight around her heart, eased a couple of precious notches.

Her parents looked . . . blank. Frowning, as if they'd forgotten something important. When her mother's eyes focused on her, Claire dredged up a smile.

"Weren't we going to have dinner?" her mother asked. "It's getting very late, isn't it? Were you going to cook, or—"

"No," Michael said. "We'll go out." He grabbed his car keys from the hook next to the door. "All of us."

TWO

There weren't a lot of choices for late-night dining in Morganville for those who weren't of the fanged persuasion, but there were a few places near the campus, most notably a twenty-four-hour diner. They ended up in an uncomfortable bunch around a table, the four of them plus Claire's parents, after an even more uncomfortably close ride in Michael's big vampire-tinted car.

The hamburgers were good, but Claire couldn't concentrate on the taste. She was too busy watching the people outside the diner. Some were college students, laughing in groups in the parking lot, ignoring the occasional pale-looking strangers walking nearby. Claire was reminded of videos of lions pacing along with antelopes as they grazed, waiting for one or two to fall behind.

She wanted to warn those kids, and she couldn't. The gold bracelet on her wrist made sure of that.

Michael, predictably, had to bear the brunt of parental conversation. He was just better at it, and he had a soothing kind of presence that made everything seem . . . normal. Claire's parents didn't exactly remember what had happened back at the house; more of Mr. Bishop's influence, Claire was sure. She hated that he'd messed with their heads, but in a way she was relieved, too. One less thing to have to worry about.

Her dad's attitude with Shane was enough.

"So," Dad said, as he pretended to concentrate on his pot roast, "how old are you again, son?"

"Eighteen, sir," Shane said, in his most blandly polite voice. They'd been over this. Repeatedly.

"You know my daughter's only—"

"Almost seventeen. Yes, sir, I know."

Dad frowned more deeply. "*Sixteen,* and sheltered. I don't like her living in a house with a bunch of hormone-crazy teenagers—no offense, I'm sure you mean to do right, but I was young myself once. Now that we're in town, with a place of our own, it's probably better that Claire move in with us."

Claire had *not* been expecting that. Not at all. "Dad! You don't trust me?"

"Honey, it's not about trusting you. It's about trusting the two adult *men* you're living with. Especially one I can see you're getting very close to, even though you know that's not very smart."

Fury burst open inside of her, and all she could see beyond the haze of red was Shane, standing between her and Eve, defending their lives while putting his own at risk.

Shane, turning away from her time after time because he was better— better by far—than she was at self-control.

Claire sucked in a deep breath and was about to let it out in a torrent of words, at top volume, when Shane's hand came down over hers and gripped it.

"Yeah," he said. "You're right about that. You don't know me, and what you do know you probably don't much like. I'm not really parent friendly. Not like Michael." Shane jerked his chin at Michael, who was trying to shake his head *no, don't do it.* "I think maybe you're right. Maybe it would be better if Claire moved back in with you for a while. Give you a chance to get to know all of us, especially me."

"What the hell are you doing?" Claire whispered fiercely. She didn't care that Dad could probably hear, and Michael certainly could. "I don't want to go anywhere!"

"Claire, he's *right*. You'd be safer there. Our house isn't exactly a fortress, in case what happened today didn't sink in yet," Shane replied. "Hell, between strangers cruising in and out, my dad's threat to come back and finish what he started—"

Claire threw down her fork. "Wait just a minute. You're telling me it's for my own good—is that it?"

"Yes."

"Michael? Jump in anytime!"

Michael held up his hands in surrender. He'd had enough, and Claire couldn't really blame him.

Eve, though, cleared her throat and waded right into the conversational swamp. "Mr. Danvers, honest, Claire's perfectly fine with us. We all look after her, and Shane's not the kind of guy who'd take advantage—"

"Wouldn't say that," Shane said, way too mildly. "I'm exactly that kind of guy, really."

Eve sent him a dirty look. "And besides, he knows we'd both kill him if he tried. But he wouldn't do it. Claire's fine where she is. And she's happy, too."

"Yes," Claire agreed. "I'm *happy*, Dad."

Michael still hadn't spoken. He was, instead, watching Claire's father with a strange kind of intensity; at first she thought, *He's trying to put some kind of vampire whammy on him*, but then she changed her mind. It was more like Michael was honestly puzzled, and trying to figure out what to say next.

Her father hadn't heard a word that anyone had said. "I want you to move home, Claire, and that's that. I don't want you staying in that house anymore. End of discussion."

Her mother wasn't talking, which was unusual, too; she just stirred her coffee slowly and tried to look interested in the food on the plate in front of her.

Claire opened her mouth to shoot back a heated, not very respectful reply, but Michael shook his head and put his hand over hers. "Don't waste your breath," he said. "This isn't their idea. Bishop planted the suggestion."

"What? Why would he do that?"

"No idea. Maybe he wants us separated. Maybe he just likes messing with people. Maybe he wants to piss off Amelie. But the important thing is, I don't think you ought to let this get to you—"

"Not *get to me*? Michael, my father is saying I have to *move!*"

"You don't," Michael said. "Not if you don't want to."

Claire's father, who'd been frowning, turned a dark, unhealthy color of red in the face. "You damn well *do*," he snapped. "You're my daughter, Claire, and until you turn eighteen, you'll do what I tell you. And *you*—" He leveled a finger at Michael. "If I have to bring charges against you—"

"For what?" Michael asked mildly.

"For—look, don't think I don't know what's going on here. If I find out that my daughter's been—been . . ." Dad didn't seem to be able to work up the words. Michael continued to watch him steadily, with no sign of comprehension.

Claire cleared her throat.

"Dad," she said. She felt color blazing in her cheeks, and her voice was barely steady. "If you're asking if I'm still a virgin, I am."

"Claire!" Her mom's voice cracked sharply across the last of her sentence. "That's enough."

Total silence at the table. Not even Michael seemed to know where to take the conversation from there. Eve looked like she was having a hard time deciding whether to laugh or wince, and finally dug into her chocolate sundae as the best possible response.

Michael's cell phone rang. He opened it, spoke softly, listened, and closed it without replying. He signaled the waitress. "We have to go," he said.

"Where?"

"Back to the house. Amelie wants to see us."

"You're coming home with us," Dad said to Claire, who shook her head. "Don't argue with me—"

"I'm sorry, sir, but she has to come with us right now," Michael said. "If Amelie says it's the right thing to do, I'll bring her to your house myself. But we'll drop you off on the way, and I'll let you know as soon as possible." It was said respectfully, but without any room for argument, and there was something about Michael in that moment that just couldn't be pushed.

Dad's face set, still red, and very hard. "This isn't over, Michael."

"Yes, sir," he said. "That much I know. We haven't even started yet."

The drive back was even more uncomfortable, and not just physically; Claire's father was livid, her mother embarrassed, and Claire herself was so mad she could barely stand to look at either of them. How *could* they? Even if Mr. Bishop had done something to them, screwed with their heads, they'd bought into it completely. They'd always said they trusted her, always said that they wanted her to make her own decisions, but when it came right down to it, they wanted her to be their helpless little girl, after all.

Well, it wasn't going to happen. She'd come too far for that.

Michael pulled to a stop in front of her parents' new house—another big Gothic-style house, looking almost exactly like their own except for the landscaping out front. Her parents' Founder House had a spreading live oak tree towering over the property that rustled like dry paper in the evening breeze, and the trim was painted what looked like, in the dark, a dull black.

Claire's dad leaned in to give her one last look. "I expect to hear from you tonight," he said. "I expect you to tell me when you're coming home. And by home, I mean here, with us."

She didn't answer. After extending the look for way too long, her dad shut the car door, and Michael accelerated smoothly away—not too quickly, but not slowly, either.

And they all breathed an audible sigh of relief when the house faded into the darkness behind the car. "Wow," Shane said. "Dude's got a glare on him. Maybe he really does belong here in Morganville."

"Don't say that," Claire said. She was fighting with all kinds of emotions—anger at her parents, frustration with the situation, worry, outright fear. Her parents *didn't* belong here. They'd been just fine where they were, but Amelie had to uproot them and bring them here. Having Claire's parents where she could control them gave her more leverage.

And now it gave Mr. Bishop leverage, too.

Shane took her hand. "Easy," he said. "Like Michael said, you don't have to go if you don't want to go. Not that I wouldn't feel better if you were someplace a hell of a lot safer."

"I don't think the Danvers house will be safer," Michael said. "They don't understand the rules, or the risks—they're too new here. I think Bishop's trying to play with Amelie's head, and whatever we think about her, he's worse. I guarantee it."

Claire shuddered. "Was it Amelie who called you at the restaurant?"

"No," Michael said, and there was a grim tone in his voice. "That was Oliver. I have to admit, I'm not feeling real good about this. Oliver's never really been on her side—maybe he's taken Bishop's. In which case we could be going home to a trap."

"Do we have a choice?" Shane asked.

"Don't think so."

"Then screw it. I'm getting tired." Shane yawned. "Let's go get eaten. At least then I can get some sleep."

Nobody thought it was funny—least of all Shane, Claire suspected—but they didn't have any better ideas, and Michael drove home. Morganville was silent outside the dark-tinted windows; Claire could barely see dim gleams of lights, and they might have been the few and far-between streetlamps, or the glow from house porch lights. It was a lot like being in a space capsule, but with better upholstery.

Michael parked and turned off the car. As Eve reached for her door handle, he said, "Guys." She waited. They all waited. "I didn't exactly get any instant upgrade on knowledge when I—when I changed, but I'm damn sure of one thing. This Bishop, he's real trouble. Trouble like maybe we've never seen before. And I'm worried. So watch each other's backs. I'll try—"

He didn't seem to know how to finish that. Eve reached out to touch his face, and he turned toward her, lips parted. The look that went between them was so naked it felt wrong to see it. Shane cleared his throat.

"We're all on it, man," he said. "We'll be okay."

Michael didn't answer, but then, Claire figured maybe there wasn't much to say. He got out of the car, and the others followed. The evening was getting cold, and the wind fluttered around Claire's hair and clothes, looking for skin to chill. Finding it, too. She wrapped her jacket closer and hurried after Michael toward the back door.

Inside, the kitchen was exactly as they'd left it—messy. Pots and pans still on the stove, though thankfully they'd remembered to turn off the burners before they'd left. The smell of stale bacon grease and rubbery gravy hung heavy in the air, barely cut by the aroma of old, overcooked coffee.

They didn't stop. Michael led them straight through the kitchen door, into the living room.

Bishop was gone. So were his two pretty hangers-on. It was just Amelie and Oliver, sitting alone at the large wooden table. They'd carelessly shoved aside plates and cups and glasses into a tottering pile, and between them was a chessboard. Nothing Claire recognized that belonged in the house; it looked old, and well used. Beautiful, too.

Amelie was playing white. She ignored their entry as she contemplated the chessboard. Across from her, Oliver leaned back in his chair, crossed his arms, and sent the four of them an unreadable look. He seemed right at home, which made Claire fume, and she could only imagine how Michael felt about it. Oliver had killed Michael—ripped away his human existence and trapped him in a twilight state between human and vampire—right here in this house. In fact, almost on this very *spot*. It had been brutal, and murderous, and Michael had never for a second forgotten who and what Oliver was, however he appeared.

Amelie had offered Michael the chance to escape from that trap, and he'd taken it even at the cost of becoming a true vampire. So far, he didn't seem to regret it. Much.

"You're not welcome here," Michael said to Oliver, who raised his eyebrows and smiled.

"Waiting for the house to evict me? Keep waiting," he said. "Amelie, you really should teach your pets manners. Next thing you know, they'll be clawing the carpet and spraying the drapes."

She didn't look up. "Do try to be civil," she replied. "You're a guest in their house. *My* house." She moved a piece on the chessboard. "Be seated, all of you. I dislike having people stand."

It had the force of royal command, and before she could think about it, Claire was sliding into one of the dining-table chairs, and Shane was settling in next to her. Eve hesitated, then took a chair as far away from Oliver as possible.

That left one empty chair, and it was next to Oliver. Michael shook his head, crossed his arms over his chest, and leaned against the wall.

Amelie gave him a glance, but didn't force the issue. "So you have met Mr. Bishop," she said. "And he has most assuredly met you. I wish this had not happened, but since it has, we must find ways to guard you against him and his associates." Oliver took one of her bishops and set it aside. She had no visible reaction. "Otherwise, I fear this house will be in the market for new tenants soon."

Oliver laughed. He stopped laughing when Amelie made her next move, and concentrated on the chessboard with a fierce, blank expression.

"Who is Bishop?" Michael asked.

"Exactly who he says he is. He has no reason to lie."

"So he's your father?" Claire asked. There was a long silence, one not even Oliver broke; Amelie raised her cool gray eyes and focused on Claire's face until Claire felt the urge, not just to look away, but to *run.*

Amelie finally said, "In a sense, at least, as you might understand such things. Both my human and immortal bloodlines flow through him. Oliver, do hurry. I feel the need to go home before the sun rises."

The sun wasn't anywhere close to rising, which must have been Amelie's bone-dry idea of a joke. Oliver moved a pawn. Amelie took it effortlessly.

Michael chimed in. "Maybe the better question is, *where* is Mr. Bishop?"

"Gone," Oliver said. "I packed him off in a nice limousine with a driver. He'll be staying at one of the Founder Houses."

"Which one?" Claire felt a sudden surge of illness, one that got worse as neither of the vampires answered. "It isn't my parents' house, right? Right?"

"I'd rather you not be aware of his exact location," Amelie said, which wasn't an answer, certainly not the right answer. She moved her white queen in a long, deliberate scrape down the chessboard. "Checkmate."

Oliver studied the board, then studied her with equal annoyance as he tipped over his doomed black king. "We need to discuss this," he said. "Obviously."

"Your tragic lack of strategic skills?" Amelie's frost-colored brows slowly rose. "I am deliberating what to do about our guests. For now, go home, Oliver. And thank you for coming."

She said it without a trace of irony—she could dismiss him like a servant, but at least she thanked him. Oliver's eyes went even darker, but he got up without comment and walked out into the kitchen. Claire heard the door slam behind him.

Amelie took in a deliberate breath, then let it out. She rose to her feet and nodded to Michael. "I think you'll be safe enough here tonight," she said. "Let no one enter, not for any reason." A quick, almost invisible flicker of a smile. "Except for me, of course. Me, you cannot stop."

"What about Oliver?" Shane asked.

"His invitation to enter has been revoked. He won't be able to bother you unless you do something foolish." Which, from the look Amelie gave him, she considered hardly unlikely. "Bishop is my affair, not yours. Go about your business, and stay out of this. All of you."

"Wait. My parents—"

Amelie didn't wait. With silent grace, she left the table and walked up the stairs, and as her luminous pale figure disappeared at the top, Shane said, "Where the hell is she going? There's no door up there."

Claire knew. She knew all too well. "However she does it, she's gone." They all looked at her, even Michael. "There must be some way out. What's she going to do, bring her pajamas and crash on the couch?"

"Do you think she has any?" Eve asked. "Because I'm betting she sleeps in the nude."

"*Eve!*"

"What? Come on. Can you really see her in flannel footies? Bunny slippers?"

Michael sank into the chair Amelie had vacated, and stared at the chessboard. He slowly reset it, but Claire could tell he wasn't really thinking about the game. "Shane," he said. "Go make sure we're locked up, would you?"

Shane nodded and left, heading straight for the kitchen first. Claire sat across from Michael, in the chair Oliver had occupied. "You're worried," she said.

"No," Michael said, and picked up the white knight, to turn it over and over in his pale fingers. "I'm scared. If this guy's got Amelie and Oliver nervous, we're way out of our league. *Morganville* is way out of its league."

He looked up at Eve, who didn't respond except to press her lips tighter together. Claire heard Shane's footsteps as he went toward the front door, checked the lock and dead bolt, and then went on to test the windows.

"We should get some rest," Michael said. "Could be a long day tomorrow."

As he got up, Eve's hand grazed his, just a very light caress, and the two of them locked stares for about a half second.

"Yeah," Eve agreed. "I should rest, too."

Claire threw a stray magazine at her. "Get a room."

"Paying for one already," Eve shot back. "And I'm going to get my money's worth, too."

She jogged up the stairs, pausing near the top to throw a glance back down toward Michael, who had the most luminous smile on his face. He shook his head, like he couldn't believe what was going through his mind, and cleared his throat when he saw Claire watching him.

"Discreet," Claire said. "You guys ought to hang a towel on the doorknob or something."

"Quiet." But Michael was smiling, and when he smiled, her heart just soared. She loved seeing him happy. He was usually so . . . focused. "If you need anything, you know where to find me."

"Yeah, you think?"

He waved and followed Eve upstairs.

Shane came back from checking all the ground-floor entry points, and dropped into the chair Michael had vacated. "Where'd they go?"

She pointed straight up.

"Oh." He knew, all too well. "So. Want to play a game?"

"I want to call my parents," Claire said. "Do you seriously think Amelie let Mr. Bishop stay in their house?"

"I don't know," he said. "Call if you think it'll help."

She pulled her phone out of her pocket and dialed information; her parents had a new listing, since they'd just arrived in Morganville. While she waited for an answer, Shane reached across the table and took her free hand in his, and the warm touch of his skin made her feel a little less nervous.

Until her mom answered the phone, at least. "Claire! I didn't expect you to call so soon. Are you ready to come home?"

She froze for a second, then said, as calmly as possible, "No, Mom. I just wanted to make sure you were okay. Everything all right?"

"Of course everything's all right. Why wouldn't it be?"

Claire squeezed her eyes shut. "No reason," she said. "I just wanted to check in and see how you were settling in. How's the house?"

"Well, it's a fixer-upper, you know. Needs some wiring, and an absolute mountain of decorating, but I'm looking forward to that."

"That's great. And—so, you don't have any guests or anything?"

"Guests?" Her mother laughed. "Claire, honey, we barely have sheets on our mattress right now. I'm not ready for guests!"

That, at least, was a relief. "Great. Well—Mom, I have to go. Good night."

"Good night, sweetheart. I'm looking forward to having you home."

Claire hung up, and Shane slipped an arm around her waist. "Hey," he said. "They're okay?"

"For now. But he could get to them, right? Anytime he wants."

"Maybe. But he could get to us just as easily. Look, you can't help them right now, but he's got no good reason to hurt them. It'll be okay."

Shane was the optimist. That was how you knew things were really bad. . . . Claire forced a smile, opened her eyes, and tried to be a brave little toaster. "Yeah," she said. "Yeah, it'll be fine. No problem."

His dark eyes searched hers, and she knew that he could see she was lying. But he didn't call her on it, probably all too familiar with the concept of denial. "So," he said. "Care for a nice, civilized game of chess?"

A thump, and the unmistakable sound of a muffled giggle, drifted through the ceiling from the second floor. Approximately where Eve's room would be.

"Hey!" Shane yelled up. "Turn down the porn soundtrack! Trying to concentrate here!"

More laughter, quickly stifled. Shane focused back on Claire, and Claire felt her lips curling into a more genuine kind of smile.

"Chess," she said. "Your move, tough guy."

Another thump from upstairs. Shane shook his head and tipped over his king. "What the hell? I surrender. Let's hook up a video game and kill some zombies."

THREE

In the morning, it was . . . the morning. For a precious few seconds when Claire woke up, nothing was wrong, nothing at all. Her body hummed with energy, and the birds were singing outside, and the sun burned in warm stripes across her bed.

She squinted at the alarm clock. Seven thirty. Time to get up if she intended to make it to her first class and still have any margin for coffee.

It wasn't until she was in the shower, and the hot water was pounding sense back into her head, that she realized that all was not well. Her parents were in town. Her parents were on the radar screen of the monsters.

And her parents wanted her to move back in with them.

That put an end to her good mood, and by the time she padded down the steps, dragging her textbook-loaded backpack and carrying her shoes, she was frowning. The house was a mess. Nobody had done the chores, including her. The kitchen was still a wreck, with breakfast congealing in the pans. She muttered to herself as the coffee brewed, dumped filthy dishes and pans in the sink to soak in hot water, and left a snarky note for her housemates. Especially Shane, who'd slacked even more than was normal.

Then she put on her shoes and walked to school.

Morganville looked just like any other dusty, sleepy town in the daylight: people out driving to work, jogging, pushing strollers, walking dogs. College students with backpacks as she got closer to the campus. The casual visitor never knew, at least during the daytime, that this place was so vastly screwed up.

Claire supposed that was the point.

She spotted some trucks delivering to local businesses; did those drivers know? Did they just come and go without incident? Was there some off-limits rule for the vamps about whom they could hunt and whom they couldn't? There would have to be. Having the state police descend on Morganville wouldn't be helpful for the vamps. . . .

"Hey."

Claire blinked. A car was idling next to her, barely keeping pace as she walked. A red convertible, harsh and shiny as fresh blood in the sun. In it, three girls with identically false smiles.

The driver was Monica Morrell, the daughter of the town's mayor. Claire's worst human enemy from day one of her tenure in Morganville. Monica had mostly recovered from her recent brush with death by drugs, or at least she looked that way—glossy as the car, and just as hard. Her blond hair was shiny and casually styled, her makeup perfect, and if she looked just a shade more pale than usual, it was hard to tell.

"Hey," Claire said, and made sure to drift farther over on the sidewalk, out of easy grabbing range. "How are you feeling, Monica?"

"Me? Great. Couldn't be better," Monica said brightly. There was something way darker in her eyes than in her tone. "You tried to kill me, freak."

Claire stopped dead in her tracks. "No," she said. "I didn't do that."

"You gave me that drug. It almost killed me."

"You *took it* from me!" The red crystals, the ones that she'd stolen from Myrnin. The ones that, however briefly, had seemed like a good idea. Not so much once she'd seen their effect on Monica, and her own face in the mirror after taking them. They hadn't hurt her, but their effect on Monica had been shocking.

"Don't give me that. You nearly killed me," Monica said. "I'd file charges, but with you being the Founder's pet and all, that won't do any good. So we'll just have to find some other way to make sure you pay. Just wanted to give you a heads-up, bitch—this isn't done. It isn't even started. It is *on.*"

She gave Claire a cold, hard smile, and accelerated away with a screech of rubber on pavement.

Claire shifted her backpack nervously and looked around. Nobody had paid attention, of course. It didn't pay, in Morganville, to get into anybody else's business.

She was on her own out here. Eve worked on campus, but Claire didn't want to drag her friends into this. They had enough problems already, and Monica was all her own.

Like it or not.

But as she passed the recessed doorway of a boarded-up shop, she sensed someone watching her.

She tried to dismiss it as imagination, but there really *was* someone watching her. She couldn't make him out for a few seconds, and then she did, with another unpleasant shock. Heroin-addict-skinny, pale, stringy hair. Wearing black. Eve's brother.

"Jason," she said, and involuntarily looked around for help. Nobody there, nobody she could turn to. Not even a passing police car—and the police definitely wanted to talk to Jason, after his run-in with Shane.

It hit her again: *He'd stabbed her boyfriend.* Tried to kill him. The cops said it was self-defense, but she knew better.

Jason took his hands out of his coat pockets and held them up. "Don't scream," he said. "Unless you really feel like it. I'm not going to hurt you. Not in broad daylight on a busy street, anyway."

He sounded . . . different. Odder than usual, and that was a pretty high standard of odd.

"What do you want?" She clutched the strap of her backpack in a white-knuckled fist. In an emergency, it would make a respectable blunt object. She might knock him down with it, or at least trip him. It was only about a block to Common Grounds—Oliver owed her Protection once she was inside the building, even from human enemies.

"Stop freaking, genius. I'm not here to hurt you." He put his hands back in his jacket pockets. "How's Shane?"

"Why do you care?"

"Because—" He frowned and shrugged. "Look, that was self-defense, okay?"

"You baited him. You threatened me and Eve. You *wanted* him to come after you."

"Yeah, well, granted, I was tweaking, but the guy took a home-run swing at my head, in case you missed it."

Uncomfortably, that was true. "What about the other people you've killed? Were those all self-defense, too?"

"Who says I've killed people?"

"You did. Remember? You left a dead girl in our basement for Shane to find. You tried to put him in prison."

Jason didn't say a word to that. He just stared at her, and in the shadows his dark eyes were like holes in his still, pale face. He looked . . . dead. Deader than most vampires.

"I need to talk to my sister," he said.

"Eve doesn't want to talk to you, you psycho. Leave us alone!"

"It's about our dad," he said, and even though Claire was walking away, leaving him and all his psycho problems behind, she slowed to look back. "I need to talk to Eve. Tell her I'll call. Tell her not to hang up."

Claire nodded, once. She didn't hate him any less, but there was something different about him right now—something that asked for a truce, but didn't get down on its knees and beg for it, either. "No promises," she said.

Jason nodded back. "Didn't expect any."

He didn't say thanks. She kept walking.

When she looked back, the doorway was empty. She caught a glimpse of a black jacket turning the corner at the end of the block. *Damn, he moves fast,* she thought, and that gave her another kind of chill. What if Jason had gotten his wish? What if someone had made him a full-fledged vampire, as hard as that seemed?

She decided she'd ask Amelie, first chance she got.

.   .   .

The morning classes came and went. It wasn't like any of them were especially difficult, even the high-level physics courses she'd tested herself into. She'd traded out some of her lame core classes for a mythology course, or rather Amelie had insisted on it—that was a fairly cool thing, and she found herself looking forward to it. No discussions of vampires just now, unfortunately. It was all about zombies, voodoo, and popular media on the subject. They were going to watch *Night of the Living Dead* next week. Claire didn't know nearly as much about zombies as most of the other students; except for the first-person-shooter game that Shane liked to play, she couldn't remember ever really paying attention to the idea.

Of course, since moving to Morganville, she wasn't ruling anything out as unlikely.

After mythology, which turned out to be a wealth of information about voodoo, if she ever needed that, Claire had a break before lab sessions began. She took herself off to the University Center. It was a sprawling building, home to a large study area with long tables and groupings of chairs, and it featured a bookstore, a cafeteria that served fantastic grilled cheese sandwiches and salads, and a pretty decent coffee bar.

There wasn't a line today. Claire paid for her mocha and moved around to the barista side, where Eve was working. Eve looked great today, and not just because of the care she'd taken with her outfit and makeup; she kind of radiated satisfaction.

Oh. *Right.*

Eve gave her an absolutely stunning smile and handed over her drink. "Hey, bookworm. Doing okay?"

"Sure. You?"

"Not bad. It's even been kind of slow and steady today, after the morning rush." That smile had a secret.

"So? How was your night?" Claire prodded. The secret wanted to be shared, and besides, she was kind of . . . curious.

"Fantastic," Eve sighed. "I just—yeah. Since I was fourteen, I've had a crush on that boy, you know? And he never knew I existed. I went to every one of his concerts, from the time he first started playing, up to the last time he headlined at Common Grounds. I never thought—I just never thought it'd work out."

"And how was . . . ?" Claire raised her eyebrows and left the question open to anything Eve wanted to make it mean.

Eve's smile got wicked. *"Fantastic."*

They shared muffled squeals. Eve did a little happydance behind the counter, dumped shots in a drink, and twirled. Claire had never seen her look so full-stop happy.

Reality came back, and she remembered why she'd come in the first place. She had the strong suspicion she was about to blow all that happiness sky-high.

Eve's smile was fading, like someone had turned down her dimmer switch. "Claire, you're wearing the worried face. What's wrong?"

"I . . ." Claire hesitated, then plunged in. "I saw Jason. This morning."

Eve's dark eyes widened, but she didn't say anything. She waited.

"He wanted me to tell you that he's going to call. It's something about your dad, he says. He says not to hang up."

"My dad," Eve repeated. "You're sure."

"That's what he said. I told him, no promises." Claire sipped her mocha, which was perfect, and watched Eve's expression. Not too easy to read, right now. "He didn't try to hurt me."

"Broad daylight, on a main street? Yeah, well, he's bug-out crazy, but he's not stupid." Eve seemed very far away, suddenly. And all her happy glow was gone. "I haven't talked to either one of my parents since my eighteenth birthday."

"Why not?"

"They tried to sell me to Brandon," she said flatly. "Like a piece of meat on the hoof. I don't know why Jason's suddenly all nostalgic about the fam; it's not like there were good times to remember."

"But they're still your parents."

"Yeah, unfortunately. Look, here's the story of the Rosser clan: we're the original nuclear family. As in, nuclear bomb. Toxic even when it doesn't explode." Eve shook her head. "Whatever Dad's damage is, I don't care. And I don't know why Jason would, either."

Another student had paid for coffee, and Eve cast him an absent, empty smile and started pulling espresso shots with mechanical precision. "It's nothing," she said. "And I'm hanging up on him when he calls. If he calls. And even if it's something, I don't give a damn anyway."

Claire just nodded. She had no idea what to say. Eve was clearly upset, a lot more upset than she'd expected her to be. She waved good-bye and took herself off to a nearby study table, and began plowing through a book she'd borrowed from the library. Somebody's PhD paper, which read like the guy had never bothered to attend a single English Composition class.

Good equations, though. She was heavily involved in them when her cell phone rang.

"Hello?" She didn't recognize the number, but it was local, and not her parents.

"Claire Danvers?"

"Yes. Who's this?"

"My name's Dr. Robert Mills. I'm the one who treated your friend Shane in the hospital."

She felt a piercing sensation of alarm. "Nothing's wrong with—"

"No, nothing like that," he broke in hastily. "Look, you were the one who had the red crystals, right? The ones that nearly killed the mayor's daughter?"

Claire's momentary relief burned away like flash paper. "I guess," she said. "I gave them to the doctor."

"Well, here's the thing: I've been looking at those crystals. Where'd you get them?"

"I—found them." Technically true.

"Where?"

"In a lab."

"I need you to show me this lab, Claire."

"I don't think I can do that. I'm sorry."

"Look, I understand that you're probably protecting someone— someone important. But if it helps, I already have approval from the Council to work on these crystals, and I really need more information about them—who developed them, how, the ingredients. I think I can help."

Amelie was on the Elders' Council. But she hadn't said anything about working with the doctor. "Let me find out what I can tell you," Claire said. "I'm sorry. I'll call you back."

"Soon," he said. "I've been told the goal is to increase the effectiveness of the drug by at least fifty percent within the next couple of months."

Claire blinked, surprised. "Do you know what it does?"

Dr. Mills—who sounded pleasant and normal—laughed. "Do I *really* know? Probably not. This is Morganville—we invented the concept of the secret around here. But I have a pretty decent idea that whatever it is, it's not designed for human consumption."

That was as much as Claire wanted to talk about on the phone, no matter how friendly he seemed. After a quick excuse, she hung up and called Amelie. She intended to leave a message, and that, she thought, would probably be the end of it.

Amelie picked up the call. Claire stammered, took a deep breath, and told her about Dr. Mills and his request.

"I should have told you last evening. I have decided to concede to your request to have additional resources on this project," Amelie said. "Dr. Mills is a trusted expert, a longtime resident of the town, and he won't make the kind of value judgments others might. He's also capable of keeping our secrets, and that is imperative. You understand why."

Claire did, all too well. The crystals were a drug that helped vampires ward off the effects of a degenerative disease—a disease they all had, one that was robbing them of their ability to reproduce. Amelie was the strongest, but she was sick, too, and the worst cases were insane and locked away in cells beneath Morganville.

And so far, few of the vampires knew about the illness. Once they did, there might be nothing to stop them from lashing out, blaming others. Innocent humans, probably.

Just as bad would be the effect on the human population. Once they knew the vampires weren't invincible, how many of them would really cooperate? Amelie had long ago figured that this could destroy Morganville, and Claire was pretty sure she was right.

"But—he wants to see Myrnin's lab," Claire said. Myrnin, her mentor and sometimes even her friend, had slipped off the edge of sanity, and he was in one of the cells. Lucid sometimes, and other times . . . dangerously not. "Should I take him there?"

"No. Tell him that you'll bring what he needs to the hospital. I don't want any human other than yourself in that lab, Claire. There are secrets that must be kept, and I rely on you to see to it. Restrict his research only to refining and enhancing the formula you've already created." What Amelie meant, in that queen-cool way, was that if Claire spilled the beans, she'd end up dead. Or worse.

"Yes," Claire said faintly. "I understand. About my parents—"

"They are safe enough," Amelie said. That wasn't the same thing as saying they were safe. "You will not see Mr. Bishop for the time being. If you happen to see his two associates, be polite, but don't fear; they are well in hand."

Maybe by Amelie's standards. Claire was a little bit more worried. "Okay," she said doubtfully. "If anything happens—"

"Discuss it with Oliver," Amelie said. "Curiously, I find the differences between us lessened dramatically once my sire paid a visit. Nothing like a common enemy to unite squabbling neighbors." She paused for a moment, and then said, almost awkwardly, "You and your friends? You are well?"

We're doing small talk now? Claire shivered. "Yeah, we're fine. Thank you."

"Good." Amelie hung up. Claire mouthed a silent *Oooo-kay,* and pocketed the phone.

As she was leaving, she saw Eve at the barista station, staring blankly at the levers as she worked. The happy glow hadn't returned. In fact, she looked grim. And scared.

Dammit. Why did I ruin her day like that? I should have just blown him off, the little psycho.

Claire checked her watch, snagged her backpack, and jogged off to her lab class.

When she met Dr. Mills later that afternoon, she did it at the hospital, in his office. He was a medium sort of guy—medium tall, medium age, medium coloring. He had a nice smile, which seemed to promise that everything would be okay, and despite the fact that Claire knew it was total fiction, she smiled back.

"Have a seat, Claire," he said, and indicated one of the blue club chairs in front of his desk. Behind him were floor-to-ceiling bookshelves—medical references in matching bindings, with some newer off-brand volumes thrown in for variety. Dr. Mills had stacks of magazines and photocopied articles on one corner of the desk, and a teetering set of patient files on the other. A framed photo faced away from Claire, so she couldn't see if he had a family. He had a wedding ring, though.

Dr. Mills didn't speak immediately; he leaned back in his leather chair, steepled his fingers, and looked at her for a while. She fought against the urge to squirm, but couldn't keep her fingers from restlessly picking at the fabric of her jeans.

"I knew you were young," he said finally, "but I admit, I'm even more surprised now. You're sixteen?"

"Seventeen in a few weeks," Claire said. She was getting resigned to having this conversation with every single adult in Morganville. She ought to just record it and play it back every time she met somebody new.

"Well, from the notes that Amelie has provided to me, you have a very solid grasp of what you're doing. I don't think I'll be so much directing your research as helping you execute your experiments. Where I see opportunities to add some value, I will. Obviously, the labs here at the hospital have much more sophisticated equipment than I imagine you have—wherever you developed your initial crystals." He flipped through the large folder open in the center of his desk, and Claire saw photocopies of her own neat handwriting. Her notes, which she'd provided to Amelie. "I took the liberty of making up a set of crystals based on your formula, using the facilities in our labs. I found that if you accelerate the drying process with heat, you can increase the strength of the dosage by about twenty percent. And I also created a stronger liquid version that can be delivered directly into the body by injection."

She blinked. "Injection." She tried to imagine getting close enough to Myrnin to stick a needle in his arm, especially when he was in one of his bad swings.

"It can be delivered through a dart," he said. "Like an animal tranquilizer, although I wouldn't use that analogy to anyone else. Wouldn't be respectful."

She managed a smile. "That'd be—very helpful. I didn't try the heating process for drying the crystals. That's interesting."

"No reason you should have. I tried it because I didn't have an unlimited time to dry them—our lab's busy, and I didn't want anyone questioning what I was doing. I've asked Amelie to provide us with some secured laboratory space at the university. More convenient for you, and safer for me. I can have equipment moved there as we need it, or requisition it through the Council." Dr. Mills cocked his head and looked at her again, brown eyes bright and challenging. Like Myrnin's, only not half as crazy. "About my request to tour the lab where you made the crystals . . ."

"Sorry. I can't."

"Perhaps if you checked with Amelie—"

"I did."

He sighed. "Then when can I examine our patient?"

"You don't."

"Claire, this will not work if I can't take baseline readings on the patient and determine what the measurable improvements are as we change the formula!"

She did see that, actually, but the thought of putting nice Dr. Mills in grabbing distance of Myrnin made her shiver. "I'll check," she promised, and got to her feet. "I'm sorry. It's getting late. I need to—"

Dr. Mills glanced at his office window. Outside the blinds, the sky was darkening from faded denim to indigo. "Of course. I understand. Here's a sample of the new batch of crystals. But before you give it to him, see if you can get baseline information—most importantly, a blood sample."

"A blood sample," she repeated. He opened a drawer and handed her a small, sealed kit. It had a syringe, gauze pads, alcohol wipes, and a couple of vacuum tubes. "You're not serious."

"I'm not saying it might not be difficult, but if you won't let me go with you to do it . . ."

She could do a lot of things, but she was pretty sure she couldn't hold Myrnin down and stick a needle in his vein. Not while he was . . . altered.

She took the kit and put it in her backpack. "Anything else?"

Dr. Mills passed her a gun—a dart gun. He opened the back to show her the fluffy end of the tube. "It's preloaded with one dose," he said. "I only made up a few—it takes some time to distill. Here are two extra, if you need them." As she stowed the gun in her backpack, he said, "It's untested. So be careful. I *think* it will be stronger and longer lasting, but I'm not sure about the side effects."

"And the crystals?"

He passed them over, too. They looked a little finer than the ones she'd developed—more like raw sugar. Those went into the backpack, as well.

"Claire," he said, as she hoisted the burden, "have you heard any rumors about a new vampire in town?"

She froze. Her gold bracelet, the one with Amelie's symbol etched on it, caught the light and glittered—not that she needed the reminder.

"Just Michael," she said. "But that's not news."

"I heard there were strangers."

Claire shrugged. "Guess you heard wrong."

She left before she had to lie any more. She couldn't stop herself from glancing back at him. He nodded and smiled a good-bye.

She felt bad, but there was only so much truth she was prepared to give, even to somebody who came recommended by Amelie.

"Did you bring the hamburger?"

Claire didn't even have time to drop her backpack on the hallway floor at home before Eve had buzzed in on her like a dark, caffeine-fueled Tinkerbell, brandishing a wooden spoon.

"Uh—what?"

"Hamburger. I sent you a text."

Oops. Claire dug her phone out and saw that, sure enough, there was a flashing message icon. "I didn't get it. Sorry."

"Crap." Eve turned away and marched back down the hall, Doc Martens boots clomping with fine disregard for the safety of the wood floor. "Michael! Guess what? You're running errands!"

Michael was playing guitar—something fast and complicated. He stopped periodically, which was unusual for him, and he ignored Eve, which wasn't normal, either. As Claire rounded the corner, she saw him standing up at the dinner table, leaning over to jot down music on a lined page.

Turned out that he wasn't ignoring Eve so much as not obeying. "I'm busy," he said, frowned at the paper, and played the same phrase again, then again. Shook his head in frustration and erased notes on the paper. "You and Shane go."

"I'm cooking!" Eve rolled her eyes. "Creative people. They think the world stops when they think."

"I'll go," Claire said. The chance to be alone with Shane, even on something as boring as a trip to the all-night grocery, was too good to miss. "Better if I do, anyway. I've got the free pass." She held up the bracelet.

Michael pulled himself away from the music in his head long enough to give her a look. He tapped his pencil in a fast, complicated rhythm on the table. "Thirty minutes," he said. "There and back. No excuses. If you guys are late, I'm coming after you, and I'm going to be pissed off."

"Thanks, *Dad*." She wished she hadn't said it—not so much because of the grimace on Michael's face, but because it made her think of her actual dad. And that the clock was running on how long he'd allow her to continue her current living arrangements.

Shane came out of the kitchen sucking on his fingertip. "What's going on?"

"You have *not* been sticking your dirty fingers in my sauce," Eve said, and pointed her wooden spoon at him.

He quickly took the finger out of his mouth. "First off, they're not dirty. I licked them first. And second—did I hear something about the store? Claire?"

"Yeah, I'm ready."

He grabbed Eve's keys from the hall table. "Then let's roll."

Shane was a good driver, and he knew Morganville like the back of his hand—of course, Morganville was just about that big, too, and there was only one all-night grocery store, the Food King, locally owned and operated. The parking lot was lit up like a football stadium. There were fifteen or so cars already there, evenly split between human vehicles and vampmobiles. Shane parked directly under a blazing set of lights and turned off the car.

"Wait," he said as Claire reached for the door handle. "It takes us about five minutes to get here, five minutes to get the stuff, five minutes back home. That gives us fifteen whole extra minutes."

She felt her heart stammer, and race a little faster. Shane was looking at her with fierce intensity.

"So what do you want to do?" she asked, trying to sound casual about it.

"I want to talk," he said, which was not what she expected. Not at all. "I can't talk about this back at the house. I never know who could be listening."

"Meaning Michael?"

Shane shrugged. "It's just never exactly private."

He wasn't wrong, but she still felt horribly disappointed. "Sure," she said, and knew she sounded stiff and wounded. "Go ahead. Talk."

His eyes widened. "You thought—"

"Just talk, Shane."

He cleared his throat. "I've been doing some research on Bishop."

The idea of *Shane* and *research* didn't seem to want to fall into the same sentence. "Where?"

"The town library," he shrugged. "Special collections. I know Janice, the librarian—she was a friend of my mom's. She let me into the back to take a look at some of the older stuff, the things they don't put out for public reading."

"The vampire collection."

He nodded. "Anyway, the only thing I could find out was a reference to a Bishop—maybe not the same one—who killed a whole lot of people about five hundred years ago."

"Doesn't sound too unusual . . ."

"Except that he wasn't killing humans," Shane said. "From the way the thing was written, Bishop was killing off his enemies in the vampire community. Making himself the ruler of the world. And then something happened, and he dropped out of sight."

"Wow. No wonder Amelie and Oliver were freaked."

"If he's been underground all this time, and has a rep for taking out anyone who stands in his way, human or vampire—yeah. I'd be freaked, too. Anyway, I thought you should know. It could be important."

"Thanks."

He nodded, gaze fixed on hers.

"Anything else?" she prompted.

"Yeah."

He leaned forward and kissed her. His weight settled toward her, leaning her back against the door, and she felt all the strength and breath go out of her body, replaced with a quivering, golden vibration. *Oh.* Shane's lips were warm and damp, soft but demanding, and she heard herself make a sound like a whimper in response. His hands knew just where to hold her—one at the back of her head, one at the small of her back, pulling her closer. Fitting their bodies together.

It felt so good, it was like swimming in sunlight. Her fingers tangled in his soft, shaggy hair and traced down his back, and for a wild second she imagined what it would be like, right here, right now, in Eve's big car. It seemed to go on forever, a dreamy eternity of heat. . . .

His hands slipped down her shoulders, traced her collarbone, then moved lower. She heard herself make a sound that was more a whine than anything else, a naked plea, as the heat of his touch reached the top edge of her bra, slid past the edge and down. . . .

Shane broke the kiss with a gasp, leaning his cheek against hers. The sound of his breath in her ear made her shiver again. *So close. God, we're so close.* . . .

"We'd—better go inside," he said. It sounded like he was fighting hard to sound normal, but he was missing by a mile, and when he sat back, all she could see was the hot focus in his eyes, and his damp, reddened, totally kissable lips. She wondered what he was seeing in her, and realized with a shock that it was probably the same thing.

Shared hunger.

"Yeah," she said. She didn't sound normal, either. She wasn't sure she could walk, in fact; her whole body felt like it had melted, especially around the knees. She took in a couple of deep breaths, then stopped when Shane's eyes focused on the rise and fall of her chest. "We should— go shop."

Shane checked his watch. "No, we should get the hamburger, throw money at the cashier, and break every speed limit back to the house if we don't want Michael calling out the SWAT team."

That sobered them up, enough to get them out of the car and into the store, but they held hands the whole way.

Inside, the place looked too bright, and yet somehow too cold. Aisles of colorful packages. There were a few shoppers pushing carts, and some of them, Claire knew, had to be vampires, but she couldn't necessarily tell which ones, at a glance. Many of them had perfected their human disguises. Was it the twentysomething girl with the red hair and the long shopping list? Or the elderly lady with her little fluffy dog riding in the child seat of the cart? Not the dad with the two small children and the harassed look—she was sure of that one.

Claire didn't really have time to gawk. Shane let go of her hand and pointed off down one aisle; she split off toward the meat section. Choosing hamburger was mainly a decision about poundage, and Eve hadn't said how much to get. Claire settled for two packages, and headed for the aisle where Shane had disappeared. The snack aisle, what a shock.

The song on the store's speakers changed to an annoying and slightly creepy song from the 1970s, something about seasons in the sun, and she was thinking about how ironic that was when she rounded the endcap display and found Shane backed up against the shelves, with a woman pressed right up against him.

It was the female vamp Bishop had brought to town. She was wearing a tight-fitting pair of blue jeans, a formfitting maroon knit shirt, and a black leather jacket. Black ankle boots, with buckles. Feminine, but dangerous. Her dark hair flowed over her shoulders in luxurious, glossy waves, and her skin was the color of fine porcelain, just a tiny hit of blush in her cheeks.

Her eyes were fixed on Shane's. He was crushing a bag of chips in one hand, but he'd clearly forgotten all about it.

The vampire leaned forward and took in a deep breath from around Shane's neck. Shane closed his eyes and didn't move.

"Mmmmm," she said in that slow, sweet voice. "You smell like desire. I can feel it curling off your skin. Poor little thing, all frustrated and wanting. I could help you with that."

Shane didn't open his eyes. "Get away from me."

The vampire's hand shot out to slam hard against the shelves next to Shane's head. The entire structure rocked unsteadily, but didn't quite go over. "Don't be rude, Shane Collins. Yes, I know who you are. You've been looking us up, so I did a little reading all on my own. You've got daddy problems, don't you? I understand. I have those, too. I could tell you all about it, if you come with me. It'd be nice to have a strong man to tell my troubles to."

As quickly as it had come, her anger was gone, and she was back to the vampire sex kitten she'd been back at the Glass House, running her pale fingers down Shane's collarbone, over his chest. . . .

"I said go away," Shane said, and opened his eyes to stare at her face. "Not interested, leech."

"My name's Ysandre, honey. Not leech, bitch, or bloodsucker. And if you want to survive my visit to this cesspool of a town, you'll learn to call me by my name, Shane." Her pale lips curled into a smile. "Or if you want *other people* to survive it. Now, let's be friends."

She leaned forward and brushed her lips lightly against Shane's, and

Claire saw him shudder and go completely still. Ysandre laughed, reached past him, and plucked a bag of baked chips from the rack.

"Mmmm," she said. "Salty. Tell your girlfriend I like the taste of her lip gloss."

She walked away. Shane and Claire stayed frozen where they were until she was out of sight, and then Claire rushed to him. When she put her hand on him, he flinched, just a little.

"Don't touch me," he said. His voice was hoarse, and the vein in his throat was beating very, very fast. "I don't want—"

"Shane—it's me. It's Claire—"

He reached out for her then, like a drowning man clutching a life raft, and his strength shocked her as he pulled her in. His head bent, and she felt the weight of it resting on her shoulder. The feverish, damp heat of his forehead against her neck.

She felt the shudder go through him, just one, just enough to tell her how horribly *wrong* he felt.

"God," she whispered, and gently stroked his hair. It was wet underneath, matted with sweat. "What did she do to you?"

He shook his head without raising it from her shoulder. He couldn't, or wouldn't, say it. His chest rose and fell, taking in breaths that felt like gasps but were too deep for that, and after what seemed like a full minute, Shane's body began to relax, uncoiling from that awful tension.

When he pulled back, she expected to get a look at his expression, but he turned away so fast it was just a blur—wounded dark eyes in a stark, pale mask. He looked down at the chips he was holding, and dropped them on the floor as he walked away.

Claire quickly put them back on the shelf and followed. He kept going, right past the registers. She shelled out cash to the impatient cashier for the hamburger, grabbed the plastic bag, and hurried out into the lamplit darkness after her boyfriend.

He was already unlocking the car and getting in. She was still at least a dozen feet away when he started the car with a roar, and she saw the flare of brake lights as he shifted into gear.

For a heart-stopping second Claire thought he was going to peel out and drive away, leaving her there in the dark, but he waited. She opened the passenger door and got in. Shane didn't move.

"Are you okay?" she asked.

He didn't so much as *look* at her.

He put the car in gear and burned rubber on the way out of the lot.

FOUR

Shane went straight to his room, and didn't come down again for the dinner that Eve made—spaghetti with meat sauce, light on the garlic for the sake of the vampire at the table. It was probably delicious, but Claire couldn't taste a thing. She couldn't keep her mind off the white, rigid set of Shane's face, and the panic and loathing in his eyes. She didn't understand what had happened, and she knew he didn't want to be asked. Not now.

"Well?" Eve twirled spaghetti around her fork as she stared at Claire. "How is it?"

"Oh—fantastic," Claire said, with so much enthusiasm she knew nobody was fooled. She sighed. "I'm sorry. It's just—"

Eve pointed above their heads. "The dean of the drama department?"

Michael looked up at her, and for a second Claire saw the blue of his eyes flicker. "He's got his reasons," he said. "Let it go, Eve."

"Pardon me, but that boy can make a paper cut seem like a mortal wound. . . ."

"I said let it go." Michael snapped it this time, and there was unmistakable command in his voice. Eve stopped twirling spaghetti. Stopped doing everything except watching him with narrowed, kohl-rimmed eyes.

"Let's review," she said, and put the fork carefully down on a napkin.

"*You* got all diva and decided you were too busy to go to the store. Next, Shane threw a tantrum and stomped up to his room to put on a one-man pity party. And now you're ordering me around like you own me. Are we under a testosterone storm warning?"

"Eve."

"I'm not finished. You may think that growing a pair of fangs makes you the boss around here, but you'd better check your playlist. You're on the seriously wrong track."

"*Eve.*" Michael leaned forward, and Claire caught her breath. His eyes were all wrong, his movements too fast, and she caught a flash of teeth that were too white, too sharp.

Eve pushed her chair back from the table, picked up her bowl, and walked into the kitchen without a backward glance.

Michael put his head in his hands. "Christ, what just happened?"

Claire swallowed. She tasted nothing but metal, as if she'd tried to chew the fork instead of the food. Her whole body felt cold, aching with the need to do . . . something.

She took Michael's bowl, stacking it with her own. "I'll clean up," she said.

Michael's hand closed around her wrist. She didn't dare look up at him. At close range, she didn't want to see the changes in his eyes, the ones Eve had seen so clearly.

"I wouldn't hurt any of you. You believe me, right?"

She heard the sudden doubt in his voice.

"Sure," she said. "It's just— Michael, I don't think you really know what you are yet. What's changing inside you. Eve thinks that showing you our weakness is a bad idea. I don't think she's wrong about that."

Michael was watching her as if he'd never actually seen her before. As if she'd changed right before his eyes, from a child to an equal.

She swallowed hard. That was a powerful look, and it wasn't the vampire part of him—it was the Michael part. The part she admired, and loved.

"No," he said softly. "I don't think she's wrong, either." He touched Claire's cheek gently. "What happened to Shane?"

"You don't think it was just another pity party, like Eve?"

Michael had never looked so serious, she thought. "No," he said. "And I think he may need help. But I don't think he'd take it from me right now."

"I'm not sure he'll take it from me, either," Claire said.

Michael took the plates from her. "Don't underestimate yourself."

Shane's room was dark, except for the dim glow that came in from the distant streetlights. Claire eased the door open and, in the stripe of warm hallway light, saw his foot and part of his leg. He was lying on the bed. She shut the door, took a slow, calm breath, and walked to sit down next to him.

He didn't move. As her eyes adjusted, she saw that his eyes were open. He was staring at the ceiling.

"You want to talk about it?" she asked. No answer. He blinked; that was all. "She got to you, didn't she? Somehow, she got to you."

For a long few seconds, she thought he was just going to lie there and ignore her, but then he said, "They get inside your head, the really strong ones. They can make you—feel things. Want things you don't really want. Do things you'd never do. Most of them don't bother, but the ones that do—they're the worst."

Claire reached out in the darkness, and his hand met hers midway— cool at first, then growing warm where their skin touched.

"I don't want her, Claire," he said. "But she made me want her. You understand?"

"It doesn't matter."

"It does. Because now that she's done it once, it's going to be easy for her to do it again." His fingers tightened on hers, hard enough to make her wince. "Don't try to stop her. Or me, if it comes to that. I have to handle this myself."

"Handle it how?"

"Any way I can," Shane said. He shifted over on the bed. "You're shivering."

Was she? She honestly hadn't realized, but the room felt cold, cold and full of despair. Shane was the only bright thing in it.

She stretched out facing him. Too close, she thought, for her dad's comfort, if he'd seen them, even though they were only holding hands.

Shane reached down on the other side of the bed, found a blanket, and threw it over both of them. It smelled like—well, like Shane, like his skin and hair, and Claire felt a rush of warmth go through her as she breathed it in. She moved closer to him under the covers, partly to get warm, and partly—partly because she needed to touch him.

He met her halfway, and their bodies pressed together with every curve and hollow. Their intertwined fingers curled in on one another. Even though they were close enough to kiss, they didn't—it was a kind of intimacy that Claire wasn't used to, being this close and just . . . being. Shane freed his hand from hers and brushed stray locks of hair back from her eyes. He traced her slightly parted lips.

"You're beautiful," he said. "When I first saw you, I thought—I thought you were too young to be on your own here, in this town."

"Not now?"

"You've made it through better than most of us. But if I could get you to leave this place, I would." Shane's smile was dim and crooked and a little broken, in the shadows. "I want you to live, Claire. I *need* you to live."

Her fingers touched the warm fringe of his hair. "I'm not worried about me," she said.

"You never are. That's my point. *I* worry about you. Not just because of the vampires—because of Jason. He's still out there somewhere. And—" Shane paused for a second, as if he couldn't quite get the rest of it out. "And there's me, too. Your parents might be right. I might not be the best—"

She moved her fingers to put them over his mouth, over those soft, strong lips. "I won't ever stop trusting you, Shane. You can't make me."

A shaky laugh out of the dark. "My point exactly."

"That's why I'm staying here," Claire said. "With you. Tonight."

Shane took in a deep breath. "Clothes stay on."

"Mostly," she agreed.

"You know, your parents really are right about me."

Claire sighed. "No, they're not. Nobody knows you at all, I think. Not your dad, not even Michael. You're a deep, dark mystery, Shane."

He kissed her for the first time since she'd entered the room, a warm press of lips to her forehead. "I'm an open book."

She smiled. "I like books."

"Hey, we've got something in common."

"I'm taking off my shoes."

"Fine. Shoes off."

"And my pants."

"Don't push it, Claire."

Claire woke up drowsy and utterly peaceful, and it took a slow second for her to realize that the heavenly warmth at her back was radiating from someone else, in the bed, with her.

From Shane.

She stopped breathing. Was he awake? No, she didn't think so; she could feel his slow, steady breaths. There was a delicious, forbidden delight to this, a moment that she knew she'd carry with her even when it was gone. Claire closed her eyes and tried to remember everything—like the way Shane's bare chest touched her back, warm and smooth where their skin connected. She'd negotiated for the removal of shirts, since she'd been wearing a sleeveless camisole underneath, and Shane had wavered enough to let it go. He'd insisted on keeping the pants, though.

She hadn't mentioned that she'd gotten rid of the bra, though she knew he'd noticed that right off.

Dangerous, some part of her said. *You're going to take this too far. You're not ready*—Why not? Why wasn't she? Because she wasn't seventeen? What was so magic about a number, anyway? Who decided when she was ready except her?

Shane made a sound in his sleep—a deep, contented sigh that vibrated through her whole body. *I'll bet if I turn around and kiss him, I could convince him. . . .*

Shane's hand was resting on the inward curve just above her hip, a warm loose weight, and that was how she knew when he woke up—his hand. It went from utterly limp to careful, tensing and relaxing but not moving from its spot.

She could feel each individual finger on her skin.

She stayed very still, keeping her breathing slow and steady. Shane's hand slowly, gently moved up her side, barely skimming, and then he moved away from her and sat up, facing away toward the window. Claire rolled toward him, holding the blanket at neck level.

"Good morning," she said. Her voice sounded drowsy and slow, and she saw a slice of his face as he turned slightly toward her. Sunlight glimmered warm on his bare skin, like he'd been dusted in gold.

"Good morning," he said, and shook his head. "Man. That was stupid."

Not at all what *she* was thinking. Shane got up, and she gulped at the way his blue jeans rode low on his hips, the way his bones and muscles curved together and begged to be touched—

"Bathroom," he blurted, and moved almost as fast as a vampire getting out of there. Claire sat up, waiting, but when he didn't come back, she slowly began to assemble her clothes again. Bra, clicked back into place. Camisole neat and demure, if wrinkled. She'd kept her jeans on. Her hair looked like she'd combed it with a blender—she was still messing with it when she heard Eve's trademark heavy shoes clopping down the hallway outside, passing Shane's door, going all the way to the end.

To Claire's own room.

Oh, damn.

Eve hammered on the door. "Claire?"

Claire slipped out of Shane's room quietly, trying not to look obvious about it, and made sure she was several steps into neutral territory before she said, "What is it?"

Eve, who'd opened up Claire's door and was looking inside, whirled so fast she almost overbalanced. She was ultra-Goth today—deep purple dress with skull patterns, black-and-white-striped tights, a death's-head choker. Her hair was up in one scary-looking spiked ponytail, and her makeup was the usual rice paper and dead black, with the addition of dark cherry lipstick.

"Where'd you come from?" she asked. Claire gestured vaguely toward the staircase. "I just came from there."

"Bathroom," Claire said. And got a frown, but Eve let it go.

"It's Michael," she said. "He's gone."

"Gone to work?"

"No, *gone*. As in, he took off in the middle of the night and didn't tell me where he was going, and he hasn't come back. I checked—he's not at the music store. I'm worried, especially—" Eve's train of thought switched tracks, and her eyes widened. "Oh my *God*, are you wearing the same thing you had on yesterday? You're not doing the walk of shame, are you? Because I totally cannot face your parents if you are."

"No, no, it's not like that—" Claire felt a hot blush work its way up from her neck to vividly light up her face. "I just—we were talking, and we fell asleep. I swear. We didn't, um—"

"Yeah, you'd better not have *umm*ed, because if you did, that would be—" Eve struggled not to smile. "That would be *bad*."

"I know, I know. But we didn't. And we aren't going to until—" *Until I can convince him it's okay.* "Whatever. About Michael—what do you want to do?"

"Go ask some questions. Common Grounds is a place to start, much as I hate it; Sam's probably there, or we can leave a message for him. I heard he's back out in public again." Sam was Michael's grandfather—and a vampire. He'd nearly been staked dead, and it had taken Amelie's help to save him. But he'd been left weak. Claire was glad to hear that he was better—Sam was, she felt, one of the best of the vampires. One she could trust. "Well? Are we going or what?"

Shane still hadn't come out of the bathroom. "Five minutes," Claire said, resigned. No chance of a hot shower, or even clean clothes—the best she had available were cleanish, and not slept in. She might be able to find that last-picked pair of underwear hiding in a drawer. . . .

There was a knock downstairs at the front door. An authoritative, urgent sort of knock. It was still early, and the number of drop-in visitors in Morganville was generally pretty small anyway; Claire dragged the least wrinkled of the two T-shirts over her head, pulled on the fresh underwear and old jeans, and hurried out into the hall still zipping up. Eve was ahead of her, already going down the stairs, and as Claire passed the bathroom, Shane opened the door and stuck his wet head out. "What's going on?"

"Don't know!" she shot back, and hurried after Eve.

What was going on was the delivery of an envelope, which Eve had to sign for. As she turned it over, Claire made out the name, neatly written in an antiquely beautiful hand: *Mr. Shane Collins.* There was even a decorative little flourish underneath his name. The envelope was heavy cream-colored paper. On the back flap there was a gold seal with some kind of shield on it.

Eve lifted it to her nose, sniffed, and raised her eyebrows. "Wow," she said. "Expensive perfume."

She waved it in Claire's direction, and she caught a hint of the dark, musky fragrance—full of promise and danger.

Shane padded downstairs, barefoot and wearing only his jeans except for the towel draped around his neck. He slowed as they both turned toward him. "What?"

Eve held up the envelope. "Mr. Shane Collins."

He took it from her fingers, frowned at it, and then ripped open the back flap. Inside was a folded card of the same expensive cream paper, with raised black printing. Shane looked at it for a long second, then put it back in the envelope and handed it back to Eve. "Burn it," he said.

And then he went upstairs.

Eve lost no time digging the card out, and since she did, Claire didn't feel too guilty about reading over her shoulder.

> *You have been summoned to attend a masked ball*
> *and feast to celebrate the arrival of Elder Bishop, on*
> *Saturday the twentieth of October, at the Elders'*
> *Council Hall at the hour of midnight.*

> *You will attend at the invitation of the lady Ysandre,*
> *and are required to accompany her at her pleasure.*

"Who's Ysandre?" Eve asked.

Claire was too busy worrying about the phrase *at her pleasure.*

They located Sam Glass at Common Grounds, sitting and talking with two others Claire didn't recognize, but Eve clearly did, from the nods they exchanged. Humans, because they were wearing bracelets. They said their good-byes and cleared the chairs for Eve and Claire.

Sam looked a lot like Michael—a little older, maybe, with a slightly wider chin. He had red hair to Michael's bright gold, but a similar build and height.

That had nearly gotten him killed, not so long ago, when he'd taken a stake meant for Michael. He still looked drawn, Claire thought—tired, too. But his smile was genuine as he nodded his greeting. "Ladies," he said. "It's good to see you. Eve, I didn't think you'd ever come in here again, not voluntarily."

"Believe me, if it wasn't for you, I wouldn't," she said, and tapped dark purple fingernails on the scarred table in agitation. "Do you know where Michael is?"

Sam's ginger eyebrows rose. "He's not at work?"

"He left last night, didn't say where he was going. We haven't seen him, and he's not at work. So? Ideas?"

"Nothing good," Sam said, and sat back in his chair. "Does he have his car?"

"Yeah, as far as I know. Why?"

"GPS. All of our cars are trackable."

"Wow, good to know in case I ever go into the grand-theft-auto business around here," Eve said. "Who's got the supersecret-spy tracking gear, and how do I get my hands on it?"

"You don't," Sam said. "I'll take care of it."

"Soon?"

"As soon as I can."

"But I need to find him! What if he's—" Eve leaned even closer, dropping her voice to a whisper. "What if someone has him?"

"Who?"

"*Bishop!*"

Sam's eyes widened, and all over the coffee shop, other heads snapped up. Mostly vampires, Claire thought, who knew the name, or at least knew *of* it. And who could hear a whisper across a crowded room.

"Quiet," Sam said. "Eve, stay out of it. It's nothing for any of you to get involved in. It's our business."

"It's our business, too. The guy was in our *house*. He threatened us, all of us," Eve said. "Can't you find out right now? Because otherwise I'm going to call up Homeland Security and tell them that we've got a whole bunch of terrorists skulking around in the dark."

"You wouldn't."

"Oh, I so would. With glee. And I'd tell them to bring tanning beds and conduct interviews at noon out in the parking lot."

Sam shook his head. "Eve—"

Eve slammed her hand down on the table. It sounded like a gunshot, and every head turned in their direction. "I'm not kidding, Sam!"

"Yes, you are," he said, deliberately quiet. "Because if you were serious, you would be making a threat against people who control the destiny of your next heartbeat, and that would be very, very stupid. Now, say you'll let me handle this."

Eve's dark eyes didn't blink. "Is this about Bishop? Why is he here? What's he doing? Why are you so scared of him?"

Sam stood up, and there was something remote and cold about him just then. Something that reminded Claire, very strongly, that he was a vampire first.

"Go home," he said. "I'll find Michael. I doubt he's in any trouble, and I doubt it has anything to do with Bishop."

Eve stood up, too, and for the first time, Claire saw her as an adult—a woman, facing him on equal terms.

"You'd better be right," she said softly. "Because if anything happens to Michael, that won't be the end of it. I swear to that."

Sam watched them all the way out of the coffee shop. So did everyone else. Some of them looked worried; some looked gleeful. Some looked angry.

But nobody ignored the two of them as they left. Nobody. And that was . . . unsettling.

They got in the car, and Eve started it up without a word. Claire finally ventured a question. "Where are we going?"

"Home," Eve said. "I'm giving Sam a chance to keep his word."

That, Claire thought, was going to involve Eve chewing the corners off the walls and pacing holes in the floor. And Claire had absolutely no idea what to do to help her.

But that was basically what friends were for . . . to be there to keep you from doing the crazy.

They'd been home for exactly one hour when the phone rang. Shane was sitting next to the phone—he'd appropriated the place, because he was worried Eve would keep picking up the receiver to check the line—and answered on the first chime. "Glass House," he said, and listened. Claire watched every muscle in his body go tense and still. "Go screw yourself."

And he hung up.

Claire and Eve both gaped at him. "What the hell—?" Eve blurted, and lunged for the phone. She flicked the contact switch.

"Star sixty-nine," Claire suggested. "Shane—who was it?"

He didn't answer. He crossed his arms over his chest. Eve frantically punched in the code. "It's ringing," she said—and then, like Shane, she went still.

She sank down in a chair.

"Should've left it alone," Shane said.

Eve closed her eyes, and her shoulders slumped. "Yeah, I'm here," she said tightly. "What is it, Jason?"

Claire caught Shane's look, and she must have seemed suspiciously in the know, because he frowned at her. "Have you seen him?" Shane asked.

Truth or lie? "Yes," Claire said, even though that definitely wasn't the path of least resistance. "I saw him yesterday morning on the way to school. He said he wanted to talk to Eve."

Oh, that look. It could have melted steel. "And you forgot about chatting with the local serial killer? Sweet, Claire. Very smart."

"I didn't forget. I— Never mind." There was no explaining the vibe she had gotten from Jason, not to Shane, whose most vivid memories of the little creep had to do with Jason sinking a knife into his guts. "I'm sorry. I should have told you."

Eve made a shushing motion at them and hunched over the phone, listening hard. "He said *what*? You're not serious. You can't be serious."

Apparently, he was. Eve listened another few seconds, and then said, "Okay, then. No, I don't know. Maybe. Bye."

She put the phone back in the cradle and stared at it. Her face looked frozen.

"Eve?" Claire asked. "What is it?"

"My dad," Eve said. "He's—he's sick. He's in the hospital. They don't think—they don't think he's going to make it. It's his liver."

"Oh," Claire whispered, and leaned across the table to take Eve's right hand. "I'm sorry."

Eve's fingers were cool and limp. "Yeah, well—he asked for it, you know? My dad was an ugly drunk, and he—me and Jason didn't exactly have the greatest childhood." She locked gazes with Shane. "You know."

He nodded. He took her left hand and stared at the table. "Our dads were drinking buddies sometimes," he said. "But Eve's was worse. Lots worse."

Claire, having met Shane's dad, couldn't really imagine that. "How long—?"

"Jason said a couple of days, maybe. Not long." Eve's eyes filled with tears that didn't fall. "Son of a bitch. What does he expect from me, anyway? To come running and sit there and watch him die?"

Shane didn't answer. He didn't lift his head. He just . . . sat. Claire had no idea what to do, how to act, so she followed his example. Eve's hands suddenly closed on theirs, hard.

"He threw me out," she said. "He told me that if I didn't let Brandon fang me, I couldn't be his daughter. Well, so he's dying, boohoo. I don't care."

Yes, you do, Claire wanted to say, but she couldn't. Eve was trying to convince herself, that was all, and in about thirty seconds she shook her head, and the tears broke free to run in dirty streaks down her pale face.

"I'll take you," Shane said quietly. "That way, you don't have to stay unless you want to."

Eve nodded. She couldn't seem to get her breath. "I wish—Michael—"

Claire remembered, with a shock, that they were still waiting for Sam's call. "I'll stay," she said. "I'll call you when I hear from Sam. I'll get Michael to come there, okay?"

"Okay," Eve said weakly. "I—need my purse, I guess."

She swiped at her eyes and walked into the other room. Shane looked at Claire, and she wondered what all this was bringing up for him—memories of his father, of his dead mother and sister, of a family he didn't really even have anymore.

You're a deep, dark mystery, she'd said to him, and now, more than ever, that was true.

"Take care of her," Claire said. "Call me if you need anything."

He kissed her on the lips, and in a few minutes she heard the front door bang shut. Locks clicked. Claire sat by the phone and waited.

She'd rarely felt so alone.

The phone rang after ten minutes. "He's coming home," Sam said, and hung up. No explanation.

Claire gritted her teeth and settled in to wait.

It took another twenty minutes for Michael's car to pull into the driveway. He crossed the short distance from garage to back door in a few fast strides, covering his head with a black umbrella he left by the steps. Even then, when he entered the kitchen, Claire smelled a faint burned reek coming from him, and he was shivering.

His eyes looked hollow and exhausted.

"Michael? You okay?"

"Fine," he said. "I need to rest, that's all."

"I—where were you? What happened?"

"I was with Amelie." He scrubbed his hands over his face. "Look, there's a lot going on. I should have left a note for you guys. I'm sorry. I'll try to keep you in the loop next time—"

"Eve's at the hospital," Claire blurted. "Her dad's dying."

Michael slowly straightened. "What?"

"Something about his liver, I guess because of his drinking. Anyway, they say he's dying. She and Shane went to see him." Claire studied him for a few seconds. "I told her I'd call when you got home. If you don't want to go—"

"No. No, I'll go. She needs—" He shrugged. "She needs people who love her. It's going to be hard, facing her parents."

"Yeah," Claire agreed. "She seemed upset." Of course she was upset. What a stupid thing to say. "I think she'd like it if you were there for her."

"I will be." Michael raised his eyebrows. "What about you? You okay to stay here?"

Claire glanced at the clock on the wall. "Could you drop me off somewhere?"

"Where?"

"I need to see Myrnin. Sorry, but I promised."

Not that visiting her crazy vampire mentor was going to be any more pleasant than going to the hospital.

FIVE

Someone had done a makeover on Myrnin's cell, and it wasn't Claire; she'd thought about it, but she hadn't been sure about what Amelie would allow him to have.

So when she stepped through the doorway from the laboratory to the cells, where the sickest and most disturbed vampires of Morganville were warehoused, she was surprised to see the glow of electric light coming from the end . . . from Myrnin's cell. As she got closer, she noted other things. Music. Something classical was playing softly, from a stereo set up outside the bars. There was a television, as well, currently turned off.

Myrnin's cell, which had been as bare as a monk's in the beginning, was floored with a plush, expensive-looking Turkish rug. His narrow cot had been replaced with a much more comfortable bed. There were books stacked waist-high in the corners of the cell.

Myrnin was lying on the bed, hands folded across his stomach. He looked young—as young as Michael, really—but there was something indefinably *old* about him, too. Long, curling black hair, a sense of style far out-of-date. He was dressed in a blue silk dressing gown with dragons on it—neat and clean.

Someone had been here before her to take care of him. She felt guilty.

His eyes didn't open, but he said, "Hello, Claire."

"Hi." She hung back, watching him. He seemed calm enough, but Myrnin wasn't all that predictable. "How are you?"

"Bored," he said, and laughed. "Bored, bored, bored. I had no idea a cell could be such a prison."

His eyes opened, and his pupils were huge. There was a fey look in his eyes that made the skin along her backbone shiver and tighten.

"Did you bring me anything to eat?" he asked. "Someone juicy?"

He was definitely not right. She hated it when he got this way—cruel and lazy, willing to say or do anything. It was as if the Myrnin she liked had just . . . disappeared, leaving behind nothing but the dark shell.

Myrnin slithered off his bed, boneless and silent as a reptile. He took hold of the bars in his white, strong fingers and fixed his black-hole eyes on her face.

"Sweet, sweet Claire," he murmured. "So brave, to come here. Come on, Claire. Come closer. You'll have to if you want to *help*."

He smiled, and even though he wasn't showing vampire teeth, she felt the predator's breath on the back of her neck.

"I have some new medicine," she said, and set her backpack down. She unzipped it and took out the bottle with the crystals—a plastic bottle, thankfully, so she could throw it without fear of breakage. She tossed it underhand through the bars of the cage. It skidded to a stop against Myrnin's pale feet. "I need you to take it, Myrnin."

He didn't even bend down for it. "I don't think I like your tone," he said. "You don't order *me*, slave. I order *you*."

"I'm not your slave."

"You're *property*."

Claire opened up her backpack, took out the dart gun that Dr. Mills had given her, and shot him.

Myrnin staggered back, staring down at his stomach, and brushed his fingers over the yellow bristle of a hypodermic dart. "You little *bitch*," he said, and sat down heavily on the bed.

His eyes rolled back as the drug delivered itself into his bloodstream, and he slumped back flat on the mattress.

"I may be a bitch, but I'm not your property," Claire said. She didn't move from where she stood as she loaded a second dart, just in case. She watched his body as his muscles twitched and contracted, then relaxed. "Myrnin?"

His eyes blinked, and she saw the pupils begin to shrink down to normal-sized black dots. "Claire?" He reached down and pulled the dart from his stomach. "Ouch." He examined the dart curiously, then laid it carefully aside. "That was interesting."

Well, he sounded saner, anyway. "How are you feeling?"

"Sore?" He brushed his fingers over the healing puncture wound. "Ashamed?" His dark gaze lifted to brush across hers. "I have the feeling I've been—unpleasant."

"I wouldn't know," Claire said. "I just got here. Hey, who brought you all the stuff?"

Myrnin glanced around, frowning. "I—to be honest, I'm not really certain. I think it might have been one of Amelie's creatures." He didn't sound at all sure. "I was cruel to you just now, wasn't I?"

"A little," she agreed. "But then again, I did shoot you."

"Ah, yes. By the way, is there any particular reason you shot me in the stomach rather than the chest?"

"Less bone," she said. "And my hands were shaking. How are you now?"

He sighed and sat up. "Better," he said. "Don't trust me, though. We don't know how long this will last, do we?"

"No." Claire put the gun away, and came closer to the bars. Not close enough to grab, though.

"That's a new formulation? In liquid?"

She nodded. "It's stronger, but I'm not sure it will last as long. Your body may break it down faster, so we have to be careful."

"Start the clock," he said. He looked down at himself and laughed softly. "My dark side dresses better than I do." He stood up and reached for clothes folded neatly on a table to the side as he loosened the tie on his robe. He hesitated, smiled, and raised his eyebrows. "If you don't mind, Claire . . . ?"

"Oh. Sorry." Claire turned her back. She didn't like turning her back on him, even with the cell door locked. He was better behaved when he knew she was watching. She focused on the faint, distorted image of his reflection on the TV screen as he shed the dressing gown and began to pull on his clothing. She couldn't see much, except that he was very pale all over. Once she was sure his pants were up, she glanced behind her. He had his back to her, and she couldn't help but compare him with the only other man she'd really studied half-naked. Shane was broad, strong, solid. Myrnin looked fragile, but his muscles moved like cables under that pale skin—far stronger than Shane's, she knew.

Myrnin turned as he buttoned his shirt. "It's been a while since a pretty girl looked at me with such interest," he said. She looked away, feeling the blush work its heat up through her neck and onto her cheeks. "It's all right, Claire. I'm not offended."

She cleared her throat. "Any side effects from the new mixture?"

"I feel warm," he said, and smiled. "How pleasant."

"Too warm?"

"I have no idea. It's been so long since I felt anything like it, I'm not sure I'd be able to tell the difference." He looped his hands loosely around the bars. "How long are you going to wait?"

"The first time, we wait until the effects start to fade, so we can have a good baseline and we'll know how long it'll allow you to be out. Safely."

"And you'll keep your dart pistol ready at all times, yes?" He leaned casually against the bars, elegant and relaxed. There was still a faint glow in his eyes, just a little unsettling. "What shall we talk about, then? How are your studies, Claire?"

She shrugged. "You know."

"They're still too simple, I would expect."

"See? You do know." Claire hesitated. "We have visitors in town."

"Visitors?" Myrnin didn't seem overly interested. "Is it homecoming already? Why on earth Amelie tolerates these human traditions, I'll simply never understand—"

"Vampire visitors," she said. That got his full attention.

For a frozen second, he didn't speak, only stared, and then he said, low in his throat, "In the name of God, who?" His fingers tightened on the bars, squeezing so tightly she was afraid his bones might snap. Or the steel. *"Who?"*

She hadn't expected that reaction. "His name is Bishop," she said. "He says he's Amelie's father—"

Myrnin's face went as still and pale as a plaster mask. "Bishop," he repeated. "Bishop's—here. No. It can't be." He took in a deliberate breath—one he didn't need—and let it slowly out. His hands relaxed on the bars. "You said visitors. Plural."

"He brought two people with him. Ysandre and François."

Myrnin said something soft and vicious under his breath. "I know them both. What's happened since his arrival? What does Amelie say?"

"She said we should stay out of it. So do Sam and Oliver, for that matter."

"Has she made any public announcements? Is she planning any public events?"

"Shane got an invitation," she said. "To some kind of ball. He—it says he has to go as Ysandre's escort."

"Jesu," Myrnin said. "She's doing it. She's acknowledging his status with a welcome feast."

"What does that mean?"

Myrnin suddenly rattled the bars. "Let me out. *Now.*"

Claire swallowed. "I—can't. I'm sorry. You know how this works. The first time we test a new formulation you have to stay—"

"Now," he snarled, and his eyes took on that terrifying vampire sheen. "You have no idea what's happening out there, Claire! We can't afford to be cautious."

"Then tell me what's going on! Please! I want to help!"

Myrnin visibly controlled himself, let go of the bars, and sat down on the bed. "All right. Sit down. I'll try to explain."

Claire nodded. She pulled over a steel industrial chair—left over from this facility's use as a prison, she thought—and took a seat herself. "Tell me about Bishop."

"You've met him?" Claire nodded. "Then you already know all you need to know. He's not like the vampires you've met here, Claire, not even the worst of us. Amelie and I are modern predators, tigers in the jungle. Bishop is from a far colder, harder time. A *Tyrannosaurus rex*, if you will."

"But he really is Amelie's father?"

Myrnin's turn to nod. "He was a warlord. A murderer on a scale that you would find it difficult to fathom. I—thought he was dead, many years ago. The fact that he's come here, now—it's very bad, Claire. Very bad indeed."

"Why? I mean, if he's Amelie's father, maybe he just wants to see her—"

"He's not here for happy memories," Myrnin said. "In all likelihood, he's here to have his revenge."

"On you?"

Myrnin slowly shook his head. "I'm not the one who tried to kill him," he said.

Claire's breath caught. "Amelie? Not—she couldn't. Not her own father."

"It's best you don't ask any more questions, little one. All you need to know is that he has reason to hate Amelie—reason enough to bring him here and for him to try to destroy everything she has worked for and accomplished."

"But—she's trying to *save* vampires. To stop the sickness. He has to understand that. He wouldn't—"

"You have no idea what he wants, or what he would do." He leaned forward, elbows on his knees, the picture of earnestness. "Bishop comes from a time before there were concepts among vampires of cooperation and self-sacrifice, and he'll have nothing but contempt for them. As you would say, he's old-school evil, and all that matters to him is his own power. He won't tolerate Amelie having her own."

"Then what do we do?"

"First, you let me out of here," he said. "Amelie is going to need her friends around her."

Claire slowly shook her head. The minutes were ticking by, and Myrnin seemed stable, but she had to abide by the rules.

"Claire."

She looked up. Myrnin's face was still and sober, and he seemed utterly in control of himself. This was a Myrnin she rarely saw—not as charming as the manic version, not as terrifying as the angry one. A real, balanced person.

"Don't let yourself be drawn into this," he said. "Humans don't exist for Bishop except as pawns, or food."

"I didn't think we did for too many of you," she said. Myrnin's eyes widened, and he smiled.

"You do have a point. As a species, we do have an—empathy gap," he replied. "But at least we're trying. Bishop and his friends won't bother."

The formula was much, much better than the last one—Myrnin's stability lasted for nearly four long hours, a score that delighted him almost as much as it did her. But once he'd tired, and begun sliding back into confusion and anger, Claire stopped the clock, made her notes, and checked the massive refrigerator in the center of the prison. She thought it had probably been built as central storage for the kitchens—kitchens that had gotten ripped out long ago—but it had the feeling of a giant, stainless-steel morgue.

Someone had forgotten to restock the supplies of blood inside. Claire made a note as she retrieved supplies for Myrnin, and tossed the blood packs into his cell. She didn't wait to watch him rip into them.

That always made her sick.

The other vampires were mostly beyond conversation—silent, reduced to basic survival instincts. She loaded up a cart and made the rounds delivering the last of the blood. Some of them had enough control left to nod a silent thanks to her; some only stared with mad, empty eyes, seeing her as just a giant, walking version of the blood bag.

It always gave her the creeps, but she couldn't stand to see them starve. It was somebody else's responsibility to feed them and keep the cells clean—but she wasn't sure that somebody did a very good job.

By the time she was done, it was late afternoon. Claire walked to the shimmering door in the prison wall, concentrated, and formed the portal back to Myrnin's lab. It was empty. She was tired and upset about what Myrnin had said about Bishop, and considered resetting the portal to take her directly to the Glass House . . . but she didn't like using it; it took too much out of her. She also didn't want to explain to the others about why she was stepping out of a blank wall, either.

"Guess I'm walking," she said to the empty lab. She climbed the stairs to the rickety, leaning shack that covered the entrance, and exited into the alley behind Gramma Day's Founder House. It was another mirror of the Glass House—slightly different trim, different curtains in the windows. Gramma Day had a front-porch swing, and she liked to sit outside with her lemonade and watch people, but she wasn't out today. The empty swing creaked in the faint, cooling wind.

The sun still felt fierce, although the temperatures were dropping steadily, day by day; Claire was sweating by the time she'd negotiated Morganville's tortuously twisted avenues and turned onto Lot Street.

The sweat turned icy as she saw the police car parked in front of the house. Claire broke into a run, slammed through the white picket fence, and pounded up the stairs. The door was shut and locked. She fumbled out her keys and let herself in, then followed the sound of voices down the hallway.

Shane was sitting on the couch, wearing what Eve liked to call his Asshole Face. He was staring at Richard Morrell, who was standing in front of him. The contrast was extreme—Shane looked like he'd forgotten he owned a hairbrush, his clothes were rumpled from sitting in a laundry basket for a week, and his whole body language screamed *SLACKER*.

A whole different person from the one who'd been so quietly concerned about Eve earlier.

Richard Morrell, on the other hand, was a Morganville success story. Neat and sharp in his dark blue police uniform, every crease perfect, every hair at regulation length. The gun on his hip looked just as well cared for.

He and Shane both transferred their stares to Claire. She felt sweaty, disheveled, and panicked. "What's happened?"

"Officer Dick dropped by to remind me I'd missed some appointments," Shane said. He had a flat, dark look in his eyes, the kind he got when he was committed to a fight. "I was just telling him I'd get around to it."

"You're months behind in donations," Richard said. "You're lucky it's me standing here, not somebody a lot less sympathetic. Look, I know you don't like this, and you don't have to. What you *do* have to do is get your ass up and down to the Donation Center."

Shane didn't move. "You going to make me, *Dick?*"

"I don't understand," Claire said. "What are you talking about?"

"Shane's not paying his taxes."

"Taxes—" It came together suddenly. The blood she'd just tossed into the cells of ravenous, maddened vampires. *Oh.* "Blood donations."

Shane held up his wrist. His hospital tag, marked with a red cross, was still on. "Nobody gets to touch me for another two weeks. Sorry."

Richard didn't move. He didn't even blink. "No, I'm sorry, but that doesn't hold up. Your hospital exemption protects you from attack. It doesn't excuse you from civic duty."

"*Civic duty*," Shane mocked. "Right. Whatever, man. Tell you what. You delivered your message. Go bust some crime or something. Maybe arrest your sister—she probably deserves it today, if it's a day that ends in *y*."

"Shane," Claire said, with just a little pleading in her voice. "Where's Eve?"

"At the hospital," Shane said. "I left her there with Michael. It's pretty rough on her, but she's coping. I came back to make sure you were okay."

"I am," she said. Not that either of them was listening to her anymore. Richard and Shane had locked stares again, and it was a guy thing. A contest of wills.

"So you're refusing to accompany me to the Donation Center," Richard said. "Is that right?"

" 'Bout the size of it, Dick."

Richard reached behind his back, unhooked the shiny silver handcuffs from the snap on his belt, and held them at his side. Shane still didn't move.

"Up," Richard said. "Come on, man, you know how this is going to go. Either you end up in the jailhouse or you spend five minutes with a needle in your arm."

"I'm not letting any vamp eat me, not even by remote control."

"Not even Michael?" Richard asked. "Because when supplies run low, the younger the vampire, the lower he is in the priority list. Michael's the last one in Morganville to get blood. So you're doing nothing but hurting your own, man."

Shane's fists clenched, trembled, relaxed. He glanced at Claire, and she saw the mixture of rage and shame in his eyes. He hated this, she knew. Hated the vampires, and wanted to hate Michael but couldn't.

"Please," she whispered. "Shane, just do it. I'll go, too."

"You don't have to," Richard said. "College students are exempt."

"But I can volunteer, right?"

He shrugged. "No idea."

Claire turned to Shane. "Then we'll both go."

"The hell we will." Shane folded his arms. "Go on, handcuff me. I'll bet you're dying to use that shiny new Taser."

Claire dropped her backpack, crossed to him, and got in his face. "Stop," she hissed. "We don't have time for this, and I don't need you in jail right now, okay?"

He stared right into her eyes, for so long that she was afraid he was going to tell her to mind her own business—but then he sighed and nod-ded. She stepped away as he stood and held out his wrists to Richard Morrell.

"Guess you've got me, Officer," he said. "Be gentle."

"Shut up, Shane. Don't make this harder than it is."

Claire trailed along behind, uncertain what she ought to be doing; Richard didn't seem interested in her at all. He used the radio clipped to his shoulder to make some kind of police call on the way down the hall, in code. She wasn't sure she liked that. Morganville wasn't big enough to need codes, unless it was something really nasty.

As she stopped to lock the front door behind them, a big, shiny black RV rounded the corner—so sleek it looked almost predatory. It had a red cross painted on the nose, and on the side, below its blind, dark-tinted windows, red letters spelled out MORGANVILLE BLOODMOBILE. In cursive script below that, it said, *No appointment necessary.*

Shane stopped moving. "No," he said. "I'm not doing that."

Richard used leverage to get him going again at a stumble down the steps. "It's this or the Donation Center. Those are your choices, you know that. I was trying to make it easier."

Claire swallowed hard and hurried down the steps. She got in front of Shane, blocking his path, and met his eyes. He was furious, and scared, and something else, something she couldn't really understand.

"What's wrong?"

"People get in that damn thing and don't come out," he said flatly. "I'm not doing it. They strap you down, Claire. They strap you down and nobody can see inside."

She felt a little ill herself at the mental image. Richard Morrell's face was carefully blank. "Sir?"

He didn't much care for her asking him; she could tell. "I can't give you an opinion, but one way or another, he has to do this."

"What if you drive us both to the Donation Center instead?"

Richard thought about it for a few seconds, then nodded. He unhooked the radio from his shoulder again, muttered some quiet words, and the engine on the Bloodmobile started up with a smooth hum.

It glided away like a shark, looking for prey. All of them watched it go.

"Crap, I hate that thing," Shane said. His voice trembled a little.

"Me, too," said Richard, to Claire's surprise. "Now get in the car."

SIX

The Donation Center was still open, even though it was getting dark. As Richard pulled his police cruiser to the curb, two people Claire vaguely recognized came out, waved to each other, and set off in separate directions. "Does everybody come here?" she asked.

"Everybody who doesn't use the Bloodmobile," Richard answered. "Every human who's Protected has to donate a certain number of pints per year. Donations go to their Patron first. The rest goes to whoever needs it. Vampires who don't have anyone to donate for them."

"Like Michael," Claire said.

"Yeah, he's our most recent charity project." Richard got out and opened the back door for her and Shane. She slid out. Shane, after a hesitation long enough to make her worry, followed. He stuck his hands in his pockets and stared up at the glowing red cross sign above the door. The Donation Center didn't look exactly inviting, but it was far less terrifying than the Bloodmobile. For one thing, there were bright windows that offered a clear view of a clean, big room. Framed posters on the wall—the same kind you could find in any town, Claire thought—listed the virtues of giving blood.

"Does any of it get to other humans?" she asked as Richard held the door open for Shane. He shrugged.

"Ask your boyfriend," he said. "They used quite a few units on him after his stabbing, as I remember. Of course it gets used for humans. It's our town, too."

"You're dreaming if you really think that," Shane said, and stepped inside. As Claire followed, she felt a definite change of atmosphere—not just the air, which was cool and dry, but something else. A feeling, barely contained, of desperation. It reminded her of the way hospital waiting areas felt—industrial, impersonal, soaked with large and small fears. But it was still clean, well lit, and full of comfortable chairs.

Nothing at all scary about the place. Not even the motherly-looking older lady sitting behind the wooden desk at the front, who gave them all the same bright, welcoming smile.

"Well, Officer Morrell, it's nice to see you!"

He nodded to the lady. "Rose. Got a truant for you here."

"So I see. Shane Collins, isn't it? Oh, dear, I'm so sorry to hear about your mother. Tragedy has come to your door too often." She was still smiling, but it was muted. Respectful. "Can I put you down for two pints today? To make up some of what you're behind?"

Shane nodded. His jaw was clenched, his eyes brilliant and narrowed. He was fighting for control, Claire thought. She slipped her fingers in his where they were handcuffed behind his back.

"You remember me, don't you?" Rose continued. "I knew your mother. We used to play bridge together."

"I remember," Shane choked out. Nothing else. Richard raised his eyebrows, got a mirrored look from Rose, and tugged on Shane's elbow to lead him away to one of the empty chairs. They were all empty, Claire noticed. She'd seen a couple of people leaving the building, but nobody coming inside.

One thing about the Donation Center, they were better than most medical places about keeping their magazines up-to-date. Claire found a brand-new edition of *Seventeen* and began reading. Shane sat stiffly, in silence, and watched the single wooden door at the end of the room. Richard Morrell chatted with Rose at the desk, looking relaxed and friendly. Claire wondered if he came here to donate his blood, or if he used the

Bloodmobile. She supposed that whatever he chose, the vampires wouldn't be crazy enough to hurt him—son of the mayor, respected police officer. No, Richard Morrell was probably safer than just about anybody in Morganville, Protected or not.

Easy for him to be relaxed.

The door at the end of the room opened, and a nurse stepped through it. She was dressed in bright floral surgical scrubs, complete to the cap over her hair, and like Rose, she had a nice, unthreatening smile. "Shane Collins?"

Shane took in a deep breath and struggled up out of his chair. Richard turned him around and unfastened the handcuffs. "Good behavior, Shane," he said. "Trust me, you don't want to start trouble here."

Shane nodded stiffly. He glanced at Claire, then fixed his attention on the nurse who was waiting. He walked toward her with slow, deliberate calm.

"Can I go with him?" Claire asked, and Richard looked at her in surprise.

"Claire, they're not going to hurt him. It's just like blood donation anywhere else. They stick a needle in your arm and give you a squeezy ball. Orange juice and cookies at the end."

"So I can donate?"

He looked to Rose for help.

"How old are you, child?"

"I'm not a child. I'm almost seventeen."

"There's no legal requirement for anyone under the age of eighteen to donate blood," Rose said.

"But is there a law against it?"

She blinked, started to answer, and stopped herself. She pulled open a drawer and retrieved a small book that was titled *Morganville Blood Donations: Regulations and Requirements*. After flipping a few pages, she shrugged and looked at Richard. "I don't think there is," she said. "I've just never had anyone donate voluntarily at the Donation Center. Oh, we take the Bloodmobile to the university from time to time, but—"

"Great," Claire interrupted. "I'd like to donate a pint, please."

Rose immediately became all business.

"Forms," she said, and thumped down a clipboard and pen.

To say that Shane was surprised to see her was an understatement.

To say he was pleased would have been a lie.

As she took the couch next to his, Shane hissed, "What the hell do you think you're doing? Are you *crazy*?"

"I'm donating blood," she said. "I don't have to, but I don't mind." At least, she didn't think she minded. She'd never actually done it before, and the sight of the red tube snaking out of Shane's arm and down to the collection bag was a little bit terrifying. "It doesn't hurt, right?"

"Dude, they're sticking a big-ass needle in your vein—of course it hurts." He looked pale, and she didn't think it was all from the fact that he was on his second pint. "You can still say no. Just get up and tell them you changed your mind."

The same friendly-looking nurse who'd called Shane to the back rolled up a wheeled stool and a cart. "He's right," she said. "If you don't want to do this, you don't have to. I saw your paperwork. You're a little young." The nurse's bright brown eyes focused beyond her, to Shane, and then back again. "Doing it for moral support?"

"Kind of," Claire admitted. Her fingers felt ice-cold, and she shivered as the nurse took her hand. "I've never done this before."

"You're in luck. I have. Now, I'm going to stick your finger and run a quick test, and then we'll get started. Okay?"

Claire nodded. Lying on the couch seemed to have effectively sapped away her will to move. The finger stick came as a sharp, bright flash, there and gone, and Claire lifted her head from the pillow to see the nurse using a tiny glass pipette to gather blood from her fingertip. It was about five seconds, and then the stick was bandaged up. The nurse did some things with items on her cart, nodded in satisfaction, and smiled at Claire. "O negative," she said. "Excellent."

Claire gave her a weak thumbs-up. The nurse took her arm and fastened the rubber tourniquet above the elbow. "Talk to your boyfriend," she advised. "Don't watch."

Claire turned her head. Shane was staring at her with dark, intense eyes. He smiled slightly, just enough, and she returned it.

"So," she asked, "come here often?"

He laughed quietly. She felt something hot slip into her arm, a jolt that faded to discomfort, and then tape being applied. A ball was pressed into her hand, and the tight pressure of the tourniquet snapped loose. "Squeeze," the nurse said. "You're good to go."

Surprised, Claire glanced down. She had a thing in her arm, and a tube, and there was red running through it. . . .

Her head fell back against the pillow, and she couldn't hear for the dark buzzing inside her skull. She thought someone was calling her name, but for the moment, that didn't seem very important. She tried to breathe, slowly and steadily, and after what seemed like hours, the buzzing faded, and the world took on edges and bright colors again. There was a poster on the ceiling overhead, one of a kitten sitting in a teacup, looking adorable. She fixed on it and tried not to think about the blood that was draining out of her. *This is what it's like*, she couldn't help but realize. *This must be what Michael felt when Oliver was draining his blood. This is what all those people feel when the vampires kill them.*

It was only a little piece of death, hardly enough to matter.

The nurse slipped a warm blanket over her, smiled down, and said, "It's okay. You're not the first to pass out. That's why the seats recline, honey."

Claire hadn't passed out—not really—but she wasn't feeling her best, either. The nurse rolled her cart and stool around to Shane.

"Done," she announced, and Claire tried to turn her head that way, but she didn't want to see the needle coming out any more than she'd wanted to see it go in. Squeamish. She was squeamish about needles, and she'd never realized that before. Funny.

A warm hand covered hers, and when she opened her eyes, she saw that Shane was standing next to her, pale and hollow-eyed but upright.

"Shane," the nurse said. "Go get some juice."

"When she's done," he said.

The nurse must have realized there was no arguing about it, because she kicked her wheeled stool over to him. "Then at least sit down. I really don't want to be picking you up off the floor."

It probably took less time than it felt, but Claire was desperately glad when the nurse came back to remove the needle and apply bandages. She didn't look at the blood bag. The nurse said something nice, and Claire tried to respond in kind but wasn't absolutely sure what came out of her mouth. Shane led her to the next room, which was a sitting area with a plasma television tuned to a news channel, juice and sodas and water, and trays of crackers and cookies and fruit. Claire took an orange and a bottle of water. Shane went straight for the sugar shock—Coke and cookies.

Claire rubbed her fingers over the purple stretch bandage around her elbow. "Is it always like that?"

"Like what?" Shane mumbled around a mouthful of chocolate chips. "Scary? Guess so. They try to make it nice, but I never forget whose mouth that blood ends up in."

She felt a surge of nausea, and stopped peeling her orange. Suddenly, the thick pulpy smell was overwhelming. She chugged some water instead, which went down cool and heavy as mercury.

"They use it for the hospitals, though," she said. "For accident victims and things like that."

"Sure. Reusing the leftovers." Shane crammed another cookie into his mouth. "I hate this shit. I swore I'd never do it, but here I am anyway. Tell me again why I stay in this town?"

"They'll hunt you down if you leave?"

"Good reason." He dusted crumbs from his fingers. She peeled the rest of her orange, broke loose a slice, and ate it with methodical determination—not hungry, no sir, but well aware she was still shaky. She ate three more slices, then passed Shane the rest.

"Wait," she said. He paused in the act of biting into the orange. "You've never done this before, have you? I mean, you left town before you were eighteen, so you didn't have to. And then you've ducked it since coming back. Right?"

"Damn straight." He finished the orange and chugged the rest of his Coke.

"So you've never been inside the Bloodmobile."

"I didn't say that." Shane got that grim look again. "I went with my mother once—didn't have to donate, but she wanted me to get used to the idea. I was fifteen. They dragged in this guy—he was crazy, out of his head. Strapped him down and started draining him. They hustled the rest of us out of there, but when we left, he was still there. I watched. They drove away with him. Nobody ever saw him again."

Claire swallowed more water. She felt weak, but she wanted out of here. The comfortable room felt like a trap, a windowless, airless box. She tossed the rest of her water and the orange peel in the trash. Shane three-pointed his Coke can and took her hand.

"Is Eve going to stay at the hospital?" she asked.

"Not all night. It's pretty uncomfortable; her dad's sobered up, and he's doing the amends thing." Shane's mouth twisted. He clearly didn't think much of that. "Her mom just sits there and cries. She always was practically a bag of wet tissues."

"You don't like them much."

"You wouldn't, either."

"Any sign of Jason?"

Shane shook his head. "If he's showing up to do his family duty, he's sneaking around in the dead of night. Which, come to think of it, would probably work for him. Anyway, Michael said he'd bring Eve home. They're probably already there."

"I hope so. Did Michael say where he was, you know, before?"

"When he was missing? Something about this damn ball," Shane said.

I should ask him about the invitation. She almost did—she opened her mouth to do it—but then she remembered how Shane had looked last night, how deeply Ysandre had shaken him.

She didn't want to see him look like that again.

Maybe she ought to just leave it. He'd talk about it when he wanted to talk.

There were two doors—one that said EXIT, one that had nothing on it at all. Shane passed the unmarked door, hesitated, and backed up.

"What?" Claire asked. Shane took hold of the handle and eased the door open.

"Just a hunch," he said. "Shhhh."

On the other side was another waiting area, and there were people standing in line. This part of the Donation Center was darker, with fewer overhead lights. Three people were standing in front of a long white counter, like at a pharmacy, and behind it stood a tall woman wearing a lab coat. She didn't smile, and she was about as warm as a flask of liquid nitrogen.

"Oh crap," Shane breathed, and about the same time Claire realized that the blond guy first in line at the counter was *Michael*. He wasn't home. . . . He was *here*.

He finished signing something and shoved the clipboard back, and the woman handed him over a plastic bottle, about the size of the bottled water Claire had been drinking.

This one didn't hold water. *Tomato juice*, Claire told herself, but it didn't look at all like juice. Too dark, too thick. Michael tilted it one way, then another, and his face—he looked fascinated.

No, he looked *hungry*.

Claire wanted to look away, but she couldn't. Michael unscrewed the cap on the bottle as he stepped out of line, put the blood to his lips, and began to drink. No, to guzzle. Claire was distantly aware that Shane's grip on her hand was so tight it was painful, but neither of them moved. Michael's eyes were shut, and he tilted the bottle back and drank until it was empty except for a thin red film on the plastic.

He licked his lips, sighed, and opened his eyes, and looked straight at the two of them.

His eyes were a bright, brilliant, glowing red. He blinked, and it went away, replaced by an eerie shine. Another blink, and it was all gone, and he was back to being Michael again.

He looked as horrified as Claire felt. Betrayed and ashamed.

Shane shut the door and dragged Claire toward the exit. They hadn't reached it before Michael came barreling in after them.

"Hey!" he said. His skin had taken on a flush, a faint pink tone, that Claire remembered seeing before. "What are you doing here?"

"What do you think we're doing? They hauled me here in cuffs, man," Shane snapped. "You think I'd be here if I had a choice?"

Michael stopped in his tracks, and his gaze flashed down to the stretchy bandages on their arms. Recognition flashed, and then he looked . . . sad, somehow. "I—I'm sorry."

"What for? Not like we didn't already know how much you crave the stuff." Still, Claire heard the betrayal in Shane's voice. The revulsion. "Just didn't expect to see you chugging it down like a drunk at happy hour, that's all."

"I didn't want you to see it," Michael said quietly. "I drink it here. I only keep some at home for emergencies. I never wanted you to watch—"

"Well, we did," Shane said. "So what? You're a bloodsucking vampire. That's not a news flash, Michael. Anyway, it's no big thing, right?"

"Yeah," Michael agreed. "No big thing." He focused on Claire, and she couldn't fit the two things together—Michael with those terrifying red eyes, gulping down fresh blood, and this Michael standing in front of her, with that sad hope in his expression. "You okay, Claire?"

She nodded. She didn't trust herself to talk, not even a word.

"I'm taking her home," Shane said. "Unless that was your appetizer, and now you're looking for the main course."

Michael looked sick. "Of course not. Shane—"

"It's all right." The fight dropped out of Shane's voice. He sounded resigned. "I'm okay with it."

"And that bugs the crap out of you, doesn't it?"

Shane looked up, startled. The two of them stared it out, and then Shane tugged on Claire's arm again. "Let's go," he said. "See you at home."

Michael nodded. "See you."

He was still holding the empty bottle, Claire realized. There was a tiny trickle of blood left in the bottom.

As the door shut between them, she saw Michael realize what he had in his hand, and throw it violently in the trash can.

"Oh, Michael," she whispered. "God." In that one gesture, she realized something huge.

He really did hate this. He really did, on some level, hate what he'd become, because of what he saw in their eyes.

How much did that suck?

The rest of the night passed quietly. The next morning, they woke up to a ringing phone.

Eve's dad was gone.

"The funeral's tomorrow," Eve said. She wasn't crying. She didn't look much like herself this morning—no makeup, no effort at all put into what she'd thrown on. Her eyes were veined with red, and her nose almost glowed. She'd cried all night; Claire had heard her, but when she'd knocked on the door, Eve hadn't wanted company. Not even Michael's.

"Are you going?" Michael asked. Claire thought that was a funny question—who wouldn't go? But Eve just nodded.

"I need to," she said. "They're right about that closure thing, I guess. Will you . . . ?"

"Of course," he said. "I can't do graveside, but—"

Eve shuddered. "So not going there, anyway. The church is bad enough."

"Church?" Claire asked, as she poured mugs of coffee for the three of them. Shane, as usual, had slept through the phone. "Really?"

"You've never met Father Joe, have you?" Eve managed a weak smile. "You'll like him. He's—something."

"Eve had the hots for him when she was twelve," Michael said, and got a dirty look. "What? You did, and you know it."

"It was the cassock, okay? I'm over it."

Claire raised her eyebrows. "Is Father Joe a . . . ?" She did the teeth-in-the-neck mime. They both smiled.

"No," Michael said. "He's just nonjudgmental."

Eve got through the day without too much trouble; she did the normal things—helping with the laundry, taking half the cleaning jobs for the day. It was her day off from work. Claire had a few classes, but she skipped three that she knew she'd already built up enough momentum in, and attended only the one that seemed critical. Michael didn't go in to teach private guitar lessons, either.

It was nice. It was like . . . family.

The funeral was held at noon the next day, and Claire found herself trying to pick out what to wear. Party clothes seemed too . . . festive. Jeans were too informal. She borrowed a pair of Eve's black tights and wore them with an also-borrowed black skirt. Paired with a white shirt, it looked moderately respectful.

She wasn't sure how Eve planned to dress, because at eleven a.m., Eve was still sitting in front of her vanity mirror, staring at her reflection. Still in her black dressing gown.

"Hey," Claire said. "Can I help?"

"Sure," Eve said. "Should I do my hair up?"

"It'd look nice that way," Claire said, and picked up the hairbrush. She brushed Eve's thick black hair until it shone, then twisted it into a knot and pinned it up at the back of her head. "There."

Eve reached for her rice-powder makeup, then stopped. She met Claire's eyes in the mirror.

"Maybe not the right time," she said.

Claire didn't say anything at all. Eve applied some lipstick—dark, but not her usual shade—and began searching through her closet.

In the end, she went with a high-necked black dress—one long enough to hang to the tops of her shoes. And a black veil. It was subdued, for Eve.

The four of them were at the church with fifteen minutes to spare, and as Michael pulled into the parking garage, Claire saw that several vampire-tinted cars were already present. "Is this the only funeral?" she asked.

"Yeah," he said, and turned off the engine. "I guess Mr. Rosser had more friends than we thought."

Not that many, as it turned out; when they entered the vestibule of the church, it was nearly empty, and there weren't many names noted in the register. Eve's mother stood by the book, waiting to pounce on anyone who came in the door.

True to Michael's earlier description, Mrs. Rosser couldn't seem to stop crying; she was wearing all black, like Eve, only it was much more theatrical—dramatic sweeps of black satin, a big formal hat, gloves.

And, Claire reflected, when you were more theatrical than *Eve*, you definitely had issues.

Mrs. Rosser had gone in heavy for mascara, and it was in messy streams all down her cheeks. Her hair was dyed blond, and straggling around her face. If she was going for the role of Ophelia in the town production of *Hamlet*, Claire thought she probably had it in the bag.

Eve's mother threw herself on Claire like a wet blanket, sobbing on her shoulder and smearing mascara on her white shirt. "Thank you for coming!" she wailed, and Claire awkwardly patted her on the back. "I wish you'd known my husband. He was such a *good* man, such a *hard* life—"

Eve stood there looking remote and a little sick. "Mom. Get off her. She doesn't even know you."

Mrs. Rosser drew back, gulping back another sob. "Don't be cruel, Eve, just because you didn't love your father—"

Which was just about the coldest thing Claire had ever heard. She exchanged a stricken look with Shane.

Michael got between mother and daughter, which was damn brave of him. Maybe it was the vampire gene. "Mrs. Rosser. I'm sorry about your husband."

"*Thank you*, Michael. You've always been such a good boy. And thank you for taking care of Eve when she went out on her own."

Mrs. Rosser blew her nose, which was how she missed Eve saying caustically, "You mean, when you threw my ass out on the street?"

"Sign us in," Michael said to Claire, and took Eve's arm and led her into the church. Claire hastily scribbled their names in the book, nodded to Mrs. Rosser—who was staring after her daughter with an expression that turned Claire's stomach—and grabbed Shane's arm to follow.

She'd been in the church before. It was nice—not overly fancy, but peaceful in its simplicity. No crosses anywhere in sight, but just now, the focus was the big, black casket at the end of the room. She was struck by the smooth curve of the wood, and how much it reminded her of the Bloodmobile.

That made Claire shiver and grip Shane's arm even more tightly as they slid into the pew beside Michael and Eve.

There were about fifteen people scattered through the sanctuary, and more arrived as the minutes ticked by. A couple of men in suits—from the funeral home, Claire supposed—set up more floral displays on either side of the casket.

It somehow didn't seem real. And the sounds of Mrs. Rosser's continued sobs and wails, responding to every mourner who entered, made it even weirder.

Eve slid out of the pew and walked up to the coffin. She stared down into it for a few long seconds, then bent and put something in it and came back to take her seat. She had her veil down, but even with the softening blur, her expression looked frozen and hard.

"He was a son of a bitch," she said when she saw Claire watching her. "But he was still my dad."

She leaned against Michael's shoulder, and he put his arm around her.

Mrs. Rosser finally entered the sanctuary and took a seat in the front row, ahead of where the four of them were. One of the funeral home attendants handed her an entire box of tissues. She pulled out a handful and continued to sob.

And a tall, good-looking man in a black cassock and white surplice, with a purple stole around his neck, came out from behind the floral displays and knelt down next to her, patting her hand. The fabled Father Joe, Claire supposed. He seemed nice—a little earnest, and younger than she'd expected. Brown hair and golden eyes that were very direct behind a pair of square gold-rimmed spectacles. He listened to Mrs. Rosser's ode to her husband with a sympathetic, if distant, expression, nodding when she paused. His glance flicked away once or twice, to the clock, and he finally bent forward and whispered something to her. She nodded.

More people had come in at the last minute, enough to fill about half the church. Claire, turning, spotted familiar faces: Detectives Joe Hess and Travis Lowe, who nodded in her direction as they took their seats at the back of the room. She recognized a few more people, including a total of four vampires in dark suits and sunglasses.

One of them was Oliver, looking bored. Of course—Eve's family had been under Brandon's Protection, and when Brandon had died, they'd come under his superior's authority. Oliver's appearance here had less to do with genuine feeling than public relations.

Father Joe stepped to the pulpit and began eulogizing a man Claire had never met, and one she doubted Eve recognized; except for the facts and figures of his life, his character seemed way better than anything his daughter had ever mentioned. From the way Mrs. Rosser nodded and cried, she was buying into the fiction wholesale.

"What a load of crap," Shane whispered to Claire. "Her dad hit her, you know. Eve."

Claire sent him a startled look.

"Just keep that in mind," he finished. "And don't shed any tears. Not for this."

Shane could, Claire thought, be one of the hardest people she'd ever met. Not that he was wrong. Just—hard.

But it helped. The emotion swirling through, amped higher by Eve's mother, washed over her and away without doing more than making her eyes sting. When Father Joe finished his eulogy, the organ started, and Mrs. Rosser was the first to the casket.

"Oh, God," Eve sighed under her breath as her mother draped herself dramatically over the wood and screamed. Bloodcurdling, theatrical screams. "I guess I'd better—"

Michael went with her, and whether it was his male presence or his angelic face or his vampire blood, he was able to pry Mrs. Rosser away and lead her back to the pew, where she sat in a complete collapse, blubbering.

Eve stood there at the casket for a few seconds, back straight, head inclined, and then walked away.

Tears dripped from under her veil and pattered on her black dress, but she didn't make a sound.

Claire filed by, but gave Eve's dad only a quick glance; he looked—

unnatural. Not disgusting, but clearly not alive. She shivered and took Shane's arm, and followed Eve as she passed her mother without a word and headed for the exit.

Eve almost ran into her brother.

Jason had slipped in the back. As far as Claire could tell, the kid hadn't changed his clothes at all—ever—and the unwashed smell of him was evident from three feet away.

He looked high, too. "Nice disguise, Sis," he smirked.

Eve stopped, staring at him, and scraped the veil back from her face. "What are you doing here?"

"Mourning." He laughed under his breath. "Whatev."

Eve deliberately looked to the side, where Detectives Hess and Lowe were sitting. "I think you'd better go." They hadn't noticed him yet, but they would. All it would take would be a raised voice, or Eve snapping her fingers.

"He's my dad, too."

"Then show him some respect," she said. "Leave."

She went around him. The rest of them followed, though Shane slowed down, and Claire had to tug at his arm to keep him moving.

Jason made a *bring it* motion. Shane shook his head. "Really not worth the trouble," he said.

And then they were out in the vestibule, away from the choking smell of flowers and the subtle smell of death, and all Claire could think was, *How is that closure?*

But Eve looked better, and that was what mattered. "Let's go have a burger," she said.

As ideas went, that one was popular, and Claire's spirits lifted as they walked out of the church and into the shaded parking structure, heading for Michael's car.

They were intercepted.

Michael sensed it first—he stopped dead in his tracks, turning in a circle as if trying to pinpoint a sound the rest of them couldn't hear.

A lithe shadow leaped down from the concrete rafters above, landed in a crouch, and grinned.

Ysandre. She rose with effortless grace and strolled toward the four of them.

"Get in the car," Michael said. "Go."

"Not leaving you," Shane said. He didn't take his eyes off Ysandre.

"Don't be an idiot. She's not after me."

Shane's eyes flicked to Michael's face.

"Go."

Claire tugged on Shane's arm. He let himself be guided to the car. Michael tossed the keys.

Ysandre flashed across the open space and plucked them out of the air. She tossed them carelessly up and down in her palm, and the cool, metallic jingle was the only sound in the garage.

"Don't get all paranoid," she said. "I just stopped by to say hello. It's a free country."

"It's car theft if you keep my keys," Michael said. He held up his hand, and she shrugged and pitched them back. "What do you want?"

"Just wanted to make sure Mr. Shane got my invitation," she said. "Did you, honey?"

Shane didn't move. Didn't speak. As far as Claire could tell, he wasn't even breathing.

"From the fast little beat of that heart, I guess you did," Ysandre said, and smiled. "See you on Saturday, then. You-all have a good rest of the week."

She walked away, high-heeled boots tapping on the pavement, and vanished into shadow.

Shane let out a slow breath.

None of them knew exactly what to say. Michael unlocked the car, and the quiet ruled for at least five minutes, until he stopped at Denny's.

"We still eating?" he asked.

"I guess," Shane said. "I'm not letting her ruin my appetite."

There was a shade awning stretching from the covered parking to the front door, which Claire had never thought about before—apparently, the local Denny's catered to vampires as much as humans even in the daytime. There were local flyers taped to the glass front doors, and Claire glanced at them on the way inside. She stopped so suddenly Shane ran into her.

"Hey! Walking here!"

"Look." Claire pointed at the paper.

It said *ONE NIGHT ONLY!* and there was a black-and-white photograph of a young man with blond hair cradling a guitar.

Underneath it said *Michael Glass returns to Common Grounds,* and the date on it was . . . tonight.

Shane ripped it off the door, grabbed Michael's shoulder, and held it up. "Hey," he said. "Ring any bells? When were you going to tell us?"

Michael looked surprised, then embarrassed. "I—wasn't going to. Look, it's just a tryout, okay? I wanted to see if I could still—I don't want you guys to come. It's nothing."

Eve grabbed the flyer and stared at it. "Nothing? Michael! You're *playing! In public!*"

"That's new?" Claire whispered to Shane.

"He hasn't played anywhere but our living room since—" Teeth-in-neck mime. "You know. Oliver."

"Oh."

Michael's face was turning pink. "Just put it back, okay? It's not a big deal!"

Eve kissed him. "Yes, it is," she said. "And I hate you for not telling me. Were you just going to sneak off or something?"

"Absolutely," Michael sighed. "Because if I suck, I don't want any of you hearing it firsthand."

Claire taped the flyer carefully back to the door. "You're not going to suck."

"Not at the guitar, anyway," Shane said, deadpan. Claire punched him in the arm. "Ow."

SEVEN

Michael spent two hours tuning his guitar, which was annoying, and he left early. Eve went with him, despite his protests that it really wasn't a big thing. That left Claire and Shane to decide on their own what to do.

She made chili dogs and was putting the shredded cheese on top when Shane, fresh from video-game triumph, came into the kitchen. "Hey," he said. "Nice. Thanks." He shoved part of the chili dog in his mouth, standing at the kitchen counter.

"You could at least sit down," she sighed. "We do have tables. They even have chairs."

"You want to go?" he mumbled. "To the thing?"

Did she? Claire ate a bite of her own hot dog, hardly even aware that she was breaking her own eating-while-standing rules, and thought about it. On the one hand, it meant going out at night, and going out to Common Grounds for recreational purposes, which was sort of not done around their house these days.

But—Michael. Out in public. Playing.

"Yeah," she said. "I would, if you don't mind. I know you don't like the place, but—"

"I like it better than Eve does, trust me. Besides, I don't want her down there alone. She needs somebody watching her back while he's neck-deep in groupies or whatever."

She laughed.

"Oh, you think that's funny? Should have seen him in high school. Guy could draw the hotties every time he picked up that guitar."

"He still can, I'll bet."

"Exactly my point. Eat up. They usually start music sets around seven."

Claire wolfed down her meal and ran upstairs for a quick shower and change of clothes. After some debate, she went with the short skirt and tights she'd last worn to crash Monica Morrell's disastrous house party, and a plain black top tight enough to match but loose enough that she wouldn't die if her parents saw her.

Shane blinked in surprise when she came downstairs. He'd thrown on different clothes, too, but they were still slacker-casual. The only sign that he was trying to make an impression was that she suspected he might have combed his hair. A little.

"You look great," he said, and smiled. She stopped on the last step from the bottom, which put them on about equal levels, and he kissed her. Long and slow. He tasted of toothpaste, at first, but then he just tasted like Shane, and that was so, so delicious that she found herself rising on her tiptoes to get even closer. "Hold up, girl. I thought we were going out. Kissing like that, you're making me think about staying in."

Claire had to admit, it made her think of it, too. Especially since the house was empty, and they were all alone.

She saw it cross Shane's mind, too, and for a second his eyes widened, and so did his pupils.

Oh, the possibilities.

"Better go if we're going," Claire said regretfully. "Only—how are we getting there?"

Shane offered her his arm. "Nice night for a walk, I hear."

"Are you sure?"

He tapped her gold bracelet, then his own white hospital-issue one. "This may be the only night we get to do it in this town," he said. "Let's live dangerously."

. . .

It was nice, strolling arm in arm with Shane and not worrying (well, not worrying too much) about which danger was about to sweep in on them from the dark.

Tonight, at least, the dangers kept their distance. It was a short walk to Common Grounds, but a lonely one; Claire felt a little unreal, moving slowly in the dark past shut houses with lit-up windows. People didn't venture out much after sunset, and if they did, they went in groups, and in cars.

Two people out in the night like this . . . seemed wrong, and when they were about halfway to the coffee shop, Claire saw someone pull a car into a driveway ahead of them and jump out. The look on the woman's face was starkly panicked as she looked toward them, and Claire realized that she'd thought they were—

Vampires. Which was both funny and sad.

The woman grabbed her groceries and hurried into her house, shutting the door with a bang and locking it with a harsh rasp of metal.

Claire didn't say anything to Shane, and he didn't venture a comment, but she had no doubt he felt the same unsettling guilt. But what could they have said? *It's okay, lady, we're not here to eat you?*

Claire was glad when the hot golden spill of light from Common Grounds' front window came into view. It was obviously doing good business—cars lined the streets on both sides, and more parked as she and Shane approached the entrance. "Going to be nuts," Shane said, but he didn't sound displeased. "Next time I'll take you someplace nice and quiet."

Claire searched her memory. So much had happened since she'd met Shane, but she was almost sure that this constituted their first real, actual date on their own. Which was startling, and sweet, and precious to her in ways she suspected Shane would never imagine. She savored the warmth of his hand in hers, smiled at him, and entered Common Grounds while he held the door for her.

The noise level was amazing. The coffee shop was normally quiet, although never boring, but as the sun went down, the excitement level rose, and tonight it was blowing through the roof. Every table was already crowded with people—humans, mostly, but toward the corners of the room Claire saw a few vampire faces she recognized, including Sam's. Michael's only family in town had come to support him. Sam sent her a smile and a wave, which Claire returned.

Michael himself was standing in the clear area behind the coffee bar, looking tense and a little bit blank. He was dressed in a plain gray T-shirt and jeans, and he had his acoustic guitar slung around his body. Claire thought the puka shell necklace he was wearing looked new—a gift from Eve? A good-luck charm?

Eve was standing next to him, and although she couldn't see clearly, Claire thought they were holding hands.

Claire and Shane pushed through the crowd to the bar. Shane nodded to Michael, who nodded back—all very manly—and then Shane went to place some drink orders, leaving Claire to fumble for words.

"You're going to do great," she finally said. Michael's blue eyes blinked and focused in the here and now.

"Man, I don't know," he said. "It was supposed to be casual—I show up and play a couple of songs. Just to get used to it again. But this—"

Somebody out in the corner of the room started clapping, and suddenly everybody was doing it, a wave of rhythmic noise.

Michael couldn't possibly get any more pale, but Claire saw the outright doubt in his eyes. Eve did, too, and gave him a quick kiss.

"You can do this, Michael," she said. "Come on. Get out there. It's what you do."

Claire nodded and smiled her support. Michael lifted the hinged section of the bar and stepped out, to a thunderous wave of applause. There was a small stage set up at the far end of the room, near the closed door that said OFFICE, and as Michael moved up on it, the stage lights caught and glittered in his golden hair, sparked an unearthly blue in his eyes.

Wow, Claire thought. That wasn't Michael anymore. That was . . . something else.

Eve ducked under the bar and came to lean next to Claire, her arms folded. She had a wistful smile on her Evil Queen–red lips. "He's beautiful," she said. "Right? He is."

Claire could only agree with that.

Michael adjusted the microphone, tested it, played a couple of fast finger exercises she knew he used to calm himself, and then smiled out at the crowd. It was a different smile than she'd ever seen from him before— *more*, somehow. More intense, more joyous, more personal. She felt a hot flutter somewhere deep inside as his gaze brushed over her, and immediately felt embarrassed about it.

But man, he was hot. She understood now what Shane was talking about, and she wasn't immune.

Shane touched her shoulder and handed her a drink just as Michael said, "I guess you all know who I am, right?"

And about eighty percent of the room cheered like thunder. The others—college students, who'd either wandered in or come because they were bored—looked lost.

Michael gave the mike stand one last, precise adjustment. His hands were sure now, moving with confidence. "My name is Michael Glass, and I'm from Morganville."

More cheers. Before they died away, Michael started to play, a fast and complicated song that Claire had heard him fooling around with at the house—but this wasn't fooling around; this was serious talent. He glittered like white gold, and music flowed out of his hands like streams of light. It wrapped around Claire like a shining net, and she didn't dare breathe, didn't move, as Michael played like she'd never heard anyone play before, ever.

She managed to glance aside at Shane, whose eyes were wide and fixed on Michael, as well. She nudged him. He gave her a dumbfounded shake of his head.

Eve was smiling, as if she'd known it all along.

Michael brought the song to a liquid, blazing finish, and as the guitar strings rang in the silence, the crowd was utterly still. Michael waited, just as motionless, and then the room spontaneously erupted in applause and cheers.

Claire thought that the smile that spread across Michael's face was worth everything about Morganville, right at that moment.

His next song was slower, sweeter, and Claire realized with a shock that it was a slowed-down version of the song he'd been writing the other night, when he'd been too busy to go to the store. It had lyrics, too, and Michael's voice transformed them into sad, aching beauty.

It was a song for Eve.

Claire realized her chest was hurting, both from the pressure of un-shed tears and the fact that she wasn't breathing. She'd never known music could have that much power. As she glanced around the coffee shop, she saw the same thing in the others' faces—common rapture. Even Oli-ver, standing behind the bar, was transfixed. And in the shadows, Claire glimpsed someone else—Amelie, nodding thoughtfully, as if she'd known all along, like Eve.

Sam's eyes were full of tears, but he was smiling.

Michael's voice drifted to a whisper, and he finished the song. This time, the applause didn't stop, and the cheers were a full-throated roar.

Michael adjusted the mike stand again. "Save it, guys," he said over the noise, and smiled. "We're just getting started."

It was the best night Claire had ever had in Morganville. She'd never felt so much a part of something—never seen so much *unity* in a room full of people so diverse. Clueless students were backslapping Morganville natives with bracelets, vampires were smiling impartially at humans, and even Oliver seemed affected by the general euphoria.

When Michael came offstage, it was only after three encores and thunderous standing ovations. He made a beeline straight for Eve, folded her in a hug, and then kissed her so deeply Claire had to look away. When they came up for air, Michael was still grinning.

"So?" he asked. "Didn't suck, right?"

Shane offered his hand. "Didn't suck. Congratulations, dude."

Michael ignored the hand and hugged him, then turned to Claire. She didn't hesitate to embrace him. He was warmer than usual, and sweaty; she hadn't known vampires could sweat. Maybe they just usually didn't exert themselves that much. "You were amazing," Claire whispered. "I just—amazing. Wow. Did I say amazing?"

He gave her a kiss on the cheek, and then turned away to the press of well-wishers coming to shake his hand. There were a lot of them, and many of them were pretty girls. Claire retreated back to Shane's side.

"See what I mean?" Shane said. "Good thing Eve's here. This can go to a guy's head."

"Even a vampire's?"

"Heh. Especially a vampire's."

It took about fifteen minutes for the rush of instant fans to die down, and by then the tables had cleared out, leaving just a few hard-core caffeine addicts to close out the evening. Claire and Shane grabbed chairs and fresh drinks while Eve helped Michael get his things together.

"Hey," Claire said, and got Shane's full attention. "Thank you."

His eyebrows rose. "What for?"

"For the best date I've ever had."

"This? Nah. Just average. I can do much better."

She cocked her head. "Really?"

"Absolutely."

"You willing to prove it?"

Somehow, his hand had taken hold of hers, and his warm fingers stroked shivers down her palm. "Someday," he said. "Soon. Absolutely."

She found herself doing the not-breathing thing again, caught in all the possibilities. Shane smiled, slow and wicked, and she wanted to kiss him right then, for a very long time.

"Ready?" Michael was standing at the table, gazing down at them. Some of the brilliance he'd had onstage had faded, and he was just regular Michael again—a little tired, too. Claire gulped down hot cocoa and nodded.

Even the best nights had to come to an end.

Claire was getting ready for bed when she heard Eve scream—not the shriek of *Stop tickling me, you jerk,* but a full-out cry of alarm, one that went through the house like a buzz saw. Claire pulled on her pajama top, grabbed her robe, and pelted out into the hall. Shane was already there, heading downstairs, still dressed in a pair of jeans and a loose T-shirt.

When they got to the front hall, they found Michael sitting on the floor, holding a bloody girl in his arms. Eve was snapping the locks on the front door shut.

"Miranda," Michael said, and moved the bloody hair away from her face. "Miranda, can you hear me?"

Claire realized with a breathless shock that it was Eve's sometime friend Miranda—just a kid, really, at that gawky stage where girls both yearned to be and feared to be women. Mir had filled out a little since the last time Claire had seen her—not quite as scary thin—but she still looked like a waif.

A wounded one. There was a gash in her head, and blood dripping down her neck to patter on Michael's blue jeans and fingers.

"Ow," Miranda whispered, and began to cry. "Ow. I hit my head—"

"You're okay. You're safe now," Eve said. She dropped to her knees across from Michael and held out her arms; Michael quickly transferred the girl over. His pupils had gone to pinpoints, and he seemed—different. "Michael, maybe you'd better go—wash up."

He nodded stiffly and pushed past Shane and Eve, heading upstairs so quickly he was just a blur.

"Ambulance?" Shane asked.

"No! No, I can't!" Miranda sounded frantic. "Please, don't send me there. You don't know—you don't know what they'll do—the fire—"

Eve kept hold of the girl, somehow, though Miranda was flailing like mad. "Okay, chill. We won't. I promise. Relax. Shane—maybe the first-aid kit? Towels and hot water?"

"I'll help," Claire said, and she and Shane took off for the kitchen. When she glanced back, she saw that Miranda had stopped fighting and was lying exhausted in Eve's arms. "What the hell happened to her?"

"Morganville," Shane said, and shrugged. He stiff-armed the kitchen door and went straight for the cabinets under the sink. The first aid kit was getting a lot of play, Claire thought as she turned on the hot water and gathered up some clean kitchen towels.

Miranda's first aid session wasn't as bad as Claire had feared—the head wound was bloody but superficial, and Eve fixed it with some butterfly bandages.

The holes in Miranda's neck looked fresh, though. When Eve asked about them, Miranda looked embarrassed and pulled up the collar of her shirt. "None of your business," she said.

"It's Charles, right? Son of a bitch." Eve had a problem with vampires who preyed on the underage—in fact, from what Claire had gathered, so did a lot of the other vampires. There were laws against it, after all. She wondered whether Amelie knew about Charles and Miranda. Or cared. "You can't let him gnaw on you like this, Mir! You know that!"

"He was so hungry," Miranda said, and hung her head. "I know. But it didn't hurt, not really."

That made Claire want to throw up. She exchanged a look with Shane.

"There's a guy who needs staking," he said.

Miranda looked up sharply. "That's not funny!"

"Do I have on my funny face? Miranda, the guy's a pedophile. The fact that he just sucks your blood instead of—" Shane paused, staring at her. "It is instead of, right?"

It was impossible to tell if Miranda even understood what he was getting at, but Claire thought she did, and it made the girl deeply uncomfortable. Miranda tried to get out of the chair they'd put her into. "I need to go home."

"Whoa, whoa, you can barely stand up," Eve said, and managed to get her settled again. "Claire, would you check on Michael? See if he's okay?"

In other words, there were questions Shane and Eve were about to ask, personal questions. Claire nodded and went upstairs. The bathroom door was closed. She knocked softly.

"Michael?"

No answer. She tried the handle. Locked.

Claire turned at what sounded like footsteps down the hall, but she saw no one. She didn't hear the door unlock, but when she looked back, the bathroom door was open, and Michael was standing about two inches away from her.

She stumbled backward. Instead of just washing up, he'd showered;

his hair was damp and curling and darker than usual, and he was wearing a towel around his waist. There was a lot more of Michael on display than she was used to, and it was . . . impressive.

Claire backed away, all the way to the wall.

"Sorry," he said. Not as if he really was. He sounded annoyed, stressed, and jittery. "She's still here." It wasn't a question, but Claire nodded anyway. "She can't stay. We need to get her out of here."

"I don't think she's in any shape to go," Claire offered. "She seemed pretty hysterical. Shane and Eve are—"

"I can still smell her blood," Michael interrupted her. "I washed it off of me. I took off my clothes. I showered. None of that matters. I can still—she has to go. *Now*."

"What's wrong with you? I thought you'd—" She hesitated, then made a drinking motion.

"I did." Michael rubbed his face with both hands. "Guess I burned it off tonight at the show. I'm hungry, Claire."

It cost him a lot to say it. Claire gulped, and nodded. "Wait here."

She went downstairs, past where Shane and Eve were still earnestly talking with Miranda, and into the kitchen. At the very back of the bottom shelf of the refrigerator sat some bottles that might have been full of beer, and weren't. There were three of them. She grabbed one without looking too closely at it and made sure it was concealed against her side as she passed the little downstairs group. Nobody really looked her way; they were too intent on keeping their own secrets.

Michael was still waiting, leaning against the bathroom doorframe, arms folded. He straightened when he saw what she had in her hand. She gave it to him silently. Michael never took his eyes off her as he popped the cap with his thumbnail and lifted the cold bottle to his lips. The contents moved more like syrup than blood, and Claire almost gagged.

Michael *did* gag. But he swallowed it. And kept on drinking until the bottle was empty.

His blue eyes flushed hot red, and then cleared back to their normal color.

She saw something like horror go through him. "I didn't just do that in front of you."

"Uh—yeah. You did." And there had definitely been some kind of challenge in it, too. Some kind of come-on, even. Which was beyond yuck and creepy, and yet . . .

And yet.

Michael wiped his lips with the back of his hand, looked down at the faint smear, and went back to the washbasin to rinse it off.

He stared into the mirror at himself for so long, Claire thought he'd forgotten she was there, and then he said, "Thanks."

Claire tried to think of something not totally idiotic to say. "Pretty disgusting, isn't it? When it's cold?" That wasn't it.

Luckily, Michael was relieved to have any kind of conversational lifeline, after that weird moment. "Yeah," he said. "But it keeps the edge off. That's what's important." He rinsed out the bottle carefully, then threw it away and took in a deep breath. "I'll get dressed. Be there in a second."

It was a dismissal, but a nice one, and Claire took it at face value this time, and went back to the living room.

Where Shane and Eve were standing together, heads cocked at identical angles, staring.

"What's going on?" Claire whispered.

"Shhh," both Shane and Eve hissed, eerily in unison.

Because Miranda was talking in a strange monotone voice, and she looked . . . dead. Unconscious. Only talking.

"I see the feast," she was saying. "So much anger . . . so much lying. All dead, walking dead, falling down. It's spreading. It'll kill us all."

Claire felt a hot snap of alarm. *Walking dead, falling down. It's spreading.* Miranda had psychic episodes—Claire knew that. It was part of the reason Eve let her hang around from time to time. Sometimes her visions were fake, but a lot of the time, they were as serious as a heart attack, and Claire somehow knew this one was real.

She was talking about the disease infecting the vampires, and she was talking about it spreading to humans. *No, that can't happen. Can it?* They hadn't even really been able to pinpoint what the disease was, only what it did, and what it did was erode the vampires' sanity, carving steadily until what was left was unable to function at all.

The first thing to go—for all the vampires of Morganville—had been the ability to reproduce. To create new vampires. Only Amelie still had the strength, and creating Michael had almost destroyed her.

It's spreading. Claire thought of all the humans in Morganville, all the families, all the young people who'd been in the coffee shop tonight, and felt cold and unsteady.

It couldn't be true.

"Feast," Miranda said again. "You're all fools, all fools—don't let him trick you. It's not just three—it's more—"

"Who?" Eve sank down next to Miranda's chair and put a hand on her shoulder. "Mir, who are you talking about?"

"Elder," she said, and now there were tears leaking down Miranda's pale cheeks. "Oh no. Oh no . . . they're turning. They're all so hungry, can't stop them—"

Michael, who was coming down the steps, paused. He looked calm again, but worried. "What's she talking about?"

"Shhh!" This time, all three of them shushed at the same time. Eve bent closer to Miranda. "Honey, are you talking about the vampires? What's going to happen with the vampires?"

"Dying," Miranda whispered. "So many dying. We think we're safe but we're not. They won't listen—they won't see us—" She restlessly turned the silver bracelet on her wrist and twisted in her chair. "He's doing it. He's making it happen."

"Oliver?" Eve asked. Because Oliver was the only male vampire Elder on the town council.

But Miranda shook her head. She didn't say another word, but she cried, cried so hard she shook herself out of her trance and clung to Eve like a thin little reed in the wind.

"Bishop," Michael said. They all looked at him. "It's not Oliver. She's talking about Bishop. He's going to try to destroy Morganville."

. . .

Miranda ended up sleeping on the couch, and when Claire came down-stairs the next morning, she found the girl huddled in a ball under mountains of blankets, still shivering but fast asleep. She looked even more frail. Her pale skin was translucent, and there were dark, exhausted circles around her eyes.

Claire felt sorry for her, but it was a distant kind of sorry—Miranda didn't really invite a lot of devotion. She didn't have any friends to speak of, or so Eve said; people tolerated her, but they didn't exactly enjoy her company. That was hard on the kid, but Claire could understand it. Miranda was a mixture of denial and outright creepiness, and even in Morganville, she was going to have a hard time fitting in.

No wonder she defended the vampire who was feeding on her. He was probably the only one who really showed her any kind of affection.

Claire paused to tuck the blankets more firmly around the girl's trembling frame before she went into the kitchen to make coffee and toast. As breakfasts went, it was lonely and basic, but the sun was barely up and none of the others were what you might call morning people.

There were times when signing up for early classes seemed like a really bad idea.

When the phone rang, Claire nearly jumped out of her skin. She leaped for the extension hanging on the wall by the kitchen door and got it before the second earsplitting jangle. "Hello?"

There was a pause on the other end, and then her mother said, "Claire?"

"Mom! Hi—what's wrong?"

"Why should anything be wrong? Why can't I just call because I wanted to talk to my daughter?" Oh, great. Now her mother sounded agitated and defensive. "I know it's early, but I wanted to catch up with you before you went off to class for the day."

Claire sighed and leaned against the wall, idly kicking at the linoleum floor. "Okay. How are you and Dad settling in? Getting all unpacked?"

"Just fine," her mother said, in so false a tone that Claire went very, very still. "It's just—an adjustment, that's all. Such a small town and all."

"Yeah," Claire agreed quietly. "It's an adjustment." She had no idea what her mother and father knew about Morganville by now, but they had to be getting some kind of—what would they call it? Orientation? Morganville was nothing if not efficient about that, she suspected. "Have you—met some people?"

"We went to a nice getting-to-know-you party downtown," Mom said. "Mr. Bishop and his daughter took us."

Claire had to bite her lip to hold back a moan. Bishop? And Amelie? Oh God. "What happened?"

"Oh, nothing, really. It was a cocktail party. Hors d'oeuvres and drinks, a little conversation. There was a presentation on the history of—of—" With shocking suddenness, Claire's mother burst into tears. "I swear, we didn't know—we didn't know or we wouldn't have sent you to this awful place, oh, honey—"

Claire could barely swallow around the lump in her throat. "Don't cry, Mom. It's okay. It's all going to be okay now." She was lying, but she had to. The sound of her mother breaking apart was just too hard. "Look, you've met Amelie, right?"

Sniffles on the other end. "Yes. She seemed nice."

Nice wasn't how Claire would have put it. "Well, Amelie's the most powerful person in Morganville, and she's definitely on our side." An exaggeration, but it was the best she could do to describe the situation in simple terms. "So there's really nothing to be worried about, Mom. I work for Amelie. She has some responsibility for me, and for you, to make sure we're safe. Okay?"

"Okay." It was wan and muffled, but at least it was agreement. "I was just so worried about your father. He didn't look well, not well at all. I wanted him to go to the hospital, but he said he was fine—"

Claire had a cold second of flashback to Miranda saying, *Please don't send me there. You don't know what they'll do.* . . . She'd been talking about the hospital. "But he's okay?"

"He seems all right today." Claire's mom blew her nose, and when she came back to the phone, she sounded clearer and stronger. "I'm sorry to lay this on you, honey. I just had no idea—it was so strange to think that you'd been here all this time and never said a word to us about—the situation." Meaning, the vampires.

"Well, to be honest, I didn't think you'd believe me," Claire said. "And out-of-town calls are monitored. They told you that, right?"

"Yes, they did. So you were protecting us." Her mom laughed shakily. "Parents are supposed to protect their children, Claire. We've done a bang-up job of that, haven't we? We really thought that it would be so much safer for you here than off in Massachusetts or California on your own. . . ."

"It's okay. I'll get there someday."

They moved the conversation to easier things—to unpacking, to the vase that had gotten broken during the move ("Honestly, I hated that thing anyway—your aunt gave it to us for Christmas that year, remember?"), to how Claire intended to spend her day. By the end of it, Mom seemed more or less stable, and Claire's coffee was hopelessly cold. So was her toast.

"Claire," Mom said. "About moving out of that house—"

"I'm not moving," Claire said. "I'm sorry, Mom. I know it's going to upset Dad, but these are my friends, and this is where I belong. I'm staying."

There was a short silence on the other end, and then her mother said, very softly, "I'm so proud of you."

She hung up with a soft *click*. Claire stood for a moment, tears prickling in her eyes, and then said to the silent line, "I love you."

And then she picked up her stuff and went to class.

EIGHT

Days passed, and for a change, there were no further emergencies. Normal life—or what passed for it, anyway—set in. Claire went to class, Eve went to work, Michael taught guitar lessons—he was a lot more in demand since the concert at Common Grounds—and Shane . . . Shane slacked, although Claire thought he seemed preoccupied.

It finally dawned on her that he was thinking about Saturday, and the invitation. And that he didn't want to talk to her about it at all.

"So what should I do?" she asked Eve. "I mean, can't he just call in sick for the party or something?"

"You're kidding," Eve said. "You think they'd buy an excuse? If you get an invitation to something like this, you go. End of story."

"But—" Claire, who was getting glasses out of the cabinet while Eve put out plates, nearly dropped everything. "But that means that creepy little bi—"

"Language, missy."

"—witch is going to make him go with her!" That made her blindly furious, and not entirely because of how upset Shane had been before. It was the whole idea of Shane going along with it. Of Ysandre putting those pale, thin fingers on his chest, feeling his heartbeat.

Shane hadn't said a word to her about it. Not a single word. And she didn't know how to help.

Eve stared at her thoughtfully for a few seconds before she said, "Well, she's not the only one who's going, of course. Shane won't be all by himself."

"What?"

"Michael's going, too. I recognized the invitation when it came in. Didn't open it, though."

Still, Eve had every reason to expect that Michael would at least ask her to go with him. Claire, on the other hand, was completely shut out.

Which made her irrationally angry again, and this time for herself. *You're jealous,* she realized. *Because you don't want him going anywhere without you.*

She *so* did not want to be that person, but there it was. And she had no idea what to do about it.

When she set Shane's glass of Coke down in front of him, she did it with probably a little too much emphasis; he glanced up at her with a question-mark expression. Eve had already settled into her chair across the table. Michael wasn't home, but Eve didn't seem bothered about it this time. Maybe he'd talked to her about where he was going.

Nice to know somebody's talking, Claire thought.

"What?" Shane asked her, and took a drink. "Did I forget to say thanks? Because, thanks. Best Coke ever. Did you make it yourself? Special recipe?"

"Got any plans for Saturday night?" she asked. "I was thinking maybe we could go to the movies, or—"

Too transparent. Shane knew instantly, and Eve choked on her forkful of microwave lasagna. The silence stretched. Claire poked at her own meal, just for something to do.

"I can't," Shane finally said. "I guess you know why."

"You're going to that ball thing," Claire said. "With Bishop's—friend."

"I don't exactly have a choice."

"Are you sure about that?"

"Of course I'm sure—why are we talking about this exactly?"

"Because—" She stuck the fork into her lasagna so deep it scraped the plate. "Because Michael's going. I guess Eve is, too. And what am I supposed to do, exactly?"

"You're kidding. Are you on crack? Because I thought you just implied that you wanted to go to the scary vampire thing. Which, by the way, I don't."

Claire tried not to glare. "I thought you hated her. Ysandre. But you're going with her."

"I do. And I am." Shane shoveled food into his mouth, a blatant excuse to end the conversation, or at least avoid it.

Eve cleared her throat. "Maybe I should, I don't know, leave? Because this is starting to sound like one of those reality shows I don't want to be in. Maybe you guys want to take turns in the confessional booth."

Shane and Claire ignored her. "I didn't tell you because there's nothing you can do," Shane said. "There's nothing anyone can do."

"Stop talking with your mouth full."

"Dude, you asked!"

"I—" Claire felt a sudden burn of tears in her eyes. "I just wanted you to talk to me, that's all. But I guess you can't even do that."

She picked up her uneaten lasagna and drink and took it upstairs to her room. It was her turn to throw a fit, slam a door, and sulk, and dammit, she was going to do it well.

She burst into tears the second the door was closed, put everything down on the dresser, and collapsed into a soggy heap in the corner. She hadn't cried like this in a long time, not over something so *stupid*, but she just couldn't—didn't—

There was a knock at the door. "Claire?"

"Go away, Shane." Her heart wasn't in it, though, and he must have heard that. He opened the door. She kind of expected him to rush to her and sweep her up in a hug, but instead Shane just . . . stood there. Looking like some mixture of annoyed and confused.

"Why is this about you?" he asked her. It was a perfectly reasonable question, so absolutely logical it made her gasp and cry harder. "I have to get dressed up in a stupid outfit. I have to pretend I don't want to shove a stake in this bitch's heart. You don't."

"But you're going! Why are you going? You—I thought you hated her—"

"Because she said she'd kill you if I didn't show up. And because I know it's not a threat. She'd do it. Happy now?"

He closed the door quietly. Claire couldn't get her breath. The hurt in her chest seemed to be smothering her, as if every heartbeat might be her last. She heard herself make a sound, but she couldn't tell if it was tears or anger or anguish.

Eventually, the tears stopped, and Claire wiped the wet streaks from her cheeks. She felt sore, alone, and utterly to blame for everything. Her dinner held no appeal, and all she wanted to do was curl up under the blankets with the biggest, fluffiest stuffed animal she could find.

But she couldn't do that.

When she opened her door, she found Shane sitting outside, back against the wall. He looked up at her.

"You done?" he asked. His eyes were red, too. Not exactly tearful, but—something. "Because it's not like this floor's real comfortable."

She sank down next to him. He put his arm around her, and her head fell against his chest. There was something so soothing about the stroke of his fingers through her hair, the soft rhythm of his breathing. The reassurance of his solid warmth next to her.

"Don't let her hurt you," she whispered. "God, Shane—"

"No worries. Michael will be there, and I'm pretty sure he'd get into it if she tried. But I want you safe. Promise me that while we're gone, you'll go stay with your parents or something. No—" Because she was already trying to protest. "No, promise me. I need to know you'll be okay."

She nodded, still miserable. "I promise," she said, and took a deep breath to push all that away. "So what dumbass costume are you wearing?"

"Don't ask."

"Does it involve leather?"

"Yeah, actually, I think it might." He sounded like he dreaded the prospect. She managed a smile, despite everything.

"I can't wait."

Shane banged his head back against the wall. "Chicks."

Her next visit to Myrnin's lab brought a surprise. When she descended the steps, she saw the glow of lamps, and her first thought was, *Oh God, he's out of his cell.* Her second was that she'd better get the dart gun ready, and she was unzipping the backpack to reach for it when she saw that it wasn't Myrnin at all.

The overcrowded, dimly lit lab—which was more like a storeroom of outdated equipment, really—held a chair and reading lamp. Seated in the chair, turning pages in one of the fragile, ancient journals, was none other than Oliver.

Claire put her hand on the butt of the dart gun, just in case, although she wasn't really sure what good a dose of antidote would do in this situation.

"Oh, relax. I'm not going to attack you, Claire," Oliver said in a bored voice. He didn't even look up. "Besides, we're on the same side these days. Or haven't you heard?"

She came down the remaining steps slowly. "I guess I haven't. Was there a memo?" Granted, he'd come running when Eve had called about Bishop, but that didn't necessarily put him in the category of ally in Claire's books.

"When outsiders threaten the community, the community pulls together against the outsiders. It's a rule as old as the tribal system. You and I are in the same community, and we have a common enemy."

"Mr. Bishop."

Oliver looked up, marking the place in the journal with one finger. "You have questions, I'd assume. I would, in your place."

"All right. How long have you known him?"

"I don't know him. I doubt anyone does who's still alive today."

Claire slipped into a rickety chair across from him. "But you've met him."

"Yes."

"When did you meet him, then?"

Oliver tilted his head, eyes narrowed, and she remembered how she'd once thought he was nice, just a normal kind of person. Not so much now.

Not so much a person, either.

"I met him in Greece," he said. "Some time ago. I don't think the circumstances would be particularly enlightening to you. Or comforting, come to think of it."

"Did you try to kill him?"

"Me?" Oliver smiled slowly. "No."

"Did Amelie?"

He didn't answer, but he continued to smile. The silence stretched until she wanted to scream, but she knew he wanted her to babble.

She didn't.

"Amelie's affairs are none of yours," Oliver said. "I assume you've been listening to Myrnin's chatter. I confess, I find it fascinating he's still with us. I thought him dead and gone, long ago."

"Like Bishop?"

"He's quite mad, you know. Myrnin. And he has been for as long as I can recall, though it certainly got worse in more recent times." Oliver's eyes took on a faraway look. "He did so love the hunt, but he was always such a pathetic weeping idiot after. It doesn't surprise me he wants to blame his own weakness on some—mythical disease. Some people simply aren't cut out for this life."

Of all the things Claire had expected, that one caught her off guard. "You don't believe there's a disease?"

"I don't believe that because Myrnin and a few others are—defective— that it means we're all declining, no."

"But—you can't, um—"

"Reproduce?" Oliver said it without any emotion at all. "Perhaps we don't wish to."

"You tried to turn Michael."

Oh, she shouldn't have said that, she really shouldn't have; Oliver's face tensed, and she saw the skull underneath that smooth, pale skin. A flicker of red went through his eyes. "So Michael says."

"So Amelie says. You wanted—you wanted your own power base here. Your own converts. But you couldn't do it. That surprised you, didn't it? Because all of a sudden you're—not able to."

"Child," Oliver said, "you should think carefully about the next thing you say to me. Very, very carefully."

He followed up with another stretch of silent staring, and this time Claire did look away. She picked at invisible lint on her backpack. "I should get to work," she said. "And you aren't supposed to be in here without Amelie knowing about it."

"How do you know she doesn't?"

"There'd be somebody else here watching you if she did," Claire pointed out, and got a small, cold smile in response.

"Clever girl. Yes, very well. Are you going to tell me to leave?"

"I don't think I can tell you to do anything, Oliver, but if you want me to call Amelie—" She took her cell phone out, opened it, and scrolled through the address book.

Oliver thought about killing her. She saw it flash across his face, plain as sunrise, and she almost dialed the phone in sheer reflex.

Then it was gone, and he was smiling, and he stood up and gave her a nod. "No need to bother the Founder with such nonsense," he said. "I'll be leaving. There's only so many ridiculous mad ravings one can read at a sitting, in any case."

He dropped the journal onto a pile scattered near the chair and walked away, moving with effortless grace around the piles of books and barriers of mismatched furniture. He didn't seem to move quickly, but before she could blink, he was gone, a shadow on the steps.

Claire let out a shaky breath, got the dart gun from her backpack, and went to see Myrnin.

"Magnificent," Myrnin said, staring down at his hands. He flexed them into fists, turned them over, extended his fingers. "I haven't felt this good in—well, years. I had numbness in my hands—did you know?"

It was a symptom Myrnin had forgotten to mention, and Claire wrote it down in her notebook. She had the countdown clock—a new addition to the lab, one she'd ordered from the Internet—up on the wall, and the red flickering numbers reminded both of them that Myrnin had a maximum of five hours of sanity from the current formulation of the treatment.

Myrnin followed her glance at the clock, and the giddy excitement in his expression faded. He still looked like a young man, except for his eyes; it was creepy to think he'd looked exactly that way for generations before she was born, and would long after she was dead and gone. *He did so love the hunt,* Oliver had said. There was really only one kind of hunt for vampires. Hunting people.

He smiled at her, and it was the smile that had won her over in the first place—sweet, gentle, inviting her to share in some delightful secret. "Thank you for the clock, Claire. That's a great help. There's an alarm feature?"

"It starts sounding a tone fifteen minutes before the clock runs out," she said. "And it has tones striking every hour, too."

"Very helpful. Well, then. Now that I have use of my fingers—what shall we do?" Myrnin wiggled his thick black eyebrows suggestively, which was actually funny, coming from him. Not that he wasn't cute—he was—but Claire couldn't really imagine finding him sexy.

She wondered if that would hurt his feelings.

"How about if we start shelving some of these books?" she said. It really was getting to be a hazard; she'd tripped over stacks more than once even when it wasn't an emergency. Myrnin, however, made a face.

"I only have a few hours in my right mind, Claire. Housekeeping seems a poor way to spend them."

"All right, what do you want to do?"

"I think we made great progress in this last formulation," he said. "Why not see if we can distill the essence further? Strengthen the effects?"

"I think we'd better do some chemical analysis on what happens in your blood before we do that."

Before she could stop him, he strode over to a table, picked up a rusty knife, and slashed open his arm. She was just opening her mouth to scream when he grabbed a clean beaker from the rack on the table and caught the drizzling blood. The wound healed before he'd lost more than a few teaspoons.

"There are—easier ways to do that," she said weakly. Myrnin held the beaker out to her. The blood looked darker than regular human blood, and thicker, but then she supposed it would—he wasn't as warm. She tried not to think about all those people donating blood, but she couldn't help it. Was Shane's blood going to end up in Myrnin's veins? And how did that work, anyway? . . . Did vampires digest the blood, or just somehow pass it whole into their circulatory systems? Did blood types matter? Conflicting Rh factors? What about bloodborne diseases, like malaria and Ebola and AIDS?

There were a lot of questions to answer. She thought Dr. Mills would be in heaven over the prospect.

"Pain doesn't matter much," Myrnin said, and yanked his sleeve down over his pale, unmarked arm after wiping away the trickles of blood that were left. "One learns to ignore it, eventually."

Claire doubted that, but she didn't argue. "I'm going to take part of this back to the hospital," she said. "Dr. Mills wanted blood samples. They've got a lot of cool equipment there, he can give us detailed information we can't get here."

Myrnin shrugged, clearly uninterested in Dr. Mills or any human beyond Claire. "Do as you like," he said. "What kind of equipment?"

"Oh, all kinds. Mass spectrometers, blood-chemistry analyzers—you know."

"We should get those things."

"Why?"

"How can we possibly operate as we should if we don't have the most current equipment?"

Claire blinked at him. "Myrnin, you don't exactly have room down here. And I don't think your current dinky little power situation is going to let you plug in an electron microscope. That's not the way scientists work anymore, anyway. The equipment's too expensive, too delicate. The big hospitals and universities buy the equipment. We just rent time on it."

Myrnin looked surprised, then thoughtful. "Rent time? But how can you schedule such a thing when you don't know what you're looking for or how long it will take?"

"You have to learn to schedule your epiphanies. And be patient."

That got a laugh out of him. "Claire, I am a *vampire*. We aren't known for patience, you know. Your Dr. Mills—maybe we should pay him a visit. I'd like to meet him."

"He'd—probably like to meet you, too," she said slowly. She wasn't at all sure how Amelie was going to feel about that, but she could tell that Myrnin had it in his head to do it whether she went along or not. "Next time, okay?"

They both glanced at the countdown clock. "Yes," Myrnin said. "Next time. Ah! I meant to ask you. What did you hear about Bishop and the welcome feast?"

"Not much. I think Michael and Eve are going. Shane—Shane says he has to go."

"With Ysandre?"

Claire nodded. Myrnin turned away from her, shoved over a stack of books with restless enthusiasm, then another. He gave a raw cry of delight and scrambled over the piled volumes to retrieve one that, to Claire's eyes, looked just like any other.

He threw it to her. Claire managed to grab it before it smacked into her chest. "Ow!" she complained. "Not so hard, please."

"Sorry." He wasn't, really. There was a subversive, dark streak in him today.

"What is this, anyway?"

Myrnin came back to her side, took the book, opened it, and flipped pages. He paused around the middle and handed it back.

"Ysandre," he said.

The book was written in English, but it was from the eighteenth century, and not easy to make out, considering the stains on the pages.

She was of a beauty so unusual and so marvelous that her grandfather was fascinated by the dazzling sight, and mistook her for an angel that God had sent to console him on his deathbed. The pure lines of her fine profile, her great black liquid eyes, her noble brow uncovered, her hair shining like the raven's wing, her delicate mouth, the whole effect of this beautiful face on the mind of those who beheld her was that of a deep melancholy and sweetness, impressing itself once and for ever. Tall and slender, but without the excessive thinness of some young girls, her movements had that careless supple grace that recalls the waving of a flower stalk in the breeze.

"Oh," Claire said, surprised. That was Ysandre; he was right. "She was—"

"A very famous murderess. She helped her husband and cousins kill a king shortly after her grandfather's death. She was hanged, in the end, but that was after she'd been made a vampire. Lucky timing, for her."

The book contained a gruesome account of the king's murder, and a whole lot of others. Claire shivered and closed the book. "Why did you show me this?"

"I don't want you to do what her grandfather did—underestimate her because she has the look of an angel. Ysandre has destroyed more lives than you can begin to imagine, starting with her own." Myrnin's eyes were dark and very, very serious. "If she wants Shane, let her have him. She'll be done with him soon enough. Amelie won't allow her to kill him."

"I think she wants other things," Claire said.

"Ah. Sexual, then. Or some version of it. Ysandre has always been a bit—odd."

"How do I stop her?"

Myrnin slowly shook his head. "I'm sorry. I can't help you. My only suggestion—which I'm quite certain you won't like—is to let him deal with this in his own way. She'll leave him alive, and largely intact, unless he resists her."

"You're right. I don't like it."

"Complain to the management, my dear." His fit of seriousness passed off, like a cloud from the sun. "How about a game of chess, then?"

"How about we just analyze your blood, because you've only got a few more minutes before I have to put you back in your, ah, room?"

"Cell," he corrected. "Perfectly all right to say so. And you work too hard for someone so young."

She worked too hard, Claire thought in frustration, because somebody had to. Myrnin certainly didn't.

By Thursday, the upcoming masked ball was the buzz of Morganville. Claire couldn't avoid hearing about it. At the university coffee shop, that was inevitable; people said the weirdest, most private things right out in public, like there was some invisible privacy wall around them. She'd heard way too much about her fellow students' sexual adventures over the past few weeks; apparently, it was mating season, now that everybody was settling in for the semester. Girls rated guys. Guys rated girls. Both wanted what they couldn't have, or had what they didn't really want.

But as Claire sipped her coffee and wrote out her physics essay on mechanics, heat, and fields—which didn't have to do with auto shops, weather, or farming—she heard something that made her pen come to a stuttering stop on the page.

"—invitation," someone was saying. The someone was sitting behind her. "Can you believe it! My God, I actually got one! They say there are only three hundred invitations being sent out, you know. It's really going to be amazing. I was thinking of going as Marie Antoinette—what do you think?"

They had to be talking about the masked ball. Claire shifted in her chair. That didn't help—she still couldn't see who was speaking.

"Well, I think somebody might have actually known her, back in the day," the other girl said. "So you might want to go with something safe, like Catwoman. I'll bet none of them know Catwoman."

"Catwoman's good," the first girl agreed. "Tight black leather is never out of style. I would look totally hot as Catwoman."

Claire spilled her coffee, more or less deliberately, and jumped up to gather handfuls of napkins from the common dispenser at the creamer station. On the way back, she got a look at the two who were talking.

Gina and Jennifer, Monica's ever-present friends. Only, this time, no Monica to be seen. Interesting.

Jennifer glared at her. "What are you looking at, klutz?"

"Absolutely nothing," Claire said, deadpan. She wasn't afraid of them, not anymore. "I wouldn't go as Catwoman. Not with those thighs."

"Oh, mee-yow."

She gathered up books and coffee, and retreated to a table closer to the actual coffee bar. Eve was working. She looked perky today, bright-eyed and smiling; she had on red, and it totally worked for her. Goth, but somehow cheerful. She still grieved for her dad—Claire saw it in odd moments, when she thought nobody was watching—but Eve had pulled herself together, and was holding it together despite all the odds.

She had a break in the coffee line, so she flashed her coworker a hand signal of five—a five-minute break, Claire guessed as Eve stripped off the apron and ducked under the bar to slip into the chair opposite her.

"So," she said, "I heard from Billy Harrison that his dad got an invitation to this ball thing, from Tamara—the vamp who owns all those warehouses on the north side, and runs the paper? And he said that vamps all over town are going, and taking humans as their—I don't know, dates? That's weird, right? That they're all bringing humans?"

"It's never happened before?"

"Not that I know of," Eve said. "I asked around, but nobody's seen anything like it. It's become the hot-ticket event of the year." Her smile dimmed slightly. "I guess Michael forgot to send me mine. My invitation. I should remind him."

Claire felt a tight little knot tug inside. "He hasn't asked you?"

"He will."

"But . . . it's the day after tomorrow, isn't it?"

"He *will*. Besides, it's not like I have to come up with some elaborate costume or anything. Have you seen my closet? Half of what I wear qualifies as dress-up." Eve glanced at her, then down. "You?"

"Nobody's asking me to go." Yeah, the bitterness was there in her voice. Claire couldn't keep it out. "You know who Shane's going with."

"It's not his fault. It's hers. Ysandre." Eve made a face. "What kind of a name is that, anyway?"

"French. Myrnin gave me a book about her," Claire said. "I knew she was dangerous, but honestly, she's worse than I thought. She might have started out just trying to get by, but she was a real player, back when politics was war."

"What about the guy? François?" Eve rolled her eyes when she said his name, doing her best foo-foo French pronunciation. "He thinks he's hotter than the surface of the sun. Who's he taking?"

"No idea," Claire said. "But—it's not a date, you know. It's—" She had no real idea what it was. "It's something else."

"Looks like a date, dresses like a date, dates like a date," Eve said. "And I intend to be arm candy for Michael and protect him from all the big, bad social climbers out there looking to grab on to the newest vamp in town."

"He's not, though," Claire said. "The newest. Not anymore. Bishop and his crew are newer than he is, at least in terms of novelty factor."

Eve frowned. "Yeah," she said. "I guess that's true."

A shadow fell across their table, but before they could look up, something hit the surface between them, and both Claire and Eve involuntarily focused on it.

It was one of the cream-colored invitations.

They looked up. *Monica.* She swept her perfect blond hair back over her shoulders, raised her eyebrows, and gave Eve a slow, evil smile.

"Too bad," she said. "I guess your hottie boyfriend knows where his social bread is buttered, after all."

Eve's eyes widened. She turned the invitation around to read it, but even upside down, Claire saw the incriminating evidence.

You have been summoned to attend a masked ball
and feast to celebrate the arrival of Elder Bishop, on
Saturday the twentieth of October, at the Elders'
Council Hall at the hour of midnight.

You will attend at the invitation of Michael Glass,
and are required to accompany him at his pleasure.

The name jumped out at her like a fanged surprise attack. *Michael Glass. Michael was inviting Monica.*

Eve didn't say another word. She shoved the invitation back at Monica, got up, and ducked behind the coffee bar to don her apron again. Claire stared after her, stricken. She could see the jittery anguish in her friend's movements, but not her face. Eve was keeping carefully turned away, and even when she went to the espresso machine again to pull shots, she kept staring down, hiding her pain.

Claire's shock thawed into a nice warm glow of anger. "You're a total bitch—you know that?" she said. Monica raised a perfectly plucked eyebrow. "You didn't have to do that."

"Not my fault you freaks can't hang on to your men. I heard Shane was boy-toying around with Ysandre. Too bad. I'll bet you never even got him between the sheets, did you? Or wait. . . . Maybe you did. Because I'll bet that would drive him straight into somebody else's bed."

Claire fantasized for a few seconds about planting her physics textbook squarely in the middle of Monica's pouty, lip-glossed smile. She glared, instead, remembering how effective Oliver's periods of icy silence could be. Monica finally shrugged, picked up the invitation, and tucked it in the pocket of her leather jacket.

"I'd say 'See you,' but I probably won't," Monica said. "I guess you can hold your own Loser Party on Saturday, with special shots of cyanide or something. Enjoy."

She joined up with Gina and Jennifer, and the three girls walked away, turning heads. The golden, fortunate girls, tight and toned and perfect.

Laughing.

Claire realized she was clenching her fists, forced herself to relax and breathe, and picked up her pen again. The details of the essay kept slipping away, because all she could see was Monica preening at Michael's side, rubbing Eve's face in the humiliation. And even when she looked past that, there was Ysandre, and Shane, and that hurt even more.

"Why?" she whispered. "Michael, *why* would you do that to her?" Had they had a fight of some kind? Eve didn't seem to think so. She acted like it had come as a bolt from the blue sky.

With a feeling that she was making a terrible mistake, she dialed the first speed-dial number on her phone.

"Yes, Claire," Amelie said.

"I need to talk to you. About this masked-ball thing. What's going on?"

For a few seconds Claire was sure Amelie would hang up on her, but then the vampire said, "Yes, I suppose we must talk about it. I will meet you upstairs at your home. You know where."

She meant the hidden room. "When?"

"I am, of course, at your convenience," Amelie said, which was winter cold and utterly untrue. "Would an hour suffice?"

"I'll be there," Claire said. Her hands were shaking, fine little trembles that were a sign of the inner earthquake. "Thank you."

"Oh, don't thank me, child," Amelie said. "I shouldn't imagine you'll find anything I have to say will be of the least comfort to you."

The house was empty when Claire got there. She checked every room, including the laundry room in the basement, to be absolutely sure. Eve was still at work; Michael was at the music store. Shane—she had no idea where Shane was, except that the house was Shane free.

Claire pressed the hidden button in the hallway on the second floor, and the paneling opened on the dusty steps leading up to the hidden room. She shut the opening behind her and trudged up, feeling sicker and more isolated with every single stair.

At the top, color spilled across the walls: Victorian lamps, all jeweled hues and pale, watery light. There were no windows, no exits here. Only a few nice pieces of dusty furniture, and Amelie.

And the bodyguards, of course. Amelie hardly ever went anywhere without at least one. There were two this time, lurking in the corners. One of them nodded to Claire. She was on nodding terms with scary bodyguard dudes. Great. She really was moving up in the social ladder of Morganville.

"Ma'am," Claire said, and stayed standing. Amelie was seated, but she didn't look as though she was in any mood to indulge the fantasy that Claire was her equal. It was hard to determine Amelie's feelings, but Claire was pretty sure that this one qualified as impatient, with a possible upgrade to annoyed.

"I have very little time for soothing your ruffled feathers," Amelie said. She shifted a little, which was surprising; Amelie was usually very still, very composed. That was almost fidgeting. There was something else unusual about her today—the color of her suit. It was still classic and beautifully tailored, but it was in a dark gray, much darker than Amelie usually preferred. It turned her eyes the color of storm clouds. "Yet you've done more than I asked with Myrnin. I am inclined to forgive your impertinence, if you understand that it's an indulgence on my part. Not a right on yours."

"I understand," Claire said. "I just—this masked ball. Myrnin called it a welcome feast. He acted like it had something important to do with Mr. Bishop."

Amelie's eyes, which had been regarding her with impersonal focus, suddenly sharpened. "You've spoken with Myrnin regarding Bishop's arrival?"

"Well—he asked me what was happening in town, and—" Claire broke off, because Amelie was suddenly standing. And her bodyguards had moved out of the corners of the room and were very close, close enough to hurt. "You didn't tell me not to!"

"I told you to stay out of my affairs!" Something pale and hungry flickered in those eyes, as scary in its own way as Mr. Bishop. Amelie deliberately relaxed. "Very well. The damage is done. What did Myrnin tell you?"

"He said—" Claire wet her lips and glanced at the bodyguards hovering terrifyingly close. Amelie raised an eyebrow and nodded, and Claire felt rather than saw them move away. "He said you both thought Bishop was dead, so he was surprised to find out that he'd come to town. He said that Bishop wanted revenge. Against you."

"What did he tell you about the feast?"

"Only that it was part of some kind of ceremony to welcome Bishop to town," Claire said. "And that you weren't going to fight him if you were putting on the feast."

Amelie's smile was quick and cold. "Myrnin knows something about the world and its politics. No, I'm not going to fight him. Not unless I must. Did he tell you anything else?"

"No." Claire sucked up her courage. "Ysandre's taking Shane. And Michael—I just found out he's going, and he's taking Monica. Not Eve."

"Do you imagine I have the slightest concern for how your friends arrange their romantic affairs?"

"No, it's just—I want you to invite me. Please. All the vampires are taking humans. Why don't you take me?"

Amelie's eyes widened. Not much, but it was enough to make Claire think she'd scored a big-time surprise. "Why would you possibly wish to attend?"

"Monica says it's the social event of the season," Claire said. She wasn't sure a joke was the way to go; she knew Amelie had a sense of humor, but it was obscure.

Today, it was apparently nonexistent.

"All right, the truth is, I'm worried about Michael and Shane. I just want to be sure—sure they're okay."

"And how would you go about ensuring that, if I cannot?" Amelie didn't wait for an answer, because there obviously wasn't one. "You want to watch the boy, to be sure he doesn't fall prey to Ysandre. Is that it?"

Claire swallowed and nodded. That wasn't all, but that was a lot of it.

"It's a waste of time. No," Amelie said. "You will not attend, Claire. I tell you this, explicitly, so that we are understood: I cannot risk you in this. You will not be at this event. Neither you nor Myrnin. Is that clear?"

"But—"

Amelie's voice rose to a shout. "Is that clear?" The fury cut like knives, and Claire gasped and nodded. She wanted to take a step back from the horrible glow in Amelie's eyes, but she knew that would be a very bad idea. She'd been around Myrnin enough to understand that retreat was a sign of weakness, and weakness triggered attack.

Amelie continued to stare at her, fixed and silent, and there was a wildness to her that Claire couldn't understand.

"Mistress," said one of the bodyguards. "We should go." He made it sound as if they had someplace to be, but Claire had the eerie feeling that he was intervening deliberately. Providing Amelie an excuse to back off.

"Yes," Amelie said. There was a husky tone to her voice Claire had never heard before. "By all means, let us be done with this. You have heard my words, Claire. I warn you, don't test me on this. You're valuable to me, but you are not irreplaceable, and you have friends and family in this town who are far less useful."

There was no mistaking that for anything but an outright threat. Claire nodded slowly.

"Say the words," Amelie said.

"Yes. I understand."

"Good. Now don't bother me again. You may go."

Claire backed away toward the stairs. She even backed down two steps before turning and hurrying down the rest, and when she was halfway there, she realized that the control to open the door from inside lay at the top, in the couch where Amelie sat.

If Amelie didn't want to let her out, she wasn't going anywhere.

Claire reached the landing at the bottom. The door was still closed. She looked back up the stairs and saw shadows moving, but heard nothing.

The lights went out.

"No," she whispered, and fear came down like a bucket of freezing water, from head to toe. Her hand reached out blindly to stroke the closed door. "No, don't do this—"

Something had changed in Amelie. She wasn't the cool, remote queen she'd been before. She was more—animal. More angry.

And Claire finally admitted it to herself: Amelie was more hungry.

"Please," she said to the dark. She knew there were ears listening. "Please let me go now."

She heard a sharp click, and the door moved under her fingertips, swinging inward. Claire grabbed the edge with both hands and pulled it open. She was suddenly in the hall, and when she looked back, the door was closing.

She collapsed against the wall, trembling.

That went well, she thought sarcastically. She wanted to scream, but she was almost sure that would be a very, very bad idea.

Downstairs, the front door opened and closed, and Claire heard the clump of heavy shoes on the wood floor.

"Eve?" she called.

"Yeah." Eve sounded exhausted. "Coming."

She looked even worse than she sounded. The red outfit that had flattered her so much before seemed to scream now, overpowering her; she seemed ready to drop, and from the state of her makeup, she'd already shed a lot of tears.

"Oh," Claire said. "Eve . . ."

Eve tried for a smile, but there wasn't much left. "Pretty stupid to be upset about Monica, right? But I think that's why it hurts so bad. It's not like he's taking somebody halfway nice or anything. He has to pick the walking social disease." Eve wiped her eyes with the heel of her hand. Her eyeliner and mascara had made a true Gothic mess, trickling in dirty streaks down her pale cheeks. "Don't try to tell me he was ordered to do it. I don't care if he was—he could have told me first. And why aren't you arguing with me?"

"Because you're right."

"Damn right I'm right." Eve kicked open the door to her room, walked in, and threw herself facedown on the black bed. Claire clicked on the lights, which mostly consisted of strings of dim white Christmas lights and one lamp with a bloodred scarf draped over the shade. Eve screamed into her pillow and punched it. Claire perched on the corner of the bed.

"I'm going to kill him," Eve said, or at least that was what it sounded like filtered through the pillow. "Stake him right in the heart, shove garlic up his ass, and—and—"

"And what?"

Michael was standing in the doorway. Claire jumped off the bed in alarm, and Eve sat up with her pillow clutched in both hands. "When did you get home?" Claire demanded.

"Apparently just in time to hear my funeral plans. I especially like the garlic up the ass. It's . . . different."

"Yeah, well, I'm not finished," Eve said. She slithered off the bed-spread, dropped the pillow, and faced Michael with her arms crossed. "I'm also going to stake you outside in the sun, on top of a fire ant mound. And laugh."

"What did I do?"

"What did you *do?*" Eve's glare was fierce enough to rip even a vam-pire's heart right out of his chest. "You can't be serious."

Michael went very still, and Claire thought the expression in his eyes was the definition of *busted.* "Monica. She told you."

"Duh. Why wouldn't she take the chance to rub my face in it, you loser? And speaking of that, *Monica?* Did you lose a bet or something? Because that's really the only reason I can think of for you to humiliate me like this."

"No," Michael said. His gaze flickered to Claire in an unmistakable plea for her to leave. She didn't. "I can't explain, Eve. I'm sorry. I just can't. But it's not what it—"

"Don't you even say it's not what it looks like, because it's *always* what it looks like!" Eve lunged forward, shoved Michael square in the chest, and drove him a foot backward, out of her room. "I can't talk to you right now. Get out! And stay out!"

She slammed the door and locked it. Not, Claire reflected, that a lock would do any good, considering how strong Michael was. But he probably wouldn't go around battering down doors in his own house, at least.

"Eve, you have to listen to me. Please."

Eve threw herself back on the bed, grabbed her iPod from the drawer, and shoved headphones over her ears as she hit the play button. Claire could hear the thundering metal all the way across the room.

"Eve?"

Claire opened the door and looked at Michael. "I don't think she's listening," she said. "You really screwed this up—you know that, right? At least Shane got ordered to do what he did. You chose, didn't you?"

"Yeah," Michael agreed softly. "I chose. But you really don't have any idea of what my choices were, do you?"

She watched him walk away, enter his room at the end of the hall, and shut the door.

Maybe he was right. Maybe it really wasn't what it looked like. Not that Eve was going to listen. Claire stood there for a while, listening to the cold and stony silence, and then shook her head and went downstairs.

Chili dogs weren't the same eaten alone.

Shane got home after dark, and the second Claire saw him, she knew something was wrong. He looked—distracted. Different.

And he barely nodded to her on his way through the living room to the kitchen. She was curled up on the sofa highlighting text in her English book, wondering for the thousandth time why anybody thought knowing about the Brontë sisters was important and multitasking by not really watching a cooking show on cable TV.

"Hey," she called after him. "I left the chili on for you!"

He didn't answer. Claire capped her marker pen and went to the kitchen door. She didn't open it, but she stood and listened. Shane wasn't making the normal dish noises of a guy desperate for dinner; in fact, he wasn't making any noise at all.

Claire was debating whether to return to studying when she heard him open the back door of the house. Voices, hushed and muffled. She eased the door open just a little, and listened harder.

"You're lucky I don't call the cops," Shane was saying. "Walk away, man."

"I can't. I need to talk to her."

"You're not coming near either one of the girls, got me?"

"I'm not going to hurt anyone!"

She knew that voice, or thought she did. But that couldn't be right, it just couldn't be.

Shane could *not* be talking to Eve's brother, Jason, especially not at the back door. She had to be imagining things. Maybe it was someone else, someone who just sounded like Jason Rosser. . . .

Claire eased the door open enough to get a tiny slice of a view.

No, that was Jason. There was absolutely no doubt about it. He was even wearing the same skanky, stained jeans and leather jacket. His hair was lank and even greasier than the last time she'd seen him, and he looked sallow and sick.

"Come on, man," he said. "Just let me talk to Claire. You keep me waiting out here in the dark, I'm lunch meat."

"Good to know."

Jason put out a hand to stop Shane from closing the door on him. "Please, man. I'm asking."

Shane hesitated. Claire couldn't really imagine why. Jason had stalked Eve; he'd killed—or at least he *said* he'd killed—innocent girls out of some misguided attempt to get the vampires to sign him up for service. He'd stabbed Shane in the guts.

Shane did swing the bat at him first, Claire's prim little voice of conscience said. She told it to shut up. Jason had engineered that fight, he'd provoked Shane into it, and it was only the fact that they'd gotten an ambulance there so fast that had saved Shane's life.

Jason didn't look like a crazy killer just now. He looked like a half-starved scared junkie kid who was terrified out of his mind. And desperate.

Claire came into the kitchen. Jason's face lit up. "Claire! Claire, tell him—tell him it's okay. I promise, I'm not going to hurt anybody. Tell him it's okay to let me in so I can talk to you."

"It's not okay," Claire said. "But he already knows that."

Shane nodded. He shoved Jason backward, off-balance, off the porch. Jason tripped over a brick and fell flat on his ass. He glared up at Shane and rolled slowly to his feet. "Claire, I'm supposed to tell you something. From Oliver."

"Oliver's got nothing to tell us that we want to hear, man. Especially from you."

"You sure about that?"

Shane grinned. "Pretty sure. Good luck with that survival thing out there in the dark."

Shane started to shut the door. He almost made it before Jason blurted out, "Bishop's setting a trap. We can tell you where and when."

Claire put a hand on Shane's shoulder, and he kept the door open, just a crack. "What are you talking about?"

"Let me in and I'll tell you." Jason looked desperate enough to claw paint off the door. "Please, Claire. I swear, I'm on the level here."

"No," she said. "If Oliver's got something to say, I'll talk to him, not to you."

Resentment flickered in Jason's dark eyes like oil on fire, and he got up and shoved his hands in his pockets. "Yeah? You gonna play it like that?"

"I'm not playing at all," Claire said.

"I think you are. So maybe we do it the hard way after all." Jason threw himself against the door with such force that Shane was knocked backward, and Claire lost her footing and ended up flat on her back on the kitchen floor. As she twisted around to try to get up, she felt Jason's hand close on her hair, painfully tight. He yanked her up to her knees and dragged her out into the night. She yelled and fought, but he had a lot of experience with making girls do what he wanted.

And she stopped fighting when he put a gun to her head.

"Good," he said in her ear, and even in a blind, black rage she thought his breath was disgusting enough to peel paint. "Calm down, I'm not going to hurt you. I was serious. You need to listen to me."

Shane followed them outside, moving slowly but never taking his eyes off Jason. Off the gun. "Let her go."

Jason laughed, and dragged her backward to the driveway, where a big black car was waiting. Shane followed at a safe distance. *Don't,* Claire mouthed. She'd seen Jason nearly kill Shane before. She couldn't stand to see it happen again. *I'll be okay.*

Jason opened the driver's-side door of the car, shoved her inside, and pushed in after. She immediately lunged for the other door.

Locked.

Jason slammed the car door and turned the key to start the engine. He took a firmer grip on Claire's hair. "Stay still!"

Something heavy fell on the roof of the car, denting it down almost to the level of their heads; Claire and Jason both ducked, and Claire yelped at the thought that panic might make him squeeze the trigger.

It didn't.

A fist punched through the metal roof of the car, grabbed the ragged edge, and peeled it back like a tin can lid. And the face that looked down was Michael's.

No—not Michael; it was *Vampire* Michael. Fangs completely down, eyes completely crimson.

Michael was *angry.* Also, *terrifying.*

He dropped through the hole in a fall of moonlight, took hold of Jason's gun hand, and yanked him away from Claire like a toy. A breakable one. Jason screamed. The gun went off, and Claire flinched and covered her head, trying to pull into a ball in the corner. The car shook as Michael *threw* Jason out, straight up through the opening in the roof. Jason screamed the whole way up, and the whole way down. He hit the ground with a sickening thud and rolled.

Michael launched himself up out of the car, landed lightly on his feet in the wash of headlights, and walked to where Jason was crawling to get away. Jason rolled over. He still had the gun.

He shot Michael six times, point-blank. Claire flinched with every loud crack.

Michael didn't.

He reached Jason, took the gun, ripped it in half, and threw the two pieces into the trash can leaning at the side of the house. Jason looked shocked, then resigned, as Michael reached down and grabbed him by the collar of his leather jacket.

Shane reached through the ragged sunroof, opened the car door, and grabbed Claire. He pulled her out and to her feet. "You okay?" He sounded deeply shaken, and he kept running his hands over her, looking for bullet holes, she guessed. "Claire, say something!"

"Stop him," she whispered, looking past him at Michael. "Don't let him do that."

Because Michael was going to bite Jason, and once he did, there'd be no going back. Shane sent her a look, one that probably meant he thought she was crazy, but she forced herself to stay still and calm, even if her insides were quivering in terror.

"Shane," she said, and tried her best to channel Amelie's cool authority. "Stop him."

She saw the reality of what was happening dawn on Shane, and he nodded and turned toward Michael, who didn't look as if he was in any mood to be talked off the murder ledge.

But Shane didn't have to try, because Michael looked up and saw Eve standing in the doorway, hands pressed to her mouth, dark eyes wide in horror, staring at her boyfriend threatening to suck blood out of her little brother.

Michael let go. Jason collapsed back to the ground, whimpering, and tried to crawl away.

Michael put his foot on Jason's back, holding him in place. "No," he said. His voice sounded low and very, very dangerous. "I don't think so. Attempted kidnapping, assault with a deadly weapon, and attempted murder of a vampire? You're done, man. It's all over but the screaming."

"You asshole!" Jason yelled. "I'm working for Oliver! You can't touch me!"

He skinned back the sleeve on his jacket, and there, on his wrist, was a silver bracelet.

Michael responded by pressing his foot harder into Jason's back. "Then you and I are going to have a talk with Oliver about how he sends his little worm to my house to shoot me," he said. "I think you're not going to like that very much. Because I'm pretty sure that Oliver didn't ask you to do that kind of thing."

"Michael," Shane said. It was a warning, and as Claire turned, she saw why—another car was arriving, a police car with lights flashing. It pulled to a stop in the driveway, blocking in Jason's half-peeled car, and Richard Morrell got out of the driver's side carrying a shotgun. Detectives Joe Hess and Travis Lowe were with him, and each of them held a drawn gun.

She'd never seen the three of them looking so grim, but she was glad to see them. At least this meant somebody would be putting a stop to Jason and his craziness at last. Michael was right: it wasn't going to be a good ending for him, but—

Richard Morrell put the shotgun to his shoulder. He was aiming at Michael. The other two men took up shooting stances.

Claire gasped.

"Out of the way," Detective Hess ordered Shane, with a jerk of his head. Shane didn't argue. He held up his hands and backed away. Michael turned and saw the cops aiming at him, and frowned.

"Let him go, Michael," Travis Lowe said. "Let's do this easy."

"What's going on?"

"One thing at a time. Let the kid up."

Michael removed his foot. Jason scrambled to a standing position and tried to run; Richard Morrell sighed, handed his shotgun to Joe Hess, and took off after him. As fast as Jason was, Richard was faster. He took him down in a flying tackle before he was halfway to the fence. He rolled Jason onto his back and handcuffed him with brutal efficiency, yanked him upright, and marched him back to where the other two policemen held Michael at gunpoint.

"What's going on?" Michael repeated. "He tries to kidnap Claire, and you come after *me*? Why?"

"Let's just say we're saving you from yourself," Detective Hess said. "You okay? You calm?"

Michael nodded. Hess lowered his gun, and so did Travis Lowe. Richard Morrell put Jason in the backseat of the police car.

"We got a tip," Hess continued, "that you'd gone berserk and were trying to kill your friends. But since I see they're all standing here alive, and well, I'm guessing little Jason is the real problem."

Richard came back, wiping his hands on a handkerchief. Clearly, he didn't like touching Jason, either. "Did he break in?"

"No," Shane said. "He pulled a gun on us and grabbed Claire at the back door. He was trying to drive away with her. Michael stopped him."

Michael, Claire realized as her heartbeat started to slow, had also been shot six times in the chest at point-blank range. His loose white shirt had the blackened ragged holes to prove it, each one rimmed with a thin outline of red. She remembered Myrnin swiping the knife carelessly down his arm, laying open veins and arteries and muscles just to get a blood sample.

She couldn't be sure, but it didn't look like there was a mark on Michael's chest under the shirt, and he wasn't moving like a man with bullets buried inside. Not even one in shock.

Wow.

"What did he want?" Detective Hess asked. "Did he say?"

"He said he wanted to talk to me," Claire said. That much was true, but she didn't want to drag Oliver into this. It was enough of a mess already. "I think he really did want to. He just knew he wouldn't be able to do it here. I don't—I don't think he really meant to hurt me." *This time.*

Shane was looking at her like she'd grown a second head, one with serious brain damage. "It's *Jason.* Of course he meant to hurt you! Wasn't the gun pointed at your head a clue?"

He was right, of course, but—she'd seen the look in Jason's eyes, and it hadn't been the predatory glee she'd seen before when he was playing his little sadistic games. This had been flat-out desperation. She couldn't explain it, but she believed Jason.

This time.

Shane was still watching her with a frown. So was Michael. "Are you all right?" Shane asked, and folded his arms around her. The warm weight of his body pressed against hers, and she realized just how cold she felt. She was shivering, and her knees felt weak underneath her. *I could collapse,* she realized. *And he'd catch me.*

But she stayed on her own two feet, pulled back, and looked him in the eyes.

"I'm fine," she said. She kissed him. "Everything's fine."

NINE

Eve hadn't said a word, but she'd allowed Michael to take her back inside once the cops had pulled away; she'd taken only one look at her brother as he'd been hauled off in handcuffs, but that had been enough. On top of the shock of her father's death, and the trouble with Michael, Eve didn't seem to have any emotion left to spare.

Through common consent, none of them went to bed. They didn't eat. The four of them crammed onto the couch, grateful for the warmth and the company, and put on a movie. A scary one, as it turned out, but Claire was glad to focus on someone else's problems for a change. Being hunted by a city full of zombies might have seemed like a relief in some ways—at least you knew whom to run from, and whom to run *toward*. She lay with her head on Shane's chest, listening more to him breathe than to the characters babbling at one another. His hand kept a slow, steady rhythm on her hair, stroking all her tension and fear away.

Eve and Michael didn't cuddle, but after a while, he put his arm around her and pulled her closer, and she didn't resist.

By the time the DVD menu came on after the credits, they were all sound asleep, and trouble was far, far away.

. . .

Fridays were usually good days, classwise; even most of the professors were in better moods.

Not *this* Friday, though. There was a weird tension in the air, along with the increasingly chilly bite to the wind. Her first professor of the day had lost his temper over a cell phone going off, and reduced some sophomore sorority girl to tears before exiling her from the class with a flat-out failing grade. Her second class didn't go much better; the TA had a headache, maybe a hangover, and was grumpy as hell—too much to bother slowing down as he sped through the lecture, or to answer any questions.

The only good thing about her third hour was that she was confident it would be over in *under* an hour. Professor Anderson had widely advertised today's supposedly pop quiz; only a complete coma patient wouldn't know to come prepared. Anderson was one of *those* professors—the ones who gave you plenty of chances, but the test was The Test, full stop. He gave only two a year, and if you didn't do well on both of them, you were screwed. He had a reputation for being a nice guy who smiled a lot, but he'd never yet allowed anybody extra-credit work, or so Claire had heard.

The history majors liked to call his class Andersonville, which was a not very funny reference to the Civil War prison camp. Claire had studied her brains out, and she was absolutely sure that she would ace the test, and have extra time left over.

She stopped off in the restroom, since she was a little early, and carefully balanced her backpack against the wall of the bathroom stall as she did her business. She was going over dates and events in her head when she heard a soft, muffled laugh from near the sinks. Something about it made her freeze—it wasn't innocent, that laugh. There was something weird about it.

"I hear there's a test in Andersonville today," a voice said. A familiar one. It was Monica Morrell. "Hey, does this color look okay?"

"Nice," Gina said, fulfilling her job as Affirmation Friend #1. "Is that the new winter red?"

"Yeah, it's supposed to shimmer. Is it shimmering?"

"Oh yeah."

Claire flushed the toilet, grabbed her backpack, and braced herself for impact. She tried to look as if she didn't care a bit that Monica, Gina, and Jennifer were occupying three out of the four sinks in the bathroom. Or that the rest of the place was deserted.

Monica was touching up her hooker-red lipstick, blowing kisses at her reflection. Claire kept her eyes straight ahead. *Get the soap. Turn on the water. Wash—*

"Hey, freak, you're in Andersonville, right?"

Claire nodded. She scrubbed, rinsed, and reached for the paper towels.

Jennifer snagged her backpack and pulled it out of her reach.

"Hey!" Claire grabbed for her stuff, but Jennifer dodged out of her way, and then Monica took hold of her wrist and snapped something cold and metallic around it. For a crazy second Claire thought, *She's switched bracelets with me. Now I'm Oliver's property. . . .*

But it was the cold metal of a handcuff, and Monica bent down and fastened the other end to the metal post on the bottom of the nearest bathroom stall.

"Well," she said as she stepped back and put her hands on her hips, "I guess you'll be finding out just how tough the little general can be, Claire. But don't worry. I'm sure you're so smart. You'll just fill in those test answers by the power of your mind or something."

Claire yanked uselessly at the handcuffs, even though she knew that was stupid; she wasn't going anywhere. She kicked the bathroom stall. It was tough enough to stand up to generations of college students; her frustration wasn't going to make a dent.

"Give me the key!" she yelled. Monica dangled it in front of her— small, silver, and unreachable.

"This key?" Monica tossed it into the toilet in the first stall and flushed. "Oops. Wow, that's a shame. You wait here. I'll get help!"

They all laughed. Jennifer contemptuously shoved her backpack across the floor to her. "Here," Jennifer said. "You might want to cram for the test or something."

Claire grimly opened her backpack and began looking for something, anything she could use as a lockpick. Not that she knew the first thing about picking locks, exactly, but she could learn. She *had* to learn. She barely looked up as the three girls exited the restroom, still laughing.

Her choices were a couple of paper clips, a bobby pin, and the power of her fury, which unfortunately couldn't melt metal. Only her brain.

Claire took the cell phone out of her pocket and considered her choices. She wouldn't have been surprised to find out that Eve or Shane had experience with handcuffs—and getting out of them—but she wasn't sure she wanted to endure the questions, either.

She called the Morganville Police Department, and asked for Richard Morrell. After a short delay, she was put through to his patrol car.

"It's Claire Danvers," she said. "I—need some help."

"What kind of help?"

"Your sister kind of—handcuffed me in a bathroom. And I have a test. I don't have a key. I was hoping you—"

"Look, I'm sorry, but I'm heading to a domestic-disturbance call. It's going to take me about an hour to get over there. I don't know what you said to Monica, but if you just—"

"What, apologize?" Claire snapped. "I didn't say *anything*. She ambushed me, and she flushed the key, and I have to get to class!"

Richard's sigh rattled the phone. "I'll get there as fast as I can."

He hung up. Claire set to work with the bobby pin, and watched the minutes crawl by. Tick, tock, there went her grade in Andersonville.

By the time Richard Morrell showed up with a handcuff key to let her loose, the classroom was dark. Claire ran the whole way to Professor Anderson's office, and felt a burst of relief when she saw that his door was open. He *had* to give her a break.

He was talking to another student whose back was to Claire; she paused in the doorway, trembling and gasping for breath, and got a frown from Professor Anderson. "Yes?" He was young, but his blond hair was already thinning on top. He had a habit of wearing sport jackets that a man twice his age would have liked; maybe he thought the tweed and leather patches made people take him seriously.

Claire didn't care what he looked like. She cared that he had the authority to assign grades.

"Sir, hi, Claire Danvers. I'm in—"

"I know who you are, Claire. You missed the test."

"Yes, I—"

"I don't accept excuses except in the case of death or serious illness." He looked her over. "I don't see any signs of either of those."

"But—"

The other student was watching her now, with a malicious light in her eyes. Claire didn't know her, but she had on a silver bracelet, and Claire was willing to bet that she was one of Monica's near and dear sorority girls. Glossy dark hair cut in a bleeding-edge style, perfect makeup. Clothes that reeked of credit card abuse.

"Professor," the girl said, and whispered something to him. His eyes widened. The girl gathered up her books and left, giving Claire a wide berth.

"Sir, I really didn't—it wasn't my fault—"

"From what I just heard, it was very much your fault," Anderson said. "She said you were asleep out in the common room. She said she passed you on the way to class."

"I wasn't! I was—"

"I don't care where you were, Claire. I care where you weren't, namely, at your desk at the appointed time, taking my test. Now please go."

"I was *handcuffed!*"

He looked briefly thrown by that, but shook his head. "I'm not interested in sorority pranks. If you work hard the rest of the semester, you might still be able to pull out a passing grade. Unless you'd like to drop the class. I think you still have a day or two to make that decision."

He just wasn't *listening.* And, Claire realized, he wasn't going to listen. He didn't really care about her problems. He didn't really care about *her.*

She stared at him for a few seconds in silence, trying to find some empathy in him, but all she saw was self-absorbed annoyance.

"Good day, Miss Danvers," he said, and sat down at his desk. Pointedly ignoring her.

Claire bit back words that probably would have gotten her expelled, and skipped the rest of her classes to go home.

Somewhere in the back of her mind, a clock was ticking. Counting down to Bishop's masked ball.

There was one comforting thing about the theory of complete apocalypse: at least it meant she wouldn't have to fail any classes.

Just when she thought her Friday couldn't get any worse, visitors dropped by the house at dinnertime.

Claire peered out the peephole, and saw dark, curling hair. A wicked smile.

"Better invite me in," Ysandre said. "Because you know I'll just go hurt your neighbors until you do."

"Michael!" Claire yelled. He was in the living room, working out some new songs, but she heard the music stop. He was at her side before the echoes died. "It's her. Ysandre. What should I do?"

Michael opened the door and faced her. She smiled at him. François was with her, both of them sleek and smug and so arrogant it made Claire's teeth itch.

"I want to talk to Shane," Ysandre said.

"Then you're going to be disappointed."

François raised his eyebrows, reached down, and pulled a bound human form from the bushes on the side of the steps. Claire gasped.

It was Miranda, looking completely terrified. Tied hand and foot, and gagged.

"Let's put it another way," Ysandre said. "You can let us in to talk, or we have our dinner alfresco, right here on your veranda."

There was absolutely no right answer to that, Claire thought, and saw Michael struggle with it, too. He let the silence stretch for so long that Claire was really afraid Miranda would be killed—François seemed glad to have the chance—but then Michael nodded. "All right," he said. "Come in."

"Why, thank you, honey," Ysandre said, and strolled in. François dropped Miranda on the wooden hallway floor and followed her. Claire knelt next to the girl and untied her hands.

"Are you okay?" she whispered. Miranda nodded, eyes as big as saucers. "Get out of here. Run home. *Go.*"

Miranda stripped off the ropes around her ankles, scrambled up, and escaped.

Claire shut the door and hurried to the living room.

François had shoved Michael's guitar out of the way and taken the chair. Ysandre sat on the couch, as comfortable as if she owned the world and everything in it. "How kind of you to ask us in, Michael. I didn't think we got off to a very good beginning. I want to start over."

François laughed. "Yes," he said. "We should be friends, Michael. And you shouldn't be living with cattle."

"Is this all you have? Because if it is, I think we're all done."

"Oh, not quite," Ysandre said.

"They're making dinner," François said. "That's ironic, don't you think? When they let ours go."

"These humans, all they do is eat," Ysandre said. "No wonder they're all fat and lazy."

Shane came out of the kitchen. He wasn't surprised, Claire saw; he must have heard them. "You're not invited," Shane said. Ysandre kissed her lips toward him.

"Oh, Shane, I really don't care whether I am or not, and you aren't anywhere near powerful enough to make me leave," she said. "It's Friday, my love. You received the costume I want you to wear for tomorrow?"

Shane nodded unwillingly, like his neck had frozen stiff. His eyes were more than a little crazy.

"You need to go," Claire said to Ysandre, with a bravado she really didn't feel.

"What do you think, Michael? Do I?" Ysandre locked gazes with him, and there was something awful in her eyes. "Do I have to go?"

"No," he said. "Stay."

Claire gaped.

They make you feel things. Do things, whether you want to do them or not. Shane had said it, but Claire hadn't imagined that they could do it to other vampires. Even one as young and inexperienced as Michael.

"Michael!"

He didn't look at her. He seemed completely caught in the web of Ysandre's attraction.

Claire dug her cell phone out of her pocket. She hesitated over the address book.

"Deciding who to call for help?" François yanked the cell phone out of her hands and threw it across the room. "Amelie won't thank you for distracting her from all her preparations. She's busy, busy, busy, making sure everything goes just right to welcome our beloved father properly."

"Maybe you ought to ask Michael what to do," Ysandre said, and laughed, showing fang. She pronounced it like *Michelle*. "I'm sure he'll help dispatch us. So *fierce*, isn't he?"

Michael's eyes were slowly turning crimson.

They can make you feel things. Do things.

"Shane," Claire said. "We need to get out of here. Now."

"I'm not leaving Michael."

"Michael's the problem."

Ysandre laughed. "You really *are* clever, *ma chérie*."

François snapped his fingers in front of Michael's face. "Dinner's ready."

Michael opened his mouth and snarled. Full fangs.

And he turned and fixed his gaze on Claire.

"Oh, crap," Shane breathed. He grabbed Claire's arm. "Kitchen!"

They retreated. Shane shoved the table against the swinging door, for all the good it would do, and they backed up toward the rear door.

Claire opened the refrigerator and took Michael's last two sealed bottles out of the back of the refrigerator. *Have to tell Michael to pick up more*, she thought, and how weird was that? Running short of blood was getting as normal as needing Coke or butter.

She was gibbering in her head, that was it. And yet, oddly calm.

Michael burst into the room and headed straight for them.

Claire stepped into his path, held out a bottle, and said, "You're not one of them. You're one of us. One of us, and we love you."

"Claire—" Shane sounded agonized, but he didn't move. Maybe he knew it would have blown everything.

Michael stopped. His eyes were still blazing red, but he seemed to *see* her.

And the red flickered a little.

She held out the bottle.

"Drink it," she said. "You'll feel better. Trust me, Michael. Please."

He was staring into her eyes.

And this time, she was the one who challenged him. *See me. Know what you're doing.*

Push her out.

His eyes flared white. He grabbed the bottle out of her hand, popped the cap, and tipped the bottle, guzzling the contents as fast as he could swallow.

He didn't look away.

Neither did she.

His eyes faded back to blue, and he lowered the bottle with a gasp. A thin line of blood dripped off his lip, and he wiped it with a trembling hand.

"It's okay," Claire said. "She got in your head. She can do that. She—"

Shane was gone. While she'd been so focused on Michael, he'd just . . . disappeared.

The kitchen door was still swinging.

It'll be easier for her the next time, Shane had told her.

Claire headed for the living room. Michael tried to stop her, but he seemed weak. Sick. She remembered how shaken Shane had been.

Why not me? Why doesn't she control me?

Maybe she couldn't.

Shane was sitting on the couch beside Ysandre, and his shirt was unbuttoned. Ysandre was running her hands up and down Shane's chest, tracing invisible lines, and as Claire watched, the vampire began to nibble on Shane's neck. Not seriously, as in not drawing blood, but little teasing nips. Licks.

Shane's face was still and blank, but his eyes were pools of panic. *He doesn't want this,* Claire realized. *She's making him.*

Claire threw the second bottle of blood at Ysandre. The vampire's hand came up unbelievably fast to snatch it out of the air before it made contact with the side of her head.

"If you're hungry, eat," she said. "And get your claws out of my boyfriend."

Ysandre's eyes narrowed. Claire felt something brush at her mind, but it was like walking through a spiderweb, easily broken.

Ysandre flipped the cap from the bottle, sniffed it, and made a disgusted face. "Don't be so possessive. Shane is at my command. The invitation said so."

"He's at your command *tomorrow.* Not *today.*"

"How charming. So young for a lawyer." Ysandre sipped from the bottle, gagged, and shook her head. "Why your vampires subject themselves to this indignity is beyond my understanding. This is rancid. Undrinkable filth." She threw the bottle back at Claire, who had no choice but to try to catch it; she did, but the contents splattered cold over her face and neck. "Remove it from our presence." Her eyes took on a horrible dull shine, angry and cruel. "And clean yourself up. You're as useless as the hospitality you offer."

"Get out," Claire said. She felt the power of the house now, gathering like a storm around her. Rushing into the cool silence, crackling with energy. "Get out of our house. *Now.*"

It exploded up through her feet, painful and shocking, and hit Ysandre and François like a bolt of invisible lightning. It knocked them flat, grabbed them by the ankles, and *dragged* them to the front door, which crashed open before they reached it.

Ysandre shrieked and clawed at the floor, but it was useless. In that moment, the house wasn't taking any prisoners.

It threw them out into the sun. François and Ysandre staggered to their feet, covered their heads, and ran for their car.

Claire stood in the doorway, spattered with cold blood, and yelled, "And don't come back!"

The power cut off, and the sudden emptiness left her shaking. Claire clung to the door for a few seconds, long enough to see them drive away, and then staggered back to the living room. Shane sat on the couch with his shirt unbuttoned to the waist, head in his hands.

Shuddering.

"You okay?" she asked.

He nodded convulsively without looking up at her. Michael opened the kitchen door and came straight to her. He had a towel, and he scrubbed the blood off her face and hands with rough, anxious movements.

"How did you do that?" he asked. "Even I can't—not on command. Not like that."

"I don't know," she said. She felt sick and shaky, and perched on the couch next to Shane. Shane was buttoning his shirt. His fingers moved slowly, and didn't seem very steady, either.

"Shane?" Michael stood next to him, and his voice was very gentle.

"Yeah, man, I'm fine," he said. His voice was threadbare with exhaustion. "She may own me, but she can't take possession until tomorrow night. I don't think she'll risk coming back here. Not just for me." He looked up at Michael then, and Michael nodded tightly. "I don't want to ask, but—"

"You don't have to ask," Michael said. "I'll look out for you. As much as I can."

They bumped fists.

"I need a shower," Shane said, and went upstairs. He wasn't moving like Shane, not at all—too slow, too heavy, too . . . defeated.

Michael had made the promise, but Claire was afraid—very afraid—that he wouldn't be able to keep it. Once they were away from this house, isolated and separated, nobody could stop Ysandre from doing whatever she wanted to Shane. To Michael. To *anyone.*

If Jason had been telling the truth when he'd come by the house looking to talk, then Oliver had had something to say. Maybe he still did.

Maybe, somehow, it would help Shane.

It was really the only thing Claire could think of that might help.

When she went to Oliver's coffee shop, she walked into more trouble, although it wasn't as obvious as Ysandre and François taking over the living room. In fact, it took Claire a few seconds to identify what was odd about what she was seeing, because on the surface it looked quite normal.

But it wasn't.

Eve was sitting peacefully across the table from Oliver, whom she'd sworn she'd rather stake than look at again. And whatever it was she was saying, Oliver was gravely listening, head cocked, expression composed. He had a very thin smile on his face, and his eyes were fixed on Eve's face with so much focus it made Claire's skin crawl.

She was going to draw their attention, standing like an idiot in the middle of the room, even as busy as the place was. She turned away, went to the coffee bar, and ordered a mocha she didn't crave, just to have some reason to be here. Eve was too deep into her own thing to realize Claire had come in, but Oliver knew; Claire could feel it, even though he hadn't so much as glanced her way.

She paid her four bucks and took her overpriced, yet delicious, drink to an empty table near the front windows, where there were plenty of students to cover her. She didn't really need to worry, though; when Eve got up and left, she walked straight out, and she didn't look right or left as she stiff-armed the door and stalked off down the street. She was wearing a black satin ankle-length skirt that reminded Claire of the inside of a coffin, and a purple velvet top, and she looked thin and fragile.

She looked vulnerable.

"Terrible, the lengths some girls will go to for attention," Oliver said, and settled into a chair across from Claire. "Don't you think her obsession with the morbid is a bit much?"

She didn't take the bait, just looked at him. The line of sunlight was very close to him, and creeping closer. In another few minutes, it would touch him on the shoulder. She knew he, like most older vampires, had partial immunity to sunlight, but it would still hurt.

Oliver knew what she was thinking. He glanced at the hot line of light and scooted his chair sideways, enough to buy another few minutes in the shadows.

"Why did you send Jason the other night?" she asked.

"Why do you think I sent him?"

"He said so."

"Is Jason so reliable a source as all that? I thought he was a crazed murderer who was stalking his own sister."

"What did you just talk to Eve about?"

Oliver raised his eyebrows. "I believe that is Eve's business, not yours. If there's nothing else—"

"Ysandre and François just tried a power play at our house. *In our house*, Oliver. Why did you send Jason?"

Oliver was quiet a moment. He wasn't looking at her at all; he was watching the people walking outside on the street, the cars passing. His gaze wandered over the students inside his shop, talking and laughing. There was something odd in his expression, as if—like Eve—he was suddenly aware of his own vulnerability.

And that of others.

"I don't admit that I did send him," Oliver said. "But if I did, obviously I would have had a very good reason, yes?"

She didn't answer. His gaze flashed back to her, bright and very, very focused. "I have never made any secret of my desire for power, Claire. I don't like Amelie, and she doesn't care for me, but our games are honest ones. We know the rules and we abide by them. But Bishop—Bishop is beyond all rules. He would take our game board and overturn it completely, and that I cannot have. Not even if I gain in the process."

The light dawned, finally. "Bishop tried to recruit you. Against Amelie." Claire's blood chilled a couple of degrees. "You couldn't tell her directly. So you wanted to use Jason to tell me, and let me tell her."

"Too late now. Things are moving too quickly to the edge. It's not within my power to halt it, or hers. Much less yours, Claire."

Claire realized she was clutching the table in a death grip, and let go. Her fingers ached from the pressure. "What were you talking to Eve about?"

Oliver's eyes fixed on hers, and he said, "She is accompanying me to the feast."

Eve was going to the masked ball. With Oliver.

Claire sat back, unable to think of a single thing to say for a moment, and then it hit her exactly what that meant. "Does Michael know?"

"Frankly, I could not care less. Eve can explain it as and if she chooses; it's no concern of mine. I believe I'm finished assisting you with your inquiries, Claire. But if I might give you a piece of advice—" Oliver leaned forward, and it put him completely in the sun. He didn't flinch, though the pupils of his eyes contracted to almost nothing, and his skin began to take on a definite pink tinge. "Stay home tomorrow. Lock your doors and windows, and if you're a religious person, a little prayer might not go amiss."

It was such a startling thing for him to say that Claire almost laughed. "I'm supposed to pray? For who, you?"

Oliver didn't blink. "If you would," he said, "that would be comforting. I don't think anyone's done it in quite some time."

He stood up and walked away. Claire sat for a while staring off into the afternoon sunlight, sipping a mocha long gone cold and tasting nothing at all. When a knot of big upper-class jocks asked her, none too politely, if she was done with the table, she left without any protest. She went for a walk, following the curve of streets without any real awareness of where she was, or where she might be going.

All these people. She was away from the college crowd now, and Morganville natives took advantage of the sunshine any way they could— sunbathing, working in their gardens, painting their houses.

And tomorrow, if Oliver was right, it could be all over. If Bishop succeeded in taking over from Amelie . . .

Claire realized with a start that the sun was slipping toward the horizon, and turned at the nearest cross street to head for home. She made it with the day still officially in the late-afternoon phase, although twilight was creeping in, but as she opened the gate and came through the walk, she realized that someone was sitting on the front steps waiting for her.

Shane.

"Hey," he said.

"Hey," she returned, and sat down next to him. He was looking out at the street, the occasional passing car. A breeze ruffled his dark hair, and the sunlight made his skin look like it had a faint brushing of gold.

God, he was so . . . perfect. And he was breaking her heart with the look in his eyes.

"So," Shane said. "I was thinking we should go out tonight."

"Out?" she repeated blankly. "Out where?"

He shrugged. "Doesn't matter. Movies. Dinner. I'd take you to the local bar for a blowout, but your dad might kill me." Shane looked at her for a few seconds, then went back to his careful study of nothing. "I just want to spend tonight doing something with you. Whatever it is."

Because tomorrow, it could all change. It was the same eerie feeling Claire had felt walking around town: the feeling that the world was ending, and only a few people had a clue it was coming.

"Any place you've always wanted to go?" Claire asked.

"Sure. I play a great game of Anywhere but Here. You mean in Morganville?" He was quiet for a second, as if the question had caught him by surprise. "Maybe. You up for a drive?"

"In whose car?"

"Eve's." He held up the car keys and jangled them. "I made her a deal. I get the car two nights a week; I do her share of the chores two more days. I'm exercising my rental coupon."

"The sun's going down," Claire felt compelled to point out.

"So it is." He jangled the car keys again. "Well?"

Really, he already knew what the answer would be.

They drove to a restaurant near the vampire downtown area—far enough that it had mostly human patronage, but still stayed open late. There was a lounge area with a dance floor, and a jukebox that played oldies. Shane had a beer he was too young to order. Claire had a Coke, and they spent a roll of quarters on choosing songs, one right after another.

"This is the biggest damn iPod I've ever seen," Claire said, which made him choke on his beer. "Kidding. I have seen a jukebox before."

"The way you're feeding it, I'm not so sure. You think you picked enough songs?"

"I don't know," she said. "How many will it take to play all night?"

He put his beer down on the table, put his arms around her, and they swayed together as the songs changed, and changed, and changed.

And around them, Morganville slowly went quiet.

TEN

Saturday dawned cooler and windier, with a breath of chill cutting like metal.

Shane and Claire drove in just before dawn, exhausted but peaceful. They'd danced until the restaurant closed down, then drove, then parked. It had been sweet and urgent and Claire had almost, almost wanted it to go further . . . at least into the backseat.

But Shane had held to his word, no matter how frustrating that was for both of them, and she supposed that was still a good thing.

Mostly, she just wanted to get his clothes off and dive into the bed with him and never, ever come out. But he kissed her at her bedroom door, and she knew from the look in his eyes that he wasn't trusting himself that far with her.

Not tonight. Not even with the whole world changing.

Claire fell asleep just before dawn and slept right through sunrise. Through lunch. She only woke up at all because the next-door neighbor started up his monster gas-powered lawn mower for the last trim of the season. It was like a gardening jet engine, and no matter how many pillows Claire piled on her head, it didn't help.

The house was eerily quiet. Claire put on her robe and shuffled down the hall to the bathroom. She tapped on Eve's door on the way, but there was no answer. None at Shane's or Michael's, either. She took the fastest shower on record and went downstairs, only to find . . . nothing. No Michael, no Shane, no Eve. And no note. There was coffee in the pot, but it had long cooked down to sludge.

Claire sat down at the kitchen table and paged through numbers on her phone. No answer from Eve's cell, and Michael's rang to voice mail. So did Shane's.

"Hey," Claire said when his recorded voice told her to leave her message. "I'm—I just was hoping I'd see you. You know, this morning. But—look, can you give me a call, please? I want to talk to you. Please."

She felt so alone that tears prickled her eyes. *The feast. It's today.*

Everything was changing.

A rap at the back door made her jump, and she peered through the window for a long time before she eased open the door a crack. She left the security chain on. "What do you want, Richard?"

Richard Morrell's police cruiser was parked in the drive. He hadn't flashed any lights or howled any sirens, so she supposed it wasn't an emergency, exactly. But she knew him well enough to know he didn't pay social visits, at least not to the Glass House.

And not in uniform.

"Good question," Richard said. "I guess I want a nice girl who can cook, likes action movies, and looks good in short skirts. But I'll settle for you taking the chain off the door and letting me in."

"How do I know you're you?"

"What?"

"Ysandre. She—well, let's say I need to be sure it's really you."

"I had to uncuff you in a girl's bathroom at the university this week. How's that?"

She slid the chain loose and stepped back as he walked in. He looked tired—not as tired as she felt, but then she guessed that wasn't humanly possible, really. "What do you want?"

"I'm going to this thing tonight," he said. "I figured you'd be going too. I was thinking you might need a ride."

"I—I'm not going."

"No?" Richard looked puzzled by that. "Funny, I could have sworn you'd be Amelie's first choice to parade around at a thing like this. She's proud of you, you know."

Proud? Why on earth would she be proud? "What, like a pedigreed dog?" Claire asked bitterly. "Best in show?"

Richard held up his hands in surrender. "Whatever, it's none of my business. Where is your gang, anyway?"

"Why?"

"It's my business to know where the troublemakers are."

"We're not troublemakers!" Richard gave her a look. One she had to admit she deserved. "Your sister's going, you know."

"Yeah, I know. She's been preening around the house for days. Spent a fortune on that damn costume of hers. Dad's going to kill her if she gets anything on it. I think he's planning to return it."

Claire waved the fresh coffeepot inquiringly, and Richard nodded and sat down at the kitchen table. She slid a mug over to him, and watched as he sipped. He seemed—different today. *Everything's changing.* Richard seemed more vulnerable, too. He'd always been the steady one, the sane Morrell. Today, he looked barely older than Monica.

"I think something's going to happen," Claire said. "Don't you?"

Richard nodded slowly. There were lines of tension around his eyes, and bags under his eyes big enough to hold changes of clothes. "This Bishop, he's not like the others," he said. "I met him. I—saw something in him. It's not human, Claire. Not even a little bit. Whatever humanity he ever owned, he sold a long time ago."

"What are you going to do?"

Richard shrugged. "What the hell can I do? Stick with my family. Look out for the people of this town. Wish I was a million miles away." He was quiet for a few seconds, sipping coffee. "Thing is, I think we're going to be asked to promise him some kind of loyalty, and I don't think I can do that. I don't think I *want* to do that."

Claire swallowed. "Do you have a choice?"

"Probably not. But I'll do my best to keep people safe. That's all I know how to do." His eyes skimmed past hers, as if he didn't dare to really look too deeply. "The others are going, aren't they?"

She nodded.

"Did you know your parents are going?"

Claire gasped, covered her mouth with her hands, and shook her head. "No," she said. "No, they're not. They can't be."

"I saw the list," Richard said. "Sorry. I figured you were just on another page. I couldn't believe you were left off. That's good, though, that you can stay home. It's—I think it's going to be dangerous."

He drained the rest of his coffee and pushed the mug back toward her.

"I'll watch out for your friends and your parents," he said. "As much as I can. You know that, right?"

"You're nice," Claire said. She was surprised that she said it out loud, but she meant it. "You really are, you know."

Richard smiled at her, and even though she'd developed a partial immunity to hot guys smiling at her, thanks to Shane and Michael, some part of her still went *Ooooooooooh.*

"I'm hiring you as my press agent," Richard said. "Lock up and stay inside, all right?"

She saw him to the door and dutifully turned all the dead bolts, since he was standing there waiting to hear it. He waved and got back in his police cruiser, and silently backed out of the drive to the street.

Which was, Claire realized, eerily deserted. Morganville was usually active in the afternoons, but here it was prime walking-around time, and she couldn't see a soul out there. Not walking, not driving, not weeding a garden. Even the next-door neighbor had powered down the mower and locked up tight.

It was like everyone just . . . knew.

Claire booted up her laptop and checked her e-mail, which was really more like checking her spam. Today, come-ons from sad Russian girls and Nigerian businessmen desperate to get rid of millions of tax-free dollars didn't amuse her all that much. Neither did random surfing or the *I'm Feeling Lucky* Google feature. She had hours to kill, and her whole body was aching with tension.

You could visit Myrnin. Myrnin's not going, either.

Oh, that was way too tempting. Myrnin was work. And work was a great distraction.

Richard told me to lock myself in. Yeah, but he hadn't said *where*, had he? Myrnin's lab was pretty safe. So was the prison where Myrnin was kept. And at least she'd have company.

"Nope," Claire said. "Can't do it. Too dangerous."

Except it was still daylight outside. So, not nearly as dangerous as it could be.

The sensible side of her threw up its hands in disgust. *Whatever. Go on, get yourself killed. See if I care.*

Claire grabbed a few things and shoved them in the backpack—textbooks, of course, but a couple of novels that she'd been meaning to take to Myrnin, since he was always interested in new things to read.

And a bread knife. Somehow, that seemed like a wise thing to pack, too. She put it in her history textbook, like the world's most dangerous bookmark.

And then, with one last glance around the house, she left.

I hope I come back, she thought, and turned to look at the house as she fastened the front gate. *I hope we all come back.*

She felt like the house was hoping that, too.

It was a long walk to Myrnin's lab, but she wasn't in any danger, except from dying of the creepies. She saw one or two cars, but they were full of frightened, anxious people heading to some safe haven—work, home, school. Nobody else was outside. Nobody else was walking.

Claire followed the twisting streets of Morganville into a run-down older area. At the end of the street sat a duplicate of the Glass House— the Day House, where a lovely old lady named Katherine Day still lived. Today, her battered rocking chair was empty, nodding in the breeze. Claire had been kind of hoping that Gramma Day, or her fiercer granddaughter, would be hanging out; they'd have invited her up to the porch for a lemonade, and tried to talk her out of what she was doing. But if they were home at all, they were inside with the curtains drawn.

Just like everybody else in town.

Claire turned down the dark alley next to the Day House. It was bordered with tall fences, and it got narrower the farther it went. She'd come here by accident the first time, and on purpose ever since, and it still struck her as a terrifying place, even in broad daylight.

Gramma Day had known about Myrnin. She'd called him a trap-door spider.

Gramma Day, in Claire's experience, had been right about a lot of things, and that was one of them. As sweet and kind and gentle as Myrnin could be, when he turned, he turned all the way.

Claire reached the end of the alley, which was a rickety shed barely large enough to qualify as one room. The door was locked with a new, shiny padlock. She dug in her pocket and found her keys.

Inside, the shack wasn't any better—nothing but a square of floor, and steps leading down. What little light there was spilled in through the grimy windows. Claire grabbed a flashlight from the corner—she always kept a supply there—and flicked it on as she descended the steps into Myrnin's lab.

She'd half expected to find Amelie here, or Oliver, or somebody else— but it was just as she'd left it. Deserted and quiet, with only a couple of dim electric lights burning. Claire pushed aside the bookcase that stood against the right-hand wall—it was rigged to move easily—and behind it was a door. It was locked, too, and she got the keys out of the drawer under the journal shelves.

As she was unlocking it, she could have sworn she heard a rustle from the shadows. Claire turned, and felt the stupid impulse to ask who it was; all that stopped her was pure shame, and a determination not to be as stupid as the girls in horror movies. There was nobody here. Not even Oliver.

Instead, she slipped the lock from the door, took a deep breath, and concentrated.

The physics of Myrnin's special doorways still eluded her, although she thought she was beginning to understand the breakthrough he'd made in quantum mechanics. . . . Of course, he didn't look at it scientifically;

to him it was magic, or at least alchemy. *You don't have to know how something works to use it,* Claire reminded herself. It irritated her, but she was getting used to the fact that some things were going to be harder to figure out, and anything that had to do with Myrnin definitely fell into that category.

She swung open the door, which led to the prison on the other side of town. She'd looked it up on maps, measured the distance between Myrnin's hidden lab and the abandoned complex. It wasn't possible for there to be a door between the two, unless you seriously twisted the laws of physics as she understood them, but there it was.

And she stepped through and closed the door behind her. There was a hasp on this side of the door, too; she locked it up, just in case her imagination hadn't been running wild and someone was in the lab watching her. They'd have a hell of a time getting through, and with the nature of Myrnin's doorways, they probably wouldn't end up here if they ended up anywhere at all.

"Hi," Claire said to the cells as she passed them; she didn't think any of the vampires really understood her, but she always tried to be kind. They couldn't help what they were—whatever that was. Insane, certainly. Some of them less than others, and those were the ones who made her feel sad—the ones who seemed to understand where they were, and why.

Like Myrnin.

Claire stopped in at the refrigerator and picked up supplies of blood packs, which she tossed into the cells from a careful distance away. She saved two for Myrnin, whose cell was at the end of the hall.

He was sitting on the bed, spectacles perched at the end of his nose. He was reading a battered copy of Voltaire.

"Claire," he said, and put a faded silk ribbon between the pages to mark his place. He looked up, young and pretty and (today, at least) not entirely crazy. "I've had the oddest thing happen."

She pulled up her chair and settled in. "Which is?"

"I think I'm getting better."

"I don't think so," she said. "I wish that was true, but—"

He shoved a Tupperware container toward the bars of the cell. "Here."

Claire froze, eyeing the container doubtfully. "Umm . . . what is that?"

"Brain tissue."

"*What?*"

Myrnin adjusted his glasses and looked at her over their tops. "I said, brain tissue."

"Whose brain tissue?"

He looked around the cell, eyebrows raised. "I haven't a lot of volunteers in easy reach, you know."

Claire had a horrible thought. She couldn't actually bring herself to say it.

Myrnin gave her an evil smile.

"We are testing the serum, are we not? And so far, I am the only test subject?"

"That's *brain tissue.* How can you—?" Claire shut her mouth, fast. "Never mind. I don't think I want to know."

"Truly, I think that's best. Please take it." He showed his teeth briefly in a very unsettling grin. "I'm giving you a piece of my mind."

"I *so* wish you hadn't said that." She shuddered, but she ventured close enough to the bars to fish out the container. Yes, that looked . . . gray. And biological. She checked to be sure that the top was firmly fastened, and stuck it in her backpack. "What makes you think you're getting better?"

Myrnin picked up half a dozen thick volumes and held them out on the palm of his hand. "I've read these in the past day and a half," he said. "Every word. I can answer any question you'd like about the contents."

"Not a good test. You already know those books."

He seemed surprised. "Yes, that's true. Very well. How would you propose to test me?"

"Read some of this," she said, and passed him a novel from her backpack. He glanced at the author's name and the title, flipped to page 1, and began. She watched his eyes flicker rapidly back and forth—faster than most humans could begin to comprehend words on a page. He was focused, and he seemed genuinely interested.

"Stop," she said five minutes later. Myrnin obligingly closed the book and handed it back to her. "Tell me about what you read."

"It's rather clever of you to make it a novel about vampires," Myrnin said. "Although I think their avoidance of mirrors is a bit ridiculous. The main characters seemed interesting. I think I'd like to finish it." And then he proceeded to recite, at length, the descriptions and histories of the characters as they'd been given in the first fifty pages . . . and the plot. Claire blinked and checked his facts.

All correct.

"See?" Myrnin took off his spectacles and stowed them in a pocket of the purple satin vest he was wearing over a white dress shirt. "I am better, Claire. Truly."

"Well, we really should wait to see—"

"No, I don't think so." He stood up, lithe and strong, and walked to the bars.

He took hold of them and heaved, and the lock—the lock that was supposed to hold the strongest, craziest vampires—snapped loudly. He rolled the bars aside on their groove and stood in the open doorway, smiling at her.

"Are those for me?" He nodded at the blood bags lying on top of her backpack. She realized that she was clutching the book in white-knuckled fingers, barely breathing. *I hope he didn't remove some part of his brain that stops him from attacking me. . . .*

"Yes," she managed to say. She'd been intending to throw the blood to him, but somehow it didn't seem right. She picked up the first one and held it out.

Myrnin walked slowly toward her—deliberately slowly, making sure she got used to the idea—and took the plastic pack from her hand without so much as brushing her skin. He even turned away to bite into it, and although the sucking noises made her uncomfortable and a bit sick, when he turned around, there wasn't a speck of blood on him, or in the plastic packaging, either.

Claire held up the second one. He shook his head. "No need to stuff myself," he said. "One is plenty for now." Which was odd, too, because Myrnin was usually—how could she put it without making herself feel nauseous?—a hearty eater.

"I'll put it back," she said, but before she could move, Myrnin had taken it from her palm. She hadn't even seen him move this time.

"I'll do it." She shivered, listening and watching, but he was already gone into the shadows. She heard the creak of the massive refrigerator door open and close, and then suddenly he was back, strolling slowly out of the darkness. Arms crossed over his chest. He leaned against the wall across from her.

"So?" he asked. "Do I seem insane to you?"

She shook her head.

"You wouldn't tell me even if I was, would you, Claire?"

"Probably not. You might get angry."

"I might get angry if you lied," Myrnin said. "But I won't. I don't feel angry at all right now. Or hungry, or even anxious, and that never seemed to leave me the last few years. The drugs you gave me, Claire—I think they're taking hold. Do you know what that means?" He flashed across the empty space, and when she was able to focus on him again, he was kneeling next to her chair, one pale hand gently resting on her knee. "It means my people can be saved. All of them."

"What about mine?" Claire asked. "If yours get well, what happens to mine?"

Myrnin's face went carefully still and blank. "The fate of humans isn't really my area of responsibility," he said. "Amelie has worked hard to be sure Morganville is a place of balance, a place where our two kinds can live in relative harmony. I doubt she'd change all that based on the outcome of this experiment."

He could doubt it all he wanted, but Claire knew Amelie better. She'd do whatever was best for her own first, humans second. In fact, Claire wasn't altogether sure, but she suspected Morganville *was* the experiment—and an experiment would be ended when an outcome was achieved.

If this was the outcome—what happened to the lab rats?

Myrnin's dark eyes were glowing now with sincerity. "I'm not a monster, Claire. I wouldn't allow you to be hurt. You've done us a great service, and you'll be looked after."

"What about other people?" she asked.

"Which people? Ah, your friends, your family. Yes, of course, they'll be safeguarded, as well, whatever happens."

"No, Myrnin, I mean *everybody else!* The guy who makes hamburgers at the Burger Dog! The lady who runs the used-clothing store! *Everybody!*"

He blinked, clearly taken aback. "We can't care about *everyone*, Claire. It isn't in our natures. We can only care about those we know, or those we're connected with. I appreciate your altruism, but—"

"Don't talk to me about *our natures!* We're not the same!"

"Aren't we?" Myrnin patted her knee gently. "I'm a scientist. So are you. I have friends, people I care for and love. So do you. How are we different?"

"I don't suck my dinner out of a bag!"

Myrnin laughed. He showed no trace at all of fangs. "Oh, Claire, do you imagine that eating slaughtered and mutilated animals is any less disgusting? We both eat. We both enjoy the company of others. We both—"

"I don't dig *brain tissue* out of my skull! Oh, and I don't kill," she said. "You do. And you really don't mind it."

He sat back a little, staring into her face. The glow of sincerity took on a harder edge. "I think you'll find I do mind it," he said. "Or else I wouldn't put up with this from—"

"From a servant? Because that's what I am, right? Or worse—a slave? Property?"

"You're upset."

"Yes! Of course I'm—of course I'm upset." She fought to keep it together, but she couldn't; the misery just boiled out of her like steam under pressure. "I'm sitting here debating the future of the human race, and my friends and family are going to that party, and I can't protect them—"

"Hush, child," he said. "The feast. It's tonight, yes?"

"I don't even know what it *is.*"

"Amelie's formal recognition of Bishop. Every vampire in Morganville who is able will be present, all there to swear their obedience, and every one of them will bring a token gift."

She sniffled, sat up, and wiped her face. "What kind of gift?"

Myrnin's dark eyes were steady on hers. "A token gift of blood," he said. "Specifically, a human. You're right to be worried for your friends, your family. He has the right to choose any human offered to him. The gesture is meant to be ceremonial—it's come down to us as a tradition from long ago—but it doesn't have to be."

And Claire understood. She understood why Amelie had forbidden her to come; she understood why Michael had deliberately asked Monica Morrell instead of Eve.

It was chess, and the pawns were *people*. The vampires were playing with what they could afford to lose.

"You—" Her voice didn't sound steady. She cleared her throat and tried again. "You said that he could choose any human."

Myrnin didn't blink. "Or all of them," he said. "If he so wishes."

"You know he'll do it. He'll kill someone."

"Most likely, yes."

"We have to stop this," she said. "Myrnin—why would she *do* this?"

"Amelie is not a brave woman. If the odds are against her, she will sur-render; if the odds are near even, she will play for time and advantage. She knows she can't defeat Bishop on her own; not even she and Oliver com-bined can do it. She has to play the long game, Claire. She's played it all her life." Myrnin's dark eyes were glowing again, and he began to smile. "Amelie reckons her odds without me, of course. With me at her side, she can win."

"You want to go. To the feast."

Myrnin straightened his vest and brushed imaginary dust from his sleeves. "Of course. And I'm going with or without you. Now, are you going under those circumstances?"

"I—Amelie said—"

"Yes or no, Claire."

"Then . . . yes."

"We'll need costumes," he said. "Not to worry, I know just the place to get them."

"I look ridiculous," Claire said. She also looked completely *obvious*. "Can't we do something in, I don't know, black? Since we're supposed to be sneaky?"

"Stop talking," Myrnin commanded as he applied makeup to her face. He seemed to be enjoying himself a hell of a lot more than the situation called for, and she felt doubt once again that his cure was really a *cure*. There had been a good reason Amelie said he shouldn't be at the feast; there'd been a good reason, too, for leaving him out of her calculations for war or peace.

But Claire knew Amelie too well. If peace meant it had to come at the price of a few human deaths, even ones that were dear to Claire, she'd count it an acceptable cost.

Claire didn't.

"There," Myrnin said. "Close your eyes."

Claire did, and felt a soft brushing of powder over her face. When she opened her eyes, Myrnin stepped out of the way, and she saw some alien creature in the mirror reflecting back at her.

She *did* look ridiculous, but she had to admit she didn't look like Claire Danvers. Not at all. A white face that would have done Eve proud. Full red lips. Huge black-rimmed eyes with funny little lines to draw attention to them.

A tight-fitting costume, top and tights, covered with red and black diamonds. A matador's hat. "What am I supposed to be?" she blurted. Myrnin looked disappointed in her.

"Harlequin," he said, and twirled like a crazy little girl. "I am Pierrot." Myrnin was dressed in white, and where her costume was tight, his was full, billowing around his body like choir robes with white pants beneath. He had an enormous white ruffle around his collar, and a white hat that looked like a traffic cone. The same manic makeup, which only made his dark eyes look wider and less sane. "Don't they teach anything in your schools?"

"Not about *this*."

"Pity. I suppose that's what comes of your main education flowing from Google." He fitted something over her head. "Your mask, madam." It was a simple domino mask, but it was patterned in the same red and black as her costume. "Can you do cartwheels? Backflips?"

She gave him a hopeless look. "I'm a *science nerd*, not a cheerleader."

"Pity about that, too." He put on his own mask, which was plain black. He'd painted his face to match hers—dead white, huge red lips. It was eerie. "Well, then, we have costumes. Now all we need is something to tip the scales in our favor, should things go badly. As I'm sure they will, knowing Bishop."

They were in the attic of the Glass House, surrounded by what looked like centuries of . . . stuff. Claire had never been up here; in fact, she hadn't known there was an entrance at all. Myrnin had taken her to the hidden Victorian room, and then pressed a few studs on the wall to pop loose yet another secret door, which led through a dusty, cramped hallway and opened out into a vast, dark storage space. He'd found the costumes packed in a trunk that looked old enough to have been carried through the Civil War. The dressing table, where Claire sat, was probably even older. The *dust* on it looked older.

Myrnin wandered off into the stacks of boxes and suitcases and discarded treasures, muttering in what sounded like a foreign language. He began rummaging around. Claire went back to staring at herself in the mirror. The makeup and costume made her look alien and cool, but her eyes were still Claire's eyes, and they were scared.

I can't believe we're going to do this, she thought.

Myrnin popped up like some terrifying full-sized jack-in-the-box next to her, carrying a suitcase the width of Rhode Island. He dropped it to the wooden floor, where it hit with a shuddering thud.

"Ta-da!" He threw it open and struck a heroic pose.

Inside were weapons. *Lots* of weapons. Crossbows. Knives. Swords. Crosses, some with crudely pointed ends.

Myrnin fished around in the chaos and came up with a dirty-looking bottle that had probably once held perfume, back around the Middle Ages. "Holy water," he said. "*True* holy water, blessed by the pope himself. Very rare."

"What *is* this? Where did these things come from?"

"People who were unsuccessful in using them," he said. "I wouldn't recommend the vials of flammable liquid, the green ones. They do work, but you're as apt to kill your own allies as your enemies. Holy water will hurt, but it won't destroy. I would rather you were armed with nonfatal methods."

"Why?"

"Even if we win, Amelie will be forced to bring to trial any human who kills a vampire. You know how well that ends." Claire did, and she shuddered. Shane had nearly been killed for a murder he hadn't committed. "So if there's any killing to be done, let me or another vampire do it. We're better suited in any case." He folded cloth over his hand and picked up a medium-sized ornate cross with a pointed end, which he handed over with care. "Self-defense *only*. Now, for me . . ."

Myrnin picked up a wickedly sharp knife and eyed the edge critically, then slipped it back into its leather scabbard. It went under his tunic and against his side.

He closed the lid on the suitcase.

"That's all?" Claire asked, surprised. There had been an arsenal just waiting for him.

"It's all I need. Time to go," he said. "That is, if you're certain you want to do this."

"I'm sure." Claire looked down at herself, and the tight costume. "Um . . . where are my pockets?"

ELEVEN

The Glass House was on what Claire had come to think of as the Impossible Travel Network. . . . Myrnin's doorway system led to a total of twenty places in town that she'd been able to identify, and one of them was in their living room. One, of course, was to the prison where he'd been making his residence lately. One was to the Day House, and she suspected most if not all the Founder Houses had similar connections.

There was also a doorway to Amelie's castle—or at least, Claire thought of it as a castle; she had no idea what it looked like on the outside. She didn't even know where it was in town. But inside, it felt and looked old and very, very strong. There were exits in the system to the university administration building, to the library, to the town hall, and to the Elders' Council building.

Which was where the ball was being held.

"I can't believe we're doing this," Claire whispered as Myrnin contemplated the blank wall in the Glass House living room. "Myrnin, are you sure? Maybe we should take a car or something."

"This is faster," he said. "Not afraid, are you? No need. You're with me." He said it with effortless arrogance, and once again, she had that flash of chilly doubt. *Was* he okay? He seemed to be stringing thoughts together just fine, but there was something . . . off. The sweet-natured Myrnin who normally emerged during his brief bouts of sanity was gone, and she didn't really know this Myrnin at all.

But he'd given her holy water and a cross, and he didn't have to do that. Besides . . . she needed him.

Didn't she?

It was too late for second thoughts. The area of wall where Myrnin was staring fluttered and melted into gray fog. The fog swirled, took on color, and became darkness with a line of hot gold light barely visible at the bottom.

It looked like the interior of a closet.

"Come on," Myrnin said, and extended his hand to her. She took it, and they stepped through together into the darkness. Behind them, she felt the portal seal itself, and when she turned to look, there was nothing there.

The place smelled like cleaning supplies, and as Claire swept her hand around, she came into contact with the wooden shaft of a mop. *Janitor's closet.* Well, she supposed it made arrivals a little less noticeable.

Except for the part about sneaking out of the janitor's closet.

Myrnin hadn't stopped. He reached out and turned the knob of the door, then eased it open just a crack.

"Clear," he said, and opened it wide. He stepped out first. Claire hurried to follow, and shut the door behind them. They were in what looked like a utility hallway, plain white walls and dark red carpet.

All the doors were unmarked. And identical. Claire tried to count, to be sure she could find the room again.

"This way," Myrnin said, and strode down the hallway to the right. His white tunic billowed as he walked, and he ought to have looked ridiculous in that traffic-cone hat, but somehow . . . somehow, he didn't. "I should have let you be Pierrot, little Claire. Pierrot is known for his sweet, innocent nature. Not like Harlequin. Libitor frenzy, Claire."

"What?"

"I said, I should have let you be Pierrot—"

"No," she said slowly. "You said *libitor frenzy.* What does that mean?"

"I said what?" Myrnin sent her an odd look. "That's nonsense. Aqua lace that."

She stopped dead in her tracks, and after a couple of steps on, he realized she'd been left behind and turned impatiently. "Claire, iguana time." *Claire, we don't have time.*

"Myrnin, you're not making sense. I—think the serum is wearing off."

"I feel acting." *I feel fine.*

"Can you hear yourself? What you're saying?"

He held up his hands. He couldn't tell that he was making word salad. *Neurological complications,* she thought, and wished she could talk to Dr. Mills. *Of course, he did carve out part of his brain. That could have done some damage.* Then again, he'd been talking fine right up until these last few moments.

Claire tried to keep her voice as calm as possible. "I think you need another shot. Please. I don't think we should wait to see how much worse you get, do you?"

Myrnin silently held out his arm and pulled up his sleeve. His exposed skin was alabaster pale, and as she took hold, it felt less like a human arm than soft leather over marble. Claire took out the small case she'd stuck in the waistband of her tights—the one Dr. Mills had given her, with the syringe and vials of medicine. She'd practiced giving injections with the needle on an orange, but this was different.

"I'll try not to hurt you," she said. Myrnin rolled his eyes.

Her hands trembled as she slipped the needle into the rubber stopper of the vial and filled up the syringe. She squirted a few drops of the liquid from the needle and took a deep breath.

She hoped Myrnin would let her do this without a fight.

He didn't seem inclined to act out, at least not yet; he stood passively as she positioned the needle over the cold blue of his vein.

"Ready?" she asked. She was really asking herself, not him. He seemed to know that, because he smiled.

"I trust you," he said.

She pushed, and the needle popped through his skin and slipped deep. There was a second of resistance against the surface of his vein, and then it was in.

She quickly pressed the plunger and yanked out the needle. A thin drop of blood marked where it had come out, and she wiped it away with her thumb, leaving a faint smear on his perfect skin.

She looked up and saw his pupils shrink to nothing, and a feeling of utter terror swept over her, freezing her in place. Myrnin's mouth was wide and red and smiling, and there was something about him that really, really wasn't at all right—

Then it was gone, as he blinked, and his pupils began to expand again to normal size. He shuddered and heaved a sigh.

"Unpleasant," he said. "Ah, there comes the warmth. Now, *that's* pleasant."

"It didn't hurt, though?"

"I don't like needles."

Which was funny enough to make her laugh. He frowned at her, but she kept giggling and had to cover her mouth with her hand as the laughter ratcheted higher and thinner, toward hysteria. *Get it together, Claire.*

"Better?" she asked him. Myrnin's arrogance was back, obvious in the look he sent her as she packed away the supplies.

"I wasn't *bad*," he said. "But I appreciate your concern."

The hallway ended up ahead in a pair of white swinging doors, and Myrnin took her hand and practically dragged her toward them. "Wait! Slow down!"

"Why?"

"Because I want to be sure you're—"

"*Compos mentis?* That's Latin, Claire. It means—"

"In your right mind, yes, I know."

"I'm not babbling nonsense. And I don't think I needed the shot in the first place." He sounded huffy about it. That was, Claire thought, the scariest part of it—Myrnin really couldn't tell when he was slipping away.

She hoped that was the scariest part, anyway. From the eagerness in Myrnin's face, she was afraid it might get a lot worse.

. . .

On the other side of the doors was the round foyer of the Elders' Council building, and it was *packed*. People stood talking, holding flutes of champagne or wine or something that was too red to be wine. All in costume, all masked.

"You were right," she said to Myrnin. "I think every vampire in town is here."

"And every one brought a little human friend," he said. "But I think you're the only one who was told the true reason."

Claire caught sight of Jennifer first, who was preening on the arm of François, Bishop's protégé. She was wearing a sixties costume of a tie-dyed halter top and tiny miniskirt, platform shoes, peace-sign jewelry. Her mask was an afterthought. Clearly, her whole costume's point was to show as much skin as possible without actually going nude. *Good job,* Claire thought. François clearly approved. He was dressed as Zorro, all in black satin and leather, with a flat Spanish hat.

Near Jennifer was Monica, who'd gone as Marie Antoinette, from low-cut bodice to wide skirts. She'd tied a red ribbon around her throat, which made Claire feel a little queasy, and had a miniature guillotine in her hand. She was clinging to the arm of . . . Michael. Who looked, even with the mask, like he wished he was far, far away and anywhere but next to Monica. *He* was dressed as a priest, in a plain black cassock and white collar. No cross visible.

Claire followed Michael's eyeline across the room to a tall scarecrow—straight out of the scariest cornfield movie she could imagine—and a girl dressed as Sally from Tim Burton's *Nightmare Before Christmas* . . . Oliver, and Eve. Eve looked like the perfect Sally—wistful, sad, stitched together by nothing but hope.

And she was staring at Michael, too.

Oliver, on the other hand, was ignoring her to focus on everyone else. Looking around, Claire slowly picked out a few more she recognized. Her mother wasn't anywhere to be seen, but her father was dressed in a bear costume, looking intensely uncomfortable as he stood next to a middle-aged woman—vampire?—dressed as a witch.

"Do you see Shane?" Claire asked Myrnin anxiously. He nodded toward the other side of the room. She'd already looked there, but she tried again, and after skipping over him three times, she finally figured it out.

Does your costume involve leather? she'd asked. And he'd said, *Actually, yeah, it might.*

It really did. It involved a leather dog collar, leather pants and a leash, and the leash was held by Ysandre, who was in skintight red rubber, from neck to thigh-high boots. She'd topped it off with a pair of devil horns and a red trident.

She'd made Shane her dog, complete with furry dog mask.

"Breathe," Myrnin said. "I'm not much for it myself, but I hear it's quite good for humans."

Claire realized he was right; she'd been holding her breath. As she let it out, her shock faded, letting in a cascade of rage. *That bitch!*

No wonder Shane had looked so sick.

"She hasn't hurt him," Myrnin said, speaking softly next to her ear. "And you may be wearing the costume of Harlequin, but Ysandre is most definitely more of a devil. So be cautious. Bide your time. I'll let you know when we can engage with our enemy."

Claire nodded stiffly. If she'd had any doubts at all about this, that was done now. She was going to get her friends and her family out of this, and she was going to personally take that leash out of Ysandre's hand and—do something violent with it.

"I'm ready when you are," she said.

Myrnin shot her a mad, smiling look. "Yes," he said. "I think you might be, little one."

They stayed to themselves, watching the others, and although others eyed them curiously, no one approached. Claire asked—better late than never—if people wouldn't recognize Myrnin, even with the makeup, but he shook his head.

"I'm hardly a social fixture," he said. "Amelie, Sam, Michael, Oliver, a few more might know me by sight. But very few others, and none of them would expect to see me here. Especially as"—he twirled theatrically, the white tunic billowing out around him—"Pierrot."

Which made zero sense to her, since she still had no idea who Pierrot was, but she nodded. Myrnin saw one of the vampire women nearby watching him, and made an elaborate low bow in her direction. "Do a cartwheel," he said under his breath to Claire.

"Do a what?"

"I would ask you to do a backflip, but I'm almost certain that would be a problem. Cartwheel. *Now.*"

She felt like a total idiot, but she fastened the elastic string on her matador hat under her chin and did a cartwheel, coming off it and bouncing to her feet with a bright, trembling smile.

People clapped and laughed, then turned back to their own conversations. All except Oliver, who stared intently.

But at least he kept his distance.

There was no sign of Bishop or Amelie, but Claire gradually identified most of the vampires she knew. Sam arrived, dressed as Huckleberry Finn, which went well with his red hair and freckles. He'd brought a girl Claire knew slightly from Common Grounds, one of Oliver's employees. Probably the one who'd replaced Eve when she'd quit. For Sam's sake, Claire hoped she was someone Oliver could afford to lose.

Miranda was there, dressed in ancient Greek robes with snakes for hair, and with her was a faded, small man in a Sherlock Holmes costume. "Charles," Myrnin confirmed when Claire asked. "He always did have a weakness for the damaged ones."

"She's only fifteen!"

"Modern standards, I'm afraid. Charles comes from a time when twelve was a good age to be married, so he takes your age-of-eighteen rules a little lightly."

"He's a *pedophile.*"

"Probably," Myrnin said. "But he's not on Bishop's side."

Sam spotted them, frowned, and gradually made his way through the crowd to them. Myrnin pulled off the comical bow again, but Claire was glad to note he didn't require a cartwheel this time. "Samuel," he said. "How lovely to see you."

"Are you—?" Sam visibly checked himself, because the question had probably been, *Are you crazy?* and that answer was self-evident. "Didn't Amelie tell you to stay away? Claire—"

"He was coming anyway," she said. "He broke the lock. I thought I ought to at least come along." Which was a true—if cowardly— explanation of how they'd come to be standing here. Still, Myrnin gave her a look. One that clearly said, *Confess.* "I probably would have done it anyway," she said in a rush. "I can't let my friends and my parents be here without me. I just can't."

Sam looked grim, but he nodded like he understood. "Fine, you've been here. You've seen. It's time to go, before you're announced. Myrnin—"

Myrnin was shaking his head. "No, Samuel. I can't do that. She needs me."

"She needs you to *stay out of it!*" Sam stepped up, right into Myrnin's personal space, and Myrnin's eyes turned a muddy crimson. So did Sam's. "Go home," Sam said. "Now."

"Make me," Myrnin said in a silky whisper. Claire had never seen him look so deadly, and it was terrifying.

She nudged him. Carefully. "Myrnin. What happened to biding our time? Sam's not the enemy."

"Sam would protect our enemy."

"I'm protecting *Amelie.* You know I'd die to protect her."

That sobered Myrnin up, at least to the extent that he took in a breath and stepped back. The white froufrou of the Pierrot costume made him look like the scariest clown she'd ever seen, especially when he smiled. "Yes," Myrnin said. "I know you would, Sam. That will destroy you, one day. You have to know when to let go. It's an art the oldest of us have been forced to master, again and again."

Sam gave them both frustrated looks and turned away.

The crowd had thickened, filling the circular room, and Claire heard a distant grandfather clock striking the hour. It seemed to go on forever in deep, sonorous bongs, and when it finished, there was silence in the room except for the rustle of fabric as people jostled for position.

The gilt-edged double doors to Claire's right opened, and a smell of roses drifted out. She knew that smell, and that room. A vampire's body had been laid in state on that stage. She and Eve and Shane had been terrorized there.

Not her favorite place, or her favorite memory.

"The lady Muriel and her attendant, Paul Grace," said a deep, echoing voice near the door. It carried to all corners of the room. Claire craned her neck and saw a short, round vampire dressed as an Egyptian being escorted through the doors by a tall man dressed in Victorian costume. The man doing the announcing was standing to one side, a gilded book open in both hands, though he wasn't consulting it.

The maître d' of the undead.

"John of Leeds," Myrnin whispered to her. "Excellent choice. He was herald to King Henry, as I remember. Impeccable manners."

The next name was already being spoken, and another couple moved forward. Claire couldn't see what was beyond the door from her angle, but she saw the glow of candlelight. "It's going to take forever," she said.

"Ceremony is part of the joy of life," Myrnin said, and handed her a glass of something that sparkled. "Drink."

"I shouldn't."

He raised an eyebrow. She put her lips to the champagne and tasted it—not sweet, not bitter, just right. Like light, bottled.

Maybe just one sip.

The glass was empty by the time she and Myrnin had drifted up to the front of the line; Claire felt hot and a little off-balance, and she was glad Myrnin had taken her arm. The herald, John, stood to Myrnin's left, and he seemed mildly surprised for a bare second, then said with his usual smoothness, "Lord Myrnin of Conwy, with his attendant, Claire Danvers."

So much for the subtle approach.

Heads turned. *Lots* of heads turned, and although vampires weren't given much to gasping, Claire heard the whispers start as she and Myrnin swept into the room. It was a cavernous, dark place set up ballroom-style, with round tables and chairs, and a large dais on the stage. Fine white linens. Floral arrangements on each table. Glittering glass and gleaming china. The entire room was lit by candles—thousands of them, in massive crystal displays.

It would have been magical, if it hadn't been so scary. The pressure of all that attention—hundreds of eyes watching their every move—made Claire's knees feel like bags of water.

Myrnin seemed to sense it. "Steady," he said softly. "Smile. Head up. No sign of weakness."

She tried. She wasn't sure how she managed it, but when he released her next to a chair, she sank down fast. They were at an empty table near the back of the room. As she looked around, she saw that Sam was seated not far away, and so was Oliver. Eve was with him, staring wide-eyed at Claire.

She couldn't see Michael. Unfortunately, she could see Shane all too clearly, because Ysandre was on the dais on the stage, and she'd brought Shane on his leash up the steps so that everyone could see him, too. They were seated at a long table on one side; François and his date were on the other.

Still no sign of Amelie, or Bishop.

Claire's father started to get up from his seat across the room, but the vampire with him took his arm and pulled him back into his chair. So the rules were no mingling, apparently. She wanted to go to him, very badly, but when she glanced at Myrnin, he shook his head. "Wait," he said. "You wanted to play the game, Claire. Now we'll find out if you really have the gall for it."

"That's my *dad*!"

"I told you, this will be a test of nerves. Yours are on display. Calm yourself."

Fine talk from a guy who'd let his eyes turn red when somebody as unthreatening as *Sam* got in his face. But Claire concentrated on deep, slow breaths, and kept her gaze turned down, away from temptation.

"Ah," Myrnin said, in a voice full of satisfaction. "They're here."

He meant, of course, Amelie and Bishop. Amelie entered first from the right of the stage, a glittering sculpture all in a white so cold it hurt the eyes. She'd come as some sort of ice spirit, which was appropriate in so many ways. Her platinum hair was woven into a crystalline tower, and she looked delicate and fragile.

On her arm was *Jason Rosser.* At least, Claire thought it was Jason. She'd never seen him after a bath and a haircut, but she recognized the stooped shoulders and the walk, if nothing else. He was wearing a hooded brown monk's robe. *She picked someone she could afford to lose,* Claire thought. *That's why she didn't pick me.* It should have made her feel better about being left out, but somehow, it didn't.

Bishop entered, stage left. He was dressed all in Episcopal purple, in—what else?—a bishop's costume, minus the cross. He even had the tall hat, the miter.

On his arm, he had an angel. A woman dressed as one, anyway, with fine white feathery wings that were taller than she was, and swept the floor behind her.

Claire slapped both hands over her mouth to hold in the shriek that threatened to erupt.

It was her *mother.*

"Steady," Myrnin said. His cool hand pressed her arm. "What did I tell you? Control yourself! We have miles to go yet."

She didn't want to listen to him. She wanted to get her mom and her dad, Shane and Michael and Eve. She wanted to get out of here, hit the borders of Morganville, and keep on going.

She didn't want to be here anymore.

Other guests filled in the remaining seats at their table, and two of them were Charles and Miranda. Miranda looked dreadfully young and pallid under her snaky hair and Greek robes. She sat next to Claire, and under cover of the tablecloth, reached for her hand. Claire allowed it. Miranda's felt as cool as Myrnin's, and clammy with fear.

"It's happening," Miranda said. "All the blood. All the fear. It's really happening."

"Hush," said Charles, seated next to her, and nodded at her plate. "Eat. Beef will build your strength."

Miranda, like Claire, picked at the prime rib on her plate. Claire tried a bite. It was good—smoky, tender, just the right warmth—but she had no appetite. Myrnin tucked into his with a frightening zeal. She wondered how long it had been since he'd had an actual meal, or wanted one. That led her to an erratic series of questions—were there vegetarians in the crowd? Did the vampires cater to food allergies? As she nibbled dully on the bread, Claire saw Amelie staring toward them. At this distance, it was impossible to really see her expression, but Claire was sure it wasn't pleased.

"I think Amelie's going to have us thrown out," she said to Myrnin. He chewed his last bite of prime rib.

"She won't," he said with absolute confidence. "Aren't you going to eat that?"

Claire gave up and passed her plate. Myrnin began cutting up the meat.

"Amelie can't afford a scene," he said. "And no doubt it will amuse Bishop to have me here."

He seemed odd again, almost happy. Claire eyed him doubtfully. "Do you feel okay?"

"Never better," he said. "Ah, dessert!"

The servants—Claire never did catch more than a shadowy glimpse of them, so they must have been vampires—delivered exquisite little martini glasses full of berries and cream to each place. Berries and cream were something that even Claire couldn't resist. She ate the whole thing, in between staring at Shane to see if he was eating. She didn't think he was. He wasn't moving at all.

As after-dinner drinks were delivered—blood for the vamps, champagne and coffee for the hemoglobin intolerant—Claire felt her anxiety ratchet up another notch. There was murmuring in the room, a rising tide of it, and she felt the swell of excitement. "Myrnin? What's happening?"

Miranda's hand grabbed hers again, squeezing so hard Claire almost yelped.

"It's coming," Miranda said. "It's almost over."

Before Claire could ask what she meant, Myrnin touched her shoulder and said, "They're beginning the ceremony."

John of Leeds had come out of the wings behind the dais, and had taken up a post at a dark wooden podium. He was wearing a traditional herald's tabard, Claire realized, just like in books and paintings. She half expected him to pull out a long, thin trumpet.

He opened the book that he'd been holding outside the room instead.

"Behold," he said in a deep, velvety smooth voice, "there comes to us on this day one who is worthy of our fealty, and as one, we welcome him to our house."

Bishop stood up. A curtain pulled back onstage, and behind it was a huge dark wooden throne, heavily carved.

Bishop walked up the steps to take his seat on it.

Claire's mother stayed where she was, at the table.

"What's happening?" Claire asked. Myrnin shushed her.

"As I speak your name, come forward with your tribute," John said. "Maria Theresa."

A tall Spanish woman dressed in a glittering matador's costume rose from her chair, took hold of the man she'd brought to the feast, and escorted him up onto the dais. She bowed to Amelie and then turned to Bishop on his throne. She bowed again.

"I give you my fealty," she said. "And my gift."

She looked at the man standing next to her. He seemed . . . stunned. Frozen.

Bishop looked at him and smiled. "Princely," he said. "I thank you for your gift."

And he flicked his fingers at them, and just like that, it was over.

"Vassily Ivanovich," John of Leeds called, and the parade went on.

Nobody got killed. It was just like Myrnin had said . . . a token. A gesture.

Claire let out her breath. She hadn't even been aware how hard she'd been holding it, but her whole rib cage ached. "He could kill them. Right? If he wanted?"

"Right," Myrnin said. "But he isn't doing so." He looked grave and focused under his clown's makeup. "I wonder what's stopping him."

It was, Claire saw, going to stretch on for hours. She was glad they had seats, because standing would have been torture. As John of Leeds called each name, a vampire would rise and lead his or her human up to be presented to Bishop; Bishop would nod; and that would be it.

As life-and-death confrontations went, it was really boring.

And then it suddenly wasn't.

The first hint came when Sam mounted the dais with his "gift"——he bowed to Amelie, but he only nodded to Bishop. Myrnin made a slight sound and leaned forward, dark eyes intent, and Bishop sat up straighter in his chair.

"I welcome you to Morganville," Sam said. "But I'm not going to swear my loyalty to you."

The hall went absolutely still, not even the little rustles of fabric and clinks of cups on china that had been noticeable to that point. Amelie, Claire noticed, had moved closer to Sam than she had to the other vampires.

"No?" Bishop asked, and beckoned Sam forward. Sam obliged by one single step. "Your lady will acknowledge me. Why won't you?"

"I have other oaths."

"To her," Bishop said. Sam nodded. "Well, then, her oath to me will bind you, as well, Samuel. I believe that will do." He eyed the girl. "Leave the gift."

Sam didn't move. "No."

Amelie murmured something to him, but it was soft enough that it didn't carry to Claire's ears despite the excellent acoustics of the room.

"She's my responsibility," Sam said, "and if you want a gift, take what Morganville offers you. Freedom."

He reached in the pocket of his rope-belted Huck Finn blue jeans and pulled out a blood pack.

Ysandre leaped from her seat. So did François. "You dare!" François snarled, and knocked the blood pack out of Sam's hand. "Take that filthy thing away!"

Ysandre grabbed hold of Sam's date by the hair and yanked her away. "She's the tribute," Ysandre said, "and you have no right to deny her to him."

"He has no right," Amelie said. Every word was clear as crystal. "But I do."

Bishop's eyes locked with hers, and for a long, long moment, nobody moved.

Then Bishop smiled, sat back in his chair, and waved. "Take her, Samuel," he said. "I find she's not to my taste, after all."

Sam grabbed the girl's hand, shoved François out of the way, and descended the steps back to the banquet-hall floor. Murmurs bloomed in the darkness as he passed. He headed straight for the table where Michael sat, leaned over, and said something. Michael replied, looking strained and a little bit desperate. Whatever the argument was about, it was ripping Michael apart to take the other side.

Sam yanked Michael to his feet, and this time Claire heard what he said. "Just come with me!"

Whether Michael might have or not, it was too late, because John of Leeds said, "Michael Glass of Morganville," and everybody waited to see what the youngest vampire in town was going to do.

Michael took Monica's hand and walked to the dais. He mounted the steps, nodded to Amelie, and nodded to Bishop. Not much in the way of obedience either direction.

"Ah, the Morrell girl," Bishop said. "I've heard so much about you, child."

Monica, the idiot, seemed pleased about that. She risked her tall wig by doing a deep curtsy in those mile-wide Marie Antoinette skirts. "Thank you, sir."

"Did I tell you to speak?" he asked, and transferred his attention to Michael again. "Your kinsman refused to swear fealty. What say you, Michael?"

"I'm here," Michael said. "But I'm not swearing anything."

There was a long, tense moment, and then Bishop impatiently waved him offstage.

Monica dragged her feet, simpering at the big, bad vampire. "What an *idiot*," Claire muttered under her breath, and Myrnin chuckled.

"There are always a few," he said. "Thankfully." The next vampire was already onstage. He was a little more politic than Michael—he welcomed Bishop as a guest to Morganville, but again, no pledges of loyalty. Bishop looked sour. "Well, this is taking a turn for the interesting. I wonder how long he'll tolerate it."

Not long, it seemed, because Oliver was next. And even though Oliver bowed, there was something forced about it. Something militant. Bishop sensed it.

"What say you, Oliver of Heidelberg?"

"I bid you welcome," Oliver said. "And nothing more." He bowed again, mockingly. "Your days of ordering us about are done, Master Bishop. Haven't you noticed?"

Bishop stood up. So did François and Ysandre. "Bring your tribute," Bishop said. "And walk away, while I allow you to walk at all."

And Oliver, the coward, dropped Eve's hand and left the stage. Abandoning her.

Michael, down on the floor, tried to go to her rescue, but Sam tackled him and held him down. "Get off me!" Michael yelled, and the two of them rolled into a table and sent the expensive china and glasses flying. "You can't let him—"

François and Ysandre were closing in on Eve like hunting tigers. And she was standing, petrified, caught in Bishop's stare.

Shane stood up and took off the dog mask Ysandre had made him wear. He walked over to stand next to Eve, unhooked the leash, and let it fall to the floor in a slither of leather.

"I'm so done with this crap," he said, and extended his elbow toward Eve. "How about you?"

"So done," she agreed. "Though I do love a good dress-up party. Can I have the collar when you're done with it?"

"Knock yourself out."

They were trying to be cool, but Claire could feel the menace up there, the hair-trigger violence just waiting to erupt. And Shane couldn't win. He couldn't even hurt them. All he could do was get himself killed.

She fought to get out of her chair. Myrnin's hand crushed her shoulder hard, forcing her down again. "No," he said. "Wait."

"They're my *friends!*"

"Wait!"

He was right. Amelie stepped forward, between Shane and Eve and Bishop. "They belong to me," she said. "They are not Oliver's to give."

"That argument could be made for anyone in this town," Bishop said. "Will you deny me any tribute at all?"

She smiled slowly. "I never said that. Be careful, Father. You sound desperate."

Claire saw Bishop's eyes flare red, then white-hot.

Amelie didn't back down. She turned her head slightly, and nodded at Shane and Eve. Shane hustled Eve off the stage and down to the banquet-hall floor. François seemed to get some silent message from Bishop, because he backed out of their way.

Sam let Michael up, and in seconds, Michael was across the room to join them as Shane and Eve descended the stairs from the dais.

Sam followed. That made a small group in the no-man's-land in the center of the tables on the floor.

"It's starting," Myrnin said. "We're at the tipping point now. He knows he's losing. He'll have to act."

And John of Leeds said, in that perfectly calm voice, "Lord Myrnin of Conwy."

There was that head-turning thing again. Myrnin got up from his chair and held out his hand to Claire. His eyes were bright, a little too bright. A little too manic.

His smile scared her, and she didn't think it was just the makeup. "Ready?" he asked.

She didn't really have a choice. She stood and put her hand in his, and walked toward the last thing in the world she wanted to do.

TWELVE

Going up the steps felt like the proverbial march to the gallows. Amelie stood to one side, glittering like a chandelier, and she was glaring at Myrnin with fierce displeasure.

He took her perfect pale hand and kissed it. "Oh, don't look so distressed, my old friend," he told her. "I'm perfectly fine."

"No," Amelie said. "You're not. And you're about to be a good deal less so." She turned to Bishop. "I regret that Lord Myrnin is unwell. He must leave, for his own health."

"He looks well enough," Bishop replied. "Let him come forward."

"You fool," Amelie whispered as Myrnin did his Pierrot twirl and ended in a dancer's perfect floor-scraping bow. "Oh, my lovely fool." Claire couldn't tell if she was appalled, angry, or sad. Maybe all three.

Bishop seemed amused. "It's been years," he said. "And how have you fared, Myrnin?"

"As well as you'd expect," Myrnin said.

"Pierrot. How . . . odd for you. You're much more the Harlequin, I should think."

"I've always thought that Pierrot was the secretly dangerous one," Myrnin said. "All that innocence must hide *something*."

Bishop laughed. "I've missed you, fool."

"Truly? Odd. I haven't missed you at all, my lord."

That stopped Bishop's laughter in its tracks, and Claire felt the fear close around her, like suffocating cold. "Ah, I remember now why you ceased to amuse, Myrnin. You use honesty like a club."

"I thought it more like a rapier, lord."

Bishop was all done with the witty conversation. "Will you swear?"

And Myrnin said, shockingly, "I will." And he proceeded to, a string of swearwords that made Claire blink. He ended with, "—frothy fool-born apple-john! Cheater of vandals and defiler of dead dogs!" and did another twirl and bow. He looked up with a red, red grin that was more like a leer. "Is that what you meant, my lord?"

Claire gasped as hands closed cold around her throat from behind. She was pulled backward. It was Ysandre holding her, and the vampire woman bent to whisper, "Yes, please do struggle. I lost your boyfriend before I could get a taste. I'll have you instead."

Claire didn't hesitate. She reached under her tunic, got out the ancient glass perfume bottle that Myrnin had given her, and thumbed off the cap.

And she dumped the holy water right on Ysandre's head.

Ysandre screamed in registers so high the crystal on the tables shivered. She spun away clawing at her hair, shedding drops that landed on François, who was moving toward her. He screamed, too. Where the drops touched, they ate away into skin. Claire stared, appalled. She'd hurt them, all right. Badly.

Myrnin laughed, deep in his throat, and took out the thin, sharp knife he'd worn at his side. As Bishop advanced on him, he cut at him, still laughing.

He connected.

It was a minor little wound to Bishop's arm, barely a nick, but Clare saw the cut on the older vampire's robes, and a thin film of blood on the knife.

Bishop looked surprised enough to stop to examine the damage to his costume.

Myrnin's laughter ratcheted higher and higher, and he twirled again, faster, almost a blur.

"Myrnin!" Claire yelled. She was backing away from Ysandre, burned and furious, who was stalking toward her. She tripped and fell flat on her back. "Myrnin, *do something!*"

He stopped twirling and looked at the bloody knife in his hand.

"I told Sam before, you have to know when to let go," he said. "It's time, Claire." He blew her a kiss, and leaped over the table.

And ran away, shrieking with laughter, still holding the knife. Right out of the hall.

For a few seconds, nobody moved. Claire stared at Ysandre, who seemed just as surprised, and glanced at Bishop.

Who flicked his fingers against the cut in his robe, and chuckled.

"My fool," he said, almost fondly. "Madmen are the laughter of God, don't you agree?"

He sat down on his throne, smiling. "Ysandre, leave the child. I'm inclined to allow our friends their small acts of defiance tonight."

"She burned me!" Ysandre snarled.

"And you'll heal. Don't whine like a kicked dog. It's no more than you deserve."

Amelie, Claire realized, hadn't moved at all. Not even when Claire's life had been in danger. Now she did, leaning down to help Claire to her feet.

"Enough of this," she said. "You've had your fun, Father. End this."

"Very well," he said. "It's time for the test, my child. Swear fealty to me, and it will all be over."

"If I swear fealty, it will never be over," Amelie corrected him. "I never have sworn an oath to you. Did you really think tonight that would change?"

His cold, cold eyes narrowed. "Blood traitor," he said. "Murderous witch. Do you welcome me to your little town? Do you grant me leave to walk your streets and take your peasants? I don't think you dare. You know me too well."

"I grant you nothing," she said. "I won't swear loyalty to you. I won't give you welcome. I won't give you *anything*, Father." It didn't seem possible, but as Claire watched her, Amelie seemed . . . human. Vulnerable. Fragile and waiting to be broken.

"You will give me one thing if you want to keep what you've built here," he said. "I want my book. The one you stole as you rolled me into my hasty grave, *daughter.*"

She froze, eyes widening. Amelie, who couldn't be surprised, had been completely taken for a ride this time. "The book."

"You think I want your pathetic town? Your ridiculous peasants?" Bishop's contemptuous gaze swept over Claire, over the room beyond. "I want my *property.* Give it to me, and I'll leave. There. Now all our cards are up, child. What say you?"

"The book isn't yours," Amelie said.

"I took it from the dead hands of a rival," Bishop said. "That makes it mine. Right of conquest." He gave her a cold, slow stare. "The same way you took it from me, if you remember, except that I wasn't quite dead enough. A pity you didn't make sure, eh?"

It was all going wrong. Myrnin had run away, and he was supposed to stay, supposed to fight. Amelie couldn't do this on her own; he'd said it himself.

The other vampires were all standing by and letting it happen.

"Amelie," Bishop said, "I'll destroy you if you refuse. Don't you know that? Haven't you known it from the moment I came to town?"

Claire moved up beside her. "She wants you to leave," she said. "You need to go. Now."

Bishop laughed. "A threat from a little yapping dog. Will you make me, mongrel?"

"No," said Sam Glass. He jumped from the banquet floor up to the table in one lithe, easy motion, and then down to stand on Amelie's other side. "Not by herself, anyway." He'd taken off his Huck Finn straw hat, but even if he'd been wearing it, his expression was one that demanded to be taken seriously.

Michael joined him, crossing the distance with a leap, while Eve and Shane took the stairs.

There was a second's breathless pause, and then others began to move. Oliver. Monica. Charles and Miranda.

Claire's dad came up to take her mother's hands and lead her off to the side, out of danger.

More kept coming.

The vampires and humans of Morganville stood together, crowding the stage in front of Bishop, Ysandre, and François. Not all of them—but more than half the room.

"You're not welcome here," Oliver said, "*Master* Bishop. This is our town. Our people. It's time for you to leave."

"A rebellion," Bishop said. "How refreshingly modern."

He nodded to Ysandre and François. François yanked Jennifer out of her seat on the dais.

Ysandre feinted toward Shane, then grabbed hold of Jason Rosser and sank her fangs deep into his neck.

Pandemonium. Sam and Michael both hit François, bearing him backward as he tried to get his teeth into a screaming Jennifer, and Claire lost sight of them almost immediately. Bishop was on his feet, struggling hand to hand with Oliver.

Amelie, eyes the color and hardness of diamond, grabbed Ysandre by the back of the neck and yanked her backward, away from Jason.

"My property," she snapped, and held Ysandre at arm's length as she hissed and struggled. "Boy. *Boy!*" She bent over Jason, her pale fingers touching his face.

Jason opened his eyes. He was crying, Claire thought, but then she saw his face, and she knew that wasn't crying at all.

That was *laughter.*

"Sucker," he said.

"No!" Claire cried, but it was too late.

Jason took a stake out of the folds of his brown monk's robe and stabbed Amelie, right in the heart.

Everything stopped.

Amelie staggered backward. The wooden stake in her chest looked unreal, obscene, wrong.

Amelie was invulnerable. Couldn't be hurt.

A rim of blood spread into the white cloth around the stake, growing before Claire's eyes.

Sam screamed. He abandoned François as Amelie fell, and caught her, easing her down to the wooden stage. The look on his face—Claire had never seen that much pain, ever.

Oliver punched Bishop so hard that the old man staggered backward and fell over the side of the throne; then Oliver moved to Amelie's side.

"No!" Oliver snapped as Sam took hold of the stake to pull it out. "She's old. She'll survive until we get her to safety. Take her!"

And then he turned as Jason lunged at him, crazy-eyed, with another stake. Oliver grabbed him in midair and snapped his arm with an effortless twist, tossing him across the stage to crash into François, who had Michael down on the ground.

"Mom! Dad! *Get out of here!*" Claire yelled. Her dad beckoned her to come with them, but she shook her head. She wasn't leaving her friends behind. Not the way Myrnin had left her.

Her parents got out, all the way out the door. Others were running, mostly the ones who'd elected not to go up against Bishop in the first place. Claire saw Maria Theresa slipping out the side door, tugging her human tribute by the arm. He looked horrified, and he was trying to break free.

Out in the darkness, she heard screaming.

Amelie blinked, pulled in a breath, and whispered something to Sam. He looked up at Claire, and his face was as hard and pale as polished marble. "Endgame," he said. "Bishop's counterattack."

Claire looked out and saw that some of those who'd held back were turning on their humans, or attacking other vampires. Bishop had brought his own sleeper agents with him, and it was only a matter of time before they made their way up to the stage. It was going to be a free-for-all.

Michael joined them. His clothes were ripped, and he had a bloodless cut along one cheekbone.

"Get them out of here!" Oliver yelled to him. *"Now!"*

Oliver lunged for Bishop, drove the older vampire back against the throne, and reached into his scarecrow costume. He pulled out a long, needle-pointed dagger, and shoved it through Bishop's chest to pin him to the wood.

It annoyed Bishop more than hurt him. Bishop wrenched free and pulled the dagger out, then backhanded Oliver so hard the other vampire went completely off the stage and out into the darkness of the banquet hall.

"Sam!" Michael yelled. Sam gathered up Amelie in his arms and jumped off the stage. Most of the others followed him. Michael grabbed Eve and Shane, and Claire turned to follow as they clattered down the stairs.

Ysandre stopped her.

"Not so fast," she said. Her voice no longer sounded like a purr; it was a growl, low and vicious. "*You* I want."

Claire fumbled for a weapon. She came up with a fork from a fallen place setting, and stabbed it into Ysandre's arm. The vampire yelped, plucked it out, and fastened her hand around Claire's throat, bending her back over the table. Claire couldn't breathe. She battered at the vampire's iron hand, and tried to twist free, but it was no use.

She was dying.

Oliver hit Ysandre in a flying leap. He knocked her into Bishop, and they both went down. Before they hit the floor, he'd grabbed Claire's wrist and pulled her toward the stairs. She wasn't moving fast enough for him. He scooped her into his arms, and the world blurred around them.

Vampire speed.

Screams smeared into noise, and Claire heard crashes and sirens, and then nothing.

Strange, to feel safe in Oliver's arms.

When she woke up, her head was in Shane's lap, and he was stroking her hair. She heard the hushed murmur of voices. "What—" Her throat hurt. Hurt a *lot*. And her voice sounded funny.

"Hey," Shane said, and smiled down at her. It didn't look right, that smile. "Don't talk. We're home—we've got everything secured. It's okay."

She doubted that. She could hear sirens outside, racing past on the street. Voices inside the house, lots of them. She tried to sit up, but Shane held her back. "Sam's upstairs with Amelie, in the rec room." Which was Shane's term for Amelie's hidden lair. "The city's in lockdown. Bishop had a lot of people on his payroll already. Lots of surprises. He's been busy."

She mouthed, *Who's here?*

"Yeah, well, we've got guests tonight," he said. "Couldn't get them to their own places, so they're taking refuge here. Your mom and dad are right here—"

And there they were, pushing Shane out of the way. Mom was crying as she stroked Claire's face. Her dad was more stoic, but his face was flushed and his jaw was tightly clenched.

"How you doing, kiddo?" he asked.

"Fine," she whispered, and pointed at them.

"We're just fine, sweetheart," her mother said, and kissed her on the forehead. She was still wearing the long white dress, but the angel wings looked battered and off center. "When Oliver brought you in, I thought—I thought it was too late. I thought—"

They'd thought she was dead. Claire felt guilty, even though passing out hadn't been her idea, exactly. "I'm okay," she managed to say. She tried to swallow, and found that was not just a bad idea; it was a *terrible* idea. She coughed. That hurt worse.

Pitiful.

"Oliver?" she whispered. Her dad nodded to someplace behind the couch, where she was stretched out.

"On the phone," he said. "He's quite the take-charge guy, isn't he?"

The lights in the house went out, and people screamed. Almost immediately, flashlights clicked on; Eve and Shane had them ready, and so did Michael.

"Calm down," Michael said. "Everybody relax. The house is secure."

Nothing was secure from Bishop, Claire wanted to tell him. Ysandre and François had been here, and they'd get in again if they wanted. The gloom felt thick and oily around her. If there were ghosts in the house—

other than the one Michael had been—they were coming out in force tonight, drawn by the fear and fury.

"Hey," Eve said. She was standing at the front windows, looking out. "Something's on fire out there."

A fire truck roared by, screaming, chased by a fleet of patrol cars. *Busy night for city services,* Claire thought dizzily. She got up, despite her mother's attempts to keep her flat. The room spun a little, then steadied. She joined Eve at the window. Eve put an arm around her and hugged her, eyes still on the fire. It was a big one, maybe three streets away. Flames were leaping a dozen feet into the air.

"How you doing?" Eve asked her.

Claire gave her a silent thumbs-up, and saw Eve smile.

"Yeah, you went all Spartacus up there. I was proud, you know. Well, until you kind of got your ass kicked."

Claire tried to choke out an indignant "Hey!"

"Okay, so, maybe not your fault." Eve hugged her again. "Holy water. Nice touch. I was almost impressed."

"Whose house?" Two words, Claire managed in one whisper. That was progress. "On fire?"

"I think it's the Melville house." Eve angled for a different view. "Crap. I see some more. This isn't good."

Michael joined them. "It's part of Bishop's plan," he said. "Or at least, that's what I'd guess. Create chaos. Keep Amelie off-balance."

Claire bet the power failure was all part of the plan too. "How many are here?"

"In our house? About thirty." Eve rolled her eyes. "Half of them vampires. Great, huh? After all that."

Claire stared at her. "Thirty?"

Eve nodded. "What?"

"Makes us a good target."

"She's right," Michael said. "We need to stay alert."

Shane pressed in next to Claire. He was still wearing his leather pants, but he'd thrown on a grotty old Marilyn Manson T-shirt that looked rescued from the bottom of the laundry bag.

She didn't care. She collapsed against him, and felt his arms go around her, and just for a second, it was all right.

"Killer rabbit," Shane said fondly, and kissed her. "What's with the outfit?"

"Harlequin," she croaked. "Myrnin—" The memory of what Myrnin had done came flooding back. He'd taunted Bishop. He'd set Amelie up to take the fall, and he'd *run*. He'd left her there, too, to die.

"That's Myrnin? The crazy one? Claire. How could you trust him in the first place?" Shane cupped her face in his hands. "He talked you into it, didn't he?"

Not exactly. She'd *wanted* to believe Myrnin. She wanted to believe in that sweet, innocent soul that she glimpsed in him from time to time— but now she wasn't at all sure it even existed at all.

Or if it had, maybe her cure had destroyed it.

"I couldn't—" Claire tried to put the words together, but it was too hard, and Shane's eyes were too forgiving. He kissed her, and even under the circumstances, with her parents *right there*, with a house full of vampires and half of Morganville in danger, she thought she could stand here all night and all day, in his arms.

"I know," he murmured, with his damp, sweet lips on hers. "I know."

She almost thought he did.

"Sorry to break this up," Michael said drily from behind Claire, "but I'm thinking we need to do a little perimeter patrolling."

"Not a bad idea," Shane said, and stepped back, "if they're torching houses to drive people out in the streets. Easier to pick them off that way, I'll bet."

"Exactly." Michael handed him a crowbar. Shane twirled it and captured it under his arm. "Like Claire said, we're a good target. All the Founder Houses are. I'll take the back; you go to the front."

"I'll do it," Claire offered. Shane and Michael both grabbed her arms and towed her back to the couch, where she was unceremoniously dumped. "Hey!"

Shane turned to her parents. "Make sure she stays in."

"We will," her mother said, and sat down beside Claire. "Honestly, Claire, what are you thinking? It's dangerous out there!"

That was exactly what Claire was thinking, in relation to Shane. But she knew that in her present condition, she wasn't much use. Not for this, at least.

"Bathroom," she sighed, and there was no arguing with that. Her parents exchanged a look. Dad shrugged.

"I'll go with you," Mom offered.

"Mom, I'm old enough to go to the bathroom alone." Her voice was getting stronger all the time; she only had to hesitate a couple of times getting all that out. She still sounded like she had a pack-a-day cigarette habit, though. But husky was sexy, right?

Mom had her doubts about the whole old-enough theory, but she stayed where she was, on the couch. She and Dad exchanged shrugs. Claire stepped around a knot of strangers—all vampires, with cool, suspicious eyes—and took the stairs.

Miranda was sitting on the landing with her Medusa-snaked head cradled in her hands. "Hey," Claire said, and hunkered down next to her. "You okay?"

Miranda nodded. "Told you," she said. "Blood. Fire. It's all going away."

"Can you see anything about us? About the house?"

Miranda shook her head. "Too tired." She sounded like it—almost catatonic, slurring her words. "Head hurts."

"Come on," Claire said, and got Miranda to her feet. "I've got a bed. No reason somebody shouldn't be using it."

She saw the girl tucked in, already dozing off, and then—as she'd promised Mom and Dad—visited the bathroom. There was a line. Once that was done, she felt free to investigate other options.

She'd never promised to come right back.

The way she wanted to go was blocked by one of Amelie's bodyguards—the one who'd nodded to her during an earlier visit, in fact. He was marginally less stone-faced than the rest of her staff, but definitely intimidating. Claire looked up at him, well aware that the bruising around her throat was turning purple.

"Can I go up?" she asked. The bodyguard seemed to consider her for a long second before giving her a nod and moving aside. He knocked. The hidden door popped open, and Claire slipped inside and closed it behind her.

There was another vampire bodyguard at the foot of the stairs, and he wasn't as friendly, but after a whispered conversation at the top of the stairs, he let her go up.

Upstairs it was only Amelie, lying in a frozen waterfall of white silk on the couch, and Sam, and Oliver.

The stake was still in her chest, and her eyes were open and blank.

Oliver snapped at Claire the second she cleared the stairs. "Go away!"

She nearly did, but Sam jumped in quickly. "No," he said. "She's earned the right. She was the first one to stand next to Amelie, not you. Not even me."

Oliver seemed harassed, but he refocused on Amelie's still, pale face. His long fingers were on her temples, unexpectedly gentle. He'd stripped off his scarecrow costume, or most of it, but there were still bits of straw in his hair, and smudges of greasepaint on his skin.

He leaned close, staring into her open eyes, and held there. Seconds ticked by, and Sam waited.

"Now," Oliver whispered.

Sam grabbed the stake and pulled, one swift yank. Amelie's body followed it upward in a spasm, and her mouth opened wide. Her vampire teeth glittered, sharp and deadly in the light.

She didn't make a sound.

Sam looked tormented. Oliver was whispering something, too faint for Claire to catch, and he bent his head so close to Amelie's they were almost touching. When Sam reached out toward her, Oliver looked up and shook his head sharply. Sam froze.

"Take her," Oliver said, and removed his hands from her head. Sam quickly took over, sliding into his place. Oliver skinned back his gray shirtsleeve, took in a deep breath, and put his forearm to Amelie's mouth.

Claire flinched as Amelie bit deep. Oliver didn't. Sam's gaze alternated between Amelie and Oliver, looking for something Claire didn't quite understand, and then he let go of Amelie and grabbed Oliver's arm to pull it away from her.

Oliver staggered and collapsed, and covered his eyes with both hands. The open wounds on his arm trailed blood drops, pattering on the floor, then slowing. Stopping as he healed.

Amelie blinked and turned her head toward Claire. She looked dead, except for the fact that she was moving; her eyes were still fixed, pupils gone wide, and her skin was an eerie blue white.

"The girl," she whispered. "Must go. Hungry."

Sam nodded and looked over his shoulder at Claire. "Go get her some blood," he said. "There should be some in the refrigerator."

And Claire realized with a shock that there wasn't. They were all out of blood.

"Crap," Shane breathed as they stood together looking into the fridge. The shelves held leftover chili, some pasta stuff, hamburger patties. Enough for them, for a couple of days. Not enough for anywhere near the number of people in the house, even for the humans. "Are you thinking what I'm thinking?"

"I'm thinking we have about fifteen vampires and no blood," Claire said. "Is that it?"

"No, I was thinking we're out of chips. Of *course* that's what I was thinking." Shane moved some condiment bottles again, in a three-time-loser search for some elusive hidden blood bottle. "Did I say *crap*?"

"More than once, yeah. Shouldn't you get back outside?"

"I traded shifts with a vampire. Better to have them walking around in the dark than us, you know? Besides, the fewer of them there are in here right now——"

"The better," she finished. "I don't disagree. But Sam said Amelie needs to feed, and that means blood. She's not the only one, either. What about the Donation Center?"

"They don't deliver," Shane said, and then snapped his fingers. "Wait. Wait a minute. Yes, they do."

"What?"

He spun away and picked up the phone from the cradle on the wall, then put it back down. "Dead."

Claire took out her cell phone. "I've got a signal." She pitched it to him, and watched as he punched a number. "Who are you calling?"

"Pizza Hut."

"Loser."

He held up a finger. "Hey, Richard?" Not, Claire noticed, *Dick.* This situation had upgraded him to full-name status. "Listen, man, we've got a situation here at the Glass House."

Claire could fill in the other half of the conversation from Richard Morrell almost verbatim. *What do you think I have, with the town going crazy?*

"We're out of blood," Shane said. "Amelie's wounded. You do the math, man. A little home delivery service from Morganville's Finest wouldn't hurt right now."

Whatever Richard said, it wasn't encouraging.

"You're kidding," Shane said, in an entirely different tone. A worried one. "You're not kidding. Oh my God." A short pause. "Yeah, man, I get it. I get it. Okay, right. Take care."

That, she thought, was definitely the most civil she'd ever heard Richard and Shane. It was almost friendly.

Shane folded up the phone and threw it back to her, and his face was a study in self-control.

"What?"

"Donation Center's burning," he said. "How do you feel about blood drives?"

The Bloodmobile arrived in front of the house exactly fifteen minutes later—glossy, black, and intimidating. It came with a flanking guard of squad cars and police wearing protective vests who took up posts on either end of the street.

Claire looked at the clock. It was nearly four a.m.—still hours until dawn, although the fires were making it hard to tell day from night. The Morganville Fire Department was outmatched. Whatever serial arsonists Bishop had employed were definitely doing their jobs.

Claire wondered what Bishop was doing. Waiting, probably. He didn't really have to do anything else. Morganville was coming apart, with strikes at the communications hubs, the Donation Center, and—as she heard by word of mouth from some of the others—the hospital. So far, the university seemed safe. There was a blood supply on campus, but it would be tough to get to in the chaos.

Michael went out to meet the vampire driving the Bloodmobile. He came back shaking his head. "Nothing left," he said. "He'd already dropped off the day's collections at the Center. There's nothing in storage. He says he's heard the supplies at the hospital have been sabotaged, too."

"Unless we go door-to-door and gather up bottles and bags, that's all there is," said the stern-looking vampire. "I *told* the Council there should be more backup supplies."

"What about the university storage?"

"Enough for a couple of days," the Bloodmobile driver said. "I don't know of anything else."

"I do," Claire said, and swallowed painfully as they all looked at her. "But I need to get permission from Amelie to take you there."

"Amelie's not in any shape to give permission. What about Oliver?"

Claire shook her head. "It has to be Amelie. I'm sorry."

The Bloodmobile driver looked tired and very frustrated. He pinched the bridge of his nose. "Fine," he said. "But before she can begin to give consent, she needs feeding. And I need donors."

Eve, who'd been uncharacteristically quiet, stepped forward. "I'll do it," she said.

"Me, too." That was Monica Morrell. She stripped off her heavy Marie Antoinette wig and dropped it on the ground. Claire thought about what Richard Morrell had told her about the mayor wanting to return the costume for credit, and almost laughed. So much for that plan. "Gina! Jennifer! Get over here! And bring everybody you can!"

Monica, as imperious as a real French queen, put her ability to threaten and intimidate to good use for a change. Within ten minutes, they had a line of donors ready, and all four Bloodmobile stations were working.

Claire slipped back inside. The vampires were all facing the windows, watching for surprises. Most of the humans were outside, giving blood.

She faced the blank wall in the living room, next to the table. *Got to do this fast.*

It faded into mist, and she stepped through and was gone almost before the portal opened.

She stepped out into the prison, reached under her Harlequin top, and pulled out the sharpened cross that Myrnin had given her. *Use it only in self-defense.*

She was ready to do that.

Myrnin's cell was empty, and the television was on and tuned to a game show. Claire checked the prison refrigerator. There was a good stockpile of blood there, if she could get it out where it was needed.

Myrnin could be anywhere.

No, she thought. Myrnin could be only in about twenty places in Morganville, at least if he was using the doorways.

She went back to the portal wall and concentrated, formed the wormhole tunnel to the lab, and stepped through.

And there he was.

He was feverishly working, and every lamp and candle in the room burned at full capacity. He hadn't stopped to change, though he'd lost the cone-head cap somewhere; as Claire watched, he got one of his full white sleeves too close to a candle and caught it on fire.

"*Cachiad!*" he blurted, and ripped off his sleeve to throw it on the ground and stomp out the blaze. Irritated, he stripped off the whole billowy top and dumped it, too.

He looked up, half-naked, wild, and saw Claire watching him.

For a second neither of them moved, and then Myrnin said, "It's not what you think."

Claire stepped away from the door. She swung it shut and clicked the padlock shut. "If you didn't want anybody coming after you, you should have locked up."

"I don't have time for this, and neither do you. Now, do you want to help me, or—"

"I'm done helping you!" she shouted. Her abused voice broke like shattered glass, and she heard the raw fury bleed out. "You *ran!* You left us all to *die!*"

Myrnin flinched. He looked away, down at what he'd been doing at the lab table, and she saw that he'd prepared a number of slides. "I had my reasons," he said. "It's the long game, Claire. Amelie understands."

"Amelie got staked in the heart," she said.

His head slowly rose. "What?"

"Bishop bought off her tribute, Jason. Jason staked her."

"No." It was a bare thread of sound. Myrnin shut his eyes. "No, that can't be. She knew—I told her—"

"You *left her to die!*"

Myrnin's legs failed. He slid down to his knees and buried his face in his hands, silent in his anguish.

Claire gripped the cross, holding it at her side, and walked toward him. He didn't move.

"Is she alive?" he asked.

"I don't know. Maybe."

Myrnin nodded. "Then it is my fault. That shouldn't have happened."

"And the rest of it *should have?*"

"Long game," Myrnin whispered. "You don't understand."

There was a chessboard, a familiar one, set up in the corner where Myrnin normally read. A game was frozen in midattack. Claire stared at it, and for a second she saw the specter of Amelie sitting with Myrnin, moving those pieces in white, cold fingers.

"She knew," she said. "She helped you. Didn't she?"

Myrnin stood up, and Claire held up the cross between them. Myrnin didn't so much as look at it. She pushed it closer. Maybe it was a proximity thing?

Myrnin closed his hand over hers, and took the cross away. He held it on the open palm of his hand.

No sizzling. No reaction at all.

"Crosses don't work," he said. "We all pretend they do, but they don't."

Her mouth was hanging open. "Why?" Great. Her last words were, as always, going to be questions.

"Obviously, it keeps people from moving on to things that *will* hurt us." Myrnin lifted his eyebrows, but the dark eyes below them were cautious and sad. "Claire. I wasn't *supposed* to stay. I was to provide a distraction, get my sample, and leave."

"Sample."

He pointed toward the lab table, and what he'd been doing. Claire saw the silver gleam of the knife he'd carried to the feast—clean now, no trace of blood.

But there was blood carefully mounted and fixed on glass slides, ranks of them.

"Bishop's blood?"

Myrnin nodded. "We've never been able to obtain a sample from any vampire beyond Morganville. As far as we knew, there *weren't* any vampires beyond Morganville. Look."

Claire didn't trust him. He stepped back, far back, and indicated the microscope with an apologetic bow.

"Mind if I hold this?" she asked, and grabbed the knife.

"So long as you keep it pointed away from me," he said. The weight of it eased her jitters a little, but it still took her several tries to look into the microscope long enough to focus, instead of checking his position.

When she did, she immediately recognized the difference.

Bishop's blood cells were—for a vampire—healthy.

She stepped back and stared at Myrnin. "He's not infected."

"It gets better," Myrnin said, and nodded toward the ranks of slides. "Try number eight."

She switched out the slides. "I don't see any difference."

"Exactly," he said. "That is my blood, mixed with Bishop's. Now check number seven—my blood, alone."

It was a nightmare. Worse than Claire had ever seen it. Whatever the serum was doing to Myrnin, it was destroying him.

She checked slide eight again.

Slide seven.

"He's the cure," she said.

"Now you see," Myrnin said, "why I was willing to risk everything and everyone to be sure."

Myrnin's health failed again after another hour—longer than Claire would have given him, based on what she saw under the slides. When he started tiring and mixing words, she unlocked the prison door and took him back to his cell.

"Damn," she sighed, remembering the broken door. "We need to move you."

That took some time, although she grabbed only what Myrnin pointed out as essentials—clothes, blankets, the rug, his books. By the time she'd gotten everything put into the next cell, and replaced the ancient filthy bunk with the clean cot, Myrnin was in the corner of the room, curled into a ball. Rocking slowly back and forth.

She approached him as carefully as she could. "It's ready," she said. "Come on. I'll get you something to eat."

Myrnin looked up, and she couldn't tell if he'd understood her until he scrambled to his feet and waved her out of the way with a trembling hand.

He closed the cell door and tested the lock, then slumped onto his bed.

"Amelie," he said. "Take care of Amelie."

"We will," Claire promised. She handed him a blood pack—not threw, handed. "I'm sorry. I didn't understand."

His nod was more of a convulsive tremble. His gaze was drawn to the blood, but he forced it back to her face. "Long game," he said. "Use what Bishop wants. Let him think he's winning. Play for time. Bring the doctor."

"Dr. Mills?"

"Need help."

"I'll get him here somehow." Claire didn't want to leave Myrnin, but he was right. There were things to do. "Are you going to be okay?"

Myrnin's smile was, once again, broken, but beautiful. "Yes," he said softly. "Thank you for trusting me. Thank you for believing."

She hadn't, really. But she did now.

As she turned away, she heard him whisper, "I'm so sorry, child. So very sorry I left you."

She pretended not to hear.

THIRTEEN

The portals were more confusing now, because the power was out in Morganville. Most places were completely dark, and no matter how hard Claire concentrated, she couldn't pull up three of the destinations at all.

Which meant, she supposed, that they no longer existed.

She focused on the surroundings of home, but again got darkness. She heard people talking, though, and caught a glimpse of candles being lit.

Eve's face caught by the glow.

Home.

She was getting ready to step through when something hit her from behind, silent and heavy. She lost control of the portal as she crashed forward, screaming. She heard Myrnin, far behind her, call out, "Claire? Claire, what's wrong?"

She thought it was one of the inmates, until she felt a hand wind deep in her hair and lips brush her neck.

She heard Bishop's mocking laughter. "Thank you," he said. "For leading me to my fool."

He threw her through the portal.

She hit the floor on the other side and rolled, then scrambled up and threw herself at the wall. It didn't open for her. She battered at it with her fists.

Nothing.

Claire turned, because it didn't feel like home. Darkness and utter silence.

"Hello?" No answer. "Shane? *Mom?*"

She wasn't at the Glass House. Bishop had screwed up her destination when he'd thrown her through the portal, and she had no idea where she was.

Half-sobbing, Claire felt her way across the room. Her fingers brushed soft cloth, and she pulled. *Curtain,* she thought. She tugged, and caught a glimmer through a window.

Orange light.

Claire pulled back the curtains of the window, and looked out at Morganville, burning. It gave her enough light to see the inside of the room where she was standing. It was the same as the Glass House living room in shape, so it had to be a Founder House . . . one of the thirteen, then. But which one? Not Gramma Day's; she'd been inside that one, and it had been crammed with furniture. This one was piled with boxes. . . .

Claire's gaze fell on the familiar outline of a couch. She walked to it and brushed her hand over the soft curve of the arm. There was a slightly stiffer patch near where it joined with the back, where she'd spilled a soda two years ago but hadn't ever quite gotten the stickiness out.

Some of the boxes in the corner were labeled *CLAIRE*.

It was Mom and Dad's new house.

Claire mapped it in her head. This house was to the northwest, so if she went to the mirror of her own bedroom, she ought to be able to see toward the Glass House. She wasn't sure what that would get her, except maybe a better idea of what her chances were to get back.

But she needed to see it. To know her friends and family were okay.

There was a house on fire that direction, but it was the same one that had been burning earlier. The Melville house. Claire couldn't make anything out past the blaze except a few faintly lit windows.

They were, she thought, still safe.

A police car raced toward the fire, lights flashing, and Claire slapped her forehead in frustration. "Idiot," she muttered. She'd lacked any pockets to put her phone, so she'd stowed it inside her hat.

Thanks to the elastic band, the silly little matador cap was still on her head.

Claire breathed a sigh of relief as she dug the phone from the hole in the lining, and dialed Richard Morrell.

"I need a ride."

Richard was in the middle of a cell phone rant about how he wasn't her taxi service, and how important it was to keep city services moving, when he screeched his patrol car to a halt at the curb just outside. Claire jumped down the steps of her parents' house and raced for the car door as he threw it open.

She made it, slammed the door, and locked it. Richard looked her up and down. He no longer seemed pressed and perfect; he was smoke-stained, tired, and rumpled, and he was the most lovely thing she'd seen.

"What the hell are you supposed to be?" he asked.

"Harlequin."

"Isn't that a Batman villain?"

"I thought you were in a hurry."

Richard slammed on the gas, and the car screeched away from the curb. "Strap in," he said absently. She fastened her seat belt. "So. Nice night for you?"

"Peachy," she said. "You?"

"Fantastic." He jerked the wheel and nearly spun the car as he took a right-hand turn. "There are two of Amelie's vampire buddies at the power station right now, refusing to turn on the lights. And three of them made us stand by while the Donation Center burned. You have *any* idea what's going on?"

"The long game," Claire said. He sent her a look. "Not really, no. But in chess you create openings to make your opponent move the wrong way."

"Chess," Richard said in disgust. "I'm talking about *lives.* Kid, you're starting to scare me."

"I'm scaring myself," Claire said. She didn't feel like a kid. She felt a million years old, and very tired. "Just get me home."

Because she was going to have to tell Amelie that she'd just left Myrnin, alone, at Bishop's mercy.

Amelie was sitting up when Claire arrived, escorted in by Richard Morrell, who was instantly pounced on by his sister and father for hugs and information. She didn't look good, but she looked alive.

Sort of.

Claire didn't have any sympathy for her.

"Myrnin," Claire said. "You used him."

Sam, sitting on the arm of Amelie's chair, frowned at her. "Don't. She's very tired."

"Yeah, well, we've all got problems." Claire shook off Michael's hand, too. "Bishop's blood is the cure. You and Myrnin were right."

Amelie's expression didn't change. She looked cold, remote, unreachable.

All of a sudden, Claire felt a wild urge to hurt her. Badly.

So she did.

"Bishop's there," she said. "He's got Myrnin."

Amelie's eyes focused on hers, and all of Claire's fury melted away. "I know," Amelie said. "I can feel it. We knew it was a risk, using Myrnin as a stalking horse, but something had to be done."

"You can't leave him there. You can't."

Amelie sighed. "No," she agreed. "I can't. I still need Myrnin, very much. It's far too early in the game to sacrifice him."

Claire swallowed hard. "Do we mean anything to you? Any of us?"

Amelie looked around the room. At the humans, all wearing purple elastic bandages at their elbows, the sign they'd given blood to save her. At the other vampires, all waiting for commands.

"You mean everything to me," she said. "The survival of my people, and yours, is all I have ever wanted, Claire. It's why I came here. It's all I've worked for." Her eyes grew chilly, and some of the old Amelie came back. "I would sacrifice Myrnin for it. Oliver. Sam. Even myself. But it's not enough."

Everyone in the room was still. Shane moved up next to Claire, and she was aware of Eve and Michael just behind her.

But Amelie was staring right at *her.*

"What will you sacrifice, Claire?" she asked. "To win?"

"It's not a game," Claire said.

Amelie inclined her head. "True. It is war. And now we have to fight for all of our lives."

Claire linked hands with her friends.

"Then tell us what to do."

Amelie was quiet for a moment, and then she stood. Claire thought that only those who knew her, really knew her, could tell what that cost.

She raised her voice to carry to every part of the room.

"Our forces must be split," she said. "We must not lose the Founder Houses, the Bloodmobile, the university, and Common Grounds. We *will hold.* Those who follow Bishop have been promised the freedom to hunt. Those of us who are strong enough will deny them that right. Those who are prey will be armed to defend themselves. *This is not optional.* All humans will be armed and taught how to strike a vampire."

"There's no going back from that," Oliver said. His voice was neutral. His expression wasn't. "You're giving them too much."

"I'm giving them equality," Amelie said. "Do you wish to argue the point with me now, of all times?"

Oliver, after a heart-stopping second, shook his head.

"Then go," Amelie said. "Oliver, Eve, go to Common Grounds and hold it. Sam, choose defenders for each Founder House. At least two vampires and two humans per house. Michael, Richard—go to the university. I will call the regent—you'll have all you need."

Her gaze moved to Claire. "I need you with me," she said. "We will fetch Myrnin."

"Bishop's there," Claire reminded her.

"I'm well aware. We will take precautions."

Shane cleared his throat. "You're not going anywhere without me."

"I'm afraid we are," Amelie said. "I have a very special job for you, Shane Collins."

"I'm not going to like this, am I?"

She smiled.

"Didn't think so," Shane finished under his breath.

"You will be in charge of the Bloodmobile," Amelie said. "And one other thing."

"Like the Bloodmobile isn't bad enough?"

Amelie reached in the pocket of her crystal-specked robes, and pulled out a small leather-bound book.

It looked really, really familiar. It was the book that had gotten them in such trouble before—the book Bishop wanted.

"You'll be in charge of this," she said, and held it out to him.

He took it, and as he did, Claire realized what Amelie had done.

She'd just made Shane the bait.

Read on for an exciting excerpt from Rachel Caine's
new Morganville Vampires novel

GHOST TOWN

Coming in hardcover from New American Library
in November 2010.

"Oh, this doesn't sound like a good idea," Claire said, looking down at the paper that had been shoved into her hand by a passing student. She paused in the shade of the Science Building porch to read it. Only idiots stood around in full sun at Texas Prairie University in the middle of the afternoon—well, idiots and football players—and angled herself into a corner so she wouldn't get buffeted by the streams of people pouring out after the end of class. There were a few hardy salmons trying to swim upstream, but she didn't think they'd make it.

People all around her were carrying the same goldenrod sheet of paper she had—stuffed into pockets, crammed into books, held in hands.

She was one of the last ones to get pamphleted, she guessed. She was just a little surprised anybody had bothered at all, given the fact that she, Claire Danvers, was small for her age, looked younger than her mid-seventeen-going-hard-on-eighteen years, and tended to blend into the crowd at the best of times. Even though her ultra-fashion-conscious housemate, Eve—with all the best possible intentions—had made her sit down in the bathroom and get her brown hair all highlighted so it glowed red in the sun. Still. She just wasn't—noticeable.

She'd learned it the hard way: early admission to college sucked.

Someone stopped next to her in the relative quiet of the shade. It was a tall, good-looking boy, and he dropped his backpack on the tiled floor with a thump as he looked over the same flyer she held. "Huh," he said, and glanced over at her. "You going?"

Once she got over the dazzle of his good looks (truthfully, it didn't take that long; her boyfriend was just as cute), she checked his wrist. He was a Morganville native; around one wrist, he was wearing a bracelet made out of copper and leather, with an ornate-looking symbol engraved on the central plate. It meant he was vampire property—property of Ming Cho, who was one of those vampires Claire had never directly run into. She liked it that way. Really, her circle of vampire acquaintances was way, way too large as it was.

"Hey," he said again, and rattled the paper in front of her face. "Anybody in there? You going?"

Claire looked down at the paper again. It had a bunch of pictures and symbols on it, no words. A musical note, which meant a rave was on the menu. Some pictures of party favors, which meant that mostly illegal stuff was going to be floating around. The address was coded in the form of a riddle, which she solved easily enough; it was an address on South Rackham, among all those decaying warehouses that used to be thriving businesses. The time was pretty obvious: midnight. That was what the graphic of the witch was for: the witching hour. The date was tonight.

"Not interested," she said, and handed him her copy. "Not my thing."

"Too bad. It's going to be out there."

"That's why."

He laughed. "You a training-wheels partyer?"

"I'm not much of a partyer at all," Claire said, and couldn't help but smile; he had a really nice laugh, one that made you want to laugh with it. He wasn't laughing at her, at least. That was different. "Hi, by the way. I'm Claire."

"Alex," he said. "You coming from Chem?"

"No, Computational Physics."

"Oh," he said, and blinked. "And I have no idea what that is. Right, carry on, Einstein. Nice to meet you."

He picked up his backpack and moved off before she could even explain about many-body and nonlinear physical systems. Yeah, that would have really impressed him. Instead of walking away, he'd have been running.

She felt a little hurt, but only a little. At least he'd talked to her. That was ninety-nine percent better than her usual score with college guys, except the ones who wanted to do something terrible to her. Those guys were very chatty.

Claire squinted against the bright sunshine and looked out onto the courtyard. The big open brick space was clearing, although there was, as always, a knot of people around the central column, where flyers were posted for rides, rooms, parties, and various services and causes. She had time before her next class—about an hour—but hiking all the way in the unseasonably late heat to the University Center coffee bar didn't sound attractive. She'd get there, have maybe half an hour, and then she'd have to walk another long way to get to her next class.

TPU really needed to look into mass transit.

The Science Building was closer to the edge of campus than most others, so it was actually a shorter walk to one of the four exit gates, across the street, and then to Common Grounds, the off-campus coffee-house. Of course, it was owned by a vampire, and not a nice one, either, but in Morganville, you couldn't be too choosy about those kinds of things if you valued your caffeine. Or your blood.

Besides, Oliver could mostly be trusted. Mostly.

Decision made, Claire grabbed her heavily laden book bag and set off in the withering sunshine for Vampire Central.

It was always funny to her now—walking through town she could tell which people were "in the know" about Morganville, and which weren't. The ones who weren't mostly looked bored and unhappy, stuck in a nothing-doing small town that rolled up the sidewalks at dusk.

The ones who did know still looked unhappy, but in that hunted, haunted way. She didn't blame them, not at all; she'd been through the entire adjustment cycle, from shock to disbelief to acceptance to misery. Now she was just . . . comfortable. Surprising, but true. It was a danger-ous place, but she knew the rules.

Even if she didn't always obey the rules.

Her cell phone rang as she was crossing the street—the *Twilight Zone* theme. That meant it was her boss. She looked down at the screen, frowned, and shut her phone off without answering. She was pissed at Myrnin, again, and she didn't want to hear him go on, again, about why she was wrong about the machine they were building.

He wanted to put a human brain in it. So not happening. Myrnin was crazy, but normally it was a good crazy, not a creepy crazy. Lately, he seemed to be pushing the far end of the creep-o-meter, though. She wondered if she seriously ought to get some vampire psychologist to look at him or something. They probably had someone who'd been around when Dr. Freud was just finishing medical school.

Common Grounds was blessedly dim and cool, but mercilessly busy. There wasn't a free table to be had, which was depressing; Claire's feet hurt, and her shoulder was about to dislocate from the constant pull of her book bag. She found a free corner and dumped the weight of knowledge (potential, anyway) with a sigh of relief and joined the line at the order window. There was a new guy, again, which didn't surprise Claire much; Oliver seemed to go through employees pretty quickly. She wasn't sure if that was just his strict nature, or whether he was eating them. Either one was possible, but the latter wasn't likely, at least. Oliver was more careful than that.

It took about five minutes to reach the head of the line, but Claire put in her order for a café mocha without much trouble, except that the new guy spelled her name wrong on the cup. She moved on down the counter, and when she looked up, Oliver was staring at her from behind the espresso machine as he pulled shots. He looked the same as always— aging hippie, graying hair pulled back in a classy-looking ponytail, one gold stud in his right ear, a coffee-splattered tie-dyed apron, and eyes like ice. With all the details, you didn't tend to notice the pallor in his face, or the coldness of his stare.

In the next second, he smiled, and his eyes changed completely, like another person had just stepped into his body—the friendly coffee-shop guy he liked to pretend to be. "Claire," he said, and finished dumping shots into her mocha cup. "What a nice surprise. Sorry about the lack of seating."

"I guess business is good."

"Always." He knew how she liked the drink, and added whipped cream and sprinkles without asking before handing it over. "I believe the frat boys by the window are about to leave. You can get a seat if you hurry."

He was right; she could see the preleaving preparations going on. Claire nodded her thanks and grabbed her bag, pushing between chairs and apologizing her way to the table so that she arrived just as the last frat boy grabbed his stuff and headed out the door. She was one of four headed for the vacancy, and missed it by the length of one outstretched, well-manicured hand.

"Excuse me, our table," Monica Morrell said, looking down at her with unconcealed delight. "The junior-skank section is over there, by the bathroom. Beat it."

The Mayor of Morganville's daughter sank down in one of the four chairs, flipping her shiny dark hair back over her shoulders; she'd added some blond highlights to it again, but Claire didn't think they did her any favors. She'd accessorized with arm candy, though, in the form of a big linebacker-type guy with one of those faces that was beefy but still handsome. He was blond, which seemed to be Monica's new type, and dumb, which was always her type. He was carrying her coffee, which he put down in front of her before taking a seat next to her, close enough to drape his big arm around her shoulders and stare down her cleavage.

It would have been the safe thing to just back off and let Monica claim her petty victory, but Claire was really not in the mood. She wasn't afraid of Monica anymore—well, not normally—and the last thing she wanted to do was let Monica spoil the one thing she'd been looking forward to during the entire walk over.

So Claire put her café mocha down at the third place and sat down, just ahead of Jennifer, who was making for the space. Gina, Monica's other ever-present girlfriend/minion, had already taken the fourth seat.

Monica, oddly, didn't say anything. She stared at Claire as if she couldn't quite figure out what the hell that was doing sitting down at her table, and then, once she got over the shock, she smiled, as if it occurred to her that maybe this could be fun. In a nasty sort of way.

Jennifer stood there glaring down at Claire, clearly not sure what to do, and Claire was acutely aware that she had her back to the girl. Never a good plan. She didn't trust any of them, but she trusted Jennifer these days least of all. Gina had kind of discovered humanity, in a vague kind of way, and Monica— Well, Monica could usually be counted on to do what was good for Monica.

Jennifer was unpredictable, and six of the worst kinds of crazy. Gina was mean, and Monica could be vicious, but Jennifer didn't seem to have any sense of boundaries at all. Plus, Jennifer had been the first one of the three to push her. She hadn't forgotten that.

Claire sensed a movement at her back, and almost ducked, but she forced herself not to flinch. Nothing will happen, not here. Not in front of Oliver.

Photo by Sharon Sams-Adams

Rachel Caine is the *New York Times* bestselling author of more than thirty novels, including the Weather Warden series, the Outcast Season series, and the Morganville Vampires series. She was born at White Sands Missile Range, which people who know her say explains a lot. She has been an accountant, a professional musician, an insurance investigator, and, until recently, still carried on a secret identity in the corporate world. She and her husband, fantasy artist R.Cat Conrad, live in Texas with their iguanas, Popeye and Darwin. Visit her Web site at www.rachelcaine.com, and find her on Twitter, LiveJournal, Myspace, and Facebook.